CAROLINA
BELLE

CAROLINA BELLE

K.I.M. Publishing, LLC
Chimney Rock, NC

Published by

K.I.M. PUBLISHING, LLC
Post Office Box 132
Chimney Rock, NC 28720-0132

Cover Photograph: Freeman Orchard, Hendersonville, NC

Published in the United States of America.

PUBLISHER'S NOTE

This is a work of fiction. Though there are numerous elements of historical and geographical accuracy in this portrait of the apple growers of Henderson County, NC, and its environs, the names, places, characters and incidents either are the product of the author's imagination or are used fictitiously, and any resemblance to actual persons, living or dead, is entirely coincidental.

PUBLISHER'S CATALOGING-IN-PUBLICATION DATA

Names: Senehi, Rose, author.
Title: Carolina belle / Rose Senehi.
Description: First United States Edition. I Chimney Rock, North Carolina : K.I.M. Publishing LLC, 2017.
ISBN: 978-0-9962571-5-2 (trade paperback edition)
Subjects: Farm life—North Carolina—History—Fiction. I Family and relationships—Blue Ridge Mountains—Southern—Fiction. I Henderson County (N.C.)—Fiction. I Women—North Carolina—Fiction. I Nature—Botany of Apples—North Carolina—History—Fiction.
Classification: PS3619.E65 C7 2017

Library of Congress Control Number: 2016910061

First Printing: Jan. 2017

For Lisa and Sean

The Southern Blue Ridge Mountains of North Carolina gently wraps its arms around the fertile plateau known as the Apple Valley. Unlike the thousands of small settlements and towns reshaped by the relentless flow of humanity, this place, in spite of decades of ups and agonizing downs, has hung on to its unique character, born the day its first settler planted an apple seed.

Orchards that endlessly unfold on the horizon bear the same names that were scrawled on the old maps and plats by the early land agents: Edney, Lyda, Freeman, Owenby, Stepp, Justus, Coston, Barnwell, Laughter, Nix. And now, more than two hundred years later, their very descendents are at the core of one of the most prolific apple growing regions in the country.

CHAPTER ONE

T HE MAP HER GREAT GRANDMA MYRTLE DREW on the kitchen wall streamed in and out of the girl's thoughts as she drove the tractor up to the end of a row of apple trees. As a kid, she couldn't understand why no one ever painted over the faded old sketch, why they just went around it with coat after coat and color after color. All the trees on the map had disappeared, even the two scrawled "for pies" and the seven marked "baking & drying."

She lowered the giant wood boxes balanced on the forklift and pulled away, mulling over the tree at the corner of the drawing that promised "Good Eating." Was it still alive and growing in some orchard, or had it disappeared from the face of the earth like thousands of other old Southern apples?

She paused a moment and took in the sight of twenty thousand trees groaning with ripe, beautifully formed fruit. Like an endless bolt of corduroy spooled open on the landscape, row after row dotted with red orbs faded into the distance.

A tide of satisfaction rolled over her, and she allowed herself a moment of serenity. This was the last day this season she could enjoy this bountiful panorama. Thirty pickers would arrive in the morning and strip the orchard of its apples by nightfall, leaving the lush carpet of grass between the rows trampled and strewn with rejects.

The foreman pulled up next to her and sank back in his seat.

Neither of them paid any mind to the squawk box blaring out chirps of predatory birds and stress calls from their prey as they drank in the sight.

"Oh, Raphael. Pap's got to be proud. Our first bumper crop out of this orchard."

"Looks good, Belle."

Belle turned to him. His swarthy looks no longer frightened her as they had as a child, for she had grown up appreciating the gentleness of his nature and respect for hard work. He took off his frayed straw hat with its sweat stained band and ran his fingers through his glistening black hair.

"I thought your grandpa was loco, putting up that new cold storage building for them. Scared me. Like he was jinxin' 'em." He nodded approvingly. "*Gracias a Dios*, he did good."

She grinned at him. "He's already got buyers lined up for every last one of them."

Then, deep in thought, Belle stared off into the distance. "You're not the only one who's been scared." She turned to Raphael. "It's the same every year. Pap's like someone with a million dollar thoroughbred about to run in the Kentucky Derby. That's all he can think about. Every dollar he's going to bring in for the year is hanging on the limbs of 70,000 apple trees."

An orchard cannon went off and a bevy of birds shot out from the trees. Raphael pulled a faded paisley bandana from his pocket and tied it around his neck, then reseated his hat snugly on his head.

She was about to crank the tractor into gear and start back for more boxes when a cool breeze swiped across her face, making her look over her shoulder. Pink and orange clouds swirled over the edge of the far northwest ridge as if snorted out by an angry bull.

She turned to Raphael. "Waddaya think?"

Deep furrows appeared on his already sweaty forehead as he studied the sky. "*No bueno.*"

A drop of rain grazed her cheek. She turned toward the misty curtain barreling towards them and shuddered from a cold gust. "Damn! All we need is one more day."

The foreman quickly took off, yelling over his shoulder, "I'll dump these boxes. You get in."

She threw the tractor into gear and bounced along the rutted lane, casting wary glances over her shoulder at the strangely colored sky. "Please God," she prayed, "don't let anything happen to this crop. Pap's got too much riding on it." Thunder boomed behind her and rain trickled down her face as the tractor raced to a nearby shed. She jumped off and ran into the musty old barn. It hadn't sheltered horses for two generations, but traces of their scent still radiated from the ancient chestnut stalls now filled with tractor parts.

She swiped her arms clear and was wringing out her pony tail when something in the sound of the rain battering the tin roof made her stop. Not breathing, she listened hard. No, she decided, taking a deep breath. Everything's okay.

Suddenly two pings pitter-pattered overhead like a knock at the door you're afraid to answer. The threat morphed into a loud metallic staccato. She spun around. Jagged marble-sized orbs bounced on the ground. As the hail piled up, a sickening feeling overcame her, like she was sinking in quicksand and about to smother. Then someone whispered in the marauder's ear that the damage was finally done, and the pelting turned into a gentle rain and stopped.

Her eyes scanned the orchard. Apples lay askew on the carpet of ice, but not as many as she had feared. Barely breathing, she cautiously inched her way toward the trees. Everything went dead quiet, no chirping birds, no hum of insects; the only sound, a ringing in her ears. All the hours of pruning, spraying and thinning flashed through her brain like scenes out the window of a runaway train.

Her heartbeat pounded against the wall of her chest with each step. Her emotions see-sawed from hope to dread as she came near enough to the big red and green orbs to pluck one from the tree. She drew it close, and a shiver ran down her spine. The face of the beautiful, perfect fruit was slashed.

PAP'S TRUCK SKIDDED TO A STOP in front of the packing

11

house. He ran in and then up the steps to his office. Belle and Raphael scrambled up behind him, taking the steps two at a time.

"Try to get those pickers in here right away," Pap yelled to Raphael as he grabbed a phone.

Raphael told him they were coming from Michigan and wouldn't get there till late.

"Then call all your cousins."

Pap looked at Belle. "Find someone who can take this crop."

Belle raced to the Rolodex and yanked out a batch of dog eared cards. Her hands shook as she dialed the processor and waited for someone to pick up. She could barely hear the ringing on the other end over the barrage of Raphael's urgent Spanish and Pap's stoic report to their insurance agent.

"We haven't checked our other orchards, but there's no question we've got damage at this one. We were all set to pick and pack tomorrow for the fresh market. Now, we'll be lucky to sell them for juice if we can get 'em picked fast enough."

He listened for a moment. "Okay, I'll be here at the farm."

Pap hung up and dialed again, then looked up at Belle. "Got anyone?"

"All the lines are busy."

"Keep trying. I've gotta get someone from Federal Crop Insurance in here to verify the loss."

He glanced over at Raphael. "How many you got comin'?"

Before Raphael had a chance to answer, Pap was back on the phone.

"It's McGrady. We got hit with hail. My agent's on his way to the valley. No telling when he's going to get to my place. Hell, we don't even know how bad our other two orchards are right now." He nodded. "Okay, we'll be here."

He hung up and listened to Belle.

"We don't know how much. We're rounding up our pickers right now."

Pap motioned for her to tell him who it was. She put her hand over the mouthpiece. "Jack Phillips out of Winchester."

He took the phone from her. "Jack, it's McGrady. How much can you handle?" He winced. "That's it?" His eyes darted from side to side. "Okay, hold onto that slot for us. We'll let you know by the end of the day how much we're shipping."

Matt, Raphael's stepson, walked in with an uncharacteristic grim expression. With blond hair and hazel eyes, he towered over the man he had called "Father" since he was five. Belle threw Matt a worried glance, which he acknowledged with a slight wink.

"Good! You're here," said Pap, patting him on the back. Pap hesitated for a split second, then as if he had come to a decision, pulled out his keys and handed them to Belle. "Go check the other orchards. Sugarloaf first, then Ridge Road. Phone me."

He looked at Matt. "I need you here."

Belle raced out of the office knowing something had just happened, but didn't know quite what. She scampered down the stairs, listening to the somber voices fade as the door slowly closed behind her. She made a dash for Pap's truck, waving to a couple of pickers pulling in.

The pickup reeled out of the compound and gunned down the road. Ted Nick raced toward her in the other lane. He had to be coming from his orchard on Sugarloaf. Belle lowered her window and waved for him to stop. He pulled up next to her.

"How's it up on Sugarloaf?" she asked.

"My Romes are cut bad. They're way too starchy. It won't pay to try and stop the decay. I'm gonna have to write the crop off."

"How many trees you got up there?"

"Fifteen thousand."

He threw her a wave and took off.

Damn! thought Belle. He was already spread thin with his two kids at NC State.

She hung on to a shred of hope as she made the twists and turns up the mountain. Their orchard grew in a narrow thermal belt that always seemed to have different weather than the rest of the mountain. She made the final turn and saw only a spattering of ice on the ground. She pulled off the road and ran to a tree. She picked an apple and scrutinized it, slowly rotating it in her hand. Nothing! Hope rising, she ran past a couple trees and picked another one. Damn! A small nick. She reached deep into the tree and twisted off an apple. Nothing.

She dialed Pap. Busy. She tried the land line and let it ring. Just as she was about to hang up, a rugged voice rasped "McGrady."

"I'm on Sugarloaf. The Galas are damaged, but no way near as bad as the Honeycrisps. Small hail pecks here and there. I tested them last week. They were almost ripe. I'm pretty sure they'll pass the sugar test for processing."

"Bring back a good sampling."

"What are we gonna do if they don't test out?"

"Spray to stop the decay until they ripen up enough to pass."

"All thirty acres?"

"Yep. Let me know about the Romes."

Belle carefully chose random apples from different trees; there was no point in fooling themselves about the crop's sugar content. After all the picking and delivery costs, it would only be rejected by the processor. She cradled as many in her tee-shirt as it would hold, raced to the truck and carefully poured them into a bushel basket.

She sped to their Ridge Road orchard and noticed a profusion of vehicles on the move. Had to be friends and relatives coming out to help. The slew of pickups parked helter-skelter at Barnwell's orchard hinted at what had to be going on back at Pap's place.

That image reminded her of the question that had been in the back of her mind ever since Pap handed her the keys. Why did he send her to check out the orchards instead of Matt or Raphael? Hell, she was just fresh out of ag school. Raphael had been foreman for as far back as she could remember, and Matt had been working for Pap ever since he was strong enough to hold up his end of an apple box.

She swung around the curve ahead, and the devastation to their Rome orchard took her breath away. Limbs were down, leaves beaten off, apples on the ground. A deep layer of hail carpeted the grass.

The intractable storm had ravaged this orchard much more

than their other two. She had tested these Romes last week. They were nowhere near ripe. Crazy thoughts shot through her brain as she raced through the lane of trees picking apples, examining them and tossing the damaged specimens to the ground. Tears welled in her eyes as the lyrics to an old Meat Loaf song streamed through her consciousness. "Don't be sad 'cause two out of three ain't bad."

She pulled her phone from her back pocket and gave Pap the news. "It's so heartbreaking, Pap. We worked so hard to make them perfect for people. I don't know. It's a pit of your stomach kind of thing."

"We'll push through, honey. We've got just about enough insurance to keep from goin' belly up. Nature does this to us every once in a while. We just take the hits."

CHAPTER TWO

Five years later

THE CHECKERED CURTAINS SWAYED silently in the soft breeze as Belle, awake in the darkness, gazed at the smoky gray glow peeking in the window. Were the sweet whistles coming from the cardinals that lived in the Leyland cypress outside her window, or from the cheeky mockingbird she'd spotted mimicking them on the fence the day before?

The aroma of coffee her grandfather was brewing downstairs in the kitchen drifted in and aroused her, luring her awake with the promise the day ahead would be good.

Everyone always said she was a born apple farmer just like Pap, the only father she ever really knew; and she believed it to be so. It was as if Reedy Creek ran through their veins, as if the sweet smell of apple blossoms lingered in a secret place in their nasal caverns, and as if their feet had mutated into roots and clawed into the earth.

She reached over and grabbed hold of the small clock she had since college, knocking over the award she'd been given as Apple Ambassador of the Year. She put the plaque, that meant more to her than any beauty queen's tiara ever could, upright next to a picture of a smiling, floppy-eared puppy. She yanked on the clock's cord to bring it near enough for her to read the now dimmed red digits. Five-thirty.

She slid out of the cast iron bed she'd slept in for most of her life and quickly slipped on a pair of jeans and a tee-shirt with a faded NC State Wolfpack logo. She brushed her long dark hair and put it in a pony tail with no regard for how it looked. It didn't matter. Over the day it could take almost any form—twisted into a bun and held with the same rubber band, or braided and slung over her shoulder.

She pulled on her field boots, reached for the iPad on the desk and tapped in her password. A glance at the calendar on the screen reminded her that today she could give G-12 its first test, triggering the passion that constantly hovered on the rim of her consciousness.

At the age of twelve, a fascination to create her own prized apple overcame her as intensely as the urge to breathe when her neighbor told her that every apple seed planted would grow into a tree that would produce a unique one-of-a-kind apple no one had ever seen or tasted before.

Now an expert pollinator, she was still searching for an apple that she could almost taste—thrillingly tangy and crisp like a cool valley morning, yet with the lingering sweetness of mountain dew. An apple born in the mountains, and by some miracle of nature, made to suck up its nutrients and flourish there. Not just an American apple, but an Apple Valley American apple.

When her sister, Missy, was a kid and heard such an apple could bring in as much as a dollar a tree royalty, it was all Belle could do to keep her from planting seeds willy-nilly all over the half acre Pap had given her.

Missy hardly talked about it anymore, just when she was in the mood to fantasize about what they could do with the millions if it were ever found and trademarked. Pretty much the only thing the apple that they were planning on calling the Carolina Belle was good for, as far as Missy was concerned, was getting her a beauty salon from a big name franchise.

Belle quickly folded the frayed cover around the iPad she called "Bubba," tucked it in the cluttered wood slat basket on her desk and started with it for the door. Careful to avoid the plank that creaked, she crept softly down the hall so as not to wake Missy, asleep behind her closed door.

She hit the staircase's last steps and spotted Pap sitting at the kitchen table in front of a mug of coffee.

"Morning, Pap."

"Mornin' Belle."

That was about all the small talk she expected to get from him. Their apples were ready to pick, and that was the only thing he could focus on. Lurking somewhere in the back of his mind had to be the heartache of the year they were hit by hail.

She poured herself a cup of coffee, then pulled out a napkin and wrapped three of the apple cinnamon donuts Pap's sister Pam had dropped off. She stuffed them in her basket and started toward the door.

"We're gonna be working the Sugarloaf orchard today," Pap called after her. "We've got three clients waiting on those Galas."

"I know. I'm going over to test one of my apples, but I'll be there by seven."

"I'll be stuck in town all morning, so tell Matt to get the grading started as soon as he can. And while you're checking on your lot, run another test on the Romes."

"I plan to."

"You gonna stop by Jake's?"

"Yeah. He hasn't been feeling too good."

She hated that, even after all these years, every time she told Pap she was visiting their old neighbor, she felt compelled to offer an excuse.

The screen door creaked open and her dog ran to her side. He had slept under her window, and hearing her stir, paced the porch, anxious for their day to begin. She made her way over the lush, dew-covered grass to a dented, mud splattered pickup that had seen its share of rough hauling. She placed the coffee on top and opened the driver's side door. McIntosh quickly jumped in and found his place on an old worn army blanket. She nestled the basket next to him and gave him a donut, which he snapped up as if it were his due.

Settled back behind the steering wheel, she took a sip of the coffee, pulled out a donut and thought about the September morning that started out as promising as this one and ended with the hailstorm that almost ruined them. She was twenty-two back then, and when Pap handed her the keys to his truck and told her to go check all the orchards for damage with Raphael and Matt standing right there, she got her first inkling that in the scheme of things, she mattered.

It had taken her a while, but she eventually figured out that if the news were to be bad in their other orchards, Pap had wanted the first heartbreaking scenes etched in her memory, and the burden of having to report it weighing heavily on her shoulders; a sort of trial by fire. With that mission, her place on the farm had been officially acknowledged: she was number two.

From the day her mother tossed a suitcase in the back of a pickup and took off, with Belle's father racing after her in a cloud of dust, everyone assumed she would eventually be handed the reins of the operation, but it was on that particular morning, with all of them filled with fear and foreboding, that Pap had decided to get it out in the open and see how she handled herself.

She shifted the squealing gears and drove down the rutted gravel road that wound erratically through their farming compound. A few million dollars worth of equipment was scattered around—sprayers, giant blowers, mowers, tractors—either tucked two deep under steel beamed canopies, parked in rustic sheds, or just sitting out in the open. That and a packing house, a refrigerated storage building and over 100,000 apple trees in the ground added up to what it took five generations of McGradys to scrape together.

The Ford F-150 turned and twisted on the back roads past endless rolling fields of apple trees awash with the pinkish morning sunlight breaking over the east ridge. A splattering of apples blown off during the last storm glistened with dew underneath them. Every once in a while, a neat country home showed its face on a flawless lawn, reflecting the deep-rooted pride of place the valley was noted for. She slowed down and pulled off onto a dirt lane, then grabbed her basket, slipped out of the truck and trudged to a row of trees with Mac trailing behind.

Mindful to test specimens from the same tree and of the same size, she carefully chose three red Rome apples and put them in her basket, then continued down the rich carpet of dew-drenched grass. They had stopped spraying a week ago, so she thought it a good idea to check a tree for sooty blotch. She eyed a black snake tightly curled around the top of the trunk—one of nature's many helpers. A sudden surge of exhilaration caught hold. This could be a good omen. Maybe G-12 would be the one she was searching for, or close to the one.

She hurried along in high spirits recalling the words that had been permanently imbedded in her brain when Jake told her how every apple seed was genetically different from all others, and in that respect, resembled humans. "Most of us are born, live and die as ordinary people, with little to distinguish us from the millions around us," he had told her. "Only occasionally does a human rise above the crowd by mental genius or exceptional ability. Who can predict when a random sorting of genes will produce an Einstein, a Michelangelo or an Alexander the Great? This goes for apples, too."

The row ended at a weather-worn sign: "Belle's Half Acre." Every row was marked with a letter that stood for a year. She went over to row G and tramped down the mowed lane to the twelfth specimen.

With only three lonely apples hanging on the small dwarf, she had better make sure it wasn't too early to test them. She put her basket on the ground, pulled out Bubba and quickly found the page for G-12. She recalculated the days since it was in full bloom. One hundred and five. Yep, it was time.

She skimmed over the data on the two antique apples from Jake's orchard she had cross-pollinated: Doctor Bush's Sweet Apple and Dula's Beauty. Doctor Bush was of "medium size, nearly round, skin yellow and covered with deep red, almost black on the sunny side." Dula's Beauty's description read: "fruit large, oblong, skin greenish yellow, mostly covered with dull purplish-red stripes and blotches."

Standing next to the tree, she decided the three apples hardly resembled either one of their parents—they were redder and rounder. After careful examination, she picked what looked like the ripest, put it in the basket with the three Romes and went back to the truck.

She pulled a cloth out of the basket and placed it on the hood. After carefully positioned G-12, she snapped several pictures with Bubba. One of the corners of its screen had a spider web of hairline cracks from the time she left it on her hood and then ran over it, yet it still managed to take good shots.

She pulled a potato peeler from the basket and took a thin slice of skin from each side of the specimen, then fished around for her pressure tester. Her shoulders slowly slumped as she studied the apple. Why did this mean so damn much to her? After over 200 tries, not one of her apples even came close to the Honeycrisp. How many times had Pap tried to drum it into her that the odds of getting a good tasting apple from a seed were one in ten thousand?

"Girl, with all the massive apple breeding programs goin' on all over the country, what makes you think you'll be the one to come up with the 'billion dollar' apple?'"

Everyone agreed it was a crazy idea. Except Belle.

Ignoring that presumption, she enthusiastically studied G-12, for she had an edge—Jake and the 400 different antique apple trees he'd spent thirty years collecting from old farms and backyards all over the South. He'd been consumed with the search, driving up and down country roads talking to farm folk and hiking through dense overgrowth, trying to save the heritage of Southern apples—trees that were born and survived in southern soil.

Belle's passion was different. She was convinced that somewhere in all his antique trees, there existed the potential for a random sorting of genes that would produce an incomparable apple, and she was bound and determined to find it.

She found it ironic that Jake wanted to rescue old apples while she wanted to create a new one. Sometimes she chalked it up to her womanhood—that deep down nurturing urge to bring something new and wonderful into being. But mostly, she suspected her intense interest in evolution had something to do with her endless yearning to know what her parents were like, especially her father. With her resemblance to her grandfather, she was comfortably seated in her mother's genetic pool, but her McKenzie link was a mystery she could only solve in her imagination. What sort of man was her father? His father? This puzzle had inspired hundreds of scenarios throughout her childhood, none of them satisfying.

She re-set the pressure tester gauge and counted under her breath as she inserted the plunger into one of the exposed sections. "1,001, 1,002." Then she tested the firmness on the other exposed section and felt her excitement rising as she noted the average of the two readings on G-12's chart.

All the money that finding the quintessential North Carolina apple would bring wasn't that important. After getting Missy her fancy salon and paying off the myriad of Pap's mortgages, she would assign the greatest portion to doing whatever it took to guarantee the valley would always be one of the country's premier apple growing regions—an unbroken heritage worth perpetuating.

Developing the Carolina Belle from Jake's orchard—a safety deposit vault of countless combinations of genes produced since the 1600s by countless settlers planting their orchards from seeds—would be the big payoff for Jake's dogged collection of antique apple trees. More than just keeping them from perishing from the earth. More than Southern history. A priceless link in man's search for the perfect fruit.

She sliced the apple in two at the equator, exposing a swirl of dark seeds, then pulled a spray bottle with an iodine mixture from the basket. She sprayed one half and watched it turn a slight blue-black on the edges. Her starch-to-sugar conversion chart told her it was nearing its ideal ripeness by a week or two.

She quickly sealed the other half in a zip-lock bag. She would save the taste test for her and Jake to do later. The Romes were tested and tasted, bringing her to the conclusion that they needed at least another two weeks. She finished putting all the data into Bubba, hollered for Mac, and they got back in the truck and took off.

Heaven knew it would get muggy soon, so she headed out to

Jake's with the window down, enjoying the cool morning breeze. Anticipation rose as she turned off onto Jake's gravel road that bordered her grandfather's compound. Mac sat up and looked out the window with his ears flicked forward. He knew where they were going.

The truck cruised along a lane that curved through a thick woods before spilling onto an open area. The sight of the house and the pastoral garden filled her with the same titillating sensation she'd felt when, at five, she laid eyes on the place for the first time.

The truck skidded to a stop. She jumped out and hurried to the house with her basket, her footsteps rustling the path's crushed stones. Birds already flitted around a smattering of feeders. She reached for the knocker just as the door swung open.

There in front of her, stood everyman in an equally nondescript outfit—wrinkled khaki shorts and a washed out tee-shirt. But, to Belle, Jake wasn't everyman. Broad shouldered and tall, with the ramrod straight back he owed to his thirty years in the army, he hardly looked his eighty-two years.

Belle pulled the bag with G-12 from her basket and playfully wiggled it in front of his eyes with a devilish grin, getting her the chuckle she aimed for.

He shook his head. "Let's take a look."

Jake's house, a Japanese-style structure built with his own hands some thirty-two years earlier, still held an ethereal quality for Belle. Everything about the place reflected the man's tempered search for excellence. So different from the sepia toned ambiance of Pap's place, half of which was built in the late 1800's.

Spying Mac peeking at him through one of the sliding glass doors, Jake let him in before pouring them both a cup of coffee and sitting down at the kitchen table.

Belle took Bubba out and booted up the page for G-12.

"Okay, girl, whaddaya got?" Jake said, rubbing his hands together.

She smiled to herself, thinking that was why he stayed so young—ever curious, ever passionate about possible discovery. She related the ancestry of the two apples she had crossed. He listened intently, especially to the test results.

"Didn't you cross Dula's Beauty before?"

"Yeah, twelve. All from different apples. Four years ago. This is the first apple to come out of the lot."

Jake reached for the plastic bag.

Belle coyly pulled it away and took the last donut from her basket. "I know Mary used to make these and how much you loved them."

It was as if she were testing his emotions. He nonchalantly reached for the donut and unceremoniously took a bite, as if memories of his beloved wife never tugged at him. He was an inveterate pragmatist. Belle put it down to his military training where acceptance of reality is a matter of life and death. Now it was a habit. This was pretty much the only characteristic he shared with Pap.

"I miss her," said Belle. "Remember those fall days when you'd bring in some of your sour apples and Mary and I would peel and slice, then lay them out on the porch to dry? I'll never forget all those fried pies we made together."

Belle stopped herself. It hurt too much. She sipped her coffee remembering how she decided to call Mary "Grandma" after being teased at school about not having one. However, Belle had known enough not to refer to her or call her that outside of her visits to their little Eden, for even at a tender age she was aware of the thorny undercurrent that existed between Jake and Pap.

Belle pulled the apple half from the plastic baggie, cut a wedge and dropped it into his outstretched hand. She watched him carefully chew as she put a wedge in her mouth.

"Flat. No zest," he said.

She nodded. "What little sweetness there is, fades right away."

"Give it a one for taste," he said.

"You don't think it deserves a two?"

"I was being generous at one."

She nodded again and inputted a score of 1.5 in the correct box in G-12's chart.

"How many is this now?" he asked.

"It doesn't matter how many," she said, snapping Bubba's cover shut. "I'm gonna live a long life, and sooner or later, I'm gonna find it."

CHAPTER THREE

"THE TROUBLE WITH THIS VALLEY is that anyone who's lived here for two generations is somehow related to everyone else," muttered Missy as she hefted a carton onto the pickup. "Remember what they told us when we started school? 'Now don't you be talkin' 'bout nobody, 'cause everybody's somebody's cousin,'" Her voice echoed in the cavernous packing house, thick with the humid night air. In the pitch black outside, a screech owl followed its spooky trill with a shrill cry.

Belle tossed on a roll of tarp and reached for their Apple Festival booth sign as a cruel rhyme played in her head: *Mandy and Randy were running away on that terrible day...* "Yep, we're just one big happy family." She gave a bitter little laugh. "I only wish those same kids thought about that before they threw what happened to Mom and Dad in our face."

Missy brushed a fluff of blond hair from her forehead. "That's why you've got to get out and meet more people. God only knows you've already been through everyone in this valley that could even remotely be considered an eligible bachelor."

Belle made a face. "I wouldn't call Matt and Jeff everybody."

"You know what I mean."

Missy stood with her hands on her hips looking at Belle. "Don't you think you should give Matt another chance now that—"

"Don't even go there, Missy. He's had his chance."

The headlights of the truck they used for heavy hauling pulled up and cast ghostly shadows of the two on the building's rear wall. Matt jumped out and rushed over to help Belle who was tugging on a rolled-up tent. Wearing khaki shorts and high top leather work boots, he effortlessly grabbed it up and hoisted it into the pickup, brandishing the kind of strength it took to manage an orchard the size of Pap's. Even at this early hour, his muscles were taut and ready to face anything that would get in the way of bringing in their crop, almost as if it were a matter of life and death.

"Anything else?" he said as he looked around.

The day had yet to dawn, but his short wavy blond hair still formed wisps of small curls on his sweaty forehead. His tee-shirt, blotched dark with perspiration, stuck to his broad chest.

"No. That's it," said Belle, dusting her hands off on her shorts.

"I've got all your apples loaded," he called out as he swung back in the truck. "I'm gonna pick up my boy and my brother. I'll meet you on Main Street."

The two girls wrestled the building's enormous door shut, then Missy climbed into the pickup. Mac wagged his tail and danced around, waiting for Belle to open her door. She crouched down and scratched behind his ears. "You stay, boy." She jumped up and broke into an impish grin. "I gotta go sell some apples." She opened her door and scooted onto the front seat.

"We need to hurry if we want to make the Kiwanis pancake breakfast at First Baptist," Missy said. "Dave's working the grill, and he'll be looking for us."

"Isn't he supposed to work at the farm stand today?"

"Don't worry, he'll make it there by nine."

Belle shook her head. "You're too much. How you got that poor devil to work for you on his vacation is beyond me."

"Have you ever heard of *animal magnetism?*"

Belle rolled her eyes and shoved the truck into gear. "I think it's more like temporary insanity."

The truck weaved through the compound cluttered with every piece of equipment they needed to bring in the harvest,

27

then through a canyon of huge twenty-bushel wooden boxes stacked twenty feet high on each side, all stenciled with a big, black "McGrady."

"About that breakfast, I can't go," Belle tossed out. "The festival doesn't start till ten, but there'll be plenty of people on the street before then."

"That's your trouble, right there," said Missy who was two years younger. "How are you gonna meet someone new if you don't go lookin' for 'em? How do you think I met Dave?"

Belle raised an eyebrow and glanced over at her. "I'll hand it to you. You lifted up every rock in this county until you finally hit on Lover Boy."

"You like him, and you know it."

The truck reached the road, and Belle glanced in the rearview mirror at the glow of the sun about to rise over the ridge. "It's gonna be a zoo on Main Street. I hope we're getting there early enough."

"Don't sweat it, Belle. No matter when we get there, it's gonna be a zoo." Missy studied her sister. "By the way, you look good in that blouse."

Belle tugged at it. "You think?"

"The minute I saw it at Target, I told myself that with all the people goin' to that apple festival there's gotta be someone my sister's not related to." She reached over and gave Belle's shoulder a playful shove. "And that blouse is just what she'll need to get 'em interested. Low enough to hint at what's under there, but high enough to say 'don't get any ideas.'"

"Really, Missy. How do you come up with all this stuff?"

"I do more than eat, sleep and breathe apples like you, girl. "

Belle threw Missy a droll look.

By the time they hit downtown Hendersonville, Main Street was jammed with anything that could possibly haul apples—trucks, trailers, vans, pickups—with everyone scrambling to get set up.

The two sisters worked in tandem pulling everything off the truck. They waved to and acknowledged members of the farming community they had worked shoulder to shoulder with at Henderson County's North Carolina Apple Festival ever since they were tall enough to stand behind a counter. They were quickly caught up in the exhilarating sense of expectation rippling through the eight blocks bustling with growers and vendors. Pride for the harvest beamed from every face. Picking was in full swing with everything running wide open at every orchard—a satisfying climax to a year of toil under the unnerving fear of what nature might do to upend everything.

Belle spotted their truck weaving through the chaos. "Here comes Matt," she told Missy. "Go park my truck and get your breakfast. Matt and I will set up. Be back by eight-thirty."

Belle opened the cab door for her sister. "Try and bring me a coffee... and say hello to Dave." She rolled her eyes in resignation. "And yeah, I like him."

Belle closed Missy's door and turned to see Matt's boy, Danny, in the front seat of the truck. It hurt her to see him, but she wasn't going to let it dampen her spirits. Had to be Matt's weekend with him. Now that Matt was divorced, she had to get used to the kid being around more often.

Matt had brought Carlos, too. As usual, Matt's fair looks appeared out of place next to one of his half-brothers; yet their bond couldn't be tighter.

The truck pulled up and the three jumped out. The two men got busy unloading cardboard boxes full of packaged Honeycrisps, stacking them at the rear of their space until they made a wall of boxes two layers deep. Then everyone pitched in erecting the tent, hanging signs, setting up counters—all with the harmony that comes from years of working hand in hand with people you trust.

Satisfied their booth looked good, Belle put on an apron, snapped on a belly pack and stuffed in a stack of bills from the cash box she'd stashed under the counter.

Matt grabbed up the empty boxes and tossed them into the back of the truck like he had no time to waste, then he signaled for the two boys to hop in. "Call if you need anything," he shouted to Belle as he reached for the truck's door.

"You gonna bring Pap with you at five?" asked Belle.

"Yeah. My dad's gonna take care of the pickers until we finish up here tonight. Then we've got to go back and move the ladders and equipment over to the Gala orchard and set up the bins for tomorrow." He turned, and for the first time that morning, took a longer moment than he should have to take her in. "You look nice."

She pinched the blouse and self-consciously pulled it away from her now sweaty skin, wishing he hadn't said that. He had broken their tacitly agreed upon rules. She hoped it hadn't anything to do with his divorce, but she would have had to be blind not to notice the subtle change in everyone's perception of his prospects, especially Pap, who had to be hoping there still was a chance they might get back together.

He opened the truck's door and slid in. Belle watched the vehicle inch its way through the maze ahead until it weaved around a stand and disappeared. She sank her hands in her apron pockets and strolled around the booth. Bag after bag of perfectly formed Honeycrisps filled her with a sense of accomplishment.

She picked one up, studied the world famous apple and thought about the mystery surrounding it. The University of Minnesota Horticultural Research Center released it thinking it was a hybrid of the Macoun and Honeygold, only to discover after genetic fingerprinting that neither of these two apples were its parents. Another of their cultivars, the Keepsake, was one of its parents. The other one was never identified and thought to be a crossbreed they had developed and later discarded.

That story still unnerved her. After years of meticulously tracking every tree she had planted, she was dead sure she knew the lineage of every apple in her half acre. But if such a highly respected institution as the Minnesota Horticultural Research Center could screw up, what were her chances?

Someone tested the P.A. system at the staging area in front of the county's historic courthouse a half a block away and shook her from her thoughts. She looked around and realized all the vehicles were gone. A cluster of official looking people stood out from the casually dressed crowd surging down the street. They headed to the stage for the opening ceremony.

Where was that Missy? Belle asked herself as a crowd suddenly charged toward the booth. A head of curly blond hair bobbed in the distance, and in minutes Missy stood behind the counter breathlessly snapping on her apron and belly pack, while Belle, in between waiting on customers, stole sips of the coffee she had brought back.

Late morning, Belle went to grab a box of apples when Missy nudged her and said under her breath, "Get a load of that guy in my line."

Belle ignored her. All she had to do was show the least bit of interest and she was headed for a Labor Day weekend from hell. While waiting for a woman to pull out her money, she cursed herself for doing it, but couldn't resist glancing over at the man.

He had the lean, leathery looks you could only achieve from being outdoors year round. She suspected he had to be a sportsman since he had the sort of confident aura possessed by those for whom life had been generous.

She stole another glimpse, and seeing he was preoccupied with the apple booth on the other corner, felt free to indulge in a keener inspection. Wavy dark hair curled around his ears, barely touching his broad shoulders, and a scar on his cheekbone added a touch of vulnerability to the too-perfect face. His outfit was casual, but studied. She knew a two hundred dollar pair of jeans when she saw one.

An elderly man suddenly distracted her.

"This is my tenth year at this here festival, and I always get a bag of those Honeycrisps of yours," he said.

Belle felt instantly connected to him, like a stream to a rock or sunlight to bare flesh. She grinned. "Thanks. We sure are proud of 'em."

Caught up in the festive atmosphere, she chatted cordially with her next two customers, yet couldn't resist glancing out from the corner of her eye at the intriguing man.

Next in Missy's line, he grabbed a sack of apples from the table and handed her sister a hundred dollar bill.

Missy eyed it. "Oh, I don't have enough change for that." She went around to the other side of Belle and bumped her with her hip so hard Belle lost her footing. "You better wait on him."

Several women in line chuckled, making Belle's eyes shoot over to the man. He smiled at her. She had no choice but to move over, reach for the bill and make the change. But she was too embarrassed to look him in the eye.

"You're a McGrady?" he questioned.

She looked up into the deepest, darkest blue eyes she'd ever seen. "My mother was."

He casually tucked his change in his wallet. "I've met your grandfather." He studied her, waiting for a response. None coming, he barely shrugged, took his apples and moved on.

Missy rushed over and whispered in her ear, "You shoulda asked him his name when he said he knew Pap." Her brows furrowed. "You're not even trying."

A hand on Belle's shoulder startled her. Her grandfather's sister, Pam, along with Helen, Matt's mother, had sneaked in from the back of the booth. Matt's mother was a handsome woman, tall and blond like him; but Pam, even though now in her sixties, was still what most folks would think of as beautiful. The two women went way back, always working as a team at every apple festival when Belle and Missy were growing up.

Pam had broken away from her apple house today to make sure her nieces got a rest and a meal. Pam had gotten the roadside store when Pap's father died and the orchards were split between him and his sister. Pap got the old house, but mostly the right to call his piece McGrady Orchards. Pam had to be content with renaming her place Apple Valley Orchards.

However, she still clung to the McGrady name. When she got married back in the seventies when women's rights were a big issue, her father-in-law was surprised when she didn't change it. "What are your kids gonna be called?" he asked.

"Williams," she told him. They'll get their father's name, just like I did."

Belle had wished her mother had been that spunky and kept the McGrady name, too.

Pam tossed a glance toward two boxes on the back counter. "We picked you up some lunch; and remember, one hour."

Missy went off with one of her friends while Belle ate on one of the bleachers in front of the grandstand and watched a group of little girls on the stage clog their hearts out. Their efforts tugged at her. Like herself, they strove to achieve something.

Just then, the shrill voice of a young man from a local theatrical group boomed from amplifiers scattered around. After an overly detailed list of his own theatrical credits, he finally got around to announcing the next act—a boy of ten who was going to play the accordion. Belle rose and looked around for Missy. It was time for them to go back to the booth.

Dave unexpectedly showed up in the mid-afternoon, telling them Matt had sent him over to help after leaving one of his brothers to supervise the farm stand.

"That's the good news," said Dave. He looked ill at ease. "You two are going to have to stay till nine. A load of bins fell on one of your drivers. He's not hurt bad, but out of commission, so Pap'll be running loads over to the processor till after dark. One of the trucks is down, and Matt's got to have it up and running by tomorrow morning."

Neither of the girls seemed moved. They were used to the shifting sands of the apple industry. However, the hot and heavy air was getting to them in spite of all the water they'd been guzzling. The counters could use a resetting, and thankfully, a lull fell on the street, giving them a chance to restock.

"How're we doing at the stand?" Missy asked Dave.

He pulled a sheet of paper from his pocket and handed it to her. She looked it over with interest, nodding her head in approval.

Missy was in charge of Pap's farm stand that was nothing more than one-hundred feet of gravel with a metal canopy over it. Being a beautician at a local salon was her only real interest, yet both girls knew without being told that giving Missy the stand was part of Pap's long-range plan. It would be her toehold on the farm, and Pap's way of making sure she'd always be dealt in on the family's legacy.

Even though cutting her hours at the salon from late August to November so she could run the stand was about all Missy did as far as the farm was concerned, both girls saw the fairness in it. The two of them made up the fifth generation. Besides, Belle might have been the image of her grandfather and dedicated to the farm as much as he was, but everyone had long accepted that Missy was his favorite, chalking it up to her being an exact duplicate of his only child, their mother, Mandy.

Missy had the stand, but the festival booth was Belle's domain, where she came face to face with all the folks she strived to satisfy. Earlier that afternoon when a little girl shyly looked up at her and said, "These are my favorite apples," she wanted to pick her up, brush back the wisp of hair that had fallen across her forehead and tell her how hard she had worked to make them perfect for her. She wanted to tell her how wonderful it was to walk through the orchard when it was in bloom and looked like it had been showered with variegated pink snowflakes. How the flowers filled the air with an overwhelming perfume of promised deliciousness. And how nature did all this just to entice the bees to pay them a visit.

"Do you want me to count the empty boxes?" Dave asked.

Belle, shaken from her reverie, quickly told him yes.

A dense crowd surged down the street and Belle braced for the new throng when Missy nudged her and tossed her head toward the booth across the street. "Look. It's that guy from this morning."

Belle saw him talking to one of the Freeman boys. "It's him all right," she said just as he turned around and caught her staring. She swept her eyes away as if she'd been casually perusing the street scene.

Missy poked her. "It's the blouse."

Belle nudged Missy back as hard as she could and still be inconspicuous and said under her breath, "Don't stare."

"Looks like Blue Eyes is coming right over to you," Missy whispered.

Belle took a deep breath, forced an amenable expression and looked in his direction. Yet, she still managed to sound threatening as she muttered between her teeth, "Don't embarrass me, Missy. I'm too hot, I'm too worn out, and I'll kill you if you do."

The man sauntered over with the easy stride one settles into when they're utterly confident their arrival is being looked forward to.

"It looks like you girls have been busy today," he said as he approached the booth.

He came to a stop in front of Belle, folded his arms and stood there, legs apart and feet firmly planted. He'd come to chat.

Belle quickly answered him. God only knew what Missy might say. "Yes, we've done pretty good."

He offered his hand. "Ken Larsen, your new neighbor. I'm buying one of the Freeman orchards."

Belle smiled and awkwardly took his hand. "Belle McKenzie. This is my sister, Missy." Just then, a swarm of people hit the booth. Crowded out, he backed away, and seeing it wasn't going to abate, he smiled and drifted off.

Dave, who had been straightening out the jumble of boxes in the back, appeared with a full box of sacks and started restocking the counter.

Missy whispered to him, "You know the Freemans, don't you?"

"Yeah, sure."

"Go find out what you can about that guy they've been talking to."

Another lull, due mostly to the closeness of the dinner hour, gave Belle a chance to straighten out the cash drawer. She crouched down behind the counter and stuffed most of the money into a bank bag, then stood up to see Dave was back.

"He's some guy who's going to start a cidery," he announced.

"Where's he from?" asked Missy.

"Virginia. His family's supposed to have a big one up there."

Missy raised an eyebrow as she gave Belle a self-satisfied little smile. "Didn't I tell you there'd be someone in all this humanity we're not related to?"

CHAPTER FOUR

THE TWO CAROLINA WRENS FLITTING about in front of him failed to break Jake's gaze as he stared out beyond the garden. Other than his heart, the doctor had said he was in great shape for his age. Everything else was working just like it always had, and he was still as strong as an ox. He ought to be, he thought, after all those years in the army, back when they used to make everyone run four miles a day.

Yet, the way he was tired all the time reminded him of how he felt before his heart failure episode six years back, and he wondered if this was the beginning of the end, like those moments that get stolen away at twilight, when you close your eyes for what seems like an instant, and upon opening them up again, find the day has mysteriously become night. He heard a jay's screech followed by the swelling song of the cicadas, and a sickening pang gripped his throat at the thought of never hearing them again.

Always the realist, he decided it was high time he got his life in order. He would call his brother, Ben, when he got back in the house. With Mary and Randy now gone, Belle was all he had left, other than Ben and his family. He pictured Belle and laughed to himself. She was tenacious like him, yet how ironic that while he was driven to preserve old Southern apples, she was as obsessed with creating a new one.

His eyes fixed on the chain-link fence surrounding his orchard. He could still see the flushed cheeks of the dark-haired little five year old in overalls peeking through, her chubby fingers gripping the wire. He had pretended he didn't see her as he worked his way down a row of seedlings, getting closer and closer, hoping he wouldn't scare her off. He had only been able to catch a fleeting glimpse of her at the funeral. Now at the end of the row, he slowly raised his lids until their eyes met.

"I like your garden," she said with ease.

The confident way she spoke convinced him she'd been watching at the fence more often than that day. He wanted to show her the way in, but Mary was still too fragile. He couldn't take the chance of letting his wife set eyes on the child, and figured if he told her no, after a while, she'd go away; but it didn't work. Even at that age she had a stubborn streak.

That summer slipped by with her coming over from time to time to show him her stuffed animals and then her puppy, always asking to come in. He'd put her off by saying he didn't think her grandfather wanted her to wander so far from home. A flicker of disappointment in her eyes would always make her look so vulnerable he'd quickly brush the comment aside.

It went along like that for most of the summer, until on this one rare occasion, Mary was feeling well enough to come out with some iced tea. One look at the child behind the fence and she dropped it, tray and all. Instantly, the painful realization of losing their son came down on him with the same blunt force it had the first time he was told about the accident. He steadied himself and was stunned to see Mary, instead of sinking into a well of despair, rush to the child.

"Come, come along here," she urged as she excitedly pointed the way to the gate. "I've got some cookies for you."

A few minutes later, he walked in the kitchen to find Mary smiling for the first time since the accident, and the child sitting on her lap.

The next day, Jake had no choice but to go see McGrady. He pulled up to the old homestead and knocked on the door exactly at the appointed time. It flew open, and there in front of him was a face as hard as any he'd seen on the toughest drill sergeant he'd ever had the misfortune to run into. There being no other women in the household except hired help, it pained Jake to think of the little girl and her sister under his thumb.

McGrady turned and went back in the house, leaving the door ajar. Jake stepped in and followed him to a small, dark parlor. A worn settee as old as the house sat in front of a stone fireplace, and an old fashioned rag rug that mountain folks loomed lay on the floor, looking like it had seen more than its share of traffic.

McGrady nodded for him to sit down on an oak rocker with its seat worn to the raw leather, then he settled down in another one that looked just as tired. Neither man spoke. A clock ticked on the ancient chestnut mantel, and off in the distance, a tractor chugged along.

Finally, McGrady broke the stifling silence.

"You got no business comin' to my home."

The brashness of the remark didn't faze Jake. He had expected the fireworks to start right off the bat.

No one said anything for a while, then McGrady's words fell from his mouth with a weary gravity. "But for Mary's sake, I'll hear you out. I'm told she's ailing."

Jake took a deep breath and forged ahead with the business at hand. "It's about Annabelle. She's been coming over by the garden fence. I keep telling her not to." He bit his lip as his resolve not to get emotional crumbled. "I know I've got no right asking... but Mary's not well." He took out a well worn handkerchief and wiped his eyes. "I can't believe how she's come alive seeing her." He wiped his eyes again. "All I'm asking, is for you to say it's okay for her to visit. We *are* her neighbors."

Just then, the fridge's compressor kicked on and the hum floated in from the kitchen. McGrady got up and went over to a window. The sunlight cast dark shadows across the deep lines on the leathery face carved from a lifetime of toil in the sun. He pulled aside the yellowed lace curtain and looked out at a row of apple trees that almost came up to the house. He pulled a bandana from his back pocket and blew his nose.

"All right. For Mary," McGrady rasped. "She was good to

my little Mandy after my wife died."

He fell silent and stared out the window. Jake got up and quietly let himself out. Except for Belle's high school graduation years later, the only time Jake ever laid eyes on him after that was when he passed him on the road.

MATT WASN'T KEEN ON GOING over to Jake's place, but Pap certainly wasn't going to talk to him about the tree. He just told them to cut it down. There already was enough bad blood between the two, so Raphael told Matt to go and get his permission first.

This wasn't going to be Matt's last chore for the day and he was anxious to get it over with. Wooly adelgid had done the hemlock in, and the tree, being over 150 feet tall and right at the edge of their property line, could rip up a row of their trellised trees if it suffered a blow-down.

Matt had always avoided Jake. Perhaps Pap's feud with him had rubbed off. He couldn't blame Pap, losing his only child and son-in-law in that horrible crash. Matt was only six at the time, but he still had no trouble conjuring up a clear image of the gory scene right there where the compound drive met the road. It wasn't till he went to school in the fall and the kids told him Pap's daughter was in the pickup with Jake's son, that he understood all the implications.

Jake's son died from burns shortly after the fiery accident, yet Belle's closeness to Jake and his wife seemed natural, seeing they were neighbors. Besides, this was a close-knit community with plenty of skeletons in everybody's closets.

Matt took the subtle undercurrent of Pap's resentment of Belle's close relationship with Jake for granted. After all, if Jake's son hadn't been running off with his daughter, she'd still be alive. More than once, Matt had heard someone remark about the justice of this eye-for-an-eye situation. McGrady might have lost his only child, but so had Jake.

Matt could never understand why Pap didn't just tell Belle not to go over there. Especially since, on top of it all, Jake was the one responsible for her fixation with all the old apple trees.

Talk about spinning your wheels. He'd given up trying to talk some sense into her a long time ago.

He took a good look around Jake's place as he approached the front door. The orchard was known to be state of the art, but it surprised him to see almost every tree a meticulously pruned dwarf. He rang the bell and waited for Jake to open the door. The man had age on him, but was still imposing.

"Come on in, son. It's been a long time."

"Yeah."

"Belle's graduation?"

"Right!"

"What brings you here?" Jake said as he led him into the main room and motioned to a chair.

Matt, uneasy about being dirty and sweaty, barely perched on the edge of the easy chair, yet he couldn't help marveling at the man remembering him.

Jake went to the kitchen and came back with a cold beer.

"Here," he said, handing it to him. "You look like you can use one."

Matt said thanks, and quickly sucked half of it down.

"So, what can I do for you?" Jake asked again.

Matt hunched forward, propping his arms on his legs, clutching his beer. "It's about that dead hemlock on your side of the property line."

"I've been meaning to do something about it, but I've been a little under the weather," Jake quickly responded.

"Don't worry. We've got it covered. We can get to it sometime this week."

"I'll appreciate that. Let me know if I can give you anything for it."

Matt's tension slowly ebbed away. This was a lot easier than he had imagined. He gulped down the rest of the beer and felt relaxed enough to take a look around. The place was a far cry from his parents' house. Or Pap's place, for that matter. His gaze leapfrogged around the room. No wonder Belle liked to come over so much. He felt suddenly disheartened. He could never come up with a place like this for someone like her.

Jake must have sensed his discomfort. He leaned back in his chair and looked around as if he were adding it all up. "I put up every stick in this place. It took me two years. My boy helped summers." He eyed the floor. "I personally crow-barred up every one of those pieces from an old department store in Asheville before they demolished the building. They're black marble Nero Marquina tiles quarried in Spain over a hundred years ago."

Jake rose, walked across the expansive main floor smattered with Persian carpets, and went to the open kitchen.

"You did a nice job," Matt yelled after him.

When Jake came back with another beer for him and one for himself, Matt guessed he wanted to talk, and he felt honored.

"Belle tells me you got an Associate Degree in business at the community college here in town."

Matt was surprised they had been discussing him and worried about how much Belle had told him. "Yeah. Pap offered to help me get a four-year degree, but I passed it up." He looked up at Jake. "Not because I didn't want it. It's just that my mom and dad had been scrimping and saving to buy their own house for as long as I could remember. I wanted to get my brothers out of that rundown trailer court I grew up in, and figured if I stayed home, worked and saved, in a couple years I could help them with a down payment on a place of their own. With all the kids and everything, I knew if I didn't, they'd never have one." He wrung his hands. "Besides, I was married with a kid and needed to get a house of my own."

"I see they got the old Asner place."

"Yeah. They've got it pretty fixed up now."

Matt looked around searching for something to say.

"If Pap hadn't talked to the bank about giving them the mortgage, it never would've happened." He chuckled. "Heck, that goes for mine, too."

Jake sank back in his chair, pulled a leg up and rested his ankle on his knee, his scuffed number twelve's testifying to years of kicking around in an orchard. "I'm glad to hear you can take care of that hemlock. I watched you guys plant all those trees on trellises and wouldn't want anything to damage them."

41

Matt shook his head. "I thought the whole trellis thing was crazy at first. I can't believe I tried to talk Pap out of it. It was a helluva gamble. One grafted Honeycrisp tree costs us ten bucks and he wanted to put in seven hundred per acre on fifteen acres." He laughed. "Man, that's high density. Then we had to come back and put in the posts to hold five lines of wire to tie the branches to. When you throw in all the labor, tree training... you're easily talking $30,000 per acre, not to mention the irrigation.

"But the old man's stubborn like Belle. Those two are willing to try almost anything if they think it'll bring in a bigger crop." He let out a cynical chuckle. "They never knew what it's like to be piss poor and hungry. It leaves you enough scared that you don't take any chances. Heck, the first week I got my driver's license, I went to the farmers' market at four in the morning to sell some apples Pap let me pick and brought the money home to my mother."

Matt finished off his beer and put the bottle down on a coaster. "When Pap had us plant the trees three feet apart, I figured, that's it. Sure enough, we're headed for a disaster."

He eased back in the chair. "I've got to hand it to those two, though, this is one gamble that's paying off. Those trees are bearing the most consistently beautiful fruit I've ever seen on a tree. All of them are getting the same amount of sun, so they're ripening pretty much at the same rate."

"I know," said Jake. "Belle talks about it all the time. She's really committed to that system."

Matt tilted his head and gave Jake a reticent smile that made him wonder what he was holding back. "Yep. That's her, all right. Really committed. And that's Pap, too. I do the books and know how much is coming in and how much is going out. The way those two are willing to take risks sometimes drives me crazy; but it's, I don't know, what makes them so cutting-edge, I guess."

Matt knew he should go. That day, they had torn up almost every piece of equipment they had. He'd been in the garage all day, with yet another tractor waiting for him to repair before the following morning. But before he could even start in on it, he'd have to help haul all the apples that weren't going to a processor over to the packing house cooler, then move all the ladders to the next orchard. But this mysterious man he'd heard about most of his life was sitting across from him, genuinely interested in what he had to say, and he couldn't pull himself away.

"Yep, putting in those Honeycrisps was a good move. Our bulk apples—the Romes—that we send to the processor, bring in fifty to a hundred dollars a bin at the most. But we get four times as much for the Honeycrisps. We're selling them direct to a lot of fruit stand people. This week we shipped thirty-eight tractor trailer loads to this guy in Gatlinburg and forty to a firm in Chattanooga."

"How many apples make up a trailer load?"

"Over a hundred thousand."

"That's one heck of a lot of apples."

"Sure is. Once the picking starts, it's pretty much a 24/7 deal to bring 'em all in." Matt paused. He got a strong feeling that Jake wanted to hear more, but of a personal nature. "That's why my wife left. If you're not born into this life, it's hard to get used to it." He let out a brittle laugh. "That and my Hispanic family. Rita tried, but she never warmed up to them."

Matt had to stop blathering, especially since it might get back to Belle.

"Want another beer?" Jake asked.

"Thanks. I'm set." He'd be working most of the night on that tractor and couldn't afford to get lulled by drink, yet he couldn't tear himself away. He looked around, trying to come up with something that would keep their conversation going. He spotted a hefty book on the coffee table: *Antique Southern Apples by Jake Gregg*. He pointed to it. "How'd you get wrapped up in all this?"

Jake eyed him for a moment, then leaned toward him in his chair, with his forearms braced on his legs like he couldn't wait to tell him his story.

"I'd gotten a degree in agronomy from NC State. In those days, it was mandatory to take ROTC for two years, so after graduating and getting married, I decided to serve in the army for a couple years; but after the stint ended, I knew I liked it, so I took a commission.

"I got out after thirty years, and after moving my family six-teen times, all I wanted was to build my own house. My brother lived in Hendersonville, so I bought out here. When I finally got the house finished, I went over to a nursery to get some apple trees and bumped into this old guy who reminisced about his early days in Henderson County. He told me that back then they had Horse Apples, Yellow Transparents, Red Junes, Magnum Bonums, Black Twigs. He said they were good eating, but you just didn't see them anymore.

"Well, I'd always been a history buff, and it kinda piqued my interest."

Jake rubbed his hands together and Matt could tell he en-joyed reliving the story.

"For the first time in my life, I realized there *were* old apples. So, hell, why not grow some? Where are they? Can I find them and grow them? I checked every nursery, every catalog. You couldn't buy a Magnum Bonum. You couldn't buy a Black Twig. But I knew if I could find one growing somewhere, I could graft it and make my own tree."

The glass doors had been slid open, and outside, the birds called to each other for the last time that day while the katydids began the night's rattling music. The setting sun had slipped be-hind the mountains and said goodnight to the orchard, leaving it glistening with rosy highlights. Inside, the aging man told his story as if he knew he was in the twilight of his life and this was his last chance to connect with the man he hoped Belle would marry.

"I was retired," he continued. "So I got in the car and drove around the back roads looking for old apple trees. I started spot-ting a few. Maybe behind a barn; or out in the pasture there'd be an old gnarly half-dead apple tree, or in the yard of a farm house. I'd go up, knock at the door and tell 'em I was interested in old apples and I'd like some to put in my orchard. When I asked what kind of tree it was, a lot of times they would say 'Well, it was there when we bought the place.' Or 'Granny knew, but she died before she could tell us about it.' If they couldn't put a name to it, I left it.

"Every once in a while an old man or an old woman would come to the door and they'd say, 'Oh yeah, that's a so-and-so apple that my granddaddy planted. It was good in its day.' Then I would ask them if I could come back in the winter and get a cutting."

A self-satisfied smile spread across Jake's face. "I talked to hundreds of Southerners and not a one of them turned me down. All in all, I've found over 400."

Jake took off his glasses and rubbed his eyes, and for the first time that evening, Matt got a inkling the man wasn't well. Matt stood up. "I'm taking a lot of your time, dropping in the way I did." He didn't mention that the visit would cost him his dinner.

Jake rose and walked him to the door.

Matt hesitated at the threshold and stared out at the orchard.

Jake smiled. "Come on, son. I'll show it to you."

They walked over to a row where Jake picked an apple and handed it to Matt.

"It's a Nickajack. Was big in the late 1800s, but you hardly hear of it anymore. Back then they found it in an old Cherokee seedling orchard."

Matt took a bite. "It's got a sort of anise taste."

"They used it mostly for cooking. Remember, those were the days when every morning started with apples fried in the drippings from sausage or some side meat."

"Do you ever get rid of any?"

"Sure. If it's a lousy apple, I'm perfectly happy to cut it down and consign it to oblivion. If it's a decent apple and it has a history that I can trace back, I'm willing to save it, because these are the apples that Southerners ate for hundreds of years. They've earned a place."

Jake strolled over to another tree. "This is the Magnum Bonum. I'd heard about it and looked for it for years. I finally caught up with it in an old orchard in Virginia." He raised a brow and eyed Matt keenly. "It was thrilling. To discover an apple you've only read about. To have looked for it for years, thinking it was gone, and all of a sudden to discover you've found it. That's a rush, boy. That's a real rush."

Matt noticed it was getting dark and said he had to go. As he drove through the woods sheltering the compound, he wished he had met the man years ago.

JAKE PULLED HIS TRUCK into the parking lot behind his brother's office building, grabbed a batch of papers off the front seat and got out. The lobby was a little overdone, but maybe that was necessary in Ben's line of work. Benjamin S. Gregg, Attorney at Law, was on the door in impressive brass letters.

The girl at the desk looked up at him and smiled as he went in. "Hello, Mr. Gregg."

"Hi, Ellie."

"Go right in. Your brother's expecting you."

Ben Gregg, in shirt and tie, stood up and greeted him with a handshake. They resembled each other, except Jake was fifteen years older and built with a lot more muscle mass; but mostly, he carried himself like someone who'd spent years in the military— self-assured and disarmingly direct, not cagey like Ben.

Jake, wearing a pair of shorts and a short-sleeve shirt he'd dug out of his closet for the occasion, sat down on one of the elegantly upholstered armchairs in front of the desk and decided they were a little overdone, too.

His brother sat down and flipped the file in front of him closed before tossing it on one of the tall piles on his desk. "It's about time you decided to straighten out your estate, but why the big rush? I hope nothing's wrong."

Not getting a response, he picked up his phone and said, "Let me get my secretary in here so she can take notes and we can get on with the will."

"I'm not here for a will," Jake casually threw out. "I don't want anything that anybody can go to the courthouse and read. Hell, or anything that has to sit in probate for six months."

Ben looked at him questioningly.

"You know I've been doctoring my heart for years. Well, it's now what they call advanced heart failure, and they've pretty much run out of treatment options. There's nothing more they can do. Brother, I just want to go to sleep and then maybe see Mary again."

He slapped the stack of papers he'd brought with him on the desk and continued, as if casually talking about the weather. "This is pretty much everything I own."

He took some sheets that he'd stapled together from under the rubber band and handed them to Ben.

"Here's a detailed list of what I've got and how I want it disbursed."

Ben took the papers and scanned the handwritten notes.

"I want you to draw up papers assigning you as co-owner of everything in there," Jake continued. "That way, when I go, you'll have a free hand to make sure everything's taken care of the way I wrote it down there."

"This isn't the way to handle it, Jake. I'm sure I can come up with a revocable living trust that won't give any secrets away."

"Ben, as my trustee, you'd only have to do what I'm telling you to do now. What's the difference? Sell the house and put the money aside along with my life insurance to help pay the nursing home. That obligation could go on for years. Get a surveyor to carve out two acres around the house. All the rest, including the five acres of the orchard, goes to Annabelle McKenzie. Ask Barbara to divvy up all the contents. Your wife's always been fair. Then let Belle take her pick of anything you or your kids don't want.

"My desk and all my research—antique nursery catalogs, seed books, everything in my office, is to go to Belle. That's important, Brother. *Everything.*"

"Jake, are you sure you want to do this? I can get Ellie in here and have something drawn up in a couple days. Sooner if I have to."

"Nope. This is how I want it. There's no one in the world I'd trust more than you to make sure everyone is taken care of." Then he paused. "And there's one last thing, and it's in there. If there's anything left after things are over at the nursing home, I want you to give it to Belle." He pulled another sheet from under the rubber band. "Here's a quitclaim deed for the whole property." He looked hard at Ben, raised an eyebrow and chuckled. "I pulled the form up on the internet and did it myself."

Jake clapped his hands together and stood up. "That's about it." He looked around. "Since I'm here, let's go to the bank and get you on all my accounts."

The stunned expression on Ben's face said he finally realized his brother was dead serious.

"What do you want me to tell Belle when I give her the orchard?"

"You don't need to tell her anything. I'm leaving her a note in my desk."

CHAPTER FIVE

BELLE STAGGERED INTO THE PACKING HOUSE office and plopped down onto a beat-up swivel chair in front of Pap's desk. He studied some papers and didn't bother to look up. She stretched her long shapely legs out in front of her, then sat up straight, arched her spine as far back as she could and let out a long moan of relief.

"Sounds like you've been helping them grade," said Pap, still reading.

"Since eight."

He looked up and pushed a sheet of paper toward her. She slapped her hand on it, pulled it over with a grunt and studied it.

"Matt worked up those figures last night. You did good at the Apple Festival. The best we've ever done."

"I know. I kept track."

He tossed her another sheet. "Here's his workup on the road-side stand."

She scooted the chair over and took a look.

"Matt's gonna have our bulk apple figures pulled together by tomorrow morning. I asked him to project them out till November."

"Pap, the way these apples are flying out of here, we won't *have* any by November."

"I know, honey. We're having one helluva year."

Just then, Raphael walked in and said, "It's about time."

They all laughed.

"You tell your wife she can count on a bonus this year," Pap said with an uncustomary grin.

Raphael's white teeth gleamed. *"Gracias,* Jeremiah. *"*

"How about me?" said Belle. "Missy won't even get in that clunker I drive."

"Okay, I'll look into a newer truck for you."

Pap opened a drawer and pulled out a batch of envelopes and handed them to Raphael.

"Here's the paychecks. With all the overtime last week, Matt says there might be some hours left out. Matt'll take care of any complaints next week."

Raphael left and the two sat with their thoughts.

Pap straightened the papers on his desk, leaned back in his chair and fingered a pencil. "You know Matt's divorce came through." He fixed his eyes on her. "He's been a real asset to—"

"Don't go there, Pap."

"Can't you, for once, swallow your pride? That boy's worth it."

She gave him a long, steely stare.

Pap tossed the pencil onto the desk. "Don't worry, I'm not gonna push you into a marriage you don't want." A pensive veil fell over his face. "I did that once before, and I'll never forgive myself." He paused. "I'm just thinking about you, gal. You're gonna be thirty next spring."

Belle sank back in her chair and folded her arms. "Don't worry, Grandpa. Missy's gonna fix me up. Heck, she's been working on it night and day."

She let out a little laugh. "You should've seen her at the festival. That guy who's buying up all the orchards stopped by, and she practically threw me at him. I don't think I've got an ounce of pride left."

Pap chuckled. "I heard about it."

Belle threw her head back and rolled her eyes toward the ceiling. "I bet it was the talk of the street."

He tossed a hand in the air. "Aw, all the tongues were busy wagging about that Jeannie Wilson walking out on Roy." He chuckled. "But you came in a close second."

Belle groaned.

"By the way, that guy called me today," Pap said as he threw some papers into his desk drawer.

"What did he want?"

"I don't know. I told him if he's got anything to say, he's got to say it to the two of us."

Belle cast him a dubious look.

"I told him early tomorrow morning. Here in the office."

The two sat quietly sifting through their thoughts.

"Dave and Missy have picked the date," Belle tossed out.

"Have they said where they're gonna live?"

"You got something in mind?"

"Well, Matt has that trailer on the corner of the Rome orchard. I thought I'd have a couple of acres surveyed out for him, and two for Missy. I could take care of the well and the drain field, and they could put in a trailer or somethin'."

He shook a finger. "Promise me you won't go tellin' her. I'll do it myself when the time is right. I don't want them thinking I'm trying to run their lives."

He stood up and picked his keys off the desk. "I'm not going to be home for dinner. Dave's out of town, so why don't you and Missy go someplace nice to eat. Celebrate. You girls deserve it." He dug a fifty out of his wallet and tossed it on the desk. "It's on me."

Belle worked at her desk for a while after he left, then went home. She came out of the shower and heard the door slam downstairs. Missy must've come in. Belle wrapped a towel around her head, went down the hall to her bedroom and slipped into a fresh pair of shorts and a tee-shirt. She stuffed the fifty dollar bill she had put on the dresser into her pocket and was towel drying her hair when she heard Missy go into her bedroom. Belle followed her in and found her flopped on the bed.

"You look bushed."

"I am. I left the salon at three and I've been at the stand till now. The bank bag's in the kitchen drawer. Be sure to take it to the office in the morning. I've got an early dye job."

Belle stepped onto the bed and slid down crossed-legged. "You should've seen Pap today. I've never seen him in such a good mood. Matt hasn't pulled together the figures for our bulk sales yet, but this is gonna be our biggest year ever."

"I hope he's gonna get you a new truck."

"He said he would." She made a face. "I'll be lucky if it's only four or five years old with under a hundred thousand miles on it." She examined her nails and picked some dirt from under one. "Jeremiah's got something else up his sleeve."

"How do you know?"

"He made me swear not to tell you. That's how I know."

As long as the girls could remember, whenever Pap wanted to discuss something with either one of them, he would tell it to the other and get them to promise not to say anything, knowing it was an impossibility. It had become his standard means of communicating delicate issues, a way in which he wouldn't have to be confronted with any emotional outbursts. The whole thing would be calmly worked out through the go-between. When the issue involved the two of them, he resorted to going through the same exercise using his sister Pam.

"Well, what is it?" asked Missy.

"He wants to give you and Dave a couple acres next to the Rome orchard. He'll pop for the drain field and the well."

"I don't know. I kinda had a little house in a nice neighborhood in mind. Maybe near town." She looked puzzled. "Hasn't he let Matt set up his trailer on that tract?"

"Yeah. He's gonna give him two acres, too."

Missy smirked. "The boy he never had."

"Cut it out, Missy. Matt deserves it."

Missy sat up and hugged her knees. "Then why don't you give him another chance?"

"Come on. After what he pulled?"

"What do you expect. He's a man, after all."

"Why do you always see everything from the gutter?"

"Your trouble is you're just like Pap. You can't forgive. Think. Mom and Dad have been gone for almost twenty-five years now, and he's still not on speaking terms with Jake."

Missy lay back down with her hands behind her head. "Jeremiah's really had a rough time of it. Having to raise our mom, then the two of us. I wonder why he didn't remarry? Imagine going all those years without someone."

Belle gave her a look. "What do you think he was doing with Beverly?"

Missy giggled. "I don't know how she put up with it all those years. I didn't blame her one bit when she upped and married Bob Bender after his wife died. Heck, her looks weren't going to last forever. It was either Big Bob Bender or spending the rest of her life waiting around for Pap to pop the question."

Missy stared blankly at the ceiling. "I wonder why he didn't do it?"

"I don't think she was ever crazy about us," said Belle "...or the farm, for that matter. That could've had a lot to do with it. He might have been afraid if anything happened to him, she'd sell out, stick us with someone and move on. That reminds me," Belle added. "Pap said something weird. Like he forced someone to get married. You don't think he's talking about our parents, do you?"

"God only knows. We don't know jack shit about those two. Dad must have been dropped from the sky. We haven't met a single member of his family. Sometimes I think he was a drifter Pap lassoed for her. And Mom? Ha! All we got are a bunch of pictures."

"I like looking at them," Belle said, wistfully. "She was like you. Same curly blonde hair, same peaches and cream complexion." She let out a short laugh. "And what did I get? Pap's genes."

"You're gorgeous and you know it. All you need is a makeover."

"I love you, Sis. You are without a doubt the shallowest person I've ever met."

Missy laughed.

Belle grabbed a pillow, fluffed it up and slid down on it. She lay there staring at the peeling plaster on the ceiling. "When I think about all the screwing around Matt and I did in those orchards. Thank God, Pap never caught us."

"Are you kidding? He knew what was going on. Heck, we all did."

Belle raised her head and looked at Missy. "Raphael?"

"I saw him pull out his rosary beads more than once when you two went missing."

They fell into giggling.

Missy reached for an emery board and casually filed a nail. "You got to face it, Belle. You've got to make an effort and pour on the allure 'cause you're not going to get anywhere in this orchard business without a man by your side. It takes a team. And Matt's not going to stick around forever if there's nothing in it for him except a paycheck at the end of the week."

"Don't worry, Missy. Pap's working on *Plan B.*"

Missy stopped filing and looked up.

"Mr. Big Shot we met at the festival phoned and said he wanted to talk to him. Pap told him if he had anything to say, he had to say it to the both of us." She smirked. "How many times has *that* happened? He's really hung up on me getting married. He went so far as to bring up my birthday next year.

"I thought I'd never get him to stop thinking of me as a kid, and now he's got me teetering on the verge of spinsterhood. He's got that guy coming over tomorrow morning, and do you believe, he actually told me to wear something nice. I don't know how I'm gonna be able to look the dude in the eye."

Belle suddenly sat up like she remembered something and scooted off the bed. "I've got to go over and check on Jake. I'm worried about him."

She pulled the money from her pocket and waved it in the air. "It's a fifty. Pap gave it to us for dinner tonight. Where should we tell him we ate?"

"Ah, Marie's will do," said Missy as she reached for it. She picked up her wallet and pulled out two tens and a five and handed it to Belle. "Here's your half."

The next morning, Belle sat in the office rearranging the papers on her desk to make it look like she had good reason to be there. Earlier, Pap had mentioned he liked her blouse. She thanked Missy under her breath, but wished her sister hadn't told her she had to do something about her hands. Now, she couldn't keep her eyes off them as she typed in the website listed on Ken Larsen's business card.

The Larsen Cidery looked like big business. The page bragged that they operated eleven orchards. This guy evidently had enough money to buy and sell every farmer in the valley. It was just a matter of who was ready to fold.

A tap on the door got a bellowing "Come in" from Pap. She quickly closed the site and looked over. The man standing in the doorway took her breath away. Other than Matt, there had never been anyone who looked so good stand on that threshold before. The way Pap stood up and reached for his hand, he had to be just as impressed.

"Sit down, Ken," he said as he motioned toward a chair. He looked over at Belle and pointed to the one next to it. "You sit there."

Ken stood waiting for Belle to be reseated, then pulled his chair far enough back to accommodate his long legs and sat down.

Pap folded his arms and looked straight at him. Belle recognized his "let's cut the small talk and get right down to business" posture.

"What do you got in mind?" he asked.

"I'm looking for more land."

"Well, you're not gonna get it from us. In fact, right now, I'm trying to buy some from my sister."

"I hear you've done well with your trellis system."

Pap barely glanced over at Belle. "Thanks to that one. She's my right arm."

Ken gave her an open face smile that had every element anyone could consider appealing, but mostly, an aura of confidence she'd never come across before. It wavered on the rim of arrogance, but his amiability let him get away with it. Pap's abrupt turndown hadn't so much as grazed his ego.

"When are you planning on getting your cidery in production?" Pap asked.

"By next fall's crop... if all goes well."

"In this business, that's a big *if.*"

"I'm not only looking for orchards; I'll need apples, too."

"What kind?"

"For good hard cider they've got to have a lot of sugar to ferment properly, but they've got to have a certain level of acid and tannins, too. You're not going to find that in those Honeycrisps or Romes all you guys are growing. My family's put a lot of their orchards into heirloom varieties—Kingston Black, Yarlington. I'm planning on doing the same here."

"It's going to be a while before you can bring in a crop."

"I know. My family's going to give me enough heirlooms to mix with the local varieties until I've got a source of my own." He waited for Pap to say something, but when he didn't, Ken looked over at Belle. But she knew enough to keep her mouth shut when Pap was negotiating.

"You got any surplus land you can put into old cider apples?" Ken asked.

"Well, seeing as the lowest valued apple is the one that's crushed into juice and the highest, the one that ends up at the local supermarket, I'm not planning on planting apples that do anything but get into that high-value category." He threw out a laugh. "Especially not those spitters that get their name from tasting terrible."

Pap stood up and offered his hand. "But I don't want to turn you down flat. Belle's the botanist. Get together with her, and if you can come up with a proposal, I'll take a look."

"Fair enough," said Ken.

Pap scribbled something on a sheet of paper and handed it to him. "Here's her number."

Belle rose, went over to the door and opened it, an obvious invitation for him to leave. She stood there with her arms folded, eyes cast down. She looked up as he passed and their eyes met.

He smiled and winked. "I'll give you a call."

She waited for him to start down the stairs, then closed the door and leaned back against it. She gave Pap a squint-eyed look. "I don't believe you gave him my number. You make Missy look like an amateur. You have no intention of doing business with that guy."

Pap was unfazed. "Sit down. The last thing I want to do is hook you up with that fella."

Belle dutifully obeyed and collapsed against the back of the chair, braced to hear about Matt again.

Pap tipped back in his chair, swung around and looked out the window.

"But this guy might have something there."

The cadence in his voice told Belle he was turning over his thoughts.

"My parents planted our Rome orchard over forty years ago. It's time we put in something new. I want you to get with Matt. Figure the cost on pushing over ten acres of them and putting in some cider apples.

"They used to grow all over this county. Hell, hard cider was safer to drink than water. Those trees pretty much went extinct once all those teetotalers went after them with their axes during Prohibition."

His chair squeaked to a familiar rhythm as he rocked back and forth. "It might not be a bad idea to have a crop of some old variety. My dad believed in it. Even though he was always putting in the newer ones, he kept the Winesap, the Limbertwig, Lodi. There's still some growing on Pam's land. My dad always said 'If you're gonna have apples, you've got to have different varieties 'cause some of 'em are gonna get killed. You never know if these new apples will be resistant to some disease they never had before, so you gotta keep some of the old ones that thrive here. That way, you always have a crop.' Marvin Owings over at ag extension told me there's only fifteen varieties grown commercially in the whole county right now."

He swung around. "Times are changing. This cidery deal could turn out to be pretty profitable. See if there are any of the old cider varieties you can get cuttings from in that antique apple orchard of Jake's you spend so much time in. Maybe it'll finally pay off."

Belle smiled to herself. There had to be dozens.

CHAPTER SIX

IT WAS STRANGE seeing a trailer sitting on the edge of the orchard where Pap always put in vegetables. Belle ran up the narrow wood stairs and knocked on the door. Seven-thirty and already getting dark. The glow from a lamp behind a curtain shown in the window. As Belle waited, the question of why she was imposing on Matt at his home crept into her thoughts.

She wouldn't have dreamt of dropping in on him to talk business when he was still with Rita, yet she refused to admit to herself that coming there that night had anything to do with his divorce. Pap and Missy took it for granted that his new status offered fresh possibilities and changed old boundaries. But she didn't. It had taken too much out of her to reset their relationship all those years back.

In one heartbreaking instant, they had gone from a madly in love young couple with dreams of together making McGrady Orchards one of the best in the state, to two people in a strained relationship between the boss's granddaughter and the company accountant who had a new wife and a kid on the way.

The worst part of the split-up was the rebound. Her two-year affair with Jeff Richardson was a fiasco from the start, but she was too proud and too stubborn to end it. She reflected on all the times she had openly made out with him whenever Matt was around, and it made her cringe.

It still embarrassed her to imagine what Pap had to have

been thinking. If there was one thing he couldn't stand, it was a laggard. He had to have been feeling pretty sorry for her to put up with Jeff's total distaste for anything that smacked of work. Everyone had breathed a sigh of relief when Jeff finally had the gumption to walk out on her. Even Raphael made a sign of the cross and threw in a *Gracias a Dios.*

Belle looked out from the porch at the forlorn remnants of a tomato patch. All that was a long time ago. She was over it now, and focused. The McGrady Orchard's spindle trees were the talk of the state's apple growing community, and she expected this venture into antique cidery apples would make as big a splash. Then there was Mr. Blue Eyes. She chuckled inwardly. Maybe it wasn't such a bad idea for Pap to give him her number.

She knocked again, but this time harder.

A curtain was pulled to the side and quickly let drop. A moment later, the door opened and Matt stood there, hair tousled, barefoot, wearing a pair of sweatpants. His bare chest and ripped abs made her look away. "I'm sorry. I woke you up, didn't I?"

"Is everything okay?"

"Yep. Nothing to worry about."

"Come on in."

He pulled a chair out from a table. "Sit down. I'll get you a beer."

He opened the fridge and the glow brightened up the kitchen, its only light coming from a small lamp in the living room. Seeing nothing but a couple lonely condiments and a few bottles of Corona Extra, she assumed he had to be eating at his parents' house.

He twisted off the cap, put the beer down in front of her and started for the hall. "I'll be right back."

He turned and she couldn't resist following him with her eyes. The feeling she got from looking at his wide muscular shoulders made her close her eyes.

She took a slow sip of the cold beer and had a look around. The place was sparsely furnished—the table, two beat-up plastic chairs and an old sofa she remembered from his parents' house. A bunch of video disks were stacked on a TV, along with a Nintendo for his son to play with. The closest the place came to décor were crayon drawings of spaceships taped to the refrigerator door.

Matt strolled back in wearing jeans and a shirt, making her realize he had noticed her uneasiness in seeing him half naked. His rolled up sleeves exposed his heavily muscled arms. He got another beer from the fridge and pulled out a chair. He put a bare foot on it, and with an arm braced on his leg, leaned toward her and said, "I've been expecting you." He barely tossed his head and gave her one of his smart-alecky grins she hadn't seen for a while. "But I hardly thought I'd be honored with a personal visit to my home."

Belle ignored the wisecrack and looked around. "Not exactly cozy."

"I'll get my stuff when my place is sold."

"Doesn't Rita want the house?"

He shook his head. "She's getting married and moving in with him."

A shadow scarcely passed over his face. This was the first time he had acknowledged to Belle the failure of his seven year marriage. Evidently, now that it was over, there was no point in him pretending anymore.

Belle looked up at the imposing figure of manhood standing in front of her, but she only saw the fair-haired little altar boy who stood out from the trio of dark skinned young men in their black robes and white tunics at the Church of the Immaculate Conception, and she knew it had to have been Rita who asked for the divorce.

It was no secret Matt felt an overwhelming debt of gratitude to Raphael for unconditionally taking him as his son, erasing— on the surface at least—the stain of being born a bastard. At five, Matt had eagerly bought into his mother's new Hispanic family; and their strict Catholic doctrine was part of the package. No. Matt wouldn't have been the one to ask for the divorce. Belle couldn't help wondering if he was still going to mass every Sunday.

Matt pulled his chair back and sat down. "I figure you're

here about the cider apples. Pap talked to me about them today." He glanced over at the laptop lying open on the counter. "I've already done some work on it."

Belle picked up a spirited tone in his voice she hadn't heard for quite awhile.

He reached over and grabbed the laptop. "Here, let me show you."

Belle bit the inside of her lip as she watched him bring up a page on his laptop. Why did she ask him about Rita, especially since she knew what was going on? One of Raphael's cousins worked at the stand and she never failed to give Missy details of Matt's contentious marriage, always muttering under her breath something about him marrying a *Gringo* when there were so many nice Hispanic girls around. "She spits on us," she would utter in contempt. Every time Missy came running back with gossip about another one of Rita's and Matt's fights, Belle felt the sting of humiliation herself. Raphael and Matt were family.

He reached over and set his laptop down in front of her. It was opened to an orchard site that sold nothing but heirlooms. "Look. This is the Harrison, one of the very finest apples for cider making." He pointed to the price. "Do you believe, thirty-six dollars a tree? I went over to talk to Jake the other day about that hemlock, and he showed me his orchard. Hell, he's got to have a ton of old cider apples in there. He's sitting on a goldmine."

Belle, grateful the sorry subject of his divorce was out of the way, looked at him and mocked a shocked face. "I can't believe it. You? Actually talking about those old apples like they were worth something? You've been pooh-poohing the whole idea ever since we were kids."

She had come over hoping to get him interested in the idea of growing cider apples, and now she suspected he was a lot more than just interested.

"Okay," he said. "I was wrong about the spindles and the value of those antique apples."

Belle gave him a skeptical look.

"People can change, Belle."

She wanted him to say more, but he didn't.

He combed his thick blond hair back with his fingers, only to have it spring back in soft waves. "Why should we knock ourselves out growing these antiques for some rich guy to get richer?" he said, slowly pacing. "Why can't we grow them for ourselves and start our own cidery? It's the fastest growing and most profitable alcohol-based business in the country."

He stopped pacing, dropped back against the counter and folded his arms. The words came slowly, as if he were taking care not to say the wrong thing. He nudged a small toy lying on the floor with his foot as he talked.

"There's fifty acres above my parent's place. I've been talking to the folks who own them."

He cast his eyes down, and for a split second Belle saw the boy she'd once shared all her dreams with.

"I want to buy that land. I can swing it with my share of the house."

He looked into her eyes with an intensity she could almost feel. "I've been working for your grandfather most of my life. You and I both know you're going to get the whole operation one of these days." He paused. "I can't see myself working the rest of my life for you and some dude you're gonna marry. I'm thirty-one. It's time I tried to make my own mark."

The sheepish look on his face faded, replaced with a glow of optimism. "I've been thinking. If you can get Jake to let us have cuttings off all the cider apples in his orchard, hell, we'll be able to go from the apple to the bottle in three to four years."

"You're serious about this, aren't you?"

"*Dead* serious."

"Does Pap know?"

"We talked it over today, and he's for it."

Belle propped herself up on her elbow and rested her chin on her fist. "Well, well. Don't we have our very own boys' club?"

"Come on, Belle. Don't be like that. You know he's been like a grandfather to me."

Belle hardly heard him. Her mind was spinning and her excitement rising. He had hit her risk-taking nerve. "It's a long shot. Do you think we can do this?"

"Why not? We'd have three years to get set up while the trees are growing. We wouldn't have to put up our own building right away. Pap said he'd let us use part of the packing house. With all the land and trees, we should have no trouble finding the money for the equipment. I can work on getting the cidery pulled together, and you can do the grafting. I'll get one of my brothers to help you."

Belle stared at him in wonderment. All this unbridled optimism coming from the person who always cautioned her and Pap to slow down. The breakup with Rita had expanded his boundaries all right—for hope.

He went over, reached around her with both arms and booted up another page. "Look, here's a school in Virginia that trains brewers. They've got courses on making it, tasting it, tax laws, licensing. The whole ball of wax."

He let one arm slip around her shoulder, gave it a firm squeeze and craned his neck to look her in the eye. "You, me and Pap—all partners. Whaddaya say?"

She pulled away from him, then stood up and stepped back. "It all depends on whether or not Jake goes for it." What she didn't say was she knew he would. "I'll talk to him."

She walked to the door and grasped the knob. She turned to say goodbye and caught herself staring into the hazel eyes she hadn't looked into so deeply in years. His moods had always been easy to read in his eyes, but never his thoughts, yet tonight she saw something in them she refused to believe—an invitation.

He neared and clasped her arms. His buoyant expression dissolved into a look so sad that if she'd let it, would make her weep.

"It would be good for the both of us if we can pull this off, and it'll validate Jake's work." He ran a knuckle slowly down the contours of her face. "And maybe mend things a little between the two of us."

They stood motionless, his words hanging in the air. For a moment, neither of them knew what to say.

She finally turned away and disappeared into the darkness from fear of betraying how much she still felt for him. She hurried down the steps and over to her truck. She opened the door and looked back at the silhouette in the doorway and knew he understood how she felt when he made an effort to sound like the only thing between them was business.

"And, hell, while we're at it, you just might come across the Carolina Belle."

THE NEXT MORNING, BELLE RACED to Jake's while turning Matt's words over in her mind. The way Pap urged her to go over and see Jake about the trees made her think this deal might help those two bury the hatchet, too.

As usual, she found Jake in the orchard. Wednesdays were the only days he wasn't there. For as long as she could remember, he and Mary volunteered that day at the VA, but Mary was gone eight years, and he now went by himself. Belle trailed behind him as he methodically checked his trees, letting the whole idea bubble non-stop out of her. Jake only interrupted her once to ask if Pap was okay with it.

Finished, she tugged at him. "Well, what do you think?"

"You done?"

She nodded readily, barely containing herself.

"Number one, you can have cuttings from every single tree I've got."

She hugged him. "Thank you. Thank you. Thank you."

He rolled his eyes. "Come on. Let's go in and figure this thing out."

She put her arm in his, squeezed it tight and hung on to him as they went back to the house.

"You get the tea and I'll get some paper," he hollered as he disappeared into his office off the entry. She noticed a jaunt to his walk and smiled.

It took until the water boiled before he reappeared and slapped a legal pad and a three-ring binder containing information sheets on all his trees onto the table.

"We should be able to pull out the cider apples without too much trouble," he said." He picked up a pen. "Let me see. We can count on at least 50 cuttings from every tree." He looked at her. "What's your goal here?"

"I couldn't sleep all last night. I figured if we graft two thousand a year, in five years we'd end up with ten thousand."

He did some calculating. "Okay. Then we've got to pick out forty trees."

The first half dozen rolled off their tongues as fast as they could talk—Arkansas Black, Winesap, Black Twig, Newtown Pippin, American Golden Russet, Roxbury Russet.

They leafed through the binder with the joy of two people looking at an album filled with photos of old friends. He'd taught her how to graft when she was twelve, and every spring, as the two of them sat inserting new heirloom cuttings into root stock, he'd tell her the stories of how he found some of his most cherished varieties—tales injected with sufficient suspense and enough down-home humor to make the work fun.

She grew up loving the wonderful names that revealed the apples' histories and personalities—the Ladies Favorite of Tennessee, the Kentucky Red Streak, the Twenty-Ounce Pippin, Aunt Rachel's Favorite. Names infused with the spirit of the farmer who found them, not impersonal monikers dreamt up by some marketing team. The quirky old-fashioned character of these names shined a light on the eccentricity of the people who long ago had the guts to forge a new world.

"I can't remember. Are there any Harrisons?" she asked.

"Sure." He thumbed through the 'H's. "Here. I found it on a farm in Virginia. It's an old cider apple they discovered in England in the late 1800s. Somebody must have brought it over here as a tree. I knew it was a famous bittersharp, so I grafted three of them and made my own hard cider for a couple of years just to see if I could do it. I'll tell ya, it was good. Later, I didn't have the heart to get rid of the extra two trees."

"There's an orchard selling them on the internet for thirty-six dollars," she said.

"In that case, let's get cuttings from all three. If we do that every year at the rate of 150 a year, by the time you hit the fourth, you'll have six hundred."

She jumped up, leaned across the desk and gave him a kiss.

The show of affection flustered him.

"You sit right back down there, young lady. We got work to do."

She slipped back in her chair with a contented smile and listened to him plan.

"We've got to start getting those cuttings, then wrap them in clingy plastic and get 'em in one of your grandfather's coolers. You've got to order all the root stock to get here by the middle of March, then you and me are gonna have to get busy grafting."

He drummed his pen on the pad. "I think we should grow them in pots for a year rather than directly in the ground. It's less risky and will give Matt plenty of time to properly prepare the land."

They spent a couple of hours picking out the forty species, and decided since Jake had a doctor's appointment in the morning, the following week they'd tag the trees with yellow caution tape so they'd be easy to find when they went around collecting the cuttings.

Belle felt like she was flying instead of driving on the way back to the office. Every once in a while a nagging vision of all the bottles of pills lined up on Jake's counter dampened her elation. She had asked him about them, but he brushed her questions aside.

She pulled up to the packing house and jumped out. Now that the season had ended, the new sorting equipment sat in the dark draped with tarps, giving the building a haunted atmosphere. She ran up the steps to the office to give Pap the news, but he wasn't there. A note lay on her desk telling her to call him.

Matt answered Pap's phone with "McGrady's."

"Where's Pap. He wanted me to call him."

"He's here, but he's settling up with our shipper."

She barely made out Pap's voice. "If that's Belle, find out how things went."

"Did you hear that?"

"Yeah."

"Well?"

"It's a go! We can have all the cuttings we want from everything he's got. In fact, we already picked out the trees. You can figure on two thousand a year for five years."

"Good job! I'll get a contract made up."

"For what?"

"Permission to access his trees for the next five years."

"We don't need a contract. He won't go back on his word."

"Belle, if you're not comfortable asking him to sign it, I'll do it. It's got to be done. This is business."

"No. I can do it. Get it to me, and I'll get it signed when I go over there tomorrow night. He's going to help me pick out the trees I'm going to cross-pollinate this spring for my orchard."

"Okay. You'll have it. And try to cross-pollinate some of his cider apples, too."

"I can't believe it. Am I talking to the good twin, or is this really Matt Sanchez?"

He laughed and hung up.

At Jake's house the following night, she waited for Bubba to load and got an inkling something was up when he pulled a bottle of whiskey from his drawer and put it down on his desk with a thud.

"Well, are we gonna discover the best apple you never tasted today?" said Jake as he poured himself a drink.

She'd never seen him so chummy with a bottle of rye and suspected he'd been at it before she got there.

Jake thumbed through dozens of small paper bags containing the seeds from apples Belle had pollinated in the spring—some from her orchard, but most from his.

Labels identified the apples the seeds had come from, along with their genetic history. Belle would soon plant them in pots and let them overwinter outside—a step necessary to set their genetic clock so they would sprout in the spring. She'd let them grow for a year, then get a cutting and graft it onto a limb of a mature tree. That way, she'd have an apple from each seed in two or three years.

Belle pushed the carton of seeds aside, then booted up the list of apples she had in mind to cross-pollinate in the spring. She put Bubba in front of Jake to review. One of his eyebrows rose like it always did when he wanted to say something but bit his tongue instead. He sank back in his chair and twiddled his thumbs.

Belle studied the look on his face. "You think this search of mine is crazy, don't you?"

"Nah. It's not crazy. Farmers have been looking for the great American apple ever since John Chapman went around planting all those seeds. Even Thoreau wrote about it."

Jake studied the list of apples on Bubba's screen and jotted down a couple additional names on a pad. He tossed it over to her and told her to take a look.

He leaned back in his chair as she studied them. "I try to imagine what it was like when the settlers started arriving in the 1600s and the only apples they found were some native crabs. I can see it now. Those hardscrabble farmers and folks like Chapman—or Johnny Appleseed, as he's called—kicking off one of the biggest evolutionary experiments this nation has ever seen.

"Can't you just picture it! Seeds being planted all over the country. Nature was having one hell of a heyday creating millions of new genetic combinations. And talk about survival of the fittest, if a tree couldn't take the cold or the soil, or just plain wouldn't germinate, it got killed off. All the rest, by their very survival, slowly made our apples more American."

Belle pulled Bubba over to her and added the apples from his list as he mused on. "But that's only half the genetic equation. It was as natural as water running downhill. All the really good trees either got grafted or their root sprouts planted, and between nature selecting the trees that would survive and farmers multiplying their favorites, little by little we got our American apples."

His reassuring words got their annual pollination selection off to a promising start. They read, speculated, imagined and argued for a couple of hours until they finally whittled down the list to fifteen varieties.

Belle snapped Bubba closed and dreamily said, "Jake, do you think I'll ever find the Carolina Belle?"

"Why not? Hell, a lot of it is sheer serendipity. Look at that Iowa orchard in 1880. How this Quaker up there kept mowing down a seedling that kept sprouting up between a row of apple trees until he finally took it as a sign and let the ornery thing live. It's amazing. That lil' ol' chance seedling turned out to be of one of the world's most famous apples." He hunched his shoulders and threw up his hands. "What's to say you won't find one as good as that Red Delicious?"

He grabbed a manila envelope from the corner of his desk and handed it to her. "Here's another ten varieties of seeds for you to plant in that crapshoot orchard you're operating. They're from some of my cider apples. I wrote what they are on their envelopes."

The gesture surprised her. This was the first time he'd showed a genuine interest in searching for a new apple himself. She spilled the contents on the desk, and as she studied the envelopes, a sudden surge of hopefulness overcame her. It was as if Jake, Pap, Matt and she were spinning at warp speed toward a vortex that would repair the wounds between them.

Jake picked up his glass and threw back the last of the whiskey, then poured himself a fresh one. He reached for another glass, poured three fingers and plunked it down in front of her.

"Go on. Have a drink," he said.

All evening Belle had a feeling something was in the air, and this clinched it. This was the first time she'd seen him have more than a couple of beers, to say nothing of offering her hard liquor.

He picked up his glass and gestured with it to a rolled up rug leaning against the wall. "It's a Shiraz. It's from my son's room. I want you to have it."

"I can't take that over to Pap's house. It's too valuable. The mice will get it."

"See to it that they don't. Put it next to your bed. That's where Randy had it." He reached into his pocket, pulled out a bunch of keys and tossed them on the desk. "And here, these are to my truck."

Belle's eyebrows furrowed. "I can't take your truck. What are you gonna do for one?"

"I've barely driven it this year. I'm too damn old to haul things around anymore. You've seen me driving Mary's old Volvo."

She shook her head in disbelief. "I can't."

He lifted his glass. "Have some, girl, or are you gonna make me drink alone?"

She knocked down a big gulp and made a face.

He tossed her the registration. "I've signed it over to you. Consider it a birthday present."

"Jake, my birthday's not until next April, and you know it. What's going on? Is something wrong?"

"No. I've had this rug in here for a couple months now and kept forgetting to give it to you. Last week, the truck insurance came up and it didn't make sense to renew it." He chuckled. "Besides, I'm embarrassed to have anyone see that bucket of bolts you drive pull into my place."

Belle gazed steadily into his eyes, her eyebrows now deeply furrowed. "What did the doctor tell you this time?"

"That I'm getting old."

"Come on, Jake. What's wrong?"

He answered her with, "Where's that orchard contract you phoned me about?"

"We don't need a contract, but you *do* need to talk to me," said Belle.

He put his hand out. "Come on, girl. Give it to me. It's good business. I'm glad to see Matt's got a head on his shoulders."

She reluctantly handed him an envelope, and he pulled out the contract and read.

"This is fine, but it needs to be notarized. I'll drop by my brother's office tomorrow and get it done."

He picked up the bottle of whiskey and poured himself another stiff drink. Spying Belle's concerned look, he said, "Honey, you reach a point in life where you start feeling like you're running out of steam and you want to straighten out all your affairs. That's all it is."

His obvious lie made her choke up. Mac, who was curled up at her feet, bounced up and licked her face. She petted his head with one hand and wiped her nose with the back of the other. "I can't stand the thought of anything happening to you."

Strangely unmoved, Jake casually pulled a tissue out of its

box and handed it to her.

"Here."

Belle took it, and then had another gulp of whiskey.

Jake scratched behind his ear and avoided her eyes. "Now that we're on the subject of propagation, have you thought about it as far as you're concerned?"

"Not you, too," she moaned.

She took a deep breath, swallowed the rest of her drink and said, "I'm gonna have to walk home."

"Just stay over."

She sniffled and he pulled out another tissue and handed it to her.

"Girl, you sure can't hold your liquor."

They fell silent and listened to Mac's tail thump on the carpet. Finally Jake said, "Matt came to see me about that dead hemlock." He cleared his throat. "I'm glad I got to know him before..." He picked up his glass and took a long swig. "He struck me as a very kind man."

Jake put the glass down and patted her hand. "So he strayed when you were at school. What's so new about that? Besides, it was a long time ago. You were just kids back then. You don't want that stubborn streak of yours to let you lose a good man." He picked up his drink and swirled it around in his glass. "I don't think he's ever gotten over you, Belle. Why can't you forgive him?"

Belle traced the rim of her glass with her finger and drifted into a trance.

"The fact is I never got over him either, Jake." Her words seemed to be suspended in mid air as she gazed past him. "Something happened between us that I never told anyone." Her eyelids narrowed and the creases at their corners deepened. "It's a day I'll never forget. I'd had a bad time in my botany class. You see, I'd gotten pregnant in my freshman year. Matt and I didn't have much choice. Everything would go down the tubes if I went ahead with it. I'd have to quit school. He'd have to leave Blue Ridge Community College and work full-time. We were both afraid of Pap and Raphael. I figured I had to let the baby go.

Matt didn't say no. If he had, I wouldn't have done it. But he didn't.

"I was never able to get that baby boy out of my head. Even after two years. There I was in class, and every time the professor mentioned genes I'd think about what he might've been like.

She sat transfixed, tears slowly tracing their way down her cheeks. "I was on my way to the dorm when I saw him. I knew something bad had happened. Why would Matt drive five hours without calling ahead? He sat me down on a bench. I saw he'd been crying and I was so scared I couldn't talk.

"Then he told me about Rita. He ran into her at a party. He'd been drinking, and now she was pregnant. I must of been screaming 'cause everyone on the quad was looking at us. When he finally calmed me down, I asked him when was she going to get rid of it. I remember as if it were yesterday. He just stared at me.

"I kept hitting him with my books and screaming that he let me lose my baby but was going to let Rita keep hers. I can't re-member walking to his truck, just his fingers biting into my arm so tight it hurt. I was hysterical in the truck, coming up with all kinds of schemes to get us out of the mess.

"Then he said Rita had gone over and told Raphael, and I knew they were married."

Jake took out a tissue and gently wiped the tears streaming down her cheeks.

"Somehow I made it to class every day, but at night I buried my face in my pillow and cried so much I lost my voice. You don't think so at the time, but sooner or later you run out of tears.

"The hardest part is when I see his boy. He's so adorable. I can't help thinking mine would have been just like him. But I never gave the little guy a chance." She dropped her head in her hands and let out a heart-wrenching wail. "Oh, Jake, I mowed my little chance seedling down."

Jake reached over and tenderly lifted her head.

She looked into his eyes. "I'm not stubborn, Jake. I just can't get over it."

CHAPTER SEVEN

IT ALL STARTED WHEN THE FIRST WHITE SETTLER dug a hole and planted an apple seed. He'd arrived under less than auspicious circumstances after fighting alongside his father for the British in the Battle of Kings Mountain. Once the bloody battle was lost and his father strung up by vengeful Overmountain men, William Mills barely escaped with his life before making his way from the North Carolina foothills into its mountain wilderness.

He holed up for months in a cave in a granite outcrop on the eastern ridge of the plateau and determined to one day start a new life in the valley below. He finally left the hideout and swore allegiance to the newly named United States, then gathered up his family and brought them to the valley. When one of his daughters married a strapping young pioneer, the McGrady clan started digging their roots into the valley.

The clan was well into its fourth generation by the time Pam's mother married Jerome McGrady in 1934. They started off with practically nothing and endured every disaster nature threw at them; yet they demonstrated a propensity for getting ahead with honest hard work.

A lot of the credit has to go to Pam's mother, Myrtle. She came from a long line of apple farmers and was married at 19 to Jerome, who at 25 was considered old at the time. The couple started out sharecropping on an apple orchard and living in a one

-room log cabin with a sleeping loft, no electricity, and water from a spring; yet Myrtle's resourcefulness and creative flair turned out to be the underpinnings of what would eventually rank them as one of the most prominent orchard farmers in the state.

Myrtle kept the money she got from eggs, chickens and butter separate, and saved for a loom; then she wove simple cotton two-treadle rugs to sell at the curb market in Hendersonville. She dyed all the material herself in an iron pot in the backyard over a fire while infant Pam sat on a blanket on the grass.

Her business progressed, and as people's sensitivity to color developed along with it, Myrtle became known for more than her business sense. Customers brought her samples to match—curtains, slipcovers, fabric scraps—and without them leaving their material behind, she'd match the color from memory. Remembering the tone, color and hue, she'd drop a mixture of dyes into the pot and come up with the right color for their rug.

Jerome and Myrtle grew up in the depression, married in the depression, and never had anything to speak of until the day Myrtle handed Jerome the down payment for their first orchard—a loan he eventually paid back.

The farm came with a house, and the couple, along with their ten year old son, Jeremiah, and Pam, who was just out of diapers, moved from the one-room cabin to a three-bedroom house with running water, electricity, a dining room, living room and kitchen. It was a big, wonderful change for them, and signaled the birth of the McGrady Orchard.

Today, Pam looked searchingly out from her kitchen window and spotted Mac loping through the orchard across the open field separating her property from Pap's. Belle couldn't be far behind. Of course. Where else would she go to mourn Jake's passing? Thank God, she found her. She'd been trying to track her down ever since Pap called. Pam pulled her jacket off the back of a chair, shouted to her husband in the other room that she'd be right back and rushed out of the house.

The field was soggy after all the rain they'd been having, and she wished she had taken the time to put on her boots. A nip in the air made her pull her jacket tight around her as she trudged across the landscape striped with cornstalk stubs.

A small flock of Canada geese that had been pecking around for leftovers took off honking as she neared, and she watched them soar into the sky. Row after row of billowy white clouds floated across the kind of glorious blue sky you see on a sunny day in the fall, reminding her of an apple orchard in full bloom. She had loved this kind of sky from the first time she saw it, when as a child she lay on that same field trying to glean figures in the clouds. The sight was like a cherished picture you stuff in a drawer and delight in every time you run across it.

She reached the crest of the hill and spotted Belle moving from tree to tree, pruning as fastidiously as her mother had thrown her shuttle through the cords on her loom. For the millionth time she was struck with how much Belle resembled Myrtle—two mavericks with an eye for business and respect for hard work.

Mac's bark caused Belle to look around and notice her. Belle finished a tree, holstered the pruner and threw a stick for Mac to fetch as she waited for Pam to approach.

Pam opened her arms, inviting a hug. "How you doin', gal?"

Belle put her arms around her, buried her head in her shoulder and dissolved into tears.

"It's good to have a place like this to come to when you're hurting," said Pam, gently running her hand over Belle's head. "Sort of like a church."

Belle somberly nodded, then looked up. Her bloodshot eyes stunned her great-aunt and filled her with the dread of having to give her more bad news.

"Come on, girl. Let's go sit a while in that truck of yours. You got all winter to go at these." She slipped an arm around Belle's waist and the two trekked toward the truck along the path of bent grass Belle's footsteps had made.

"We're a lot alike," said Pam. "I grew up always surrounded by orchards just like you. In fact, the first vehicle I ever sat in or operated was a tractor. When I was around eight, my job was to move it from row to row with a trailer behind as my dad and

Pap—we called him Jeremiah in those days—loaded the apples. It saved them from having to get on and off the tractor."

"I had to fight to drive one," said Belle as she kicked a rotting apple that had rolled onto the path. "Matt taught me. One day Pap hollered for Raphael to put our new Deere in the barn, and I got on it and drove it right in. I was ten. Just once in a while I might've seen Pap smile, but he grinned at me all that day."

A sharp gust of wind swirled Belle's ponytail in the air. Pam stopped, then Belle. Pam pulled a soft scarf from her pocket and wrapped it around Belle's neck and stuffed the ends in her jacket. "Land sakes, girl, you've been wearing this same 'ol ratty thing since you were in high school." She pulled a tissue from her pocket and gently blotted the tears on Belle's cheeks.

"I can't believe he's gone," said Belle. "I remember the first time I saw him. Pap and Raphael were with the pickers in the orchard and I wandered off. I went through the woods until I got to this fence and saw him working in his garden." She looked puzzled. "There was something about that place. I was only five, but I knew something wonderful was happening in it." She crouched down, took the stick from Mac and gave his head a vigorous rub. "Missy says there's no way I can remember that far back, but I do." She looked up at Pam. "As if it were yesterday."

Pam grasped Belle's arm and coaxed her up, then they continued arm in arm along the path.

"Of course, you can remember it," said Pam. "The earliest thing I remember, and I know this was before I could walk, was when my mother went to the curb market and left me with my dad. I remember he was working in the field and put me on the mule's neck and told me to hold on to its mane. That was when I was maybe a year old. Can you imagine that? I was a *baby* hangin' on to this mule while he plowed."

Belle laughed softly.

"I remember seeing its ears," Pam continued. "That's how I know I was that little. I wasn't conscious of anything else, only that my view of the world was being blocked by those two mule ears. People tell me it's impossible to remember that far back, too, but *I do.*"

They reached the truck and Belle put down the tailgate for Mac to jump in, then the two slid in the front.

Pam looked around. "Jake gave you this?"

"Uh-huh. A rug, too."

Pam couldn't stall any longer. Belle was going to hear the news, and it had to come from someone who loved her. She took her hand and squeezed.

"Honey, Jake's property is up for sale."

Belle gave her an incredulous stare. "What are you talking about?"

"You don't think that place is just going to sit there, do you?"

"The funeral was two days ago. I haven't had a chance to think about anything." She clutched the back of her neck and groaned. "How do you know?"

"Pap found out this morning and called me."

TEN MINUTES LATER, Belle raced to the compound. She pulled up to the packing house, ran up the stairs to the office and threw the door open. "Pap!"

He put his pen down and leaned back in his chair. "I see Pam's talked to you."

"How long have you known?!"

Her question was met with silence.

Belle put two hands on his desk and leaned toward him. "You've got to buy it!"

"They're asking too much. It's more than I can come up with."

She threw up her hands and paced, then suddenly stopped, swung around and exploded. "Get a mortgage! You've got so damn many now, what's another one?!"

"We can't handle another one."

Matt opened the door, rushed in and came to a sudden stop at the sight of Belle, clearly under strain and miserable. She sank down on a chair and he pulled one up and sat facing her.

"Belle, I know you're upset about Jake, but can I ask you something?"

She nodded.

"Did you get that contract signed?"

"He took it to his brother to be notarized."

Belle noticed Matt give Pap a look.

"What? What is it?"

"That's who put the property up for sale," Pap answered.

"Well, if Jake took it over to him, even if he sells the property, we'll still have the rights to the trees for five years, won't we? That's enough time for me to get cuttings from every single tree in that orchard. I'll be able to save it."

Pap got up, went over to the window and jangled the change in his pocket.

Belle's optimism dissipated. "What is it, Pap?"

"Pam's brother-in-law, the one who's a real estate broker, called me this morning. That's how I know. I've had him looking around for acreage for us to put up more spindles. I told him about the contract Matt had drawn up and he checked with the listing agent. She said there were no contracts, easement, liens or any sort of encumbrance on the property whatsoever." Pap was trying hard to be positive for Belle's sake, but he'd been in business long enough to know something wasn't adding up.

Belle's expression went blank. In less than a day she'd gone from mired in bottomless sorrow to horror-stricken.

"I'll call Jake's brother and see if he's willing to cut away the orchard," said Pap. "I think we can handle that." He paused. "One way or another."

She jumped up and wanted to hug him, but his back was to her.

"Pap?"

He turned.

"Thank you."

She put a hand on his shoulder.

"Can I do the calling?"

BEN GREGG PUT THE RECEIVER BACK in its cradle and pressed the intercom button. "Annabelle McKenzie's coming to see me tomorrow at ten."

"You want me to open a file for her?"

"No!" He dropped his head in his hand, weary. "I'm sorry. I didn't mean to speak to you like that, Ellie. Please do me a favor and get my realtor on the phone."

After a moment, a button blinked. He held his breath until his secretary's voice came over like a threat. "It's your stockbroker."

He put his hand on the receiver and waited a moment, then picked it up. "I'm working on it Ralph."

"So are the regulators."

"Calm down for Pete's sake. I'll have the money in ten days."

"Jesus Priest! You've been saying that for two months! Ben, I'm telling you, they're sniffing around. Our auditors weren't supposed to be here till after they finished with the Charleston office. I talked to one of their brokers today. He said something about their not getting there for a while because they're going somewhere else on Monday. Where in the hell do you think they're going?! I need that $796,000 by Friday. If I go down, buddy, believe me, I'm taking you with me."

Ben eyed another blinking button. "I've got to go, Ralph. Sit tight. You'll get the money."

"Your realtor's on the line," floated from the intercom.

He picked up the receiver and pictured the woman sitting in her big white Cadillac, gripping the phone with her chubby fingers loaded with the rings she'd finagled from her last two husbands. The main reason he used her was because she was always good for another contentious but lucrative divorce he could easily handle.

"Where are we with that damn contract?"

"They're writing it up now."

"Call that agent. I've changed my mind. I don't want to sell the orchard. Take if off and let them have the rest."

"Is this because of that call I got over the tree contract?"

"Of course not."

"We've got it listed as a complete unit and by all—"

"Save it! Just do as I say. How much do you think we can get if we cut out the orchard?"

"The whole value of the property is in the house. That orchard is only five acres and it's more of an eyesore than anything. I can tell them you'll knock off twenty-thousand if they take it without the trees."

"Do it! And let me know by nine tomorrow."

The next morning, his secretary greeted him with, "Your realtor called."

He glanced at the note she handed him, went into his office and gave the woman a call. It took only a moment for her to pick up, but as he feared, her car was floating in and out of a dead zone. He barely made out what she was saying.

"For Christ's sake, tell me about the orchard," Ben screamed at her.

She had pulled off the road. "Is this better?"

"Yes. Yes. What did they say?"

"His client wants the orchard. He's buying 'em up all over the county. Ben, if you don't take this deal as is, I'm afraid this guy's gonna move on to something else."

Ben ran his fingers through his thinning hair and pictured himself in a courtroom, only this time as the accused. He pushed back a strong urge to vomit. "How fast can they close?"

"It's a cash deal and they're not asking for an inspection. All we need is the property search and a survey. A week."

"That's not good enough. Tell them we've got to close by Friday, then bring me the contract."

He must have sat there for an hour wringing his hands and pouring over Jake's portfolio. It was ironic that his brother, after serving in the military most of his life, was worth more than he was. He remembered laughing to himself when Jake told him he and Mary were writing a book about antique apples. That and all his subsequent speaking engagements had given them more than they would ever need.

He couldn't get the face of the heartbroken young woman who'd shortly be sitting across from him out of his head. He pictured her grandfather and sister holding her up during the memorial service. When she called, she couldn't have sounded more desperate if she had been begging on her hands and knees in front of him. The prospect of having to watch her in person plead for the use of something she already owned, would have been a fitting punishment for all the crap he'd ever gotten away with; that is, if he had a heart.

He'd have given the orchard to her outright just to get rid of her, but he was at the end of his rope. Damn that realtor. He didn't care how many divorces he was passing up, he was never going to use her again. He suspected that all she wanted was to get her greedy little hands on her commission by the end of the week. It wouldn't surprise him if she hadn't even tried to talk them out of the orchard.

Why in God's name didn't he just laugh off Ralph's proposal? Him, of all people. He was one of the county's premier defense attorneys with intimate knowledge of the long arm of the law. It still gave him the creeps when a jail door slammed behind him, even though all he had to do was signal to the guard after listening to another lying bastard insist he was innocent. Yet, he was still able to turn off that little voice in his head when the chance to gamble and win big was dangled in front of him.

His mind wandered to his family. If he went to jail, Barbara would carry on. She was a trouper. But his two girls would never be able to face their friends at the country club again without wondering what they were thinking. He envisioned Ralph in a prison jumpsuit. At least, he'd have the satisfaction of seeing him get what he had coming.

Just like he'd been doing a lot lately, he thought about how much chance played a part in determining one's fate. How a person's future can pivot on a single event that strikes like a bolt of lightning from out of nowhere. Moments before Jake walked in his office and slapped everything he owned on his desk, he had actually been considering suicide.

Then, as he skimmed over the list of his brother's holdings, what little he'd ever felt about brotherly love and ethics flew out the window, and an irrepressible desire to survive flew in. Why in the hell had he urged Jake to establish a health care trust to cover the nursing home? Now, there was only one way he could touch that money—another death in the family.

But the here and the now is what he'd better concentrate on. He'd gotten almost $50,000 out of Jake's two bank accounts, and $500,000 from the life insurance policy Jake had foolishly assigned to him as his executor, but he still needed $250,000 of the $300,000 from the sale of the property. If he didn't come up with the money by Friday, he'd wind up on the front page of the *Times-News* like all the other crooks. But if he did come up with it, this whole nightmare would go away as if a crime were never committed. The slate wiped clean. Saved from disgrace.

If he wanted to make sure his fate pivoted in the right direction, he had better put on one hell of a convincing show for Annabelle McKenzie. The last thing he needed was some hysterical girl asking a lot of questions, especially one with a powerful grandfather. The curtain was going up shortly, so it was time to buck up. Then all he'd have to do was hang tight for a few more days and he'd be in the clear.

His secretary poked her head in the door, startling him.

"It's your ten o'clock."

The woman stepped to the side and Belle walked in. She was clad in jeans and a blouse, but he only noticed the intense expression she wore on her face. He rose and gestured for her to sit down, relieved to see she had pulled herself together since the funeral. She neared the desk and he noticed a glint of recognition as she eyed Jake's handwritten pages lying on his open file. He quickly slapped the folder closed and dropped it in a drawer.

He sat down and casually rested his folded hands on the desk. "I don't know what I can do for you, dear. As I told you on the phone, I know nothing about a contract. And to be absolutely sure, I reviewed everything in Jake's file again this morning."

She dropped her head in her hands with a soft sigh, raising his concern level a notch. She looked up at him and the angst on her face brought back all the times he had let his wife down.

"Mr. Gregg, I don't know how much you know about your brother's orchard, but it contains a priceless collection of antique apple trees. He spent thirty years of his life searching for them all over the South. I can't believe he didn't make *some* arrangement for them."

He didn't like her tone, but there was nothing she could do. Jake's handwritten letter was definitely the only one. It contained all his edits and additions. Some of the inserts had been crossed out and rewritten twice. If he had a cleaner copy, he would've brought it in. And he knew Jake didn't have a copy machine, because he always came over to use his. So he let her accusation slide.

"Certainly, I am aware of how important that orchard is. My wife and girls cherish his book. Dear, I wouldn't be selling the place unless it was necessary, but he left a lot of obligations that have to be met."

"Then can you sell us just the orchard? We can't come up with the money for the house."

Despite a lifetime of being cool under pressure, her intensity was getting on his nerves. He resisted an urge to press his temples with his fingers, and instead, forced a sympathetic manner. "Miss McKenzie, I know you meant a lot to my brother. He told me so. And if there was any way I could do as you ask, I would."

She lunged forward. "Please. I'm begging you. Jake *is* that orchard. If anything happens to it, it's like he's dying all over again."

He knew she was distraught, but he didn't expect her to be so impassioned. He had dealt with women in this condition in enough divorce cases to know he had to nip it in the bud. She leaned at him, her face inches from his. Her eyes were bloodshot, her forehead grooved in deep wrinkles and her mouth set in a militant clamp, yet she was still beautiful and strangely vulnerable. It was a combination that demanded he summon one of his strongest talents—the ability to tell a bald-faced lie with heartfelt sincerity.

"I'm so sorry, dear. It's already sold."

A killing look flashed on her face and he had to readjust a slight upturning of his lips. Her eyes moved from side to side, then suddenly froze on him.

"Who bought it? I'll get *them* to sell it to me!" She pounded her fist on the desk. "Tell me! Who!?"

Her militancy stunned him. "I can't. Not until it closes." By the glint in her eye he realized he had said the wrong thing.

"You mean it's not final?"

The sound of the door opening made the both of them look over to Ellie who had poked her head in.

"Is everything all right, Mr. Gregg?" she asked, somewhat meekly.

"Yes! Close the door!"

Ellie took a quick look at Belle and swiftly closed the door. Loud altercations in Ben's office hardly bothered her anymore, but there was something about the way her boss had reacted to the young woman's call the day before that worried her. She was at her desk, when moments later Barbara Gregg walked in the office.

"Ben and I are having lunch," she sang out as she went over and reached for the door to his office.

"He's with someone," Ellie quickly offered.

Muffled bits of Belle's emotional pleading drifted from under the oak door. Barbara listened intently.

"How many times do I have to tell you I can't sell you the orchard!" Ben shouted, making one of Barbara's eyebrows arch.

"Sometimes he has difficult clients," Ellie apologetically offered.

Barbara looked at her. "You don't have to soft-pedal it, dearie. We both know he hasn't been himself for weeks."

The door flew open, and Belle, tears rolling down her cheeks, ran out, threw open the door to the office and was gone. Ben appeared in the doorway and took a look at Barbara.

"You're here."

"Well, don't act so surprised. You did offer to take me to the club for lunch."

"That's off." He turned to his secretary. "Give her the keys to my brother's house." He looked back at Barbara. "It's sold and you've got three days to get everything you want out of there."

"Three days?"

"You heard me. Three days."

"What do you want me to do with all the stuff in his office? The last time I saw it, there were cartons stacked to the ceiling."

Ben suddenly remembered Jake mentioning he'd left Belle a note. "Get your handyman to drag it all out and burn it."

He shot back to the secretary. "Ellie, I want you to go over there tomorrow and get his computer, discs, thumb drives, all that shit."

"What do you want me to do with it?"

"Bring it here." He thought for a moment. "And put it in the closet in my office."

He turned, went back in and slammed the door shut.

The secretary shrugged her shoulders sympathetically, embarrassed for Barbara. She pulled a box of keys from her drawer, thumbed through the tags and handed her one. Barbara took it as Lucy Bishop, the firm's accountant, walked in. Barbara gave her a polite nod of recognition, said goodbye to Ellie and left.

Lucy handed the secretary an envelope. "Here's your check. I'm closing the books for the month tomorrow, so if you've got any invoices kicking around, make sure I get them."

She gave the door to Ben's office a glance. "How's Attila doing today?"

"Well, I'll tell ya," Ellie whispered. "Some women don't have any backbone. If my husband ever treated me the way he treated his wife today, I'd leave him."

BARBARA MEANDERED INTO BEN'S DEN wearing a robe and fluffy slippers. She wanted to get a legal pad so she could work up a list of questions for Ben while he showered. She'd been sifting through Jake's belongings all afternoon and had a pretty good idea of who was going to get what.

She took a sip of Ben's Manhattan, and out of habit, picked up one of the sheets lying on top of an open file and read. Ten minutes later, she was leaning against the doorway of their bedroom, clutching Jake's letter and glaring at her husband. He sat on the bed, putting on a slipper.

Without looking up, he said, "Well, are you just going to stand there?"

"I can't believe you're doing this to that girl."

He looked up. "What girl?"

85

She waved the letter. "This one!"

He flung the slipper across the room. "*Ssshit!* I should've burned that goddamned thing the minute I walked in the house."

"Ben, I'm warning you. God will strike you down dead if you do this."

"If I don't, he won't need to. I'll do it myself."

She went over, sat down next to him and put her arm around his shoulder.

"Ben, darling, I know you're in trouble, but this isn't like you. You're not that mean."

"For Christ's sake, Barb, do you think I'd do this to that girl if I had a choice? I'm in such deep shit, it's going to take every dime Jake left to keep me out of prison." He stood up and paced erratically. "I'm going to make it up to her. I just can't do it now."

"Ben, tell me. What have you done?"

"It's that sonofabitchin' Ralph Reynolds' fault. This summer we had a couple of drinks at the club after a golf game and, I don't know, he had this deal we could go in together. He was so sure of it. He had inside information about this start-up company that was ready to announce a big contract with China. He said I could buy futures and make a killing after the deal went public."

"Ben, you promised me you'd never gamble again."

"Honey, I wasn't gambling." He pounded his fist on the dresser. "Ralph said it was a sure thing."

"How much did you lose?"

"Ralph said their shares would go up from $52 to at least $75 once the official announcement came out. I bought 20,000 on margin, so all I had to come up with was a little more than a hundred thousand."

"Where did you get it?"

He took a deep breath and slowly let it out. "You got to remember, Barb. I'd be making almost a half a million, less the twenty percent I had to kick back to Ralph."

"Do we still own this house?"

"Yes. But it's mortgaged to the teeth."

Barbara grabbed the footboard and braced herself.

"The China deal went south when they arrested some general in their army in a big bribery sweep. The scandal trickled back to the U.S. and it really hurt the company I had all the stock in. Well, to make the whole damned story short, by the time the contract came due, the shares had fallen to $7." He ran his hands through his hair and winced. "I bought long, so I had to come up with another eight hundred thousand. Ralph's been holding off a margin call by fudging the books so it looks like I paid it, but the auditors are coming next week."

He went over, sat down next to her and took her hand.

"Honey, my brother's property's going to close in four days. If I don't give Ralph the money by Friday, they're gonna get him for insider trading and the both of us for fraud."

"You're not going to get enough money from the sale, are you?"

He looked into her eyes.

She put her trembling fingers to her mouth. "You haven't taken the money from the trust fund, have you?"

"Of course not," said Ben, even though he would have if he could.

Barbara's face was rigid with torment. "What else have you done?"

"I'm using the money from Jake's life insurance." He didn't think it was wise to mention the bank accounts.

Barbara sat dumbfounded. "Weren't you supposed to put that in the trust fund?" She sat shaken. "I can't believe this, after what Jake said about you in his letter—'There was no one in the world he trusted more.'"

MIRED IN A CLOUD of bewilderment while waiting to find out who bought Jake's place, Belle decided to drive over there for what could turn out to be her last look. She came around the curve and saw a Mercedes parked by the door. Next to it, two men wrestled a huge oak headboard into a truck.

Why didn't she think of it before? Of course, if they're planning on selling the house it had to be emptied. Her heart beat in her throat. What was going to happen to all Jake's research—

thousands of newspaper clippings going as far back as the 1700s, all the old nursery catalogs, agricultural bulletins and pamphlets? Everything! Her whole world unraveled right in front of her.

She pulled up behind the Mercedes and jumped out. The silence struck her as dismal, nothing but the creaking of empty bird feeders swaying in the breeze. She headed for the propped open front door and went inside.

Barbara stood at the table wrapping a piece of china with newspaper. Even with all the clutter around her, the woman looked put together. The turtleneck with a single string of pearls and the sharply creased slacks were evidently her version of work clothes.

Barbara looked up.

"Hello," Belle said, masking fears bordering on hysteria.

"Hello, dear," responded Barbara. She didn't seem surprised to see Belle as she gently placed the wrapped article into a carton and casually picked up another dish.

"I came over to take one more look," said Belle. "It's kinda hard for me to stay away." Belle ran a hand over the dining room table she had sat at so often and felt her eyes pool as she groped for the words to beg for Jake's research. "What are you planning on doing with Jake's files?"

Barbara studied Belle's face for a long moment as if she were considering her answer. "We're going to—"

One of the workers appeared at the threshold and yelled, "Can we clean out the office next? We gotta get started if we're gonna get all that stuff burned today."

It took a moment for his words to sink in, then Belle covered her face with her hands and shrieked as if sorrow was spewing from the very core of her being. "Oh, God! Please don't let this happen! It's a man's life work."

Barbara put an arm around Belle's waist and pulled her close.

Belle slowly took her hands away from her eyes and looked at her, wild-eyed.

"Darling, can you get a truck here right away?"

Belle's mouth sagged open.

"Can you?" Barbara asked again, this time more urgently.

"It's outside."

Barbara turned to the men. "Put all the cartons in her truck."

The older of the two scratched his head. "Your husband called me last night and told me to be sure to burn every scrap of paper in that room and bring the contents of whatever's in the desk to his office. And he used pretty colorful language."

"Listen, Leo, you either put those cartons in that truck and keep your mouth shut, or so help me, when I get finished with you, neither you nor any of your family will ever work for me again... or for anyone in my club."

The man shrugged and the two of them trooped into the office and started hauling out the cartons with Belle watching in disbelief. It wasn't until the room was almost empty that she stopped being afraid that the whole thing was a dream.

Barbara came into the office and nodded approval. She looked over at Belle who was standing next to the desk, then she suddenly turned around and left. She came back in moments with an empty carton, dropped it on the floor and pulled out a drawer.

"Help me empty these," she ordered, then swiftly tipped over the drawer and dumped the contents into the carton. "He wants whatever's inside, and he's gonna get it."

After the men hauled out the last of Jake's cartons, Leo came back in and spoke to Belle. "We had to stash two of 'em in the front."

Barbara pointed to the carton on the floor. "That's everything in the drawers. Now, put the desk on the truck."

He rolled his eyes, then motioned for his helper who was standing at the door to grab one end. As they carried it out, he looked at Belle and said, "I hope you're not going far."

"Come on," Barbara told Belle.

Belle followed her into the main room where Barbara hefted up a carton and handed it over to her.

"I want you to have this set of china. Both of my girls have three already. One of these days you're gonna get married and it'll come in handy." She grabbed up another carton and started with it for the door. "Let's see if we can squeeze these two, plus that other one, in the front seat."

Belle stood frozen. "Why are you doing this?"

Barbara turned around and looked at Belle, a mixture of pride and self-righteousness on her face. "Because Jake said that I'd always been fair."

CHAPTER EIGHT

"GIMME YOUR HAND," said Missy. She sat cross-legged on her bed with a tray cluttered with beauty products on her lap. Belle lay next to her, staring mindlessly at the ceiling. Missy picked up one of Belle's fingers and started to file the nail, then dropped the file on the tray and dug around for her clippers.

"I think I'm just going to trim them," she said as she snipped off a jagged piece of nail. She picked up a bottle of polish, examined it, then put it back down. "We're gonna need something more neutral." She picked up another bottle and held it in front of Belle's face. "What do you think about this color?"

"How could this have happened?" Belle said in a pathetic weepy voice.

Missy shrugged, then put the bottle back on the tray and grasped the next finger. "If anyone needs their eyebrows plucked, it's you. We'll do that next. Okay?"

"He was the sweetest, nicest man in the whole world," whimpered Belle.

"If there's one thing a woman has to do is make sure her eyebrows have the right arch." Missy picked up the next finger and casually clipped a nail. "You don't want to have a surprised look permanently pasted on your forehead. It's creepy."

"The whole thing doesn't make sense. I know Jake. He never would've abandoned his orchard."

91

"Look at Pam. At her age she's still fabulous. You know why? Because she's always looked after herself. It's good to look natural, but there's no harm in—"

Belle grabbed her hand.

"You know, Missy. There was something about Jake's brother that I picked up on, but I can't put my finger on it."

Missy stopped snipping. "Tell me about it. Lucy Bishop, you remember her from school. She's his accountant. She said he's a beast."

"Is Lucy that girl in your class who won that big scholarship to Duke?"

"Yeah. But she couldn't go. Her dad died in an accident at the baby-food plant, and she had to stay home and help out. That's how she got the job. Mr. Gregg represented her mom when she sued the company. When they lost, he felt sorry for the family and hired her."

"Then why doesn't she like him?"

"He treats her like dirt. His wife, too. From what she says, the guy's an arrogant bastard."

"Has she ever questioned his honesty?"

"Not really. Just that he handles a lot of divorces and defends the worst scum in the county. A lot of them pay in cash, and he makes *her* take the money. She's sure the bills are covered with meth powder." She reached for Belle's hand. "Gimme the other one."

"He had a file open on the desk, and I saw some notes written in Jake's own hand. If only she could—"

"Uh-uh. Nothing doing. I'm not going to ask her to do anything crazy."

Belle sat up. "You've got to call her and get her to meet me for lunch!"

Missy was taken aback. This was the first time since Jake died that her sister registered any emotion other than anguish. Missy was suddenly willing to make a date with the devil if it would pull her sister out of her misery.

"Okay. I will. Now lie down." Missy picked up the tweezers. "After your eyebrows, I'll give her a call."

Belle grabbed her hand. "Oh, no, you don't. No call, no eyebrows."

Missy reluctantly put her tray on the bed and left for the kitchen to look up Lucy's number.

The next morning, Belle sensed a mood in the office the minute she walked in, and it made her ill at ease. The way Matt and Pap had suddenly stopped talking, it was obvious she had interrupted something. She gave her desk a once-over and told the two she was going to check out the old barn. She turned to leave and noticed the look they gave each other.

"Well. What is it?"

"Ken Larsen's been calling. He says you don't return his calls."

"Just stall him, Grandpa." She was angry with herself that she couldn't purge the defensiveness out of her voice.

"It won't hurt for you and Matt to see what he's got in mind," said Pap.

The room became quiet, and after a long moment, Pap mentioned they had to do something about all Jake's cartons she had left downstairs in the packing house. Belle knew his casual attitude was intended to mask the fact that he was hiding something from her. Next, he told her Matt and Raphael could put them in the loft of the old barn. Then, Matt wanted to know what they should do with the desk, and she told him to put it in her bedroom.

She expected something was afoot, but was still jolted when Pap told Matt to bring her old one to the office, and then pointed to the corner.

"Put it there," he said. "It's about time you came up here. Raphael can use your desk downstairs."

She crossed her arms and glared at them. "So what else are you two cooking up?"

"I talked to my sister. There are quite a few of our father's old cider trees at the back of her orchard that she's willing to let us get cuttings from."

Belle fought back her rising anger and told herself to keep her head. But instead she heard herself say, "For God's sake, can't you two wait until we find out who bought Jake's place? Believe me, I'll get whoever it is to sell us the orchard, or at least honor the contract."

She regretted the outburst and slumped against the door.

"I'm still hoping you can," said Pap, before casually mentioning that he had enrolled Matt in a cidery course in Virginia and wanted her to go, too.

"I'll be too busy collecting my cuttings from Jake's orchard!" She turned and left, slamming the door behind her, then started for the barn.

She didn't know how she was going to do it, but those four hundred trees born in the South, some hundreds of years ago, had to be saved. She had called Jake's brother to ask him if the property had closed, but when he wouldn't talk to her, she pleaded with his secretary who finally told her it was closing that Friday at nine.

Belle walked through the compound with Mac at her side, wondering if Pap was embracing Matt so openly because he had given up on her ever getting married. No, it was more likely he was engineering it so sooner or later Matt's and her life would be so intertwined they'd have to get together. And that little move about her going with him to Virginia! How convenient. The two of them together in the same hotel for a week.

What part was Matt playing in this little scheme, she wondered. The other night when they talked about the cidery, she saw the same burning ambition she'd seen when the two of them would lie on the grass in the high part of the Rome orchard and dream. That was back when it was a given that she and Matt would marry and eventually run the farm.

She had noticed something else new, too. Before his divorce, he'd never allow himself to look her up and down the way he had that morning at the festival. Damn! She wished he hadn't noticed her blush when she saw him bare-chested at his trailer.

Pap and Missy were right about the boundaries changing since his split with Rita. It wasn't entirely impossible to believe he now figured he had a shot at getting everything—the cidery, the orchards, and her. The wound he'd inflicted was supposed to be healed by now, but the resentment she'd buried years ago suddenly reared its ugly head.

Why, God? Why did he go and ruin everything? She fought back rage as she neared the barn, then she went in, fell against the wall and slid down to the floor, fighting back the guilt that haunted her. Why, God? Why wasn't I strong enough to face Pap about the baby? A familiar sickening regret washed over her, for she knew if she had, she and Matt would be married and she wouldn't have been punished every night with the knowledge he was sleeping with someone else and tenderly caring for Rita's child instead of hers.

Mac climbed on her lap and gently placed a paw on her arm. She wrapped her arms around him and buried her face in his fur. His whimpers made her wipe her tears with her shirt, get up and face the work ahead. She spread out a bunch of pots that were stacked one inside the other on the floor next to a huge mound of rich potting soil. She intended to graft a couple dozen trees onto dwarf root stock. She'd planted them from seed two years ago and they were ready. She picked up a shovel and started to jab it into the pile, then stopped and put it back against the post.

She slapped her leg. "Come on, boy. Let's get out of here."

They left the barn, jumped into her truck and took off. She pulled off the road at the Rome orchard and climbed out. The air had the kind of chill that usually revved up her body's engine and made her feel alive, but not today.

Huge masses of clouds crept across the sky, blocking the sun and giving the orchard the grey, black and white palette of *Guernica,* interrupted by lone ribbons of green running between the rows. Belle felt the most at home in this orchard. There was a beauty about it—a textured rhythm in the orderly rows of dark rugged dwarfs, that after decades of pruning so their limbs would hang down, resembled Siamese dancers with their weirdly twisted arms and fingers.

The spindles, on the other hand, in the winter looked more like a fence than anything. Their limbs were tied flat against row after row of wires that ran from one big, heavy post to another. When she mentioned their ungainliness to Pap, he had told her,

"Honey, we're growing apples, not trees."

She took her loppers out of the truck and began cutting the new upward growing shoots when Pam's SUV pulled off the road and set Mac to barking. Pam got out and came toward her.

"I suppose Pap sent you," said Belle, who continued pruning.

"He's worried about you, gal."

"For once, I'd like to see him talk to me directly. The closest he ever comes is when he fusses about me getting married. I'd give anything to be a fly on the wall when he and Matt get together. You know, I can't remember him ever saying he loved me."

"Oh, he does, honey. You can be sure of that."

"It seems like he's more comfortable on a man-to-man basis with someone like Matt."

"Agriculture is a man's world in general, Belle. But don't get any ideas about them being chauvinistic. I don't think there's a man whose wife is involved who would be that way. It's a team and family thing. You grew up without a mother and father and pretty much landed at the tail end of Pap's career. You never saw the whole thing up close."

Pam dug her hands in her pockets and thought. "There's the family, and then there's the bigger family. I can go to another county, state even, and after talking to another orchard farmer's wife feel like she's my sister. Only they know what it takes to make a living at this, and the devotion you have to put into it."

Pam started uphill along the lane and motioned for Belle to follow. "Come. Let me show you my favorite place in the whole wide world."

Belle leaned her loppers against the tree, and together they climbed toward the crest of the orchard, both knowing exactly where that place was.

"Your grandpa wasn't always like he is now. What happened to your mother broke him into a million bits. If it hadn't been for her leaving you and Missy behind, I don't think he'd of made it."

"That doesn't excuse him from being so distant."

"He doesn't trust himself, is all. He was too heavy-handed

with your mother and doesn't want to misstep with you two."

"I was afraid of him when I was little. He was never harsh. Just detached. Yet, I'd see him tenderly pick Missy up when she fell, or get a contented look on his face when he'd rock her to sleep in front of the fireplace, holding her in his arms way past when she fell asleep, and I knew he was kind. It took a while, but he finally got a soft spot for me, too." She let out a soft chuckle. "It helped once I stopped screaming that I wanted my mother every time he came near me."

They reached the crest, meandered over to a huge rock that was well known to the both of them and sat down on the grass.

"You're just like him," said Pam. "And it comforts him knowing you'll keep this farm like he and our mom and dad did."

"It's no fun being the heir apparent. Every day I feel like I have to earn the right all over again."

"Well, that thing about you finding someone and getting married isn't such a bad idea. Our parents were a great team, and we wouldn't have everything you see in front of you now without them working hard together to get it."

Pam shivered and pulled her jacket tight around her. "I love this orchard." She turned to Belle. "Have I ever told you the story of how we got it?" Belle shook her head. "My parents got their first taste of what it might be like to be known for their orchard when my mother scraped together enough money to buy the land on Route 64. It came with a store. Think of it. Myrtle now had road frontage on a highway with customer opportunity. It was real uptown for her in those days, even though it was nothing more than a wood shack with a potbelly stove and a big Coca-Cola sign across one whole side. My apple house sits on that very spot.

"My mother would take me with her and we'd sell apples from it during the season. At the same time, my father and Pap would put apples on a horse-drawn wagon and take them to the market at Travelers Rest in South Carolina. Back in the '40s and '50s it was a good place to attract people from Greenville or catch folks on their way to the mountains."

"I'm glad Pap's gonna give our roadside stand to Missy," said Belle. "I can picture her running the place with a couple of her kids helping out. Maybe even putting up a nice little apple house. There's enough land behind it to have a picnic ground."

"Is she still interested in being a beautician?"

Belle threw up both hands with fingers splayed apart so Pam could see her painted nails. "Do you believe?" She traced her brows with her fingers. "I hope she got my arch right." She sighed, wistfully. "That's Missy for you. She wanted to cheer me up, and that was all she knew to do."

Pam threw her head back and laughed. "You two have always been tight."

"We had to be."

"Pap and I were never close when I was a kid, being ten years apart and all. Funny how it all changed in that one day I was telling you about. It was in '59. By that time, my father had a truck and was still going down to Travelers Rest. He'd go early Saturday morning and camp overnight. If he had any apples left, he'd put them in a couple of buckets, and him and Pap would sell them door to door in Greenville.

"This one October Sunday—I was around seven—my mother and I worked hard all day in the store selling our apples. It got dark, so we finished up and went home to make dinner and count our money. We had over two hundred dollars, the most we ever made.

"That was the big turning point for us. My father never made that much in a weekend at Travelers Rest, and that winter he and my mother, along with Pap and me, planted every single tree in this here orchard you're lookin' at, so we'd have more apples to sell. My father never went back to Travelers Rest after that. We didn't have to go down the mountain anymore to sell our apples. We had a market right here."

Pam reached an arm around Belle and squeezed. "You gonna be all right, girl?"

Belle nodded, and her great-aunt said for her to let Pap know she wasn't mad at him, then kissed her goodbye. Tonight Belle would make fried chicken and biscuits for dinner. His favorite.

She had her own way to give him a wordless message.

Pam walked back down the hill with Mac prancing around her like he wanted her to stay. Halfway down the row he gave up and ran back to Belle. The sun had come out from behind the clouds, casting the trees' weird shadows across the green carpet. Pam went over the crest of the hill, and with every step, slowly sank from sight. Yet, in the distance, the row kept falling and rising up again, until the undulating landscape stopped at the far-off horizon.

Belle's emotions were rubbed raw, and she felt herself seep into the earth. Never had she been so aware of being one with the land and all it stood for. She looked out at the bare trees and thought about the thousands of apples they had borne, then the thousands of people who had eaten them who would always be invisible to her and Pap, just like she and Pap would always be unknown to them. Yet, she felt a kinship with them and a special kind of pride, for McGrady's Orchard had done its share in linking the bounty of the earth to the river of life.

CHAPTER NINE

LUCY BISHOP HAD ALWAYS BEEN a timid girl, but everyone figured with her brains and predilection for hard
work she was sure to amount to something. All that changed the
day her mother lost her battle with the canning company, and
Lucy had to pass up college and go straight to work.

Her office—that is, if you could call the eight foot by eight
foot cubby hole with a network of exposed pipes overhead an
office—was at the end of a narrow back hall next to the opulent
suite of Benjamin S. Gregg, Attorney at Law. Every time she had
to go in there, the lavish décor only made her feel that much
more demeaned.

She checked her watch. She'd better get going. She put her
desk in order, stopping at the picture of her parents. It was hard
to believe her mother ever looked like that. She was so beautiful
in those days. But she was never the same after being denied the
satisfaction of punishing the company whose negligence killed
her husband. Not only was her mother unable to work again, but
her mushrooming medical bills were eating them alive.

Lucy picked up her purse, locked the door behind her and
started for the restaurant. She looked forward to having lunch
with Missy McKenzie's sister and walked the three blocks to
Main Street with anticipation. She only knew Belle enough to
say hello and was intrigued when Missy said her sister wanted to
ask her a favor. What could it possibly be? Whatever it was, she

was pleased to have an opportunity to pay back even a little of all the kindnesses the McGrady's had shown her and her mother.

Missy always managed to drop off a box of apples from their orchards every fall and come up with some plausible explanation for bringing it, like wanting them to try out one of their new varieties. Missy always took the time to sit down and chat with her mother over a glass of iced tea, one of the few occasions anyone came to visit. She always knew Missy had stopped by when her mother greeted her at the door with a smile on her face.

Being eleven-thirty, most of the tables in the restaurant were empty. She settled down at one in a corner where they could talk. The door opened and Belle rushed in and looked around, not recognizing her. But Lucy knew who she was, one of the beautiful McKenzie sisters. Missy was fair with delicate features, but Belle's dark sultry looks always made her stand out. Lucy waved her over.

"Thank you so much for coming," Belle said rather breathlessly as she pulled out a chair.

"It's nice seeing you again," was Lucy's guarded response. She didn't want to sound like she was making out that they were old pals just because Belle wanted a favor.

The waitress appeared and took their orders—a sandwich, fries and a Coke each, a signal that neither had much time.

"What can I do for you?" Lucy asked.

Belle appeared nervous. "I don't know where to start." She looked around, then spoke in a low tone. "It's about Mr. Gregg's brother, Jake."

"I know who he is. I do the books for the company's trust accounts."

"I was in the office last week and it didn't turn out too well."

"About his house?"

Belle nodded.

"I heard about it but didn't know it was you."

The Cokes arrived and Belle quickly unwrapped a straw and took a sip. "I saw a file on Ben's desk. I know it was Jake's because I recognized his handwriting." She reached over and grasped Lucy's hand. "I know this is asking a lot, but can you get me copies of everything in that file?"

Lucy suppressed a look of surprise. This meeting was turning out to be much more interesting than she had imagined.

Lucy's silence was hard for Belle to interpret, so she kept pushing. "This whole thing of his property being sold doesn't make sense. He has an orchard in there that represents his life's work. There's no way he would ever have let it go this way. I'm sure of it. Something's very wrong here." Belle pounded a fist on the table. "I don't know how I'm gonna do it, but I've got to save those trees."

The order arrived and Lucy picked up half of her BLT and had a bite, not taking her eyes off Belle who wasn't touching her food. This wasn't the first time she'd heard a story about Ben Gregg where someone claimed it didn't make sense. Her mother had insisted the same thing was true about her lawsuit ever since she ran into one of his co-workers after the trial.

He had mentioned he saw the whole accident and was willing to testify that he had complained about the faulty safety switch on the conveyor belt to the manager several times, and couldn't understand why her lawyer never called him to the stand. Her mother's gnawing suspicion, that the man who was supposed to represent her made a backroom deal with the canning company, had a lot to do with her mental state.

"The files are locked in a cabinet in the office every night, and I don't have the keys. I don't even have the keys to his office, just the door to the building."

Belle bit her lip and shook her head. "Do you have *any* of Jake's records?"

"Just his trust fund. There really wasn't much activity on his account, just a check for four-thousand dollars every month made out to one of Mr. Gregg's management accounts." She thought for a moment. "An odd thing did happen a couple days after his brother died, though. Mr. Gregg told me to stop drawing out the money."

Belle leaned toward her, wanting to hear more.

"I keep my mouth shut and never question anything, but some things you can't help being curious about. The next day he called me in again and handed me his personal check for fifty thousand dollars and had me put it in another one of his clients' trust accounts. That never happens. The money comes from someplace else. Not a personal check from the trustee. It made me wonder, especially since he had taken that same amount out of that account a couple months earlier."

Belle didn't touch her sandwich and sat there mulling over what Lucy had told her.

"What was the four thousand dollars for?"

"I don't know for sure, but two weeks ago, Ellie, his secretary, called me and said someone was on the phone from a nursing home asking for $7.77." She raised an eyebrow. "That's a figure you don't forget. Anyway, Ellie wanted me to write them a check from the office account since Mr. Gregg would be in court all week, and that was the only check she could sign."

"What does that have to do with Jake?"

"I talked to the woman on the phone and asked her what the money was for, and she told me it was all that was left on a closed account and she wanted to zero it out. At first, I was kinda leery. No invoice or anything. Then I remembered, once when Ellie couldn't get Mr. Gregg's management account to balance, she asked me to do it.

"I had to go back three months to straighten everything out. At the time, I thought it was interesting when I saw debits for four thousand dollars to a nursing home right underneath the four thousand dollars he had me write him from his brother's account every month. So, I figured he owed the nursing home the money, and told the lady we'd remit the balance that day."

Lucy's eyebrow raised. "But I was curious, and asked her if the person died. Her answer was kinda weird. She said, 'No, they transferred the poor soul to a nursing home that accepts people with nothing but Medicaid.'"

"I wonder who it is," said Belle. "Where is this nursing home?"

"I don't know. Ellie told me to make out a check for the $7.77 and she'd do the rest. But don't worry. When it comes back from the bank, I'll find out and let you know."

"Can't you just ask Ellie?"

"Are you kidding?" She wrung her hands. "Mr. Gregg is really paranoid, dealing like he does with all those desperate people. You don't dare ask questions. If I lose this job, I don't know what my mother and I will do. We're barely hanging on now."

Lucy studied Belle's anguished face, and it reminded her of her mother's after she lost her case. There *was* a way she could still help get the file, if only she dared. She looked around to make sure no one was listening and whispered, "I know where the keys to the cabinets are kept during the day." That remark brought a spark to Belle's eyes. "In the secretary's desk. Last week when Mr. Gregg was in court, Ellie had me sit at her desk while she left on a personal errand. She's getting married in May, and I think she's getting her wedding plans organized."

"How long does she go for?"

"That was the first time she let me sit at her desk, but it was for most of the afternoon. He's got another trial coming up in a few days and she might need to go out again. If I get back in the office, I'll look through the files and let you know what I find."

Belle jotted something on a napkin. "Call me at this number."

"Aren't you going to eat your sandwich?" Lucy asked.

"No, I'm not hungry." Belle rose. "I've got to run. They closed on the property last Friday and I'm waiting to hear who bought it." She started to go, then turned back around and hugged Lucy. "Thank you."

Belle went to the cash register to pay her bill, then waved to Lucy mouthing "I got it" and ran out.

Lucy motioned for the waitress and asked for a container for Belle's sandwich and fries. It would be a nice treat for her mother that night.

THE NEXT MORNING, BELLE rearranged the apple novelties that lined the back of her desk for the second time, then rested her chin on her fist and absentmindedly spun a small wooden apple. Sensing Pap was near, she turned and looked up at him. He reached over and snapped up the apple.

"You're no good to anyone here today. Why don't you go check the irrigation lines over at the spindles. Matt and Raphael can fix the leaks later."

Belle, all stiff and dug in, stared stubbornly at the wall in front of her.

"Pam's brother-in-law will call me the minute the deed is processed on the courthouse books. He knows people there."

"But the closing was on Friday."

"These things can take a couple days."

Grudgingly, she grabbed her phone and left. She came down the stairs, and Mac got up from his blanket in the corner of the building and ran to her as she went outside. Just then, Matt pulled up. She couldn't help noticing how quickly he got out so they'd meet as she passed in front of his truck.

"How are you doing?" he asked.

"I'll survive."

He reached in his pocket and gave Mac a treat, something she'd never seen him do before. He crouched down, let Mac put his paws on his shoulders and gave him a vigorous rub. That takes the cake, she said to herself. He's even trying to win over my dog.

He looked up at her. "How about you and me going fishing tomorrow." He rubbed Mac all over. "You like that, don't you boy?" He looked up at her again. "You need some time away from this place."

"It's not this place I need time away from," she shot back. A hurt flicker in his eye made her instantly regret it.

"I'm sorry, Matt. I didn't mean that."

He stood up and dug his hands into his back pockets, then tossed his head and gave her his half smile that always left her wondering what he was thinking.

"Belle, I don't want to get in your face. If my moving up-stairs bothers you—"

"It's okay, Matt. It makes sense with the cidery and all."

She was aware he was watching her as she leaned into her truck bed to make sure she had the caution tape to mark the leaks. He held her door open for Mac to jump in, then waited for her to climb up before closing it. She turned the ignition key and glanced over at him. Instead of a stalwart grown man in jeans and a Carhartt, she saw a skinny blond kid in an ill-fitting jacket borrowed for the prom, and she was ashamed of her rudeness.

She tossed him a little wave, but the eager smile he tossed back made her instantly regret it. Now that his divorce had come through, she could see he was thinking she was now fair game and was planning on tearing down the invisible wall between them. She jammed the truck into gear and took off for the spindle orchard. He had another think coming.

THE FAR CORNER of the orchard where they had planted the spindles lay at the crest of the rolling hillside overlooking the compound and edging a woods. This morning, the sun was coating the earth with an inviting warmth, yet there was an unnatural quiet. It was as if all the creatures were hiding from something lurking in the nearby forest. A truck rose up on the dirt road from below the hill and rolled to a stop at the start of the farthest row.

The creak of an opening door broke the silence. Inside, Belle studied the motionless scene and listened to the eerie quiet. The sky was empty, yet she sensed hidden eyes all around her. She knew the smells and sounds of the farm at every time of day and every season of the year just like the wild animals that lived there, and now every sensor she possessed told her to be wary.

Belle shook off the feeling, grabbed her gloves and slid from her seat. Jake's property thirty yards ahead stared her in the face. The beckoning woods brought so many memories streaming back that her eyes pooled, and she got back in. Remembering that this morning before she rose she'd promised herself she wouldn't shed another tear, she took a deep breath and climbed out again. She went to the back of the truck, dug the basket of caution tape strips from the cluttered bed and tramped with it to the in-ground spigot that fed water to the row.

She crouched down, lifted the lid and turned it on, then the spigot for the next row, which she'd check on the way back. Oddly, Mac wasn't off on his usual hunt for rabbits and squirrels. Instead, he stuck to her, his sights set on the opening in the woods that led to Jake's place. She reached over and gave him a pat. "You miss him, too, don't you boy?"

She grabbed the basket and trudged along, checking the hose secured to the bottom string of wires that was now dripping as it should. Up ahead she could see water spurting out. She went over and wound a long strand of tape tightly around the break to stop the leak enough to allow the hose to drip up ahead. She finished the row and came back checking out the one next to it. So Matt would know there was a leak in the line, she tied a tape around the post next to the spigot with the break, before turning both of them off.

She was about to move on to the next two rows when she heard a distant clatter. She looked around and listened. It had to be coming from Jake's place. She suddenly recognized the rumble of what had to be a bulldozer. She dropped the basket and raced behind Mac to the now overgrown path through the woods. All those years back, curiosity had lured her to this place, its foreboding darkness filling her with trepidation. Today, terror drove her.

Her heart pounded as her urgent footfalls sounded through the woods. Terrifying scenarios of what could be happening to Jake's orchard ripped through her brain like a strip of barbed wire.

She saw past the overreaching hemlock boughs slashing across her face and caught a glimpse of billowing exhaust. Breathless and her chest aching, she sped ahead with the urgency of a mother racing to save a drowning child.

She reached the clearing and stopped dead. The fence lay in a twisted jumble and the gnarled roots of three apple trees loomed above her. She suppressed an urge to scream. The rumble of the bulldozer and Mac's frantic barking came from behind the huge clumps. She raced around the mass and saw the monster was getting in position to push another one over. She furiously waved her hands and shouted. The driver, cocooned in the enclosed cab, heard nothing but his radio blaring out... *down, down, down and the flames went higher...*

The huge yellow hulk paused for its gears to be shifted. She ran up its tracks and pounded on the window. The stunned driver saw the frantic face and cut the engine, causing the tracks to jolt and throw her off.

She lay in the torn up turf trying to catch her breath as the man jumped from the cab. Anger mixed with fear twisted his red, flushed face.

"Are you crazy? You almost got killed!"

Too breathless to answer, she stood up, her chest heaving.

"What the hell do you think you're doing?"

Unable to catch her breath enough to speak, Belle beat on the bulldozer.

"Listen, girl. I've got a job to do. Now clear out!"

Belle jumped on the tracks again, reached in the cab and snatched the key. He grabbed her leg, and she spun around and flew on him, wrapping her legs around his chest and pounding with her fists. He put up both arms to fend her off.

"Murderer!"

He got hold of her and pulled her off, tossing her to the ground. She quickly thrust herself back on her feet, threw her arm back and hurled the key.

"Goddammit!" the driver shouted. "We're never going to find that key in this mess." He flipped open his phone and pounded on a button, all the while glaring at her. "Joe, it's me, Don. I need you to bring me another key for the 'dozer." He listened. "It's a long story. I've got this crazy lady who just tossed it in a bunch of trees." Another pause. "Okay, I'll be here. And hurry. I want to get this done today."

He flipped his phone closed and turned to her. "Listen, sweetheart, you either clear out of here, or my next call is to the sheriff."

She stood with arms folded. "Good. Call him. My grandfather plays poker with him every Thursday night."

He shook his head. "What is it with you? Are you the town nut?"

She glared at him.

"Lady, this rig here is costing somebody a lot of money, and when that key gets here I'm gonna push these trees up."

"Over my dead body."

He stomped his feet and twisted in frustration. "Oh, boy. I don't need this." He took a step toward her, but his eyes suddenly shot over to Mac who was baring his teeth and growling with his hackles raised and seventy-five pounds of muscle poised to lunge.

Belle took advantage of the distraction and jumped back on the bulldozer's tracks. "You lay one hand on me or my dog, and I'm going to scream assault."

"That takes the cake. *Me* assaulting *you?*" He looked at her as if he was summing up the situation. "That does it. I'm getting the sheriff in here." He flipped open his phone again. "Joe, is the key on the way?" He listened. "You better get the sheriff here, too. This lady's not gonna leave." His eyes roamed the orchard as he listened. "What do you mean, we don't own this property? We've got a contract." A veil of acquiescence fell across his face. "Okay, when the key gets here, I'll load it up and go over to the next place."

He slapped his phone closed, found a patch of grass that hadn't been torn up and sat down. He looked up at her. "You know you've screwed up my day. I've got till Saturday to clear three orchards and I'll have to work until dark tonight, or I won't make it."

The sound of a truck skidding to a stop made them both look over to the driveway. A man slid out and walked over.

"I got the key." He put his hands on his hips and looked up at Belle in a cocky manner, then at the driver. "You mean to tell me you're letting this li'l 'ol gal hold up this job?" He jumped on the tracks and gave Belle a menacing look, then grabbed her arm and threw her off.

He looked over at the bulldozer driver. "That's how you do it, pal."

Before he could gloat another moment, Belle got hold of his foot, yanked it from under him and tossed him to the ground. With all this commotion, none of the three noticed a truck pull in the driveway.

The man got up from the ground, brushed himself off and

grabbed her. Mac dug his teeth into the man's pant leg and ripped off a big chunk of denim while Belle struggled to pull away from his grasp. Suddenly two hands reached from behind her, grabbed her around the waist and yanked her away.

Belle turned and looked into piercing blue eyes, absolute astonishment on her face.

"Call off your dog," demanded Ken.

"It's you!" she spit out from lips contorted in hate. "You don't deserve this place!" She pointed to the orchard. "You're destroying a man's life!"

"I said, call off your dog!"

Belle slapped her leg, and Mac, who was shaking a chunk of denim like he wanted to kill it, froze.

Ken let go of her and gave the man a stern look, making him cautiously back away.

"It's okay, boys. Call it a day. I'll get hold of you later."

The sound of doors slamming shut and trucks leaving calmed Belle. She dropped down on her knees in the dirt and leaned back on her haunches, exhausted. Ken crouched down and looked at her. Dried tears had made streaks on the splotchy, dirt smudged face framed with long unruly wisps of hair.

"I've been trying to get hold of you. Why didn't you answer my calls?"

"Do you have any idea what you're doing!? You blew into this valley like a damn carpetbagger and think you can buy whatever you want!"

She covered her face with her hands. What was she doing? This would get her nowhere. She pulled her hands away and grabbed his shoulders. "I'm sorry. I didn't mean that. I'm begging you. Please sell us the orchard."

He took hold of her arms and lifted her up. An easygoing smile spread across his face as he brushed a clump of dirt from her shoulder.

"Okay, let's talk about it."

The tranquility in his manner eased her fears, yet her tone was terse. "Good! Let's go. Pap's in his office."

He raised both hands. "Whoa, girl. Not so fast."

Belle's face registered alarm until a nonchalant laugh rippled out of him.

"If I'm gonna talk, I'm gonna do it over a nice quiet dinner. Can I pick you up tonight around seven?"

Belle bit the inside of her lip and wiped the sweat off her forehead with the back of her hand as she thought. "Okay about dinner. But I'll meet *you* somewhere."

"Fine. Then come over here."

"Of course, you got the house, too."

"I moved in yesterday. I'm not unpacked, but I can whip us up some dinner." He eyed the rip in her jeans and noticed the blood trickling from her scraped knee. "Why don't you come in and let me take care of that."

"That's okay. I've got something in my truck." She slapped her leg for Mac to follow and started for the path.

"Let me at least give you a lift," he called after her.

She turned to him. "I'll be fine. See you at seven."

She waited till she was safely out of Ken's sight, then wincing at the painful scrape, she crouched down, clamped Mac's head in her hands and said, "good boy."

As she came out of the woods, her phone rang. She pulled it out of her pocket and saw it was Pap.

"Pam called. It's all over the valley you stopped Don Black from bulldozing Jake's trees. Are you all right?"

"Pap, listen to me. Ken Larsen bought the place, and he's willing to talk to us about selling the orchard."

"Good. Bring him right over."

"I tried that. He wants to talk it over tonight at dinner." A pause. "Don't worry, Pap. I can handle him," she said with more than a little contempt.

"YOU SHOULD'VE TOLD HIM you could go out with him tomorrow instead," said Missy as she rushed into Belle's bedroom. "It's a good thing I could reschedule my last appointment." She held her hands as if in prayer. "I can't believe it. An actual date with Mr. Blue Eyes."

Belle sat on her bed in a faded chenille robe that had been

her mother's. Her wet hair hung in straggles. Missy rushed over and examined her eyebrows through squinted lids. "A little touch up is all these need." She picked up one of Belle's hands, shook her head in disgust and let the hand drop. Seeing Belle in a thoughtful gaze, she snapped her fingers in front of her face.

"Back on this planet, Sis. You've got less than two hours."

Belle moved, and the robe slipped enough to expose a raw knee.

"How in the world did you get that?" asked Missy. "You can't wear jeans with that mess." She disappeared and came back ten minutes later laden with an armful of dresses and braced for major resistance from Belle. Bubbling with excitement, she dropped the pile on the bed and held one up for Belle to try on. "Didn't I tell you he was interested? Pap's got to be thrilled."

"I wouldn't call it thrilled."

"What do you mean?" mused Missy as she lifted a dress over Belle's outstretched arms. "This guy's perfect for you."

"It's not exactly a date," said Belle. "I'm going over there to talk to him about buying the orchard."

Missy's euphoric mood slowly ebbed away as Belle told her about the afternoon. Missy helped her in and out of several dresses, but as she watched Belle throw herself into the effort as if it were a life and death situation, it struck her as too dangerous for her sister to go over there in her emotional state.

Belle stood in front of the mirror carefully considering how she looked in a silky black dress. It had long sleeves and a cling-ing bodice that revealed her figure before spilling out into a full skirt. The last time Missy saw Belle in a dress was when Matt took her to her high school prom, and it touched her. The poor kid was willing to do anything to get her hands on that orchard.

Belle looked sideways at the low neckline.

"This one's not bad," she said. "But are my ribs showing too much?"

"I can fix that." Missy pawed through one of her drawers, finally dangling a bra in the air.

Belle pulled off the dress and squeezed herself into it. The sudden appearance of cleavage brought on a snide little smile.

Belle's deliberate manner worried Missy. She was obviously equating getting the orchard with keeping her old friend from slipping away. Her obsession with Jake and finding the Carolina Belle among his heirlooms was beginning to look like a stampede towards the edge of a cliff. Belle was a risk-taker like Pap, and Missy didn't doubt for an instant that she'd be willing to put everything she had on the line to get that orchard.

Missy grabbed Belle's arms and looked into her eyes. "Honey, you don't have to do this. If all that guy wants is to talk business, he can come to the office. You don't want to be dragged into one of those deals." She waved her hand in the air groping for words. "What's it called?"

"Quid pro quo?" Belle casually interjected.

Belle put the dress back on and studied herself in different poses, her jaw set tight. She fluffed up her hair, then her eyes shot over to Missy. "You've got to fix this."

That settled it. Belle had resisted her pleas to let her do something about that ponytail since she started beauty school. This girl was definitely in no shape to go over there tonight. Missy folded her arms and leaned back against her dresser. "This is crazy. I'm not cutting your hair. You've gotta put the brakes on. You may not know it, girl, but you're on the verge of falling apart. For God's sake, you almost got yourself killed today."

Belle pawed through the tray on Missy's dresser and picked up a pair of Missy's hair cutting shears, then lifted a clump of hair from her forehead.

Missy grabbed her hand and snatched away the scissors. "Take the dress off and let's go outside." She got a comb and a tunic from a drawer and went with Belle to the middle of the driveway where she sat her on a chair. She bent around and looked at Belle. "Aren't you gonna ask me what I'm gonna do?"

Belle sat unmoved.

Missy shrugged and stoically trimmed the thick dark hair by four inches and gave her sweeping, ragged bangs. She led her in the house and blow dried the cut so it had a graceful glistening swing. Missy's misgivings grew as Belle feverishly tried on shoes, finally choosing an open-toed wedgie she'd dug out of her closet.

Belle's hand shook as she put on a light coat of lipstick and dabbed some rouge on her cheeks, almost breaking Missy's heart. She studied Belle and thought, one way or another, she was going to get that orchard. There was no way to stop her.

"What time is it?" Belle asked.

Missy glanced over at her clock. "Almost seven."

"You got a purse I can use?"

Missy found a black clutch bag and tossed it on the dresser.

Belle snapped it up, threw in a lipstick and headed for the stairs.

Missy followed her down, hoping Pap would be in the kitchen and stop her from going. He was in the kitchen, all right, and so was Matt. Belle walked in and the two of them fell speechless as they took her in. Matt, at the window, turned his back to her and looked out. It took a minute for Pap to catch his breath enough to say something.

"Pam wants you to call her."

"I'm going to be fine, Pap." She reached for the door. "I'm a big girl now," she said, and left.

The poignancy of her sister's mission made Missy want to sit down and cry, but instead, she told Pap everything would be fine and went to the stairs. Hearing Pap say something to Matt, she paused on the second step and listened.

"Son, you better hurry up and make your move. That there fella is one handsome dog... and he's sweet on her."

CHAPTER TEN

B ELLE WOBBLED to her truck, wondering if the wedgies were such a good idea. She didn't look back but was aware of Matt's eyes. Mac came running and she told him to stay, then left with him sitting solemnly at attention with a wrinkled forehead, convincing her that even he was worried.

Earlier, Pat had told her to get Ken down to his lowest price and he'd take it from there, and that was all that was on her mind as she pulled up to Jake's. She winced at the sight of the rutted landscape and the three overturned trees in the distance as she scanned for the bulldozer. Finding it gone, she sighed in relief and got out. This was a good sign. Ken must have had the driver come back and take it away after she left. He wouldn't have had him go through the trouble if he planned to let him finish the job.

Ken stood at the door. Even in jeans and a sweater he looked like a fashion plate. She was definitely overdressed, and wished she had listened to Missy. With each step toward the door she wondered what message she was sending. Her sister was right about another thing. She *was* on the verge of falling apart. But that was all right; she was about to fix it.

She approached the door, dreading having to look at Jake's place destroyed, and was relieved to see a lot of his furniture still in place—the easy chairs, dining table, a huge sideboard. Ken must have read her thoughts. He poured her what looked like a glass of wine and told her he had negotiated the purchase of quite a few of the larger pieces.

She took a tentative sip and the taste confused her.

He laughed. "That's my brother's hard cider. What do you think?"

She took another sip and nodded approval. Hearing something, they both glanced over and saw Mac with his paw on the window. Ken strolled over, rolled it aside and let him in. Belle, wondering which one of the three back at the compound had sent him over, with a stern expression on her face, snapped her fingers and pointed to the corner. Mac hung his head and obediently trotted over and sat down.

Ken gently touched Belle's shoulder to guide her to a chair, making her flinch.

"Girl, you're really up tight." He waved towards an easy chair. "Sit down, and let's get the business end of this over with."

She made her way to the chair trying to disguise a limp.

"First of all, I'm sorry about the bulldozer," he said. "I wasn't here when it arrived, or this never would've happened. Don got his wires crossed. He was supposed to start on the Freeman property." He reached over, picked an envelope off the coffee table and handed it to her. "I had my lawyer draw this up and email it to me this afternoon after you left."

She pulled out two sheets and studied them.

"It's a signed agreement," he said, "to let you take any cuttings or trees from the orchard till the end of March. I'm sorry, but I can't sell it to you."

Her brows wrinkled as she read. She looked up. "It doesn't say anything about a charge."

Ken threw his hands up. "What can I say? We're neighbors."

She examined the second sheet. "It's the same thing."

"It's my copy. Both of them have to have our signatures."

She took the pen he handed her and hesitated, then tapped her fingers on the arm of the chair. There was nothing she wanted more than those cuttings, but she didn't want to get them dishonestly, a strange determination considering she would die if she didn't get them. "I want to be fair to you. If I take them, I'm going to use them to build up my own orchard of cidery apples. We're planning on putting one up ourselves."

He threw his head back and laughed. "Welcome to the club, darlin'. I just hope you won't regret it."

"I don't think I will."

He pointed to the paper in her hand. "It's okay to sign it. The only caveat is that I won't be responsible for any accidents to you or any of your employees, or any damage to your equipment."

Belle studied the utterly disarming look on his face. She finished reading the agreement, put both sheets on the table and signed. She picked up her purse, stuffed in her copy and snapped it shut. She took a deep breath, slowly let it out and eased back in the chair.

"You'll have almost two months. Then we're tearing them out. Face it, sweetheart, a lot of those babies are getting old and need to be replanted."

"I know."

He took a sip of the cider and sat back in his chair. "You're going to need a lot of help getting started. It's important you get an experienced cider maker. I can help you with that. In fact, you can come over while I'm setting up so you'll know what you're in for. Maybe even spend some time at my parents' operation."

"That's very generous of you."

"Why not? The more of us that get into the hard cider business, the more this area's going to be known for it." He paused for a moment. "By the way, who are the 'we' in your operation?"

"Me and my grandfather... and Matt Sanchez."

His eyelids tightened slightly, making her wonder if he'd heard all the gossip. She changed the subject. "You know, quite a few of those trees out there produce the most desired cider apples on the planet. Why don't you want them?"

He stood up and reached for her hand. "I'll tell you at dinner. Come and help."

He pointed to a carton on the floor and told her to dig out the dishes and tableware. She found them and set the table while he worked on the dinner in the kitchen. He had put on a Miles Davis disk, and the cool jazz floated through the room, but her head was spinning too fast to melt into a mellow mood. She couldn't wait to get out of there and give Pap and Matt the news. She had a lot to think through. Tomorrow she had to get organized so they could start getting the cuttings. It was already February.

"Bring over the plates," hollered Ken, distracting her from her frantic planning. She kicked off her shoes, and took the plates into the kitchen.

He eyed her bare feet. "I wondered how long you'd last in those things." He lifted the lid of a steamer, revealing two thick slabs of salmon with rosemary twigs lying across, and winked at her. He hadn't shaved for a couple of days, and the dark haze of beard set off the blue in his eyes.

He took a plate from her, dished up some sautéed vegetables from a wok and carefully placed a piece of salmon on top. He set it down and did the same with the other, then looked at her and slowly raised an eyebrow. "And now for the *pièce de résistance:* Larsen's cider *crème* sauce."

His amusing attempts at appearing debonair made her smile.

He poured a ladleful over each dish and took them to the table, calling out to her to bring the salad and rolls. He pulled a chair out with a flourish then stopped. "*Attendez!*" he exclaimed with a good deal of bravado. "*Où les chandelle?*"

She laughed out loud. "I hope your cooking is better than your French."

He winked at her again. "Dig them out from the box behind you, and I'll get some matches." He swept up her dish and moved it to the far end of the table. "And you're not getting one bite till you find them."

She laughed to herself as she got out the candles and holders and listened to him bang drawers shut in the kitchen, while singing along to a new disk he put on.

He came back shuffling to the tune. *"Blue Moon, you saw me standing alone, without a..."* He struck a match and smiled at her.

"Billie Holiday?" she asked.

"Uh-huh. She's my girl."

He lit the candles and didn't overlook the dish sitting in front of her, nor the smug grin. He laughed and poured them both cider and sat down.

"Here's to you and all your enterprises," he toasted.

She raised her glass and swelled with a delirious surge of happiness for the first time since she had gotten the call about Jake. She suddenly felt him in the room.

Ken stared at her with a fork in one hand and knife in the other. "You're beautiful."

She made a face.

"I didn't mean to embarrass you. It's a fact, is all." He dug into his salmon. "You remind me of my brother."

She tossed her head. "Come on. You don't even know me."

"Oooh, but that's where you're wrong. You're a legend in these parts."

"So what insane asylum is your brother in?"

"Nobody said you're crazy. *Obsessed?* Maybe. But not crazy." He laughed. "Anyway... that was before your antics this morning." He watched her take a bite of her salmon. "Good?"

She nodded.

"The sauce is my brother's recipe. Actually, he was my twin. He died last year with his wife and kid in an auto accident. The poor guy. He was only thirty-six. I don't think my mom's ever going to get over it."

"Oh. I'm so sorry."

"That's why I'm here. I'm kinda carrying on for him. Before that happened I was pretty much nothing but a surf bum."

"What beach?"

"All over the world—San Juan, Canary Islands, Panama. My claim to fame is winning the big-wave surfing contest in California they call the Titans of Mavericks. My name's even on a brass plaque in good 'ol downtown Half Moon Bay." He chuckled. "That's my ace in the hole. When my grandkids don't think I'm cool anymore, I'm gonna take them there and show it off."

"Do they give out prize money?"

"It depends. The biggest purse I got was for the Titans. One hundred and twenty thousand. But after my brother died, I couldn't get into it anymore. I kept wiping out." He rubbed the scar on his cheek. "That's how I got this."

"*Awww...* and all this time I thought some irate lady orchardist did that to you."

"No. All the irate lady orchardists I know concentrate on 'dozer drivers."

"Pap says it's all over the valley. I wonder if I'll ever live it down."

"Not a chance."

He helped himself to the salad and then looked up at her. "I don't blame you for fighting to save those trees. In fact, I'm impressed. When the locals told me about you and Jake and your work with antique apples, I couldn't believe it. That's exactly what my brother was doing. He'd been pollinating different cultivars looking for that 'billion dollar' cider apple since he was fifteen. He was all set to open his own cidery."

"Here?"

"He and his wife had rock-climbed in the area, and when he discovered this apple valley, he was hooked. There are over 10,000 small trees sitting in his orchard right now. He planned to replant them once he found the land. That's why I don't need the ones out there."

"Then why did you ask us to grow some cider apples for you?"

He averted her gaze, embarrassed to have to admit he wanted to get to know her. "Well, the answer to that is pretty obvious, isn't it?" He started back on his food.

"That was a little extreme, wouldn't you say?"

"Hey, I tried friendly." He flashed a smile. "But after the way you brushed me off at the festival... no more Mr. Nice Guy."

She finished her cider and held the glass up for him to pour her another. "First you tell me I'm crazy... no... *obsessed,* then you accuse me of being outright mean. And all that coming from the man responsible for getting three antique trees knocked over that were found on a lifelong quest by one of the nicest persons who ever lived."

"Come on," he said as he poured. "I was saving them for you. That's why I kept calling." He stopped pouring and looked at her, "I'm mad at myself for not coming over in person. When I think you might have gotten hurt today..."

They fell silent as they ate, laughing every time one of them looked up and caught the other one staring. The room slowly grew dark with the flickering glow of the candles now casting deep chiaroscuro shadows across their faces.

"I never got a chance to ask my brother what it was about his antiques that made them mean so much to him," he said in a subdued tone. "It had to be more than just making good cider."

He looked at her as if he wanted her to give him the answer. Her brain was clouded by the alcohol, but not enough to diminish the fervor of her core passion.

Belle crossed her arms on the table and leaned into him. "Ever since I was a kid I wanted to come up with the best apple anyone ever bit into, and one of these days I'm going to find it in those trees out there." She pushed a piece of salmon around on her plate with her fork.

"Today, people go in the grocery store and take their pick from maybe seven or eight apple varieties that can come from as far away as Washington State, Michigan, New York, even Chile. They have no idea about the thousands of apple varieties that were born in the South. We've either forgotten, or worse yet, never knew anything about our agrarian past."

She put her elbow on the table and sank her chin onto the palm of her hand. "Our unique Southern heritage is more than the restored mansions on Charleston's Battery, or heart-pine floors, or Coin silver. It's an old apple with a name like 'Aunt Susan's Favorite' dreamt up by some farmer in an isolated valley in the mountains, or Bloody Butcher corn, Red Ripper peas, Moon and Stars watermelons, Greensboro peaches, Gold Dollar tobacco, James grapes.

"No one ever told those people in the grocery store about how farm families used to store their apples through the winter in unheated rooms, nor how their aroma perfumed the whole house. They've never seen apple slices drying on a tin roof, nor do they know the least bit about making cider and vinegar.

"But most of all, they never had the thrill of strolling through their backyard orchard and enjoying the incomparable taste of a freshly picked Southern apple baked right on the tree by a long, hot Southern summer."

She sat up erect and her tone become more matter-of-fact. "We're living in the last days of the Southern apple. In fact, most of them have already passed into history. Maybe ninety percent are now extinct. There's only four hundred out there in that orchard, but Jake found them, grew them and decided they were worth keeping."

"You should be proud of yourself," he said.

"Not really. If the story of these apples has heroes, it's all the men and women who have gone out and found them and gathered their grafting cuttings—like Jake, and Lee Calhoun, Elwood Fisher, Henry Morton... the list goes on."

In a reminiscing mood, she trained her eyes on him with a relaxed smile on her face. "Jake taught me to graft when I was twelve. The tree was called the Accordian. I remember my hands shook so much as I started to cleave it that I was afraid he would make me stop before I cut myself.

"Instead, he calmed my nerves with his soft story-telling voice and told me about the tree my cutting came from. I can still hear him telling me how it originated with the Vernon family of Rockingham County, North Carolina, and was propagated by root sprouts by the same family for over a hundred years. Can you imagine that? Over a hundred years. The instant he showed me a photo of it with ribs running from top to bottom as if it were pleated, I knew how it got its name."

She crossed her arms and leaned on the table. "One of my most cherished memories was the fall that tree bore its first apples and his wife, Mary, made a pie from them. I can still see the three of us sitting down at this very table and enjoying it with a dainty cup of tea. I love that apple tree." She pointed to the window. "In fact it's right out there. They had a little brass marker made that said 'The Accordian, Belle McKenzie's First Graft at the age of Twelve.' Someday I'm gonna drive to that farm and see if the tree it came from still grows there."

Belle took a slow sip of her cider. "You know how you said

you're here because you're carrying on for your brother, well it's the same for me; I'm carrying on for Jake. I wish you had gotten to know him." She put a finger on the edge of her glass and slowly traced the rim. "You have no idea what it means to me to have those cuttings. I can't help thinking that as long as I have all those wonderful old apples he worked so hard to gather, he's still here." She looked up at him. "Thank you from the bottom of my heart."

"If my brother were here, he would have done the same."

She finished eating, except for a small piece of her salmon.

He reached for her plate. "Can I give this to Killer?"

She made a face. "That there is the sweetest dog in the world."

"Tell that to the guy who limped out of here with one of his pant legs missing."

"Hey, he doesn't know how lucky he was. If I had given Mac the command to sic him, he'd of lost more than his pant leg."

They both laughed and she found herself staring into his eyes.

"You can give him the salmon. I saved it for him."

"I figured," he said as he put the plate on the floor. "Here, boy."

Mac sat panting with his tongue hanging out, staring at Belle. She gave him a nod and he ran to the plate.

Ken offered to make coffee.

"I'd rather sample some more of your brother's ciders."

"You're on! I'll clear the table and you set up the bar." He pointed to a carton. "We're gonna need seven glasses out of that one." He pointed to another. "And one each of all the bottles in that one. There should be seven different kinds."

KEN RETURNED FROM THE KITCHEN to find the large balloon-shaped glasses and seven ciders sitting on the table. He carefully arranged the bottles in a row and put a glass in front of each, then read the labels, thumbed through a stack of index cards and put one face-down in front of each. He uncorked the first bottle with the confidence of a skilled bartender, then poured about a half-inch in the glass and told her to sniff.

"Lesson number one. If you're going to open a cidery, you need to get the hang of tasting." He took the glass away and swirled the cider around before putting it under her nose again. "Now give it another sniff." He waited a moment. "Notice the difference?"

"Yes. It's more full bodied. More aromatic. This time I smelled blackberries."

"Swirling adds oxygen. Lets it breathe and develop its flavor."

He read the card. "You nailed it. My brother blended our Harrisons with blackberries for this one."

Belle did well with the guessing game until they hit the fifth bottle.

"It's familiar, but I can't put my finger on it."

She reached for the card but he snapped it up, then poured more in her empty glass. "Okay, we're gonna do this once more. Take another whiff."

The room had grown dark and the reflection of the candlelight flashed in her pale green eyes. He studied her face as she closed her lids and slowly inhaled. Her high cheek bones and straight, slightly turned up nose gave her an aloof classic look, yet the full lips seemed to suggest what everyone had said about her.

"All right. Now give it a swirl and sniff it again."

She did as he said, then rose and strolled around the table as if she were considering the taste. She stopped at his chair and suddenly grabbed the card from his hand. He drew her onto his lap and wrestled her for it. She turned and their eyes stayed locked until he let her go.

He stood up and said, "Okay, you hit your limit. No more cider for you." He took her hand and walked her to his stereo. He pawed through his CDs, pulled one out and waved it in front of her eyes. "It's Frank Sinatra time," he said and slipped it in the stereo. He took her hand and pulled her close. She almost fell into his arms, making him laugh. "Oh, boy. I can see now I'll have to find you a taster, too."

She placed the side of her head against his chest as they barely moved to the slow beat. She slurred her words. "I see a pattern here. First you loosen 'em up with jazz... then mellow 'em out with Billie... and put 'em to sleep with Frankie."

"It works every time."

The candles neared the end of their wicks, and as they flickered out their last dying moments, they made the shadows of the two figures leap wildly around the room. A head taller than her, he easily rubbed his cheek across her hair. She grew heavy in his arms, and he found himself holding her tighter and tighter.

He craned his neck and looked into her face. She opened her eyes and barely blinked. She looked so tired it was painful to see. The brave little girl who had fought so valiantly to save an orchard was falling asleep in his arms. He hated himself for giving her so much to drink. Now, instead of them talking for hours, she was hopelessly fading from the magic of the evening.

There was no way she was going to make it home, so he swooped her up in his arms and carried her to his bed, the only light coming from the full moon outside. She was asleep as he laid her down and found a blanket to put over her. She threw it off with an annoyed grunt, then sat up, wrestled off her dress and tossed it.

"I can't sleep in this," she slurred out, sounding like a cranky four year old. Then she took off her bra and fell back in the bed murmuring "That's better. That thing was strangling me."

The moonlight revealed more than Ken's imagination had been able to conjure up, and he stood there absorbing every detail. He finally pulled himself away and retrieved the blanket from the floor. He spread it over her again, and tucked it under her chin.

Suddenly aware of him, she reached up and ran her hand along his face.

"Kiss me," she said.

He wanted her, but not like this. He would wait until this wildling fell in love with him. He bent down and gave her a gentle kiss and listened to a whisper that was filled with yearning. "I love you, Matt. I love you."

125

He stood up, heavy with disappointment, and watched her curl up in the bed and drift into unconsciousness, then he turned off the lamp and left the room.

THE NEXT MORNING, BELLE felt her head ache even before she awoke. She opened her eyes not knowing where she was. It looked like Jake's bedroom, but how could that be? She looked down and saw she was naked except for her panties. Ken appeared at the door with a tray, and she spontaneously pulled the blanket up to her chin.

"Breakfast is served," he sang out.

She looked around wild-eyed. "Where are my clothes?"

He put the tray on a table, picked up the dress from the floor and dangled it in the air with a grin. She lunged forward with the blanket clasped to her chest and snapped it from his fingers.

"Turn around," she screeched. "No! Get out!"

She waited a few moments after he left, then quickly put on the dress. She tiptoed to the door and held an ear to it. If he was a gentleman he wouldn't be out there. Not hearing anything, she swung it open and found him staring her in the face. She looked at him coldly.

He raised his hands and gave her a patronizing smile. "Hold on, darlin'. I need to tell you something."

She pulled her arm back and slapped his face. Her eyes blazed at him as he slowly rubbed his cheek.

"I can't believe I actually thought you were nice. I wonder if you even *had* a brother." She rushed to the coffee table, pulled the agreement from her purse and quickly checked it over, then stuffed it back in. Belle composed herself enough to hide her embarrassment and said, "We'll be here tomorrow to start with the cuttings."

He laughed out loud at her effort.

"What's so funny?" The confidence she had been feigning appeared with a vengeance. "I don't care what happened last night." She waved her purse. "I've got your agreement and I'm coming back for those cuttings."

"Hey, have at it, sweetheart. I'm leaving for Virginia and

126

won't be back for a couple weeks."

She glared at the grin on his face and wanted to run over and slap him again, then she remembered Mac. "Where's my dog!"

He pointed to the front door. Mac peered in, wagging his tail.

On the way back to the compound, she wanted to cry but was too angry to do anything but pound on the steering wheel. She glanced at the clock on the dash. "Oh, my God, it's already ten," she squealed. She eyed Mac with distain. "Why didn't you wake me up!?"

Thinking it best to use the back way into the compound, she swung onto a rarely used lane. She looked around as she drove slowly enough so as not to kick up any dust. She crept around the final turn that would take her to the side of the house, and there in the driveway leaning against Pap's truck were Matt, Raphael and Pap.

She pulled up next to them, took the agreement out of her purse and felt around for her shoes. *Shit!* She'd left them behind. She closed her eyes for a long moment, gathered the nerve she needed to face them and got out. Steeling herself, she walked over to the three and handed the agreement to Pap. He read it and then gave it to Matt. Pap looked down at her bare feet, said nothing and headed for the office with Raphael. While Matt read the agreement, she said, "I've got to get in there and get those cuttings as soon as possible in case he changes his mind and comes up with something to keep me out."

Matt looked at her. "Why would he? You earned them."

She pulled her hand back and swung. He caught her wrist and his eyes became slits. He gazed steadily at her for a long moment and the hurt in his eyes made her want to cry. He finally let her go, turned and left.

Belle stood stunned. In less than twenty-four hours her life had gone from insane desperation to joyful ecstasy to utter humiliation. And during the emotional rollercoaster she'd wielded her wrath on four men, and let Pap down. Yet, in spite of the mess she'd left in her wake, she filled with pride. She had made a difference. She had done something that mattered. Four hundred heirloom trees and the essence of a man's life had been saved.

She pictured her old friend and smiled to herself. "I got 'em, Jake. I got 'em."

CHAPTER ELEVEN

BELLE PUSHED OPEN THE DOOR to her bedroom with her knee, staggered in under the weight of the carton she was carrying and dropped it on the floor. She stood there for a moment, her eyes lingering on Jake's desk. She slowly looked around the room, readjusting her semblance of the place.

She eyed the contents from her old desk scattered in stacks on the floor and quickly moved a couple of piles lying between the desk and her bed. She went to the closet, fetched the rug Jake had given her and unrolled it. She went back to the doorway and took in the room again. It looked so right—the desk that belonged to the man she'd never forget, and the rug that belonged to the man she wished she'd met.

She went out to her truck to get an extra computer they had at the office, and was on her hands and knees plugging it in when Missy entered and noticed the new furnishings.

"Well, well... aren't we getting uptown. What's goin' on?"

"I'll be working from here for a couple days," Belle answered. She crawled from behind the desk and sat hugging her legs. "I've got to get everything arranged for my cuttings, and the mood in the office isn't exactly uplifting."

"Is Pap still upset?"

"More like disappointed."

"How about Matt?"

"He's so overworked, he's numb. Pap has him taking out

129

half the trees in the Rome orchard so they can put in three thousand more spindles. He's been operating that old bulldozer of ours until it's so dark he can't see anymore."

Belle got up and put some things in the desk drawers while Missy went over and sat on her bed. "A lot of nights he's got to take it into the shop and make repairs before the next morning. He's going to a cidery school two weeks from now and those trees have to go in before he can leave."

Missy ran a hand over the ornate iron bed. "I love this thing."

"You ought to. You slept in it with me till you were six. I remember the first night I made you sleep in your own room and found you lying on the floor against my door the next morning."

Missy laughed. "That little stunt got me a couple more weeks in bed with you."

Belle put a stack of her hanging files in one of the drawers and heard the crunch of paper as she slapped it shut. She pulled the drawer out as far as she could, reached her hand under and felt a sheet stuck in a crack. She pulled it out and gave it a quick glance. Seeing it was one of Jake's familiar check lists, she tossed it on the desk. She would look at it later.

"Is Pap playing poker tonight?" asked Missy.

"Are you kidding? The only Thursday night he misses is Thanksgiving."

Missy got up and said she'd make dinner and bring it in so they could talk. By "talk," Belle assumed that meant she was going to question her about the other night.

Belle sat down at her desk, reached into one of the boxes on the floor and retrieved a cylinder of disks Jake had made for her in the fall. She shuffled through them and cried out loud when she found one marked "Book of Antique Apples." She placed it in the computer's drive and booted it up. All the pages picturing and describing his apples lay before her eyes. She quickly uploaded it into the computer, then into Bubba.

Missy arrived with a tray, scooted with it onto the bed and motioned for Belle to join her. Belle sat on the bed and folded her legs under her while Missy took a bite of her grilled cheese sandwich. She looked up at Belle, and muttered, "Go on. Tell me."

"There's nothing to tell. I can't remember a thing."

"How convenient."

"It's true. I'd had a lot to drink, and the last thing I remember was dancing with him."

"Well somewhere between that dance and you getting back here, I'd love to know what happened to my bra and wedgies."

"Jake said I couldn't hold my liquor. Damn! He was right."

"You know, Belle, this story isn't any different from what Matt did back when you were in school. I hope you didn't do it to get even with him."

"Is that what you think?"

"No, but I wouldn't be surprised if Matt does."

"It's not the same," said Belle, irritated. "I don't think we did anything. I would know."

"I wouldn't try to sell that story to Matt if I were you."

Belle rubbed her forehead and grimaced. "I don't have to sell it to anyone... especially not him."

Missy put her grilled cheese sandwich down. "If it makes you feel any better, I don't think Pap gives a damn about your little pajama party. Heck, look how he ignored it when Jeff was hangin' around. It's just that I think he was counting on you and Matt getting back together again." Missy twisted her lips. "I'm afraid that's not gonna happen now."

They sat quietly for a while until Belle said, "What did you and Dave do last night, or shouldn't I ask?"

"We had fun. But, of course, you wouldn't know what that's like. We went to the Rusty Bucket and had some drinks with friends." She examined her nails. "And speaking of Matt, guess who he walked in with as we were leaving?"

Not getting a response, she continued.

"You remember that girl in school who was always in the papers for winning those tennis championships? Marsha Johnson?"

"Yeah."

"She works for an advertising agency here in town. It looked like they were really getting it on. I've never seen Matt look so good. He actually had on a nice pair of pants." She paused for a moment. "You may not have noticed what a hunk he is, but ever since word got out he's divorced, there's a lot of Matt fever goin' around."

Belle ate in silence, picturing him at the door of his trailer.

"I want to talk to you about something," said Missy.

"What?"

"I never wanted to say anything to you or Pap, but Dave hasn't been happy in his job. Actually, it's not the job. He likes welding. It's having to go out of town all the time. For instance, he left for Charleston today, and for the next two nights he'll be sleeping in some fourth-rate motel."

Belle ate and listened intently, happy to focus on something other than Matt and the Rusty Bucket.

"He worked on a couple of breweries in Asheville and kinda got interested in them." Missy put a hand on Belle's arm. "Belle, we want to be dealt in on the cidery."

Belle choked on her sandwich.

"I can't believe it. *You...* interested in the cidery?"

"Between the two of us, we've got twenty-five thousand put aside. We were planning on putting it down on a house, but last night we talked about the cidery for hours. Dave would be good at it. He could do the welding when it's getting set up, and there's nothing he can't fix. Think back. How many times has he come over and helped Matt repair equipment?" She grasped Belle's hand. "This morning we went and asked Pap if we could buy his share."

"Well I'll be damned. What did he say?"

"Yes, if it's okay with you and Matt." She gave Belle a wry look. "Then he finally got around to telling us about the two acres and threw in a trailer. We're okay with it." She bit her lip and paused for a moment. "Dave talked to Matt before he left for Charleston, and he said yes. In fact, Dave said Matt was pretty excited about it. We just need an okay from you."

Belle slowly examined her nails as if she were thinking it over. She suddenly let out a howl, leaped up on her knees and hugged her. "Yes! Yes! Yes!" She sank back down. "Did Pap get the money from you yet?"

"No, he didn't want it."

"I knew he'd just give you his share."

Missy let out a humph. "You bought that? He told me if you two agree, bring him the check right away 'cause George, one of his poker buddies, is setting up the corporation."

Missy rose and said she was going to take a bath and go to bed. Belle smiled contentedly to herself, thinking her sister would soon be on the phone with Dave, spinning dreams of their future together. Belle wondered how painful giving up her dreams of a salon had been for Missy. The way she had talked, it was obvious she was throwing herself into the cidery for Dave's sake. Her sister's unselfish sacrifice for the man she loved touched her.

Belle worked into the night, and while waiting for the last sheets of Jake's apple book to finish printing, she went to the window and pulled the curtain aside. Her forehead rested against the cold pane as she watched the mesmerizing snowflakes slowly drift down.

A light was on in the garage. Matt had to be in there working on the bulldozer. She pictured the glint in his eyes as he talked about the cidery—the same one she'd seen when he'd tell her about how they'd grow Pap's orchards once they got married. She wondered if the loss of that dream was as painful for him as it had been for her.

The printer stopped and she let the curtain fall back. She picked up the sheets and added them to a stack of labels she'd run off to put on the bags that would hold the cuttings. Matt kept creeping into her thoughts as she worked, and she admitted to herself it was getting harder and harder to ignore the buried yearnings clawing their way to the surface. Maybe she could shake him out of her head by straightening her desk.

She picked up the sheet she'd found in the back of the drawer. A number "eight" was circled at the top. Had to be the eighth page. She read the words scrawled in Jake's hurried handwriting. *After things are over at the nursing home, anything left goes to Belle.* There was that nursing home again. She'd been thinking about it ever since Lucy told her about the four-thousand-dollar payments. Who could be in there? Whoever it was had to be alive when Jake wrote the note.

Something began to nag at her. She never understood why there hadn't been any visitation for Mary. No service, no time out for mourning, nothing. Just a phone call to her dorm from Jake telling her she was gone. It was as if she had vanished off the face of the earth. Then when she came home, he gave her Mary's favorite ring, a ruby with two small diamonds. Belle wished she would hear from Lucy soon. She needed to look at that file. Too many questions demanded answers.

Meanwhile, a hundred yards away, Matt was finishing replacing the head gasket on the bulldozer. It had been leaking oil, and he hadn't dared let another night go by without fixing it. He collected his tools and put them where they belonged, then he squirted out some hand cleaner and rubbed it in. He pulled a rag from his pocket and wiped his hands as he strolled over to the open garage door and looked out into the night. The light shone from Belle's room, making the snowflakes sparkle as they fell across her window. He could barely make out her silhouette beyond the curtains, then the light went off and left him with a feeling of sudden loss.

He remembered going into her bedroom that morning to empty her desk before his father and brother brought Jake's over. Memories had cascaded at the sight of the old iron bed. A vision of Belle kneeling on it in pigtails and overalls, holding her Monopoly deeds with a devilish grin on her face, entered his mind again. In those days, everything had been so natural and wholesome between them.

An avalanche of regret overcame him as he pictured the look of betrayal on her face that afternoon on the quad. Sickening scenes of her cavorting with Jeff shot through his brain like a horror film streaming in fast-forward. He had shared her shame, for the hurt he had heaped on her drove her to look for solace from the first man she met. The other night it had almost torn his heart out to watch her walk to her truck on her way to see Ken, yet he couldn't blame her. She was driven and broken at the same time.

For the millionth time he asked himself the question that defined him. Why was he still at McGrady Orchards? Where could it lead? Then he saw the innocent, trusting face looking up at him as Belle lay on the grass underneath him, her hair loose and glimmering, and it answered his question.

BELLE WAS ONLY ABLE TO GET A CHARLOTTE STATION on the radio in the barn basement, so she listened to the news as she checked out her grafting supplies. An announcer was dispassionately reading off an account of a house invasion gone right. A Charlotte housewife who happened to be a Marine back from Afghanistan shot the two intruders dead. Chalk one up for the good guys, Belle told herself. When the newsman went on about a Chinese firm that was building a new cotton mill in North Carolina, she snapped it off. Pap was already buying too much equipment and chemicals from them. She still found it hard to grasp that China had more apple trees in the ground than the rest of the world combined.

Three thousand plastic pots stood stacked near a long workbench set up on sawhorses, and a mountain of specially blended potting soil sat to the side. She was arranging the pots when she heard a truck pull up. Mac lifted his head and listened, then put it back down again. It had to be Pap. Moments later he walked in the door, came to the table and casually leafed through the box of labels she had brought over.

"I see you're getting ready to graft."

"I'll probably start getting the cuttings tomorrow if it doesn't rain. I'll process them at Jake's place. He's got a nice workbench right there in the orchard."

"That's what I came to talk to you about. Our trees have been shipped and should get here in two days."

This was the first time Pap had talked to her since she came back from Ken's, and she was surprised his tone wasn't as cold as she would have thought. Missy was right.

"Has Matt finished fitting out the ground?" she asked.

"Pretty much. He's disking it right now, and Raphael and the men are pulling out the roots. When the trees get here, you're gonna have to drive one of the tractors so we can get them all in before Matt has to leave for Virginia."

"Just let me know."

Pap looked around at the concrete block walls. "When I was a kid, before there was cold storage, we'd go to the ice house and get these huge blocks of ice and drag 'em in here." He pointed to the far end. "We'd put them right over there and cover 'em with straw. We could keep our apples for weeks, sometimes months, that way.

"It was real tough to get ahead in those days. Mostly you concentrated on surviving. Nobody had their own cold storage buildings or their own markets. We had to take our crop to the packing houses and they'd do the sorting, grading and packing, and we'd just get paid our percentage. I was already fourteen by the time my father built our first packing house."

"Hey. We're big time now," said Belle.

"We sure are, honey. We sure are."

"Pap?"

"I don't want to talk about it, honey. I only hope you'd fight as hard to save this place."

She looked straight ahead. "I didn't mean that." She looked up at him. "I'm glad about Missy and Dave." She paused. "You know that was mostly Missy's salon money. She's been saving it since she was in high school."

"Good. Now she's invested," he said, and left.

Belle was on her way to their cold storage building with Mac, thinking about how much it mattered to Pap that Missy was finally being drawn into the farm, when her phone rang. It was Lucy, and she was sitting at the secretary's desk as she spoke.

"Did you find the file?" asked Belle.

"It's not here. I couldn't find my mother's, either. It's strange. These files go back to his first case. They should've been here. And believe me, I looked everywhere, even in Mr. Gregg's desk drawers. I was so scared he might walk in, my knees are still shaking."

"Why do you want your mother's file?"

"I think she was right all these years. I think he cheated her."

Belle suddenly realized why Lucy was so committed to her

search, and it made her more comfortable about disclosing what was worrying her. "I found the strangest notation in Jake's desk. It said something about when things are over at the nursing home I was to get whatever was left. How much is in that trust fund?"

"Over five hundred thousand."

"Phew! That's a lot of money." Belle fell silent as she tried to make sense of everything. Was Mary in the nursing home? Why would Ben stop sending them money? Had she died?

"I'm worried, Lucy. Things are piling up. There's a lot more here than the question of why Jake would let his life's work fall to chance. I think there's someone out there that needs my help. I've got to find out what's going on."

"I wonder if there's anything on his computer that would help you," said Lucy.

Belle leapt at the remark. "Do you know where it is?"

"In my office. I got it out of his closet yesterday. He wants me to have someone come over and swipe it clean and didn't want some no-body technician sitting in his reception room. Do you believe that?"

"Can I come and look through it?"

"I don't know, Belle. Ellie told me that Ben said she was never to let you come into the office again. If she walks in and sees you, I could lose my job."

Belle thought fast. "Okay. Then can you put everything on a thumb drive for me?"

"Are you kidding? I don't even know how to turn the thing on. I do all the books by hand."

Belle searched her brain. "What if I sent someone over to pick it up? If anyone notices, you can tell them he's from the computer shop."

Belle crossed her fingers and held her breath.

"Do you have someone who can pass for a delivery man?"

She didn't, but she'd think of someone. "Uh-huh."

"Okay, but you gotta do it tomorrow. He'll still be in court."

"I'll have someone pick it up around three-thirty."

Belle hung up and continued through the compound until

she reached their cold storage building. Piles of wire for the new spindles sat on skids in the outer room. She rolled open the door to the cooler, pushed aside the clear plastic strips hanging from the ceiling and went inside.

The room's thirty-five degrees would keep the buds on her cuttings dormant by tricking them into thinking it was still winter. She checked the stainless steel wire shelving she would put her cuttings on and was satisfied everything was in order.

She left the building and walked back toward the barn, intending to find Jake's orchard plans in one of the cartons she'd gotten from his office. It would be a lot easier if she could put the labeled plastic bags in the same order as the trees.

Rafael came out of the packing house and walked towards her. Since all the cartons were piled in the barn loft, she asked him if he would help with the lifting. *"Cualquier cosa por ti,"* he told her with a fatherly smile. Her Spanish was deplorable considering all the Hispanics she worked with, but she'd heard him say "Anything for you" all her life and cherished the endearing way he always said it.

They went in the barn section above the basement and climbed the ladder to the loft. They easily fell into the routine of Rafael lining up cartons, her going through them, and him re-stacking after she was finished. The way her luck was running, it didn't surprise her that the very last carton contained the plans.

Belle hadn't been in the loft for years and she marveled at all the remnants of her life piled in its dusty corners. She lifted up Missy's pink doll buggy for Raphael to see, and they both laughed. She casually picked through the items heaped one on top of the other. The suitcase didn't interest her the first time she eyed it, but it kept tickling the back of her mind as she pawed through the junk.

She went back to take another look and struggled with a tricycle entangled in a jump rope until she was able to reach in and pull the suitcase out. Made of tough cardboard with leather edging, one corner was crushed as if it had been thrown from some distance. She crouched down to open it, when Raphael grabbed it up. He stood there holding it with an expression she'd never seen on his face before—a mixture of panic and determination. *No, no se puede.*

She stood up and reached for it, but he stepped back. "Why not, Raphael?" She reached for it again. He suddenly grabbed it with both hands and heaved it on top of the pile, and they both watched as it slid down behind the heap. Her deep respect for him held her back from challenging what he'd done. She picked up her plans, thanked Raphael for his help and climbed down the ladder, and for the rest of the day couldn't shake the incident from her head.

She worked in the barn until Mac's restless pacing told her it was time to go home and eat. She got ready to leave, when Pap phoned and said he was putting dinner on the table. It had been a long time since he'd done that. He was sending her a message, and she walked to the house with Mac, trying to figure out what it was.

His telling her that he hoped she would fight for the farm as hard as she did for Jake's trees kept floating to the surface. That *was* the message. No matter what she did wrong, the only thing that held sway with him was his belief, that no matter what happened, she would continue the legacy of the McGrady Orchard.

Pap ate his dinner in front of the TV, while Missy ate in her room and talked to Dave on the phone. Belle barely touched hers. She had to go over to Raphael's house and talk to his son, Miguel.

Her truck pulled off Sugarloaf onto a steep dirt road that climbed upward. It made a sharp turn, and the lights of a house shone ahead. Belle pulled up next to Raphael's truck. A dog that looked more like a wolf barked viciously in her headlights.

Suddenly a door to the house opened wide and cast a light across the yard. Someone hollered out in Spanish and the dog vanished. Belle looked over at Mac. "You stay here, boy." She got out and walked toward the doorway packed with kids shoving each other to get a good look.

A waft of warm air mixed with cold brushed across her face as she walked the twenty yards. The property Matt was buying for the cidery apples was even higher up the mountain where the heat would rise from the valley below as the cold fog settled in the low areas. Perfect for an orchard.

Raphael appeared and shooed the kids away.

"Buenas noches, Belle."

He held the door open for her as she entered. Helen wiped her hands on her apron and gave Belle a big hug, the signal for all her children to greet her with hugs and kisses. Alfredo, the youngest, took her hand and led her to the couch. Minutes later, one of their daughters appeared with a tray laden with Mexican cookies. Belle helped herself to an elephant ear, making them all laugh.

This was the first time since Matt's marriage that Belle had stepped foot in Raphael's house, for fear of running into Rita and her baby. It hadn't offended Helen and Raphael, for they knew that was how it had to be. The eager smile on Helen's face embarrassed Belle. Evidently she hadn't heard the gossip about Ken and her, and hoped that now that Rita was gone, she and Matt would get back together again.

Belle's eyes roamed around the spacious room, a far cry from the crowded trailer she knew as a child when Helen would babysit with her and Missy. Helen was no more than a child herself when Matt was born out of wedlock. Raphael met her five years later at the local cantina where she washed dishes, and they married two months later. With no family to speak of, Helen, surrounded by his plethora of Hispanic relatives, was now as at home with the culture as Matt.

After getting caught up with what all the kids were up to, Belle rose. "I came over to ask Miguel if I can pick him up at Immaculata tomorrow after school. I need him to help me with something downtown."

The family was so pleased to have the fourteen year old invited to help, it took a while for her to pull away from all the hugs and get out of the house. She drove away with the whole family crammed in the doorway, waving her off.

Her now cold pickup rumbled along the dirt road in the black of the moonless night, yet she still felt embraced with the warmth of the loving family. How lucky those kids were to have a mother and father. Everyone was right. She should get married and start a family of her own. Why didn't she listen to Pap and swallow her pride while she still had a chance with Matt. Her head told her he was right for her, then the image of his little boy snaked into her head like it had a thousand times before, and she pounded the steering wheel and swallowed a scream.

CHAPTER TWELVE

THE WEATHER HAD TURNED WARM for February, dredging up the valley's annual fear of the trees budding too early and getting hit with a frost. Belle spread out the orchard plan and arranged all the labeled plastic bags in the same sequence as Jake's trees, then grabbed up the carton and left the barn.

No one was stirring in the compound yet, and the sun was still on the rise as she tossed the carton into her truck. She yelled for Mac who came bounding, and they took off for Jake's. The trees for the new spindle orchard would be there in a day or so, and she had to get all the cuttings before they arrived.

If Ken hadn't changed the locks, she knew where Jake hid a key to the house. If she found it, she could turn on the orchard's lights and work all night if she had to. Hopefully, Ken wouldn't show up and catch her in the act.

Grafting almost three thousand trees would be the hardest way to start their cidery, she thought as she carted her materials to the workbench in Jake's orchard, but it made sense. Trees comparable to Jake's would cost thousands.

The key to the house was where it had always been, and she hung it on a nail at the workbench. She'd start with the cidery apples since she and Jake had already flagged them with strips of caution tape.

All the cuttings had to be from new wood and the diameter

and length of a pencil. She cut fifty from the first flagged tree and took them to the bench. She ran five of them under the tap and shook out as much water as she could, then wrapped them in Saran Wrap before tucking them in the properly labeled bag.

She planned to stop work at three and pick up Miguel. She could use the time with him to see if he would be willing to work for her every day after school while she was grafting. With Miguel's help potting, she could graft at least four hundred a day, and they'd be finished in a week.

By three, she had finished ten of the forty trees and only cut herself once. She quickly packed up and left for Immaculata to pick up Miguel, only stopping at their compound for a moment to put the cuttings into the cooler.

THE COMPUTER SAT ON THE FLOOR of Lucy's office, and a bag containing all the disks and thumb drives from Jake's office lay on her desk. She kept glancing up at the clock. Belle's delivery man would be there any minute. She was tempted to phone Ellie again and ask her if Mr. Gregg was back so she could get some checks signed, but she'd already done that twice that day and it might get Ellie suspicious, especially after she promised she would call her the minute he arrived.

She tried to keep busy, but kept looking up at the clock. Damn, he was already fifteen minutes late. A knock on the door startled her. She got up and opened it. A look of disappointment swept across her face. It was a kid.

"How come you're so late?"

"Soccer practice ran over."

She rolled her eyes and sighed, then pointed to the computer. "There it is."

He picked it up and started for the door.

"Wait!" She grabbed the bag from her desk. "Let me go first in case anyone sees us and gets suspicious."

His brows wrinkled with a look of concern.

"Hasn't Belle told you anything?"

"Just for me to get the computer."

"If we run into anyone, you've got to tell them you're picking it up for Computer City."

"But I'm not. I'm getting it for Belle McKenzie."

She went over to him and looked straight into his eyes. "Listen, kid, we're just borrowing it for a couple days."

His wide-eyed look concerned her. Thinking he was about to cry, her tone became more conciliatory. "There's nothing to worry about. Follow me down the hall. I'll make sure no one's coming, then all you have to do is walk to the door and leave."

She opened the door, and seeing the narrow hallway empty, said "Let's go." She remembered something, went back in and came out with a piece of paper. She folded it and tucked it in his shirt pocket. "Belle wants this address. Be sure to give it to her."

Before they reached the end of the hallway, Lucy stopped and turned to him.

Startled, he jumped back. "What? What is it?"

"*Shush!* Do you want to get us in trouble?"

He threw his head back and murmured. "Oh, my God."

She quickly helped him wrap the handle of the plastic bag around his wrist as he balanced the computer on a knee.

"Belle wants these, too."

She peeked around the corner to check out the entry hall, and her eyes locked onto Ben's. He let go of his office doorknob and came over, looking at her questioningly. Then the boy. Then the computer.

"What are you doing with that?" he said to Miguel.

Lucy quickly stepped between the two. "He's picking it up for Computer City."

"I told you I wanted them to come here."

"They have to use the equipment in their office to erase everything from the hard drive."

He side-stepped her and looked at Miguel. "I want *everything* erased. Do you understand?"

"I... I just pick up and deliver."

Lucy gave Miguel a nudge and he hurried down the hall toward the entrance.

Ben shook his head. "These Hispanics will do anything for a buck. I bet that kid's not old enough to drive."

THE NEXT MORNING, Belle eagerly started collecting her cuttings. She wore fingerless gloves, and had to keep blowing into her fists to keep her hands warm. It didn't help that she'd been up half the night looking through Jake's computer. She studied the east ridge, hopeful that once the sun rose things would start to warm up.

Mac barked at a vehicle skidding to a stop. Belle's eyes shot toward the driveway, and she recognized Matt's truck. He slid out and walked toward her with a stride that was meant to send a message. He stopped less than a foot in front of her, his broad chest almost in her face.

He tossed up two fingers holding a folded note.

"This is for you."

She snatched it.

"You let *me* know when you're finished with that computer. Understand? *I'll* take it back." He turned to leave, then stopped and looked at her over his shoulder. "I don't know what you're up to, Belle, but nothing you do surprises me anymore." He shook his head, and his tone plunged from angry to disgusted. "I thought I'd seen it all, but you never fail to amaze me. Miguel's only a kid."

She ran ahead of him, stopped and faced him with her fists firmly on her hips. "He was just picking it up. If anyone would have gotten into trouble, it would've been me. I was in my truck ten yards away. I'd never let anything happen to him."

"You don't understand, Belle. He's a Latino. They'd of come down hard on him."

After he pulled out of the lot with his tires spitting gravel, Belle tried hard to ignore the incident and concentrate on getting the cuttings. She could see why Matt couldn't understand why she was taking these risks. It was her fault he could never fully understand how unlikely it was that Jake would ever leave his life's work to chance, or the depth of the love and responsibility she felt for Mary. She should have drawn Matt into her life with them back when they were kids. Instead, she had made sure their paths never crossed.

Maybe it was because she didn't want to share Jake and

Mary with anyone else, or maybe it was because she was childishly jealous of the way he could run to a loving mother and father when anything happened, while all she had was Pap and Pam who always seemed to operate on the outer rim of her existence. Somehow, she had to resolve the mystery of finding Mary without cutting Matt off again. But she was too afraid to go there. Just like Pap, if he tried to stop her, she'd never be able to forgive him. It would be a final betrayal.

More than any time before, their relationship—love, wanting, needing, whatever it could be called—was hanging in the balance. It was as if both of them were waiting for some pivotal event, that if it went well, would cleanse them of regret, suspicion and unrelenting bitterness. And if it didn't, would wrench them apart forever. She was a gambler, but this time the stakes were too high. She was going to keep her secrets from Matt.

She threw herself into her work, and by six, had gotten and wrapped all the cidery cuttings. The sun had slid behind the mountains, yet its rosy glow lit up the clouds overhead. She took the key off the nail and opened the door to the house, then reached in and turned on the orchard lights. Now she was going to start getting the cuttings from every tree for her personal heirloom orchard. To be safe, she had decided on two each in case any of her grafts didn't take. She quickly fell into the rhythm of getting two cuttings from ten trees at a time and putting them in the proper bags before wrapping them at the bench.

Mac barked, and she looked up to see car headlights pull in the driveway. Belle held her breath until she recognized Matt's mother getting out with a basket. Belle went to greet her, and Helen put an arm in hers as they strolled together to the bench.

"I went to the garage and brought Matt his dinner," Helen said, "but he wouldn't take it and told me to bring it to you."

The last morsels to pass Belle's lips were two donuts at five that morning. She threw open the cloth napkin and grabbed one of the meatball sandwiches with her red, raw fingers protruding from wet, dirty gloves. She tore off a chunk and gave it to Mac.

"*Umm,*" she moaned as she devoured it. Her cheeks were red, and straggles of hair that had escaped from her wool cap stuck to her sweaty face. She pawed through the basket and pulled out a bag of cookies, greedily wolfing them down as Helen talked.

"It's my fault Matt spoke to you that way today. Last night, Miguel was so worried that I called Matt and made him come and talk to him." She reached up and ran her hand down Belle's face. "I know you would never do anything to hurt any of my children."

Helen reached for the thermos and poured some coffee. "Here," she said, handing it to Belle. Helen's eyes roamed over the house, now looming in the spotlights. "So that guy who's buying up all the orchards owns this place, too."

The doleful way she said it, gave Belle an inkling Raphael had finally told her about her night with Ken.

Helen grasped Belle's hand. "Belle, there's something that's got to be said."

Belle's eyes locked on hers.

"I want you to know Raphael is sorry he made Matt marry that woman. I want you to know, too, that Matt had no choice. The way he was born and the way Raphael took him as his son and gave him his name, Matt could never go against him. I begged Raphael on my hands and knees not to do it... for both yours and Matt's sake, but he's from a world where faith is un-compromising."

She wiped her eyes with the napkin. "Matt's a good man, and he respects you." Helen paused for a moment. "I remember when he was a little boy and he came home from playing with you. 'I'm gonna marry her when I grow up,' he told me." Helen put an arm around Belle and squeezed. "Things don't always work out the way you want, do they?"

Helen left, and Belle worked through the night, getting the last cutting as the sun was about to rise over the ridge. She put everything in the cooler at the compound and went home to get some sleep.

She woke around seven that evening to find Pap standing next to her bed with a tray.

"You got 'em all?"

She nodded and took the tray. Pap clasped her shoulder with his massive hand. "Good. The trees came this afternoon and we're gonna start putting them in tomorrow."

He left, and Belle finished the meal before getting up and starting back on Jake's computer. Well after midnight, Belle heard Missy's car pull in. Moments later she tiptoed into Belle's room.

"Why don't you just move in with him?" Belle threw out.

"Are you kidding? His parents would drop dead." Missy studied Belle's face. "You look like hell. When's the last time you got some sleep?" She took one of Belle's hands and shook her head in disbelief. "Good grief."

"You haven't seen anything. Wait till I start grafting."

Missy tapped a manicured nail on the computer. "Is this the one you stole?"

"I didn't steal it. It's going right back."

Belle pulled a thumb drive from the computer and tossed it on a pile, then hit delete. "That's it. They're all erased." She pointed to the four thumb drives lying on her desk. "And everything's in those." She thought for a moment. "But I didn't find what I was looking for."

"What do mean? All you wanted were his files."

Belle handed her Jake's note and waited for her to read it. "If that was page eight, there had to be a heck of a lot in front of it." She showed her the nursing home address in Winston-Salem. "Ben sent them four thousand dollars every month, but it stopped after Jake died."

Missy stomped a foot and rolled her eyes. "Don't you have enough to worry about? You gotta let Jake go and concentrate on the farm and the cidery."

Belle leaned back in her chair and eyed her. "Lucy said there's over five hundred thousand in the trust account the money was coming from."

"Come on, Belle. If there was any hanky-panky with Jake's money, do you honestly believe you're gonna pin anything on his brother? He's a lawyer, for God's sake." Missy picked up an open bag of potato chips from Belle's desk and sank down on the bed looking a little dejected. "At least you got the rug and the truck."

"You don't get it, Missy. Something's really wrong here. Lucy said Jake was paying that nursing home to take care of someone; and whoever it is, has been shipped to another place that accepts Medicaid patients. Something tells me it isn't quite as nice as the one that costs four thousand dollars a month." She pressed her fingers to her temples. "Damn! I'm sure it's Mary."

"Now I know you're nuts. She's dead!"

"This whole 'four thousand dollars a month to the nursing home thing' started just before she was supposed to have died. Who else could be there? Think back. I was still at NC State. We never saw her in a casket. Jake just told me he had her cremated."

All kinds of scenarios had been running through Belle's thoughts ever since the call from Lucy, and only one made sense. "You remember how proud she was... always making an effort to look good. Those last years had to tear Jake apart, her mouth sagging open and dribbling all over herself." Belle fell into a stony gaze. "I can see her begging him, in the few lucid moments she had, to take her someplace where no one would see her like that... especially not me."

"I don't believe you," said Missy. "You're getting too wrapped up in all this."

"I called the nursing home, but they wouldn't divulge any patient information. There's no way I can take a day off to go to Winston-Salem right now, but once I finish grafting, I'm gonna go there, and one way or another I'm gonna find out where she is. I don't care what it takes, I'm not going to rest until I know she's okay." She bit her lip and made a face. "I kinda lost it with them. I shouldn't of done it. Hopefully they won't remember the call."

Belle jotted Ben's office address and Lucy's phone number on a Post It and slapped it on the computer. "Matt's going to take it back," she said as she unplugged it and put it on the floor. "I wish I could do it myself, but if Ben catches me with it, he'll put two and two together and Lucy'll lose her job." She plopped down on the bed, fluffed up her pillow and sank back with her hands locked behind her head. "There's something else."

"What?"

Belle told her about the suitcase, but failed to mention she intended to retrieve it from the loft the first chance she got.

"Do you think it's our mother's?" asked Missy.

"Who else's? Can you imagine Pap going anywhere?" She reached for a chip and slowly munched on it while mulling everything over. "There's too many loose ends, Missy. Tell me, how many times have you wondered why our mother would run off with Jake's son and leave us behind? Jake has the answer, and I think he's trying to tell me what it is."

CHAPTER THIRTEEN

B ELLE SENSED THE EXCITEMENT the minute she stepped out of the truck. The crew shook hands and patted each other on the back with broad grins, as they joyfully looked forward to a solid week of twelve-hour days in the off-season.

Everyone gathered in the middle of the field. Two tractors attached to wagons loaded with metal posts stood at the ready. Matt meted out instructions in fluent Spanish, and the crowd slowly dissolved as the men took up their tasks. Matt pointed to one of the tractors. "Belle, you drive that one and work with Carlos."

She looked over at Carlos. A big spool of string lay on the ground next to him. He and another farmhand measured a ten foot row, marked it and moved on. She got on the tractor and drove over to the two men following behind them. She let the tractor creep slowly along with the men pulling the posts off the wagon and pounding them in the ground. Two teams worked from the center of the field, going in opposite directions.

It was a glorious day with a clear Western North Carolina blue sky. The work went along smoothly, and when they finished stringing the rows, the crew jumped in their pickups and headed out to the Mexican food truck on Route 64 to get some lunch. Belle decided to go home and grab a sandwich. On the way to her truck, she felt a tap on her shoulder and turned to face Matt.

"I was rough on you yesterday. I owe you a lunch."

"We're even. I owe you a dinner."

They walked along together without a word until they reached his truck. He took hold of her arm with one hand and opened his door with the other.

"Get in."

She looked into his bloodshot eyes and said, "You look like hell." She braced for a smart comeback. He stared at her for a moment as if he were going to say something, then motioned for her to climb in.

Belle gazed out the window as the truck sailed past row after row of bare apple trees and headed toward Route 64.

"Pap said you've got all the cuttings in the cooler."

"Yep."

"Miguel will come after school and help you with the grafting."

"Aren't you afraid I might corrupt him?"

"*Are you kidding*? Wild horses couldn't get him to go anywhere with you."

"Ha, ha."

He pulled off the road onto a graveled lot with two lone picnic tables and a big red food truck. Belle started to get out.

"You stay right where you are. I'll get it. With your Spanish, God only knows what they're gonna serve you."

Matt came back holding a plate in each hand and motioned for her to come out. The crew made room for them at one of the tables, and Belle ate listening to their playful Spanish banter.

One of the Hispanics, who was new to the crew, said something that made Matt blush and the others look solemnly downward. Belle imagined what that might have been. Raphael, who was sitting at the other table, turned and spoke to the man in a way that wiped the smile off his face. The only word Belle recognized was *respeto,* which she knew to mean respect.

On the way back, the full stomach and warm sunshine made her groggy, and she closed her eyes and sank back in her seat. The next thing she knew, the truck wasn't moving, and Matt stood at the open door. She looked around and saw he had parked at the house.

"Go in and get some sleep."

"Pap wants me to help."

"We'll get an extra hand from Miguel every afternoon when he gets off the school bus, and that'll loosen someone else up to take your place, but we'll need you to drive a tractor up until then."

She slid out, all stiff. "Wait. I'll go get the computer."

"Where is it?"

"My bedroom."

"You stay right here. I'll get it."

Belle smiled inwardly as she leaned against the truck and waited for him to return. In spite of all that had gone on between them, those eight years in a Catholic school had given him a clear set of rules.

He came out and put the computer on the floor of the truck. She pulled off the Post It and slapped it on his chest.

"This is where it goes. Call Lucy first."

He pulled it off and read it, then put the number in his phone. She started to say something, but he interrupted her.

"I know. If anyone asks, I'm to tell them I'm from Computer City."

She watched him back up his truck and turn it around. He stopped in front of her and lowered the window.

"I hope to hell you know what you're doing."

The next morning found the new orchard buzzing with activity. Belle skillfully positioned the tractor at the beginning of a row. Carlos sat on the planter attached to it. Clumps of four-foot trees were stacked on either side, their damp roots rubbing up against him. The window at the back of the tractor's cab was up, with Belle inside looking over her shoulder and waiting for the signal to start.

Carlos pulled a tree off the pile, got it into planting position and shouted for her to go. She dropped the blade and slowly advanced with it cutting a deep swath. Carlos handed the tree to someone walking behind, who stuck it in the trench. A chain with a marker three feet from the end dragged behind, indicating where the next tree should go. Belle looked ahead to make sure she was driving in a straight line while listened acutely for the order to halt.

A heavy-duty flat-bed truck held the three thousand trees in bundles of fifty. Their roots were covered with damp peat moss and tucked in black plastic bags to protect them from the direct rays of the sun. Someone stood by ready to untie and shake out the next batch when needed.

Belle didn't realize how late it had gotten until Pap pulled in with lunches from the food truck. Keeping the trees from drying out in the sun was too critical to risk taking an hour to eat. Raphael gave the order to stop, and everyone streamed to Pap's tailgate to grab a Styrofoam box. Belle eased off the tractor and spotted Pap coming towards her with a lunchbox.

"I had them make this up special for you," he said as he handed it to her.

She took out a sandwich and ate as they trudged over to Matt and Raphael.

"Looks like you'll have these planted in plenty of time for your trip," Pap said to Matt. "They're not calling for rain for five more days."

Belle drifted over to a chest tucked under a tree and helped herself to two bottles of water. She stuffed one in her jacket pocket and opened the other, guzzling it down as she strolled over to Pap who was still talking with Matt.

Pap looked at Belle. "I was just telling Matt that I don't know how he did it, but Dave got the week off so he can go with him to the cidery school."

"That's good," she said.

"I figured it would give him enough of a taste of the business to see if he really likes it before he gets in too deep," said Pap. He looked at Matt for a moment, and then Belle. "I asked them if they could take one more, and they said yes. Do you think you can put the grafting back a week?"

"No. The root stock is coming next Monday and I've got to get it heeled in, and then start potting so they'll get off to a good start."

"In another couple weeks we're gonna be in full-swing. You

won't be able to go again till fall."

"That's okay, Pap. The grafting can't wait."

Raphael shouted for everyone to get back to work, and the routine got cranked up again.

Clouds had been crawling across the sky all afternoon, and now a cold wind kicked up from the north. Belle reached the end of the row that landed at the crest of the orchard in front of the big rock where she and Pam had sat. Carlos called out for her to stop, then yelled for more trees.

It would take a while for them to be brought up and situated on the planter, so Belle sat back and looked down over the slope, now barren except for row after row of thin little trees. Gone was the exotic beauty of the contorted old Romes, soon to be replaced by trellises with their posts and wires.

She'd been fighting it ever since she had to stop, but she now let her eyes rest on the crest of the hill where Matt had made love to her for the first time, before she left for college. An irrepressible urge made her scan the field for him, and she caught him staring back at her.

Their eyes stayed locked, and the pain of him being ripped away from her pierced her heart all over again. Then an intense fear grabbed her from behind. The picture in the *Times News* of Marsha Johnson holding a trophy shot into her head, and she wanted to vomit.

Just then, Raphael came up the hillside and said something to Carlos in Spanish, then he reached up to help Belle come down before climbing on himself.

"Miguel's here. I'll take over now," he said.

Belle lamented how much her mood had plunged since the morning as she walked down the rolling hillside where the crew was already putting in the ten foot posts in the planted rows.

Noticing Miguel busy tapping down the dirt around a tree with his feet, she walked over and startled him as he turned her way.

"Your brother told me you want to help me graft."

He nodded eagerly.

"Good. I'm going to start right after we finish these trees, then we'll go straight through until we're finished. How long can you work after school?"

"My mother said till seven."

"Good. I'll let you know."

Exhausted, Belle trudged to her truck and drove to the office. Her phone rang, and she was excited to see it was Lucy.

"Did you find anything in the computer?" Lucy asked.

"A lot of good antique apple stuff I can use, but not what I was looking for."

"I've thought of something else."

Belle was amazed to see this timid person so solidly invested in this risky enterprise. She was seized with a feeling of kinship—two women with nothing in common except their passion to help someone they loved and for whom no other aid existed.

"What is it?"

"It's odd that both Jake's and my mother's files are missing, and I think I know where they might be. Ben has a storeroom halfway down the hall from me. Actually, three other people in the building have one, too. He doesn't go in there much, just every once in a while."

"Can you get the key?"

"Ellie had me watch the office last Friday, so I sneaked out and tried every one she had, but none of them worked. I bet he's got the only one."

Belle didn't say anything. She was confident Lucy had a plan, and she was also sure that getting her hands on her mother's file was the reason for her keen interest. She wouldn't be surprised if Lucy wanted to reopen her mother's case, and if that weren't possible, go after Ben some other way. She had already told Belle the transcriptions of the all the depositions concerning her mother's suit would be in the file.

"It wouldn't take much to pry open that door, but it has to be done at night," said Lucy.

"I don't know, Lucy. Borrowing the computer was one thing... It could get dicey."

"Not really. I can give you the key to the front door and mark the one you need to pry open. All you'll need is a crowbar and a flashlight. If I remember right, there's a light in there. It'd be a good idea to pry a couple others open to make it look like a druggy did it. That way, Mr. Gregg won't get suspicious."

"What if a cleaning person shows up?"

"They won't. All the offices are cleaned by this one firm, and they come around five in the morning. I know this because Mr. Gregg owns the building and we hire them."

Belle bit her lip and thought. "I don't know if I can do that sort of thing, Lucy. Especially with all we've got going on. I'd be putting a lot at risk. Our orchard, the cidery, our family name. I need to think about it." Belle hung up and sat mired in conflict, but what bothered her the most was the dead certainty that she couldn't turn her back on Mary.

CHAPTER FOURTEEN

THE FIRST APPLE SEEDS to dig their roots into the New World were planted in Jamestown, Virginia, years before the Pilgrims landed at Plymouth. And for the next two centuries, with no nurseries to turn to, if a Southerner wanted an apple tree—a highly prized food source in those days—he had to plant a seed. The hard cider and vinegar produced from apples were essential, and no other fruit could be kept fresh in the winter by being stored in caves or pits like apples.

These seedling trees produced many different varieties. Some were too small or sour and were fed to the hogs or mules, some were mediocre and used for cider and vinegar, but a few seedling trees would have good apples that would be prized for cooking and eating.

People would say of these apples, "I wish I had a tree like that." Grafting was a rare skill in early America, but these seedling apple trees sent up sprouts from their roots that had the same genes as the tree itself. Settlers and farmers dug up the sprouts from these good trees and gradually improved their orchards. They spread from one community to another and were given names—Red June because it was red and got ripe in June, Sheepnose because that's what it looked like, the Albemarle Pippin because that's where it came from, or Payne's Late Keeper named after the man who discovered it.

The appearance of a middle class was the impetus for the

emergence of nurseries in the late 1700s. These people didn't want to bother with planting seeds and taking potluck with seedling apple trees. They wanted to buy a good tree.

Beginning at the end of the Revolutionary War, small nurseries, using grafting cuttings from good local apple trees, popped up all over the South. The early apples that are called heirlooms today can be found listed in the old nursery catalogs—Black Twig, Winesap, Red Russet, along with scores of others. And on this day, in the mountains of North Carolina in an ancient barn with its chestnut beams and poplar siding, a young woman was preparing to save four hundred of them.

Belle put her grafting knife on the table and unpacked the metal tags she'd brought from her bedroom. It had taken the whole weekend to carefully print on the names identifying every one of the two thousand trees that were going into the cidery orchard, plus the eight hundred for her personal collection—and she had the sore fingers to prove it.

The chugging of a tractor made her go outside. Carlos sat behind the wheel and Raphael stood on the foothold with a hand braced on the back of the seat. Stacked on the trailer behind it were bundles of rootstock that had been shipped from Oregon.

Belle, cheeks rosy and hair flying in the wind, helped unload, then thanked them and waved as the tractor disappeared behind the garage.

She went in the barn, dragged a bucket over to the table to the left of her stool and filled it with water. Then she dragged another bucket to the other side and put in just enough water to cover the roots. After opening a can of black, sticky grafting compound and setting it on her table, she was satisfied all was in order and went back out. A nuthatch perched in a huge black locust pierced the silence with its loud, throaty song. She untied a bundle of fifty rootstocks and shook out the damp peat moss before taking them in the barn.

She dropped them in the bucket and left for the cold storage building across from the barn to retrieve a bag containing fifty of the cidery cuttings she'd gotten from one tree. Before she got started, she tore off several four-inch strips from a roll of masking tape and stuck them on the edge of the workbench.

With an old towel spread on her lap to catch the drippings, she picked up a cutting and cut off a piece about three inches long, then she sharpened the bottom end with her pruning knife and lay it on the table. She picked a root stock from the bucket, cut off the stem a few inches from the root bundle and split it open, then pressed the sharpened end of the cutting into the cleft before pulling off a piece of the masking tape and winding it around the graft. Being paper, it would eventually rot off. She covered the tape with tar, tagged the tree and carefully stood it up in the shallow tub so the roots wouldn't dry out before it was potted.

She grafted and potted non-stop right up to mid-afternoon when Miguel arrived. After she showed him how to plant the grafted trees, everything sped up. They were working on the cidery twigs, so she told him to stick a white stake in each pot so they wouldn't get mixed up with the trees for her orchard. The careful way he handled the grafts and conscientiously kept all the sets of fifty neatly in their own separate section relaxed her enough to enjoy the work.

By the next afternoon, she realized Miguel was working out better than she had expected, and she trusted him enough to let him fetch the cuttings from the cooler. It wouldn't be a bad idea to show him how to graft during one of their breaks. It might come in handy some day. After all, Jake had taught her to graft when she was only twelve. Finished with a batch and needing to stretch her legs, she told him to set up another fifty pots and left for the office to get Pap's grafting knife.

She strode across the compound and spotted Pap's truck in front of the packing house. Good, she thought. He sometimes carries his grafting knife attached to his keys. She ran up the stairs and opened the office door to find his chair empty. She glanced over at Matt's desk. Pap was leaning over Danny and looking at his drawing.

Pap patted him on the back and came over to her.

"What is he doing here?" she asked.

Pap rubbed his forehead.

Her voice rose another decibel. "I asked you, *What* is he doing here?"

Pap grabbed her arm, led her out onto the landing and closed the office door. "Rita dumped him off at Raphael's last night and told him she was gonna be gone for two weeks."

She jerked her arm from his grasp. "Then why in the hell doesn't he go to their house after school?"

"He was supposed to, but he got off with Miguel." Pap looked into her eyes. "Listen to me Belle, give the kid a break. What Matt did to you isn't his fault. I tried to put him in the truck and take him over there, but he started crying and told me he was ashamed to face the other kids. He doesn't think his mother's ever coming back."

Belle rolled her eyes. "Great! Matt's in Virginia, so now the kid's our problem."

"Don't worry. He's either going to be with me, Raphael or Carlos, and it's only for a week. Belle... he's Matt's boy."

Belle got the knife and left. She wasn't in the mood to teach anybody anything, so she and Miguel worked together quietly in tandem until Raphael picked him up at seven. Besides, she had bigger things gnawing at her. She couldn't waste a moment finishing the cuttings so she could go find Mary.

By the third day of grafting, typical of an Apple Valley spring, the temperature had dived from fifty degrees on Tuesday to thirty-five that morning. Even Mac had to be coaxed out of his warm spot in the corner of the kitchen. Belle hurried through the deserted compound with the icy wind cutting through her jacket. She reached the barn and flipped on the radio, then poured some coffee from her thermos before starting back on the grafting. By mid-morning, the big heater that hung from the rafters stopped kicking on as the sun showed its face and the temperature slowly climbed to forty.

By three, she had done quite a few grafts and gotten up to date on all the random acts of violence that had befallen the folks in Charlotte. She switched off the radio and looked forward to Miguel showing up. He was due any minute. Mac raised his head and listened, then ran to the door wagging his tail. It opened, and in walked Miguel; and a few paces behind, came Danny.

Miguel's face was painted with guilt as he came near and spoke low enough so Danny wouldn't hear. She glanced over and saw the boy crouched down petting Mac.

"I was supposed to take him to the office, but he wouldn't go," said Miguel. "He wants to stay with me." He wrinkled his forehead. "Is that okay? I promise he won't be any trouble."

Her phone rang and she saw it was Pap.

"Belle, do me a favor and when Miguel gets there, send him over to the office to tell Danny I'll be there in a couple hours. The crew's running behind and Raphael can't get away, either."

She looked at Miguel, then Danny who was now trying to get Mac to shake his hand. "He's here. He wants to be with Miguel."

"Can you handle that?"

"Just today."

Pap thanked her, told her to be nice and hung up.

She sensed Danny standing next to her, but kept on grafting. "You can't play with the dog in here," she said without looking up. She pointed to what were by now almost a thousand potted trees. "And don't you dare go near them."

She caught a glance of his slumped shoulders out of a corner of her eye.

"Can I play with him outside?"

"Yes, but don't go far."

Having any little kid around her grafting operation would make her uneasy, but Danny unsettled her even more. Once he left, she and Miguel quickly got back into the rhythm that worked so well for them the two days before. When it came time to tool up for the next set of fifty cuttings, Belle told him she'd run to the cooler for the next batch while he set up the pots and rootstock.

She let the door of the barn swing shut and didn't see Danny. She hurried over to the cooler and got a stack of cuttings, pleased to see how much the pile had gone down. On the way back, she looked around for Danny and Mac, and not seeing them, called out. Mac came bounding from behind the barn. She was about to call out a second time when Danny appeared and leaned against the corner with his head hung down.

Damn it, she said to herself, I've gone and hurt his feelings. She went over and crouched down, then looked him in the eye. This was the first time in the six years of his existence she had looked directly at him, and the face her eyes now rested on took her to a time and place a long time ago, and for an instant she wanted to stay there.

She reached for his hand. "It's okay. You can come in."

He folded his arms. "No. You don't like me. I can tell."

Her mind raced. Oh, my God. What have I done? She clutched his shoulders and looked into his eyes. "I do like you. I like you very much." She stood up and took his hand. "Now come on in and I'll find a place for you to play, and let you give Mac a treat."

Miguel came out to get more root stock. Danny ran to him and tugged on his arm. "It's okay. She said she likes me a lot."

Just then, Raphael pulled in and picked Danny up.

The next morning, the alarm woke her from what she thought was a nightmare, until she felt her sore fingers and the throbbing pain told her it wasn't a dream. She quickly dressed and looked out into the darkness from the window. The light in the kitchen cast a pattern across the driveway with Missy's shadow moving in and out like a silhouette in the fog. The aroma of bacon frying on the grill wafted up the staircase as she hurried down.

Missy, still in her pajamas, looked up at her for a second, then continued pouring Pap a cup of coffee.

"Sit down. I made you breakfast."

Belle's eyes shot over to Pap's. His lips curled ever so slightly. This was the first time in Missy's entire twenty-seven years she had made breakfast, and it made Belle chuckle as she pulled out a chair. It had to be her letting go of all that beauty salon money for the cidery. Pap was right. Missy was definitely invested.

Belle scarfed down the breakfast and filled her thermos with coffee before giving Missy a quick hug.

"Belle," Pap said. "Raphael talked to Danny last night. You have nothing to worry about. He won't be coming to the barn again."

Belle thanked him, then Missy handed her the lunch she had made, and Belle took off for the barn with Mac. The cold bit her the moment she opened the door, and she ran through the compound, gripping her collar tight around her neck.

Once in the barn and out of the wind, she flipped on the lights and then the radio. The barn was cold enough that it would be safe to get three packs of cuttings from the cooler and bring in the same number of root bundles. Dreading going back out, she opened the door, and the wind almost tore it off its hinges.

It was an hour before she was finally able to settle down and get back to grafting. She listened as the news came on the radio. The announcer ran through a litany of all the mayhem that had been heaped on Charlotte the night before, and it made her wonder if there ever was or would ever be a morning with nothing bad to report. She couldn't hold back a cynical laugh. When that day comes, she said to herself, I'll give them a call and let them in on the mess my life's become.

She reached over and turned the dial, searching for a station that would keep her mind off Mary. The way the nursing home had stonewalled her with such cold professionalism when she phoned, she was starting to fear she might never find her.

Belle kept picturing her lying in some desolate room with no one caring for her. Those low-end nursing homes operated on such narrow margins, they paid as little as they could get away with and were notoriously understaffed.

And where was she going to get the money to move Mary back to where she was, or how was she going to get her moved in the first place? If Ben was the guardian of Jake's estate, he probably controlled where she was sent.

She wondered how long nursing homes kept their old files, then how long Ben would store everything in that hall closet. She took several long, deep breaths until the urge to hyperventilate subsided. She had no choice. After she finished the grafting, she was going to break into the closet and get all the answers. A stoic resolve rolled over her as she realized she had crossed a threshold. But she wasn't going to do it alone. Lucy had to go with her in case something did go wrong. At least she could claim some reason for them being there.

She began to settle down when a picture of Matt in the Rusty Bucket with the prim and proper Miss Tennis Champion loomed in her thoughts. She pictured mug shots of her and Lucy in the *Times News* next to one of Marsha holding another trophy. If the two of them did get arrested, the least she had to worry about was her reputation. It was already ruined. By now, every one of Raphael's cousins had heard the story about her night with Ken. How could Matt face them if they ever got back together? Everyone had known about his brawls with Rita, but up until she met her new husband, she hadn't dared do anything that even smacked of adultery.

By the time Miguel showed up, Belle was cold enough to seriously consider calling it a day, but the enthusiastic way he dove into his work energized her. It was odd the way they didn't fall into the usual give and take between two people sharing a long, monotonous task. She chalked it up to his either being wary of her after the computer fiasco, or following orders from Matt.

She found herself talking to him, even though she understood she was mostly talking to herself. Yet somehow she sensed this young man was going to work with her the rest of her life, and she felt an urge to lure him into the world of heirloom Southern apples just like Jake had her. She decided she had to make him love them and care about them before she'd ever trust him to graft.

"You know," she said. "Most of the trees we got the cuttings from started out as chance seedlings."

Miguel took a finished graft from the tub and went about potting it without responding.

"In fact, a lot of the apples you find in the grocery store come from the seeds of apples that just fell to the ground a long time ago. Or maybe they were dumped behind a cider press, or tossed from a settler's apron after she finished preparing apples for a pie." She waved her knife at Miguel, now standing in front of her. "Take the Golden Delicious. It was a chance seedling discovered on a family farm in West Virginia. That farmer made himself a bunch of money when he sold its propagation rights to Stark Brothers Nursery in the early 1900s."

She finished dabbing a graft with tar and put it in the tub. "A couple of years ago, an Italian lab decoded its complete genome and found it had fifty-seven thousand genes, the highest number of any plant studied to that date."

Belle got an inkling he was listening by the way he hesitated for a moment before picking up another graft. "The McIntosh was another chance seedling. John McIntosh discovered the tree in a field way back at the beginning of the 1800s in Ontario, Canada."

She was surprised when Miguel spoke. "My dad said you're looking for an apple and gonna call it the Carolina Belle. Is that true?"

"Uh-huh. If all these great apples can grow up from a seed by chance, why can't I find one?" Belle's instinct was to tell him more. Wasn't that the way Jake had done it with her? "The Rome was another chance seedling discovered around the same time on a farm in Rome Township, Ohio. The Black Twig was found on a farm in Arkansas, and the Jonathan in New Woodstock, New York."

Miguel stood listening and holding a graft. She looked up at him, and he quickly turned and got busy putting it in a pot.

"My favorite story is the one about Maria Ann Smith. I like her 'cause she was spunky like my great-grandma, Myrtle. She and her husband propagated fruit trees on their farm in Australia. She found a seedling that had sprung up near a creek where she had dumped the cores of French crab apples from Tasmania. She let it grow, and it bore apples that were good for cooking and eating, so she took it upon herself to propagate it and sell its apples from a stall at a street market in nearby Sydney. She had some age on her by then, so they called it the Granny Smith; and today it's among the world's top selling apples."

"If you don't find yours till you get real old," said Miguel. "They'll probably have to change its name to the Granny Belle."

Belle smiled. This was the first time the boy had joked with her.

"Have you heard about the one that was discovered just down the road from us?" she asked, but didn't wait for an answer. "Will Dalton found it in his orchard in 1935 and for a time it got pretty popular all over the South, especially for making pies and thick, creamy applesauce. He called it the King Luscious."

"How about calling yours the Queen Belle?"

"No. It'll be born and bred in the Carolinas and that's what it's gonna be called." She smiled. "You wanna know how it got its name?"

He nodded with interest.

"Char Wojcik, the Yankee gal who lives in that big house down the road with her husband, thought it up. I was around fourteen when she came over to get some apples from Pap and I told her about my search for the perfect apple. When she asked me what I would call it, I just figured to give it a letter and a number. But she wouldn't have it. 'It's got to have your name on it,' she said. Belle snapped her finger. "...and just like that, she named it the Carolina Belle."

They both lapsed into silence until Miguel said, "We're running low on potting soil. We'll have enough for today and tomorrow, but we might not make it through the weekend."

With this being Thursday, Belle realized that she had better tell Raphael right away so he could make arrangements to have some delivered the next day. She couldn't get him on his cell, and had no luck with Pap, either.

"Miguel, I've got to run over to the new orchard for a minute. Set everything up for two hundred pots." She grabbed her coat and ran out with Mac at her heels.

One good thing about the dip in the weather, she determined as she drove to the orchard, her fingers were so cold she hardly felt her two cuts. But she wasn't as bad off as the crew pulling the wires. It had to be murder out there.

She pulled off Ridge Road and stopped next to a cluster of

vehicles. She spotted Raphael halfway up the slope, and as she started the climb, swore she saw something move in Raphael's truck. She looked in and saw Danny curled up on the front seat like he was hiding. She opened the door.

"What are you doing here? Why aren't you with Pap?"

He sat up and looked down at his folded hands. "He had to go to the bank. He said it was important."

"Aren't you cold?"

"A little."

She noticed the red light on the dash. It must have stalled. She pointed to her truck. Mac was sitting up staring back at them. "Go get in it. It's warm."

She saw him off and continued up the slope. Raphael noticed her and met her part way down.

"What's the boy doing in the truck?"

"I left it on with the heater running."

She wanted to ask him why he didn't bring him to the barn, but knew the answer. She told Raphael about the potting soil, and before turning to go, asked him how late they'd be working.

"Till dark. We need to start spraying and thinning, and this has to be out of the way."

"You can't leave that kid in the truck. I'm taking him with me. I'll bring both of the boys over to your place when I'm done."

Pap phoned as she walked back.

"Pap, this kid was sleeping in a cold truck."

"I got a call from the bank and needed to get one of my notes extended by the close of business today. I tried to take him to Raphael's house again, but he wouldn't go. I had no choice. Didn't Raphael keep the truck idling?"

"It stalled. I'm taking him to the barn."

"I'm sorry, honey."

"It's okay."

"I'll be playing cards tonight. See you in the morning."

Miguel had everything set up when she returned. She gave Danny some treats for Mac, then pointed to the corner and told Mac to get in his bed and stay. Their routine began to flow again, however, Belle kept catching herself looking over at Danny who was sitting with Mac. He caught her looking at him a couple times and smiled; but try as she might, she couldn't find it in her heart to smile back.

By six, Belle had finished grafting all the cidery cuttings, and together, they finished potting all the grafts in the tub. While Miguel straightened up his work area, she put away the left-over white stakes and got out the pink ones. Tomorrow she would start on her heritage orchard trees.

Before heading out to Raphael's, she dropped the truck's tailgate for Mac to get in, but he wouldn't budge from Danny's side, and they ended up driving with the four of them packed in the front seat.

She turned off Ridge Road and pulled onto the dirt lane that led to Raphael's place. They hadn't gone but a short way when Danny started kicking and screaming that he didn't want to go there. Miguel made matters worse by trying to calm him down. Belle stopped the truck and looked at Miguel.

"What's wrong? Why doesn't he want to go to your house?"

Miguel stared wide-eyed at her. Danny stopped kicking and folded his arms in a stubborn pout.

"I'm not going there. They said mean things about my mother."

Belle looked for an explanation from Miguel, who took a deep breath and exhaled through puffed cheeks.

"It's my little brother, Alfredo. He's not a bad kid. He's just jealous of Danny."

Belle started the truck again and drove to the house. This time, two wolfish looking dogs greeted her. Miguel opened his door and hollered at them in Spanish, and they both lay down on the dirt.

Belle slowly drummed her fist on the steering wheel, remembering Pap telling her "He's Matt's boy." She turned to Miguel.

"Tell your mother he can stay at our house tonight. Missy can take him to school in the morning. What time does he have to be there?"

"Seven-thirty."

Miguel reached for the door and patted Danny's leg. "You be good. Your dad will be home in a couple days."

Miguel got out, and Belle turned the truck around and headed for the house. Every once in a while she stole a peek at Danny who sat with an arm around Mac. They could see Missy cooking in the kitchen when they pulled in. Belle got out and went to the door with Danny trailing behind.

"Aren't we getting to be the homemaker," Belle dryly sang out as she entered. She went up to Missy and whispered in her ear. "Don't ask me what's going on. I'm too tired. Can you just feed him?"

Missy nodded, confused.

Belle wolfed down a big plate of spaghetti while leaning against a wall and watching Missy get Danny's coat off. As she seated him at the table, Belle could see there was a definite change in Missy since she and Dave became partners in the cidery. Everything to do with the farm and all the characters in it were suddenly more important.

Belle put her empty dish in the sink and headed for the stairs. "I'm beat. I'm going up and taking a hot bath."

"Where's he gonna sleep?" asked Missy.

"With you."

"No way. My bed's too small."

"Okay. Put him in Pap's. He'll get in so late, he won't even notice him."

Belle stopped in the bathroom on the way to her room and started the bath in the ancient claw-foot tub. Half undressed by the time she hit her bedroom, she wanted to curl up in the iron bed the minute she spotted it, but resisted the temptation. Chilled to the bone, it would take half the night to warm up if she didn't soak in the hot tub first. She kicked off her boots, peeled off her socks and wriggled out of her jeans and long underwear.

The small bathroom was filled with steam. She slipped off her robe and squealed from the hot water as she eased herself in. She lay in an almost catatonic state with the back of her head resting on the rim, listening to Missy coax Danny into getting undressed and into one of her tee-shirts. Belle laughed to herself.

Missy had no idea who she was dealing with.

Missy pretended to cry and mournfully wailed, "please," making Belle laugh out loud. Missy'd been pulling that stunt on her since she was three.

"Okay. I'll get undressed if you go out and close the door," Danny meekly replied.

Damn, Belle said to herself. It works for her every time.

She wrapped her toes around the hot water knob and turned it on for the third time, but the cold water streaming on her ankle made her turn it off and get out. Her bedroom was cold, and she raced to get into her pajamas and under the covers.

By the sound of it, Missy seemed to be making headway with Danny. She evidently coaxed him into Pap's bedroom. It had grown quiet again and Belle imagined Missy was now putting him to bed. A few minutes later, she heard her in the hall saying good night.

Missy popped her head in Belle's room. "I put his clothes in the washer. When you get up tomorrow, be sure to put them in the dryer."

"Remember, he's got to be in school by seven-thirty," said Belle.

"Got it. Wake me up before you leave."

As exhausted as she was, Belle couldn't fall asleep. After tossing for a half hour, she carefully slipped out of bed, so as to trap the warmth under the covers, and tiptoed down the stairs to the kitchen. As usual, Missy had left the light on for Pap. She expected to find Mac curled up on his bed in the corner breathing noisily like he always did in the winter, but he wasn't there.

She poured herself a couple fingers of Pap's whiskey and gulped it down. Suspecting Mac was up in Pap's room with Danny, she climbed the stairs and peeked in. Mac lifted his head and looked up at her. She whispered for him to come, then pointed towards the stairs. He rose and obediently lumbered down the hall hanging his head before descending to the kitchen.

She slipped under the still warm blankets, and lay there waiting for the drink to kick in. A long, low creaking noise made her eyes shoot towards the door. She reached over and turned on the light. Danny stood sleepy-eyed with Missy's tee-shirt drooping below his knees and hanging off one shoulder. He looked like a waif.

"What do you want?" she asked.

"I want to come in bed with you."

It was so late and he was so stubborn and she had so much work facing her in the morning, she lifted a corner of the covers and said, "All right. Get in."

She turned off the light and lay there looking up at the dim reflection of the light from the kitchen window on the ceiling. The furnace kicked in and the curtains above the floor vent barely fluttered. Matt's little seedling was close enough for her to hear him breathe, close enough to feel the heat from his body, close enough to hear him softly cry.

"Now, what's wrong?"

"My mother doesn't love me anymore."

His words hung in the darkness waiting for her to chase them away. She tried, but her throat had tightened and nothing came out.

She finally said, "Oh, I'm sure she does, honey."

"It's my fault. I'm not a baby anymore." He wiped his nose with his arm and sniffled. "She's real happy she's going to get a new one."

Belle listened to his plainspoken words and felt for him with the whole of her heart.

"I'm sure she'll love you just as much."

"She's not going to come back 'cause I've been bad."

"I don't think you could be bad."

"I was. She caught me speaking Spanish on the phone to my grandpa and gave me a whoopin'."

Belle threw off her covers, bound from the bed and ran into the bathroom. She grabbed a towel and buried her face so deeply, she barely heard her muffled sobs. She sank to her knees and cried in the towel until her shoulders ached. "Oh, Matt, what has she done to your little boy?"

The door opened and the sight of the little silhouette against the dark broke her heart. She wrapped her arms around him and pulled him close to her, crying softly as she rocked him in her arms.

She reached for a box of tissue and blew her nose and wiped her eyes. She rose and tenderly gathered him up and carried him to her bed. She put an arm around him and hugged him tight to the arc of her body and fell asleep.

CHAPTER FIFTEEN

B ELLE WOKE BEFORE the alarm went off and carefully slipped her arm from under Danny's before reaching for the shutoff button. She tenderly brushed aside the thick, silky blond curls sticking to his sweaty forehead. She lifted the blankets and slipped out of bed, careful not to step on Mac, asleep on the floor. Mac awoke and ran out ahead of her as she snatched up some clothes and tiptoed from the room. She quickly dressed in the bathroom, then went into Missy's room and gently nudged her awake.

Once downstairs, she put on coffee before tossing Danny's clothes in the dryer. She eyed Mac, and deciding he needed a scolding, crouched down and looked into his big brown eyes. "What were you doing upstairs in the bedroom? And why didn't you get in the back of the truck last night like I told you?"

It had been years since she had shaken a finger at him, and he looked away in shame. She spontaneously hugged him. "I know why. You like him, too, don't you, boy?" She ruffled his short butterscotch fur and got up, then stuffed some of Missy's snack packs in a bag, filled her thermos and left with him for the barn.

This morning the news from Charlotte wasn't all that bad. No one got murdered, just some guy threatening to kill himself unless his wife came back. Somehow this dramatic close-up of someone's messy life affected her more than a murder would have. Dozens of scenarios streamed through her head—he had been unfaithful, or she had been unfaithful and was running off with a lover. She dismissed gambling too much, or drinking too much, and determined the whole mess stemmed from love lost or betrayed. After all, wasn't she an expert on the subject?

She came back from checking the cuttings still left in the cooler, estimating that by Saturday night she'd be finished, when Pap dropped in with a coffee and donut he'd picked up for her in town. He mentioned they were almost done setting up the trellises for the spindles, and Carlos and Raphael would finish off whatever was left. He eyed the trees and patted her on the back.

"You've done a yeoman's job, girl."

It wasn't like Pap to wile away his time chatting, and she wondered how long it was going to take him to get around to the real reason for his visit. He fell silent, waiting for her to give him her attention.

She stopped grafting and looked him square in the eye. "What?"

"I talked to Danny this morning. He said he slept with you last night."

"That's right. And I want him to come over here after school."

"Belle, don't get too close to that boy unless you intend to mend things with Matt. It could only hurt the both of you."

Belle was stunned. This was the very first time Pap had talked to her from his heart. She swallowed hard. "Don't worry, Pap. I've been hurt so much, I won't even feel it."

He shook his head.

"And by the way," she added, "the same goes for that kid."

He left, and all her fears crept out from their hiding places. She picked up her phone and punched in Lucy's number. She answered on the second ring.

"Lucy, I've thought about it, and I want to get Jake's and your mother's files out of that storeroom before they get destroyed."

"Good."

"There's a hitch, though."

"What?"

"You've gotta come with me."

"Oh, no. I can't."

"Do you want your mother's file, or don't you?"

After what Miguel had told her, she pictured Lucy nervously biting her nails.

"Okay. When?"

"Sunday night. I'll meet you in the parking lot at midnight."

"No," she said emphatically. "Park on the street in front of the apartment building. I'll be in my car."

Belle hung up, hoping the file would tell her where they sent Mary. If so, it'd save her the trip to Winston-Salem. After the call, she found herself checking the time every five minutes, anxious for Miguel and Danny to show up and take her mind off Mary.

The sun was now in the west and light streamed through the panes in the door, slowly dissipating the dampness in the barn. Miguel and Danny would be getting off the bus soon. She dropped the root she was about to start grafting back in the water and jumped up.

"Come on, Mac, let's go get 'em," she said as she grabbed her hat and coat.

The air outside was crisp, yet the sun felt warm on her face. The only thing that moved in the deserted compound was a barn cat slinking around the bins. The scraggly old tom had a bent tail and had been around for years, but still wouldn't let anyone near him, yet he ran up to Raphael every time he saw him.

She reached the edge of the compound and stood looking down the hill. The winding lane unfurled in front of her and ended at the place where the bus would stop—the exact same spot where her mother and father were killed. It used to bother her when she got off the bus in grade school, but that was so long ago she hardly thought about it anymore.

From this vantage, she could see the main road lying across the mountain like a casually discarded ribbon. Across the road, monochromatic rows of apple trees ran up a rolling slope; and beyond, Sugar Loaf Mountain rose as if to wrap its arms around the valley and shield it from the harsh northern winds.

The bus emerged from behind a row of Leyland cypress and rolled to a stop. Without taking her eyes from it, she told Mac "Go get 'em, boy!" and laughed with glee as he charged down the hill. The door to the bus opened and Miguel stepped out. She caught herself holding her breath until she saw Danny jump down and race towards Mac. That's how it had always been. A faithful dog greeting the school bus and getting his just rewards from a faithful friend.

She hugged herself and watched the boys trudge up the hill. The lonely little words Danny spoke the night before had echoed in her head all day. She wondered how many times Matt had lain next to his precious little boy and had the same painful words kill his heart.

Danny's curls fluttered in the wind as he looked up at her and waved. Mindful of Pap's warning, she was careful not to show how happy she was to see him, even as he ran up to her and threw his arms around her legs and pressed his cheek against her. She knelt down on one knee, pulled off her hat and fit it snugly on his head.

"I'm supposed to take him to the office," said Miguel.

She looked up at him. "It's okay. I told Pap he could stay with us today."

Belle took Danny's hand in hers and the three walked towards the barn. Belle didn't see Pap and Raphael come out of the packing house lugging more wire for the crew. She didn't see Raphael notice them and nudge Pap. She didn't see Pap's eyes turn into slits, or Raphael make the sign of the cross.

"I see the dirt got here," said Miguel as he walked into the barn with the confidence of someone who knew they were an important member of a team.

Belle passed snack bars around, sank down on her stool and poured the last of the coffee from the thermos. She took a sip and her eyes landed on Miguel, who was efficiently, yet skillfully potting a graft like someone who had caught the apple orchard fever. She smiled to herself and plunged back into her work.

Danny leaned against the table watching her.

"You want to go out and play with Mac?" she said, smiling.

"No. I want to stay here with you."

Belle caught sight of a big grin on Miguel's face and smiled back even though she was blinking back tears. Danny was so hungry for motherly love, he was hanging on for dear life to the little bit of affection she had shown him. The hurt she'd felt for him last night exploded in her heart like a ripe abscess. Tears ran down her cheeks as she realized the boy had been damaged just like her, and by the same perpetrator. Only, he hadn't learned to hide it yet.

She'd only seen Rita a dozen times since Matt married her, but if she walked in the barn at that moment, she'd tear her to pieces. One at a time, she swiped her arms across her face, then became aware of Miguel watching her.

"Are you okay?" he asked.

Belle wiped her nose with the towel on her lap and forced a smile for both boys.

Danny rolled his eyes up at Miguel. "She cries a lot."

The ho-hum tone of his remark broke the tension and made Belle and Miguel laugh out loud. Danny watched her for a while longer, then pulled some toy trucks out of his backpack and played on the floor. Belle and Miguel worked straight through until Raphael came to get Danny.

"I'll bring him out in a minute," Belle told him.

Once Raphael left, Danny looked at her pleadingly. "Do I have to go?"

She told Miguel to get Danny's things together, then pulled the boy over to her. "You don't want to hurt your grandma's and grandpa's feelings, do you? You've got to be a big boy and learn to live with things you can't change. Go on with your grandpa. It'll make your daddy happy."

They hugged, and Miguel handed him his backpack and walked him to the door.

"See ya around, buddy," Belle called out after him.

He turned to face her, waved goodbye and left, leaving Belle remembering the cruel taunts she and Missy had to learn to live with. The thought of her parents' accident reminded her of the suitcase in the loft.

"Miguel, before we get started again, I need you to help me." She got a flashlight from her truck, then started up the ladder to the loft. "Come with me," she told Miguel.

"Wow," said Miguel as he stepped onto the loft. "You sure got a lot of junk up here."

She flashed the light into the mass of items Pap didn't have the heart to throw away and spotted the suitcase sticking out from behind an old icebox in the back. She showed Miguel what she was after, and as they lifted off rusted bikes, iron beds, and even an old wooden hay rake with all its wood tines intact, Belle couldn't help thinking that there was more to learn about her grandfather from the things he couldn't part with than anything he'd ever told her about himself.

Miguel lifted off an antique wood scythe. "Boy, would this be great for Halloween. I could go as the Grim Reaper." He looked over at Belle. "Do you think I can borrow it?"

"Are you kidding? Nobody's supposed to know I'm going through this stuff. Especially not your father."

They finally got deep enough into the pile for Miguel to reach in and grab the suitcase, then they started putting everything back. Together they lifted an old metal bed spring and leaned it against the barn wall.

"I don't want you to tell anyone about this," she said.

"I know. I'd be in trouble. Matt said I wasn't supposed to do anything for you without getting his permission first. Just help with your grafting."

She wrestled a barrel against the pile. "Then why did you?"

Miguel didn't answer.

"Well, why?"

"The way you were so mean to Danny, I told my mother I didn't want to work for you anymore." He hefted a rolled up rug onto the pile with a grunt. "Then she explained about Matt marrying Rita instead of you, and I kinda felt bad about you getting dumped and all... and I really liked the work, so I came back."

"At least you're honest," she said as she slapped the dust off her clothes.

"Oh, don't get me wrong. I like you now. You were really nice to Danny yesterday." He laughed. "I don't know how he did it, but he sure won you over."

Belle tied a rope around the suitcase handle and lowered it to the barn floor. She'd bring it in the house after Pap went to sleep and hide it under her bed until Missy and she could look at it together.

Sunday morning, Belle was in the barn alone. She and Miguel had finished everything but a few bundles on Saturday, and knowing Miguel would have to go to mass, Belle had told him not to come in on Sunday. She pulled out the last root and clipped off the top. She was concentrating on her cut when Mac's bark made her look up to see Matt walk in with Danny.

She smiled at the boy, then looked at Matt. "I thought you weren't coming back till tonight."

"My mother called, so we told them to mail our certificates and took off yesterday after the last class. All we missed was a dinner."

He strolled around, sizing up the mass of potted trees, then came over to her workbench. Belle could tell he wanted to thank her for taking care of Danny, but found it hard in front of the boy. Danny put a small red crystal apple on the table and pushed it toward her.

"Here. My dad got it for me, but I seen the stuff on your desk and want you to have it."

She took it up and saw it was etched with the name of the cidery school. Knowing it had to be a freebie, she glanced at Matt and gave him a slight wry smile, then looked back at Danny.

"It's beautiful. Thank you."

He rushed to her side and hugged her. She didn't want Matt to think she was insinuating herself into his little family, but she couldn't resist hugging him back. She held him tight until she became aware of him being pulled away. It made her feel a little foolish, and she bit her lip and looked off to one side.

"Come on, son. We got to go to Grandpa's. They're holding up lunch for us."

Belle looked up and into Matt's eyes and saw a tinge of something that, if she wasn't so sure he despised her for spending that night with Ken, she might have mistaken for love.

Danny reached the door and waved. "See ya around, buddy," he said, making her laugh.

Once the sound of the truck faded, she reached over and turned on the radio and scanned the stations. She snapped it off again. All she could find was church music, hardly appropriate for someone who was planning to commit a crime that night.

Belle worked in the barn until Mac got restless for dinner and they went home. She ate with Pap and told him she was tired and wanted to go to bed early. However, she set her alarm for eleven before lying down. It was dark when she woke. A glance at the clock told her it was ten-thirty. Plenty of time to stop at McDonald's and get a coffee before she had to meet Lucy. She turned off the alarm button, grabbed her jacket and tip-toed down the hall, careful not to wake anyone.

A hand clasped her shoulder and she caught her breath.

"Where on earth are you going this time of night?" whispered Missy.

Belle took hold of Missy's arm, swiftly pulled her back in her room and closed the door.

"I'm gonna meet Lucy."

"What for?"

"She thinks Jake's file might be in a closet in her hallway."

"And you two crazies are going to break into it."

"I've got to do this, Missy."

"What if you get caught?"

"Jake's brother owns the building, and we'll get him to drop the charges."

"How in the hell are you gonna do that?"

"I don't know, but we will."

Moonlight streamed in from the window and Belle caught a glimmer of tears pooling in Missy's eyes. "Don't worry, Sis. I would never do anything like this unless I was dead sure Mary needs me."

Belle gave her a quick hug and left. She crossed the kitchen and Mac suddenly appeared next to her. She patted his head and told him to stay. If anything did go wrong, no telling what might happen to him. She slowly opened the door so it wouldn't creak and ran to her truck. Before starting the engine, she made sure the bag she'd packed with a crowbar and flashlight was still on the front seat floor, then turned the key and took off.

Matt was so tired he thought the ringing phone was part of a dream until Danny shook him awake. He got up, reached for it and said a groggy hello.

"Matt, it's me. Missy. I'm sorry to call you in the middle of the night like this, but I'm worried about Belle."

He sat up and ran a hand through his hair. "What's wrong?"

"She's crazy. Totally, utterly crazy. Her and Lucy are going to break into a storeroom in Jake's brother's office building."

"Don't let her go. I'll be right there."

"She took off five minutes ago."

"The same place I took the computer?"

"Yeah. Matt, she's obsessed with a note she found in Jake's desk."

"What did it say?"

"That someone was in a nursing home and when they died, any money left was to go to her. She's convinced it's Mary."

"Jake's wife? The one who's supposed to be dead?"

"Uh-huh. That's not all. Someone at the nursing home told Lucy that she'd been transferred to some cheapo place after Jake died. Belle's going to Winston-Salem tomorrow to talk to them. You know what she's like, Matt; she'll stop at nothing until she finds her."

"Have you told Pap or Dave?"

"Are you kidding? Pap would try to stop her. Can't you just picture that?" She caught her breath. "As for Dave, if I were him and found out what a crazy family I was marrying into, I'd back out of the wedding."

That would never happen, thought Matt, as he pictured the big-hearted guy who did nothing but talk about Missy all the way back from Virginia.

"Okay, I'll do what I can."

He got dressed and swooped Danny up in a blanket. Five minutes later, the dogs at his parents' house woke everyone up. The door opened and Matt handed Danny to Raphael and told him he'd pick him up in the morning, then without an explanation, he rushed back to his truck and left.

BELLE FOUND A PARKING SPACE in front of the apartment building and was sipping coffee as a car pulled up behind her. She put the cup on the dashboard and looked in the rearview mirror. Recognizing Lucy getting out, she grabbed the duffle bag and followed her to the building's door. A car cruised on Main Street two blocks up, but it quickly disappeared behind the row of buildings.

Lucy handed Belle a pair of latex gloves with a command for her to put them on, then Lucy's hands shook so much, it took her forever to get the key in the lock. She opened the door and they slipped in. A streetlamp lit the entry, and they didn't need a flashlight until they reached the dark narrow hall to Lucy's office.

Belle stopped and shot a beam down one wall. "Which one is it?"

"Right there. The second one."

"You stay here and keep an eye on the front door till I get it open."

Jimmying the door was nothing compared to stretching fence wire. She popped it open and felt around for a light switch. A minute later, the two of them were inside with the door closed. Three old dark olive-green file cabinets stood up against one wall. Lucy raced to the first one with a swiftness that startled Belle, then she flicked through the files with the speed of someone who'd won a three minute shopping spree.

"Look for Bishop and Gregg on the tabs," ordered Lucy as Belle opened a drawer of the last file cabinet. The musty scent emanating from it attested to the age of the files within.

Belle reached the third drawer, and noticed Lucy was almost finished with the second cabinet. Lucy suddenly stopped her frantic search and pulled out a file.

"Oh, my God. I actually have it," she said as she browsed through a hefty file. "It's got all the transcripts." She waved a tape at Belle. "It's even got the actual interviews."

Belle was happy for Lucy, but her concern was growing. She stepped aside so Lucy could complete her search. Lucy finished without finding Jake's file and told Belle she was going to go through the drawers again. Ben might have changed the file name and put it under something like Jake, or brother, or even Belle, Annabelle or McKenzie. But when Lucy started back for the third time, Belle tapped her on the shoulder.

"Stop. It's not here."

Lucy shook her head in bewilderment. "I can't understand it. It's got to be somewhere."

"Not if he took it home or destroyed it."

Lucy thought for a moment. "I wonder if he could've put it in that box they brought over from Jake's house. The one that has everything from his desk."

"Do you know where it is?"

"Yeah. It's in the closet in his office. When I went in to get the computer, 'Jake's desk' was scrawled on it in big black letters."

"Was the closet locked?"

"Yeah, but Ellie got the key from her drawer." She saw Belle's hopeful expression. "Don't get any ideas. I can't get us in there."

"Can't we jimmy the door open?" Belle stopped and sighed. "What am I thinking? That's too crazy."

"Mr. Gregg is so paranoid that if we did anything like that he'd get someone in here and launch a full investigation."

Lucy gathered up her mother's file while Belle collected her tools.

"Don't worry, Belle." The next time Ellie has me take care of the office, I'll get in there and get half the stuff out of the carton so if he opens it he won't suspect anything. And when you're finished looking it over, I'll put it back and get the rest."

"Okay. Let's get out of here," said Belle.

"Not until you pry open two more doors."

Belle rolled her eyes. "I hate doing this."

"Hurry. His insurance will cover it."

Belle quickly popped open two more doors with Lucy muttering, "I hope it raises his rates."

Belle followed Lucy as she turned the corner to the main hall, when she suddenly pushed Belle back into the dark corridor. The echoing of the entrance door opening and slamming shut was accompanied by a rustling.

Lucy pressed against the wall grasping her files. Belle backed up, hitting her tool bag against the wall with a clink. She shut her eyes tight and held her breath, listening intensely. Alarmed by Lucy's deep breathing that threatened to turn into hysteria, Belle whispered in her ear, "Calm down and don't make a sound."

The erratic footsteps coming from the entry were strange, not like someone walking with a purpose. There had to be two people, one wearing high heels. As they neared, Lucy squeezed Belle's arm. The intruders had stopped and were now right around the corner, a few feet away. Belle could make out that they were kissing.

"Oh, Joey, you're such a bad boy. What would your wifey, mifey say if she knew where your hands were right now?"

Hearing that, Belle's fear level went down a notch. If those two did discover them, they were hardly going to tell anyone. The clicking of the high heels started up again. Belle stared out at the hall and felt Lucy's hand grip hers so hard it hurt as the two intruders staggered past. Even at ten feet, the odor of alcohol was pervasive. Moments later, the sound of a door opening and then closing down the hall made Belle rest her head against the wall and take a deep breath.

Not hearing anything more, the two rushed to the door and carefully opened it. They peered nervously out onto the street. Finding nothing moving, they hurried to their vehicles.

Belle drove down Route 64 with her heart beating against her chest. The highway was practically deserted, except for a cop car coming from the other direction. She was convinced those two in the office hadn't detected them, and was sure if they had, they wouldn't have called the police; yet after the cop car passed, she kept glancing at the rearview mirror to make sure it wasn't turning around.

She swung onto Sugar Loaf Road and was beginning to calm down when the beams from a vehicle behind her bounced off her rearview mirror, almost blinding her. She sped up. When that didn't work, she gave it more gas, and so did the driver behind her. The headlights were high enough to be on a van or a truck.

Don't panic, she told herself. Academy Road was two turns ahead. She slowed down, and just as she was about to pass the road, she swerved onto it, sending her truck careening out of control with the tires squealing and her fighting to straighten it out. When she finally got it on an even keel, a suffocating wave ebbed over her and she fought off fainting.

She hadn't gone very far when a set of headlights appeared behind her in the distance. The vehicle was going slow enough that she easily gained on it. Nearing the compound, she glanced in the mirror. All black. The vehicle had to be behind the curve. She switched off her headlights, then made the turn onto the compound's road.

She drove up the hill lit only by the moon and pulled up next to the barn. Cocooned in the safety of the farm buildings, she put her elbows on the steering wheel and grasped her head with her hands, waiting for her heartbeat to slow. After a few moments, she started for the house on foot. Just as she turned the corner of the garage, she heard a car door slam. She fought an impulse to scream. It had to be from the vehicle chasing her. She stopped breathing and stared in the direction the sound had come from. A man came from around the corner.

She'd know that walk anywhere. It was Matt. He came up to her, grabbed her arm and thumped her against the wall.

"For Christ's sake, are you crazy?"

She yanked her arm from his grip. "Thanks for scaring the hell out of me."

"I didn't mean to."

"Did Missy call you?"

"Yes."

"How much did she tell you?"

"Enough. She thinks you're going off the deep end." Regretting his flash of anger, he stepped back. "At least you didn't risk some little kid this time. I hope you got what you're looking for."

"Jake's file wasn't there."

He put his fists on his hips, turned and walked a few steps. He stopped to face her, and threw up his hands in a gesture of exasperation. "Just what are you planning on doing in Winston-Salem tomorrow?"

"It's none of your business."

He walked back. "That's where you're wrong, sweetheart. We're partners now, and the business isn't going to look too promising with you in jail."

She was leaning against the garage with her arms folded. There was enough light from the security lamp on a lone pole in the middle of the compound for him to see she was trying to appear self-assured, but the troubled look he saw in her eyes told him otherwise. Missy was right. She was going off the deep end.

His tone softened. "Okay. You win. But I'm going with you."

"No. The last thing I need right now is listening to you trying to talk me out of it."

He braced a hand against the garage and ran a knuckle slowly down her cheek. "I worry about you, girl."

She turned away and for a moment they both stayed silent. She looked back at him. "Matt, I gotta do this. Mary needs me. She was the nearest I've ever come to having a mother." They fell quiet again. "Matt, please don't say anything to Pap. If he tries to stop me, it'll never be the same between us."

Matt knew it to be true. "All right, but I want you to promise me if you need my help you'll come and ask for it."

"Thanks. I will."

She gently pushed him away and started for the house. "Don't worry, I'm not planning on breaking into anything else."

"Why is it I'm having a hard time believing you?"

As his truck drove out of the lot, she was overcome with determination. She wasn't going to break into anything; Lucy was.

CHAPTER SIXTEEN

S PRING CAME EARLIER TO WINSTON-SALEM than it did to the mountains, and the flowering Bradford pear trees lining the nursing home's long drive billowed with snowy-white blooms. Belle parked in the lushly landscaped lot dotted with drifts of colorful azaleas, and went in.

Her eyes roamed the spacious reception area that looked more like someone's parlor than what she imagined a nursing home to be like. The walls were papered with the same subtly toned grasscloth that covered most of the walls in Mary's and Jake's house. Two nicely dressed elderly ladies sat on a settee chatting. Belle pictured Mary next to them, looking as nice.

Belle went to the glassed-in counter, and it seemed strange that with the generally friendly atmosphere the entry was designed to project, the staff was barricaded behind a glass wall. She was quickly noticed and someone stepped to the window and slid it open.

"Hello," Belle told the woman. "I would like to talk to someone in the admitting department."

"Can you tell me what it's about?"

"It's personal."

The woman handed her a clipboard. "Please fill out this visitor's form."

Belle filled in the usual lines, except she put "admitting director" after the question asking which resident she was visiting.

She signed it and handed the clipboard back.

The woman looked it over, and Belle noticed her eyebrow arch slightly.

"Someone will be with you shortly."

Belle sat down in an easy chair across from the two smiling women and smiled back.

"Are you here to visit someone?" one of them asked with the same sweet Southern lilt as Mary's.

Belle bit her lip and thought for a moment. "Yes," she said. "Mary Gregg."

The women asked each other if they knew a Mary Gregg. Neither of them did.

"She was here, but left about two months ago," said Belle with an emphasis meant to sound encouraging.

They both shook their heads with sympathetic smiles. Belle figured their memories were slipping. Damn, why didn't she bring a picture? She went over to the settee and sat down next to them. "She's around eighty. Slender and tall. I'm sure you must have—"

The two women looked up at someone standing next to her, and she turned to see an authoritative figure in a feminine yet "in charge" suit peering down at her.

"Please come with me, Ms. McKenzie."

Belle recognized the same impersonal voice that she had argued with on the phone. She started to rise, and the two women grabbed her hand as if they didn't want to see her leave. They wished her well and told her to be sure to come back and visit soon. Belle followed the woman to a door marked "Director," and they went in.

"Please be seated," the woman said as she went over and sat down at a huge desk, bare except for a leather bound calendar lying open and what looked to Belle like her visitor's form. The woman waited for Belle to be seated, then opened a drawer and took out a business card. She pushed it toward Belle and tapped her nails on the desk as Belle glanced it over.

"Ms. McKenzie, I see from my notes you called me a few weeks ago. I told you then we don't discuss our clients with unauthorized persons. I also told you if you get Mr. Gregg to release the information you're requesting, we'll be happy to give it to you. That remains the case at this time. However, as of yet, we haven't heard from him in this regard, so I'm going to have to ask you to leave."

Belle winced at the perfunctory statement. "Wait a minute. You haven't let me say a word."

The woman picked up her phone and spoke into it with the same offhand efficiency she would use to ask someone to bring in a coffee. "Send in security, please."

Belle stood up, put both hands on the desk and leaned into her. "I'm not asking for any information, *just where you took Mary Gregg!*"

The door opened and Belle looked over her shoulder. Two men in business suits walked in and took their place on either side of her. She turned back to the woman. "Please, you have to help me."

"I'm asking you to leave now, or I'll have no choice but to call the police."

Belle glanced at the security guards, standing solidly with their hands crossed in front of them. She pounded the desk with her fist. "Please, I beg you!"

The director picked up her phone and Matt's warning streamed through Belle's head: "The cidery isn't going to do that well with you in jail."

Belle gave the guards a hint of a sneer and left with the woman's words trailing behind her. "Walk her to her vehicle and make sure she leaves the premises."

From the corner of her eye, Belle saw the two sweet ladies watch with mouths agape as she was escorted out the door. She went to her truck, and through her rearview mirror, saw the two men standing at the door watching as she swept down the driveway.

She went a few blocks, drove into a fast-food joint and pulled up behind a car waiting in line to order. The head of a little girl bobbing in the back seat drew her attention. She had to be chatting with the elderly couple in front. It reminded Belle of the game she played with Mary and Jake as they drove through the countryside looking for old apple trees. The first one to spot one got to choose where they would eat. Mary was the one with eagle eyes and always managed a clever hint so Belle could make the discovery.

By the time she parked with her order, she'd decided to go back to the nursing home. There had to be an entrance for deliveries. If she could only get in, she'd find someone who could remember Mary, maybe even someone who wrote to her and knew her address.

She drove slowly past the entrance until she spotted a small sign with "Deliveries" printed on it and an arrow pointing to an asphalt driveway. She pulled in and circled behind the building to a parking lot, then nestled her truck between two SUVs and waited for someone to either come out of one the building's two doors, or go in. A man who was having a smoke on the loading dock paid no attention to her, and after a while, put his cigarette out and went inside.

One of the doors opened, and a woman in a uniform who looked old enough to be a resident of the home herself shuffled out like she'd had a long day. She stopped at a two-toned Ford Fairlane with a sagging rear that had to be over fifty years old.

Belle rummaged through her wallet and found two twenties. She stuffed them in her pocket and got out, then hurried to the car as it started to back out of its space, sputtering a dark cloud of exhaust. The woman, noticing her preparing to knock on the window, stopped and buzzed it down.

She flashed a toothy smile. "What, darlin'?" she asked.

"Can I talk to you for one minute?"

"Honeychild, you can talk to me for two."

Two people came out of the building, and Belle nervously looked to make sure they weren't security.

"Child. You in a bit of trouble?"

"No. But can I get in the front seat so we can talk?"

"Sho' nuff. Come on in, darlin'."

Belle raced around and slid onto the front seat. She locked onto the woman's dark brown eyes that seemed to melt on her, and for the first time in a long time felt comforted.

"I'm looking for... my grandma. Her name is Mary Gregg. She left this place two months ago, and they won't tell me where she went."

The woman's tenderly melodic Southern drawl purred, "Honey, nobody ever leaves this place unless they're *dead*. It's like the Garden of Eden in there."

"Do you know Mary Gregg?" Belle persisted.

The woman pressed a finger on her mouth and thought for a moment. "No. I can't say as I do... and I know just about everybody. They call me Granny Jo, 'cause I always take the time to make some kind of fuss over everyone, 'specially all the bad cases."

"Think back. She left two months ago."

"Child, the only person who's left this place to go somewheres else other than the undertaker was a man. Poor soul." She raised a hand to her mouth as if a thought struck her. "I'm gettin' so I don't remember hardly anythin'. *His* last name was Gregg." She looked at Belle. "Randy Gregg."

Belle was thunderstruck.

"Do you know who I'm talking about, darlin'? He's got to be an uncle of yours."

Belle couldn't clear her head enough to respond.

"Me, oh my, that poor man. How his mama loved him." She laid her spread fingers across her chest. "Why, of course! His mama's name was Mary."

Belle felt the hair on the back of her neck rise.

"Yessiree. She was ailing bad and couldn't come every Wednesday like his daddy done. That man spent the whole day readin' to him mostly. Then the mama took sick and didn't come no more."

"Why was Randy here?"

The woman barely rocked back and forth as she spoke. "Oh, Lordy. That poor fella was a quadriplegic. He'd been in another place ever since some awful accident, but he took a turn for the worse and got brought here with pneumonia... seven, maybe eight years ago. His mama died no more than a couple months after that. It broke my heart when they told him. The whole time he was here there was a *Do Not Disturb* sign on his door, and he never said nothin' to nobody but his parents, but he done cried when he heard his mama had passed. I know 'cause I was in the hall and I heard him.

"I go through every room pickin' up twice a day, *Do Not Disturb* sign or no *Do Not Disturb* sign. If no one was around, I always talked to him, gentle like, while I straightened up. Everybody was told that he didn't want anyone lookin' at him, but the way I saw it, every God's child needs someone to show 'em some love."

"Why in all this time didn't he get any better?"

"Land sakes, girl, you don't understand. He had to be hand fed and everything done for him. All his burns were healed but he was scarred bad. It's a real shame. His father told me he wasn't but a young man when it happened... and good lookin', too."

Belle put her elbow on the armrest and dropped her head in her hand.

"When he was took away from here, I figured his father died and there wasn't money for him to stay."

Belle looked over at her. "Where'd they take him?"

"Honey, I wasn't here that day. But I tell ya, if it wasn't a right nice place like this here, he won't last long. Not without his daddy visitin' regular to make sure of things. Like him gettin' taken out of bed and put in his wheelchair... and that breathin' tube of his gettin' cleaned proper. Things like that."

Belle reached in her pocket for the money, put it in the woman's hand and clasped it shut. "Please find out where they took him." She grabbed up a paper napkin and pen from a tray hanging from the dashboard and quickly jotted down her name and phone number. She looked over at the woman and asked for hers and wrote it down before tearing the napkin in two. Belle handed her the piece with her information.

"Please, it's important."

The woman took Belle's hand and put in the money. "Honeychild, Granny Jo don't need your money. I's gonna help you like I do everybody else. I do know all the people in there, and somebody's gonna tell me where they sent that poor man." She studied the napkin Belle had given her. "Annabelle. That's a right nice name."

"Everyone calls me Belle." She glanced at the name she'd written on the napkin. "Billie Jo." She looked up at her. "That's a nice name, too."

The woman squeezed Belle's hand. "Just call me Granny Jo."

Belle reached over, put her arms around the frail bony frame and couldn't let go.

The woman patted her on the back. "Bless you, child. Don't fear. I'm gonna help ya." She pulled away and looked Belle in the eyes. "The government might be regulatin' this place, but it ain't regulatin' me and it ain't gonna do no harm bringin' kin together." She patted Belle's hand. "I do hope when we find him, you'll make sure he's taken care of like his daddy done. Granny Jo's goin' to church now and she's gonna pray for you and Randy like I do for everyone in that place."

Belle was halfway home and just getting used to the stunning revelation when her phone rang. It was Lucy, asking her where she was.

"I'm on my way back from visiting the nursing home."

"What'd you find out?"

"That it's not Mary who was in there, and that Ben Gregg is a bigger bastard than I thought."

"Who was it?"

"Jake's son, Randy."

"I thought he was dead."

"So did everyone else. He was badly burned in that accident with my Mom and Dad and I guess he didn't want anyone to visit him or see him." Belle didn't tell Lucy that Mary probably didn't want anyone to see what had happened to her beautiful boy, either. She wouldn't understand.

They were silent for a moment. "Have you had a chance to look over your mom's file?"

"Uh-huh."

"What'd you find out?"

"That Ben Gregg is a bigger bastard than *I* thought. I couldn't believe it when I read through the transcripts of his interviews with men working on the same shift as my dad, only the man who talked to my mother wasn't included. We couldn't find his interview on the tapes either, just whole sections that had been erased."

"How does he get away with all this?" asked Belle.

"Come on. He figured my mother was just a country bumpkin and wouldn't know what was going on. I'd like to talk to an attorney and get some legal advice, but Mr. Gregg's chummy with every lawyer in town. All one of them has to do is give him a call and I'm out of a job. Belle, I'm living from paycheck to paycheck, my mom really needs her medicine, and I haven't got a shred of proof."

"You haven't gotten into his office closet yet, have you?"

"Not yet."

"Call me when you do. I'm praying there's something in there we can use to nail him."

CHAPTER SEVENTEEN

THE FIRST DAY IN APRIL can usually be counted on as the start of what apple growers call a two-week death watch, and this spring would be no exception. Fear of a killing frost when all the trees are in bloom is as endemic to an orchardist as the fear of a hurricane is to a coastal fisherman out to sea. There's no way to stop it; they brace themselves and pray to God they'll make it through.

Belle's truck came over the ridge and the rolling hills blanketed with white fluff spooled out in front of her. She pulled off the road and trekked into the orchard. The bountiful clusters of beautiful blooms against the bluest of blue skies brought tears to her eyes. If she lived to be a hundred, she'd never see anything more beautiful.

She weaved deep into the orchard, carefully twisting and bending so as not to disturb the branches. She stopped to study a heavy cluster. The blossoms were just as they should be, five white petals kissed with a delicate hue of the deep, rich pink of the buds.

An army of bees industriously flitted from blossom to blossom, picking up pollen from male anthers and leaving them on female pistils. At that very moment in that very orchard, millions of male sex cells from the pollen were making their way down the blossoms' pistils to the female sex cells in the base of the flowers. The energy of the orgy going on all about her took hold of Belle and awakened the yearning she was feeling more and more these days, a yearning for Matt.

It was as natural as the eternal dance swirling around her. Just like the trees, she was in bloom and felt the urge to fulfill the destiny of nature. Was that why she made all the effort getting dressed that morning, she wondered?

Her breathing quickened, and a streak of fear coursed through her. She knew by the way Matt had been looking at her, he was feeling the same; and she also knew she didn't have much time before he finally gave up on her and found someone else.

After checking the orchard, Belle drove to the packing house and pulled up next to Pap's pickup. She saw Matt's service truck parked nearby, and was pretty sure one of the reasons Pap had brought him into the office was to get the both of them used to each other, like stock you put in adjoining pens to get them ready to mate. He was willing to try anything.

A tractor pulling a sprayer headed for the upper trellis orchard. Beyond, gray clouds swirling over Mount Pisgah worried her. She ran up the steps to the office and saw Pap and Matt peering at their computer screens.

"How does it look?" Belle asked.

"A 50/50 chance it's gonna dip as low as the mid-twenties tonight," answered Pap.

He swung his chair around to face her. "What do you want to do about your seedlings?"

"I don't trust that heater to keep the barn warm. Not with our cidery and Jake's orchard riding on it."

Matt turned to them. "I called Tractor Supply. They're holding a kerosene forced-air heater for us."

"Will it do the job?" asked Belle.

"It can handle three thousand square feet. That should more than do it."

"I'll go pick it up," she said.

Matt got up and went to the door. "I better make sure there's plenty of gasoline in the wind machines."

He left, and Pap leaned back in his chair and rocked. "Belle, most of those forced-air deals need electricity to kick on. Go 'round and get some of our old kerosene heaters as a back-up in case we get a power outage. There's four or five in the storeroom downstairs along with a box of supplies. They haven't been used for a while, so let me know when you get 'em in the barn and I'll have Raphael check 'em out." He picked up his phone and got Matt.

"Belle's gonna round up some heaters for the barn, just in case. Fill up plenty of those five-gallon jugs with kerosene and take them over there when you get a chance."

Pap hung up, and before Belle was out of the office, he was on the phone giving orders to someone else. She found the heaters and piled them in her truck, then dropped them off at the barn before heading to town. On the way back, Matt called and said he'd meet her at the barn to set the heater up.

Matt and a couple of their farm hands were hauling in the kerosene as she pulled up. The minute she came to a stop, they swarmed to the truck and lugged the heater into the barn.

Matt got the workers busy filling it, then shot a glance over to Belle. "That baby will run for ten hours on ten gallons." He put his fists on his hips and studied the ocean of potted grafts. He looked over at Belle. "You've really accomplished something."

Belle, wearing a new pair of stretch jeans Missy had gotten for her months ago and a leather jacket her sister had lent her, leaned back against her workbench. Matt's eyes lingered on her for a long moment, then he plugged in the heater and showed her how to fire it up. He let it run for a while, then sent the men to take gasoline to two of their six wind machines, leaving him and Belle alone in the barn and creating an awkward few moments.

"How did everything go in Winston-Salem?" he asked.

"I didn't get arrested."

"Don't worry. I checked to make sure you got back."

"I found out Mary was never in a nursing home."

"What else?"

"Nothing." Belle didn't think it would be a good idea to let him in on her plans—not if she wanted to dispel his impression of her as a loose cannon.

"So that's it?"

"Pretty much." Her eyes roamed his gently sculpted face and locked onto his eyes. She was filled with a sudden surge of yearning so close to desperation that she quickly turned away so he couldn't read it in her eyes.

"Good. Now you need to go to that school for a week and get your mind on the cidery."

"How can I? We're going to be running wide open from now until November."

"I don't know how to tell you this, darlin', but this place will survive a week without the Carolina Belle."

Belle wondered briefly when was the last time he called her that, and a tide of hope washed over her. She was convinced he wanted her, but just couldn't stop fighting it.

Matt brought the instruction package he'd gotten off the heater and handed it to her. The way he kept track of every warranty, it was something he would never part with, and it told her he wanted an excuse to be near her. He stood close enough for her to pick up his manly scent.

"You look nice," he said.

He held his gaze for what seemed forever. Finally, she looked away and then back at him, and said what needed saying. "He's a nice kid."

He took hold of her arms and tenderly rubbed them with his thumbs. "It was really kind of you to let him sleep with you, Belle. Rita never—"

The door opened and their eyes shot over to Raphael who looked as surprised.

"Perdón. Jeremiah wants me to check out the old kerosene heaters. I come back later."

"That's okay, Dad. I was just going." Matt's hands slipped from Belle's arms and she stepped away.

"Yeah," said Belle. "Let's get it done now in case anything needs fixing."

"Dad, let me know if you want me to scare up any more," Matt said as he walked out the door.

That night, Missy made dinner and served it on the dining room table they only used for Thanksgiving and Christmas. It was obvious she was putting on a show for Dave's sake. It had to have taken her an hour just to clear off all the junk. Belle wondered what she'd done with the jigsaw puzzle Pap had been working on for the past two months.

Missy plunked a steaming bowl of mashed potatoes on the table and sat down next to Belle. When she asked Pap to say grace, Belle's eyes locked onto his. It was another thing they only did on those two holidays.

Belle tried hard to engage in the conversation, but only came up with a few "uh-huhs" and an occasional nod. The weather occupied her thoughts. It didn't help that Pap kept checking his phone every five minutes, making announcements as if he were the weatherman on the nightly news.

Pap's and Belle's preoccupation made way for Dave to chatter endlessly about the cidery school. He kept mentioning "Matt this" and "Matt that," leading Belle to believe the two of them were getting on better than anyone had hoped.

"Matt wants you to go to that cidery school as soon as you can," Dave said to Belle.

She thought about it for a moment, then nudged Missy. "I'll go if you go."

Missy bounced up and hugged her. "Whoopee! I thought no one was ever gonna ask!"

That got Pap's attention. "Well I'll be hogtied. You are a McGrady after all!"

Missy beamed as everyone enjoyed a good laugh. After dinner, Dave and Missy went out and Pap went into the living room and started a fire, while Belle stacked everything in the dishwasher and fed Mac.

Belle finished up and found Pap asleep in his big oak rocker in front of the fire. She slipped into hers, pulled up her legs and wrapped her arms around them. Mac had wolfed down his meal and was already snoring at Pap's feet. The paper slipped from Pap's lap and fell on the floor, waking him.

Shadows cast by the flames danced around the darkened room as Belle listened to the lulling rhythm of Pap's rocking. It stopped, and only the crackling of the burning ash logs sounded, while Belle waited for Pap's deep craggy voice to break the silence.

"What were you and Matt talking about in the barn today?"

Belle rubbed her toes through a thick sock. "Don't you and Raphael have enough to worry about with this freeze coming?"

"Whether the freeze is coming or the freeze is not coming, life will go on, or at least I hope it will." The familiar creaking of his chair started up again. "Helen told Raphael that Matt was still sweet on you."

"I know he is, Grandpa, but I'm worried he's never going to let himself come after me."

"Girl, you haven't figured it out yet, have you? That boy's stuck on you."

"Sure, Pap. Especially since I'm such a shining example of feminine virtue."

"Let's not talk about that, honey. Like I told you before, as far as I'm concerned, it's water over the dam." He leaned forward and craned his neck to look directly at her. "Just don't let it happen again."

"I never did it to begin with, Pap. I would know if I had."

He rocked in silence as if he had put what she said in his pipe and was smoking it. The rocking stopped and Belle got up and tugged on his arm.

"Come on, Pap. Let's go to bed."

As they trudged up the stairs, Belle asked him if he checked the temperature alarm. He mumbled he'd set it at thirty-six degrees and disappeared into his room.

Less than four hours later, the alarm blared and woke the both of them. Minutes later, Raphael phoned Pap, and seconds later, Matt called Belle. She wriggled into a pair of long johns and quickly dressed. She almost bumped into Pap in the hall and ran down the stairs behind him. The light was on in the kitchen, and the sight of Dave with tousled hair and stocking feet putting on his shoes surprised them. Belle and Pap pulled on their boots as he talked.

"I thought I'd stick around and help Belle in the barn."

"Welcome aboard, Son," said Pap as he put on his coat and

started for the door.

Missy suddenly appeared, looking half asleep. "Don't you guys want any breakfast?"

"You can fill up all the thermoses with coffee and bring them over to the office in a couple hours if you want," said Pap on his way out the door.

Missy looked up at the clock. "Geez, it's only two."

Dave rode to the barn with Belle. She turned on the light, and he got his first look at all the grafted trees.

"Wow!"

"You, sir, are looking at our cidery," she said with a trace of pride as she went to check the new thermometer. She lifted it off its nail and her forehead wrinkled.

"What does it say?" asked Dave.

"*Shit!* Thirty-two degrees."

The overhead heater had been running since they walked in.

"The temperature outside's gotta be plunging. This unit can't handle it."

"Don't worry. I'll get this big baby going," he said as he went over to the new heater and began turning it on.

"You've used these before?"

"Sure. All the time when we're working on new construction. The only problem is you need electricity to get 'em on."

"I set the thermostat for forty degrees," said Dave after he fired it up. "We should be okay in about ten minutes."

Belle put the new thermometer on the table where she could keep an eye on it. She pulled two chairs close enough to the heater to keep warm, and they both sat down and waited.

MEANWHILE, MATT WAS DRIVING up to the highest section of the compound's trellised orchard. He kept glancing at the truck's exterior temperature gauge. Forty-five degrees. Good. The sooner he cranked up the wind machine, the sooner it would grab the warm air in this inversion layer and pull it down to the lower end of the orchard.

His phone rang. It was Pap.

"Get that machine going as fast as you can. It's almost down to twenty-nine degrees here at the bottom, and frost is starting to lie on the petals."

Matt told him he was on his way, and sped down the lane that led to the wind machine positioned at the halfway point. Its lone thirty-five foot blade, fully extended, was as high as the top of the slope. He left his headlights on, jumped out and raced over to the engine. He turned the key they always left in the ignition, but it didn't kick on. Anxious, he kept trying until the battery ground down.

Matt began to fret; he better find out what was wrong fast or they could lose all their Honeycrisps. He jumped on the back of the truck, threw open the service bed and dragged out the jumper cables. He stuffed a bunch of tools he figured he was going to need into his pockets, along with a can of starter fluid, and jumped off.

He raced to get the cables set up, quickly sprayed the plugs with starter fluid and turned the key again. Still no luck! He wrenched off the distributor cap and shone his flashlight on the points. Damn! They're stuck! He pulled a file out of his pocket and hurriedly cleaned them. He wiped the sweat pouring from his forehead with the back of his hand, then held his breath and turned the key.

He was never happier to hear an engine kick on. He tossed his tools in the truck and checked to make sure the blade was turning. In moments, the wind blew his hair straight back. He took off for the next orchard with his heart thumping against his chest.

Halfway down the hill, the compound suddenly went dark. He got Pap on the phone. "I got it going, but the power's out. Where are you?"

"On my way to Sugarloaf."

"I'll stop by and see if Belle needs help."

"No! You got to get over to Ridge Road. She's got Dave in there with her. Those two are just gonna have to handle it."

Matt tried to get his dad on the phone. He was working on the wind machine at the far end of the orchard. When he didn't pick up, Matt assumed he was scrambling to get it started and couldn't take the time to answer the phone. He got to the bottom of the hill and wanted to check on the two in the barn, but Pap was right. They were on their own. He headed for the Rome orchard, recalling all the times Dave had helped him with repairs, and he felt more confident. Then he thought about Belle. There was no way in hell she was going to let anything happen to Jake's heirlooms.

"DAMN! WHERE IN THE HELL ARE those old heaters?" Belle bemoaned as she crawled along the floor. "Dave, I'm gonna try to find the door and get my flashlight out of the truck. Whatever you do, don't knock over any of the grafts."

"Shit!"

"What happened?" asked Belle, alarmed.

"I burned my hand on this damn big heater."

"Don't try to restart it until I get back!"

Belle staggered ahead with her arms outstretched. She hit a wall, then felt along until she found the door. "I got it!" She hollered. She went outside to see the truck's silhouette barely visible against the moonless sky.

She quickly retrieved her flashlight and first-aid kit from the glove compartment and rushed back in.

"Flash that light over here," Dave hollered.

She noticed a kerchief wrapped around the palm of his left hand as she stood over him with a beam on the big heater. After several tries, he looked up at her and shook his head.

"This baby's not gonna start."

Belle flashed the light around the barn, and the minute it landed on the old heaters the two of them raced over.

Dave flew into getting them started, ignoring his hand, while Belle found the new thermometer. Not a half hour had passed and the temperature had already dipped to thirty, frightening her.

Dave finished adjusting the last kerosene heater, went to a cluster of seedlings and flashed the light on the one Belle was now holding. She studied it for a moment, then sank onto one knee, put it down and picked up another. Dave slowly ran the light along the cutting.

"So far, everything looks okay," she said, "but we won't know for sure for a couple days." She carefully put the seedling down with her mind racing. There was still time before her agreement with Ken would expire. If she lost the seedlings, she could go for more cuttings, but it would be slim pickings. Fighting off an impulse to have a good cry, she stoically sat down in front of the bank of kerosene heaters instead. As she watched the seedlings' eerie shadows dance on the walls, Belle asked Dave what happened to the new heater.

"When the power went off, it was in idle. Its thermostat must've called for it to go on again, and somehow it wouldn't kick on. It could be a sort of safety switch or a malfunction. I'll look into it later."

Belle put some salve on Dave's hand, already starting to blister, and wrapped it in gauze, then phoned Pap.

"How's everything in the barn?" he asked.

"You saved the day by having me gather all these heaters. Once the power went out, we sure as hell needed them." She held her breath and waited for him to tell her how the orchards were doing.

"All the wind machines are up and running. Matt said he had a lot of frost on the Romes, but once he started the machine, it melted off. Hopefully, we've saved them. I'm heading to the office. There's nothing more we can do except wait it out and hope like hell we didn't lose too many."

CHAPTER EIGHTEEN

T HIS WAS THE FIRST MOMENT of peace Belle had in weeks, and she was savoring it. The cidery seedlings had made it through the freeze undamaged, and more than ninety percent of their apples escaped the frost. Thankfully, it looked like their highest dollar crop, the Honeycrisps, came through totally unscathed.

She studied a pair of high heel booties on her screen and shook her head. She'd break her neck in those things. That wasn't what she was looking for anyway. She hit the button for riding boots and a tall leather one with a side zipper and double straps at the ankle caught her eye.

She filled in her size and put them in her shopping cart. Next, she found a page for the kind of leggings Missy always wore and got two pair. A row of sweaters ran along the side of the page, and remembering how blatantly the leggings showed off the shape of Missy's rear, she picked out two that would reach below her hips, and sent in her order. She laughed to herself, thinking she'd just spent more on clothes in the last five minutes than she had altogether for the past five years.

No one else was in the office, so she listened to Granny Jo's message again, picturing the kind woman's warm brown eyes and smiling brown face. Of all places, Randy Gregg had been taken to a nursing home in Asheville.

She picked up the crystal apple Danny had given her and

rolled it around in her palm as she thought about the man. If it weren't for him, her mother and father might still be alive. Yet, the thought of someone sitting immobile and watching the world go by for most of his life, tugged at her. Remembering Granny Jo's warning, she decided she owed it to Jake and Mary to go check the place out the first chance she had. But right now, she was going to go over to Jake's place and take one final look around.

The scene was deserted as she pulled in. It was easy to spot the cidery trees she'd taken all the cuttings from. There were hardly any blooms on them. Beyond, dark clouds promised rain later on. Mac ran off, and she wandered leisurely up and down the rows for a while. She meandered over to the orchard workbench, thinking how she would love to have it, when someone pulled in. Recognizing the truck and the bulldozer it was pulling, she strolled over.

"We're not headed for trouble again, are we?" said the driver as he jumped down.

"No, Don. Everything's fine."

"Well that's a good sign," he said wryly. "Can't see ya beatin' up on me now that we're on a first name basis."

Mac appeared from out of the orchard, giving the man a start.

"Don't worry about him," she said with a slight smile.

She folded her arms and casually strode alongside the driver as he went about unfastening all the chains latched to the bulldozer.

"Are you gonna start right now?"

"No. Just unloading. He doesn't want me to do anything till Monday. I haven't got anything lined up till then, so I thought I'd get set up now."

"Did he say anything to you about that workbench?"

"Nah. Just told me to wait. He's gonna be here on Friday. Why don't you ask him yourself?"

Somehow hanging around the place didn't feel the same with the din from the bulldozer, so she hollered for Mac and left.

The Ford Taurus pulled in at an angle to the trucks in front of the packing house, and the woman inside slammed on the brakes. She got out and looked the building over, her gaze lingering on the office windows. Casually dressed in jeans and a sweater, she paused and tapped her pursed lips with a fingernail, then promptly entered the cavernous building.

Hearing a conversation in Spanish drift from an office in the corner, she marched over and shoved the door open. Raphael sat at his desk talking with a couple of farmhands. She glared at him with her upper lip quivering.

The room fell silent.

"Where is he!"

Raphael didn't answer.

"Don't you understand English? I said *w h e r e i s h e!*"

A shuffling foot sounded from above. She sneered at Raphael, then shared it with everyone else in the room and left. She found the steps to the upstairs office and raced up. She fluffed up her hair and went in.

Pap saw her first. "Rita."

Matt's eyes shot across the room.

"What are you doing here?"

"I've come to talk business."

"Rita, please leave. I'll come and see you tonight."

"You're through giving me orders. I'll see you when and where I want to see you." She looked around, pulled Belle's chair out and sat down.

Matt rose and dragged the chair next to his desk over to her.

"Get out of that chair."

Rita studied the apple souvenirs on the desk behind her for a moment. *"Excuse me!* Am I sitting in the chair that belongs to the love of your life?" She ignored the one he'd brought over and glared at him, her face hard.

"Are you back for good?" Matt asked.

"This shitty town? My husband's got a new job and we're just here to pack up our things."

He squinted at her. "Where are you going?"

"Arizona."

"You know you can't take the boy out of state."

"Isn't that too bad. I guess he's your problem now." She patted her belly. "I got something else in the oven." Her face twisted with contempt. "Someone that's never going to speak a word of *Spanish!*"

Matt gave Pap a quick glance. He was leaning way back in his chair with his arms folded, taking it all in.

Matt was still squinting at her. "Then what do you want?"

"You're not going to get away with it. I got an earful from my hair stylist. I've got half of your share in that cidery coming to me."

"You got everything you're gonna get. We're done."

"That's what you think. You kept it from me so I wouldn't get my share. It's conspiracy, and a collision, too."

Pap laughed out loud and they both looked at him. His smile faded. "It's collusion, Rita. Not collision. Now quit wasting our time." He let out a humph. "I've got to hand it to you, your shamelessness knows no bounds." He stood up and towered over her. The sudden fury on his face stunned Matt. "But you're not getting any more out of this boy... or from any of my kin than you've already helped yourself to. Now get your sorry ass out of here; and if you ever step foot on this property again, I'll sic my lawyers on you like a pack of mad dogs."

She grabbed her bag and didn't take her eyes off him as she backed out of the office and hurried down the steps. Pap went to the window and watched her drive off.

"Can she do anything?" Matt asked.

"Nah! Haven't you read your divorce agreement?"

"George went over all the major points with me."

Pap sat down in his chair and slowly rolled a pencil between his thumb and finger. He raised an eyebrow in a rakish arch and chuckled. "What do you think we talk about in those poker games every Thursday night?"

He didn't expect an answer.

"Your divorce agreement was the *número uno* topic of conversation for four weeks in a row. George may be a crummy poker player, but he's one hell of a lawyer. He covered your ass for every possible contingency the whole band of us could come up with. You can thank your lucky stars Rita was the one itching for the divorce. It made negotiating on your behalf a hell of a lot easier for old George."

He stopped rolling the pencil and tossed it on the desk. "That divorce agreement was your 'Get out of jail free card.' Just pray she doesn't come back. After she's out of state for six months, she relinquishes all rights to that boy of yours... and then Danny gets his 'Get out of jail free card.'"

The door opened and a worried Raphael timidly poked his head in.

"Come on in and sit down, Raph," said Pap.

"Todo está bien," added Matt.

Pap clasped his hands behind his head, leaned way back in his chair and rocked. "Son, we got bigger fish to fry than that two -bit hustler."

"Pap," said Matt. "I don't like to come down too hard on Rita. I feel sorry for her. I tried... hell, we both tried, but she knew I didn't love her. That had to be hard for her to take. I think that's why she treated Danny the way she did. It was the only way she had to get back at me. I'm glad she's finally found someone who really cares for her."

"You're right about feeling that way, son," said Pap. "But right now, we need to talk."

Pap and Raphael exchanged glances, with Raphael nodding in agreement. Matt sat down, now squinting at Pap.

Pap cleared his throat. He looked at Raphael as if to confirm a prior understanding, and then at Matt. "Both your mother and Raphael are okay with you marrying Belle."

"Si, si," said Raphael, nodding again.

"What she did over at Jake's place," added Pap, "was wrong... it was the drink." He stared hard at Matt. "That isn't too far from what you did, now is it?" Matt looked away. "That girl's been carrying the torch for you for years. Ask yourself, why hasn't she gone and found someone like Missy did? God knows she's pretty enough. And now that Rita's out of the picture, she's comin' 'round. All she needs right now is for you to forgive her."

Matt rose from his chair, knowing Pap was waiting for a response. He went to the window and looked out. "There's nothing to forgive. This whole damn mess is my fault. I did this to her."

"That's settled," said Pap, relieved the delicate subject was dispensed with.

Matt turned and looked at him. "It's not that easy, Pap. There's something between us she can't get over. More than just Rita. Every time I think she's falling for me, she gets a look in her eye and can't let herself go. We won't have any kind of marriage unless she forgives me. There's been enough regret between the two of us."

The room became still, broken only by the rhythmic squeaking of Pap's back and forth rocking. A sad expression was now clouding his face as he slowly twiddled his thumbs. "It happened in her freshman year, didn't it, son?"

"Yeah."

"Did she give it away... or what?"

"She never had it."

"I knew it was something like that," said Pap. "The way she felt about Danny wasn't right. She hasn't got a mean bone in her body." He rocked a while longer. "Matt, I think she's over it now. Look how she's taken a shine to that boy. I never thought I'd see the day." He scratched the back of his neck. "And have you noticed how she's been getting all gussied up? It sure ain't for that motley crew we got downstairs."

A slight outline of Matt's dimples appeared.

The creak of Pap's chair was the only thing that sounded for a while until Matt spoke.

"I'm already giving it another chance, Pap; but if it doesn't work this time, it'll be best for the both of us to move on to someone else."

Pap swung his chair around to face Matt, now perched on the edge of the window sill. "I'm telling you to go for it, son. Believe me, once she's got your baby suckling on her breast, she's gonna forgive you for everything."

Matt thought about that for a moment, then got up and said

he needed to bring another wire puller to Carlos. As he drove his truck out of the compound, he couldn't get Pap's words out of his mind. He suddenly picked up his phone and punched Belle's number.

"What do you want, Matt?"

"Where are you?"

"Picking up some office supplies."

"Are you coming back to the office?"

"I'm gonna spend a couple days at the house organizing my new desk and updating my apple records. Why?"

"Well, I... ah... want to ask you if you'll go out with me Friday night."

There was a long pause and then a teasing lilt to her answer.

"It all depends on where you're gonna take me."

He cracked a smile. The last time he'd heard that impishly taunting voice was when he'd asked her to his junior prom. "How about the Rusty Bucket? They usually have a good band Friday nights."

"Just how usual is usually?"

"Usual enough for me to give them an endorsement."

"When do you want to pick me up?"

He wanted to say "in five minutes," but blurted out six o'clock instead.

"Much, much too early. If I'm gonna make my premier appearance at this valley's version of Austin City Limits, I'm gonna do it when it's packed." She told him to pick her up at eight on Friday and hung up, chuckling.

He dropped off the wire puller, and on his way back to the compound, was drawn to the barn—something that was becoming a habit. Was it because the place and everything in it brought him closer to Belle than if she were standing next to him? He went in, and the dust specks dancing in the sunlight streaming in from a skylight gave the massive space a cathedral-like aura.

The sight of the three thousand tiny seedlings filled him with such high hopes he thought his chest would burst. As he studied the army of pots, a feeling of respect for Belle surged through him. It took the kind of drive she had displayed for as far back as he could remember to pull off such a feat.

He strolled over to her workbench, picked up her pink plastic radio and pictured the two of them practicing their dance steps to the tinny sounding tunes pouring out of it. He put it down next to her old metal lunchbox lying open with her grafting equipment inside.

An avalanche of regret rolled over him. How could he have hurt her the way he had? He couldn't remember one minute of that fateful night, just the sickening shock of waking up the next morning in bed with Rita. That one senseless act had damaged Belle and made the past seven years of his life hell, to say nothing of the harm it had done Rita and little Danny.

The image of Belle in a wrinkled dress and mussed hair stepping barefoot from her truck inched its way into his head, and a niggling thought entered his mind. Did she do it just to pay him back? If that was her way of punishing him, he accepted that he deserved it.

He remembered Danny—the symbol of all she'd lost—laying in his arms and contentedly murmuring "she said she likes me a lot." No. He had to chase away these suspicions. Belle didn't have the heart to do anything that vindictive; she was just blindly driven to get Jake's orchard.

Suddenly, her rosy-cheeked face encircled with a fluffy wool cap glistening with early morning dew loomed in his thoughts. He had been angry enough to want to shake some sense into her for sending Miguel to get the computer, yet as she stood at Jake's workbench in the pre-dawn chill wearing those ridiculous fingerless gloves and that fervent expression of hers—aggravating and appealing at the same time—all he had wanted was to make love to her so much his heart hurt.

He picked up her grafting knife from the table, put it in her lunchbox and gently latched it closed, then he emptied the two buckets with root bits floating on their surfaces and stacked them in the corner. He smiled to himself, recalling her playful tone after he had asked her out. There was no question; she'd been waiting for him to call. A bolt of uncontrollable desire shot through him, and he was suddenly like a marathon runner who just managed to summon the strength and fortitude for a last ditch effort to pass the leader and win the prize he'd dreamt of capturing his entire life. He gave the mass of seedlings one fleeting look and left, remembering Pap's urgings for him to "go for it."

FRIDAY AFTERNOON, BELLE stopped by the office to pull some files from her computer, but mostly to see if the clothes she ordered had arrived. One of the crew poked his head in the door, waving a box.

"Is this what you're lookin' for? It just came."

She thanked him, grabbed a letter opener and quickly pried the box open. She pulled out a pair of leggings and a sweater and hurriedly put them on in the bathroom where she could catch a glimpse of herself in the mirror. She ran her fingers through her hair and shook it, pleased at the way it bounced. Now at her desk, she picked up a boot and wriggled in her foot. She zipped it up and twisted it in the air in front of her. Perfect for the Rusty Bucket.

Her cell phone rang and she recognized the caller. Ken Larsen. She was about to ignore it, when she remembered the workbench.

"Hello," she said in the civilest tone she could muster.

"I'm back in town. Can you come over? I want to review everything with you before we start bulldozing."

"I'll be right there."

She ran down the stairs, and as she was leaving the building, Carlos walked in with the rest of their crew. She felt their eyes on her back and sang out, "It doesn't hurt to dress up once in awhile, guys," and bustled to her truck.

SHE WASN'T GONE TWO MINUTES before Matt pulled in and caught a glimpse of what looked like Belle's truck headed for the east exit. All day he'd been thinking about their date that night, his emotions see-sawing from sheer elation to a desperation he hadn't known since the day he had to tell her he was married. They weren't kids anymore, and that morning he knew he wasn't aiming just for a date as he changed his sheets and made arrangements for Danny to stay with his parents for the night.

He had prayed for this moment, yet a fear gripped him—tonight, if he couldn't tear down the barrier she'd put between them, he'd probably lose her forever. Did this evening mean as much to her, he wondered.

He ran up to the office to get the paychecks from his desk and noticed the open package on her desk. He went over and fingered a sweater and smiled. She'd evidently come to the office to pick up some clothes she had ordered to wear that night. He whistled happily as he went downstairs and strolled into Raphael's office, crowded with everyone looking for their pay.

"Was Belle just here?" he casually threw out as he handed out the checks.

The grins all around puzzled him, then a comment about Belle from one of the new hands drew his glare.

He handed Carlos his check and gave him a questioning look.

"She was dressed real nice, like she was going to meet someone," he whispered.

"Where's Dad?"

"On his way."

"When he gets here, have him tell that new guy, over there in the plaid shirt, we won't need him anymore."

Finished, Matt meandered outside. He stared stonily out at the threatening sky as the wind whipped through his hair, replaying the remark the man had made about Belle looking like she was headed next door for another night of fun. A sickening feeling rushed through him as he remembered how she got all dressed up the last time she went over there.

His stomach churning, he pulled out his phone and started to punch Belle's number, then put it back.

One of the workers emerged from the office mumbling angrily to himself.

"What's the problem?" asked Matt.

"My wife and kids are waiting for me to take them shopping, and Carlos wants me to go get the sprayer I left in the orchard."

"Go to your family. I'll get it," said Matt. "Where is it?"

"In the spindle orchard. On the last row, next to the old Gregg place."

BELLE PULLED INTO JAKE'S place, looked around and saw an electrician's truck parked next to a gently used Volvo. Ken, who was walking the man to his vehicle, threw her a wave as she slid from her truck. With all the gossip floating around the valley about Ken and her, Belle wished the electrician hadn't seen her drive in.

He got in his truck and pulled out, but not before giving her a keen look. Ken walked over to Belle, and after taking a moment to size her up, smiled approval.

"I see you got the cuttings."

"Yes. Thanks."

"Are you all set, then? We're planning on pushing everything over on Monday."

"What are you gonna do about that workbench over there?"

"You want it?"

She nodded.

"Then it's yours. You just got to get it out of here by Monday."

"That's gonna be tough. The whole crew has been looking forward to the weekend."

"Okay. I'll have them drag it over to the far side of the parking lot. Get it when you can." He hesitated for a moment. "You want that shed, too?"

Belle immediately pictured both of the items in her heritage orchard. "Actually, I do."

"I'll have them drag it over there, too."

He leaned against his Volvo with his arms folded and legs crossed at the ankles. "I heard two of your people were at the cidery school."

"You know the folks at the school?"

"Oh, yeah. They said one of your guys did the welding at the two new wineries in Asheville."

"That's Dave Collins. He's marrying my sister, and the two of them are coming in as partners in the cidery."

"Maybe I can use him. You guys won't be up and running for quite a while, and it'd be good experience for him."

"We'll talk it over and let you know."

She looked over at the orchard. This would be the last time she would see it as it always was.

"Take a look around if you want."

He walked with her as she strolled over to the Accordian apple tree, sitting in view of the windowed wall of the house. She grasped a piece of yellow caution tape streaming from it, and looked at him, puzzled.

"That's so they don't bulldoze it away. I'll have them put a fence around it before they start."

Belle swallowed hard and batted back tears.

"It was that little brass sign that got to me," he said, shaking his head. "I'm putting in a perennial garden over here, and it'll add some height."

She threw her arms around him and gave him a smack on the cheek, then pulled away. "Damn it," said Belle. "I want to hate you... and then you go and do something like this."

"When it bears apples, I expect you to make me a pie."

She laughed, and they stood facing each other for a long moment.

"I never laid a hand on you that night."

Belle looked away. "I didn't think you had." She gave off a bitter little laugh. "But I'm afraid you and I are the only ones who'll ever believe it."

"They'll get over it. I've never heard so much gossip in my whole life. That cleaning lady of mine dished out enough local dirt this morning to qualify as a mudslide."

A tear trickled down Belle's cheek. He wiped it off with his hand, put his arms around her and pulled her close. She buried her face in his sweater and put her arms around his waist. He kissed her tenderly on the forehead. "Don't let it get to you, kid. We've got to look like a couple of amateurs next to some of the things Mrs. Gordon swears is going on around here."

Belle pulled away. "That's not what's making me all teary eyed." She turned to the orchard and threw up a hand. "It's this place. It's gotten me all emotional." She took a deep breath and then exhaled. "I gotta go before I make a fool of myself."

He started to walk her to her truck and then stopped. "How's everything between you and Matt?"

Her face suddenly lit up and she coyly rolled her eyes. "He's taking me to the local dive tonight." She giggled. "In valley speak, that kinda means we're goin' together." Her tone was playfully suggestive as she added, "What more can I say?"

"So the two of you are getting it on, huh?"

Belle couldn't believe she was in such high spirits. "We'll know tonight." A soft, contented laugh trailed her words.

They reached her truck and he opened the door for her. Before she got in, she took one long last look at the house and the orchard and saw Mary and Jake and a motherless child walking hand in hand. She heard their laughter echo through the trees, and she knew that this place, and those two, and those times would always be with her, no matter what happened to the orchard.

She pulled out of the lot and wouldn't allow herself a look back. She wouldn't see Ken's shoulders slump as he kicked a stone and wistfully turned toward the house after she disappeared around the bend, nor would she see Matt stoically hitch the sprayer onto the back of his truck by the row of cypress that separated Pap's property from Jake's.

CHAPTER NINETEEN

P AP WAS COMING OUT of the house as Belle was going in. "I'll be late tonight, honey." Then he called out to her as he climbed into his truck, "Why don't you have dinner with Missy and Dave?"

Belle hadn't told him about her date with Matt. God only knew how much pressure Pap would put on him. Mac looked up from his bed in the kitchen as she walked in. She dished out his food and ran upstairs to the bathroom, still steamy from Pap's shower. She'd give the water a few minutes to reheat.

She got undressed and caught sight of herself for the second time that day; but this time the face in the mirror looked unfamiliar. It was joyous. She stopped and stared, and every trace of euphoria slowly slipped away like a toy sailboat from the grasp of a child on the edge of a pool—for she knew that in one split second, in one chance twist of fate, love can be snatched away.

Her glistening green eyes glazed over as she felt the empty spot in her heart for the parents she never knew. The killing moment on the college quad suddenly surfaced, and she whispered aloud, "Oh, God, please don't let anything go wrong this time."

She took a long soak in the tub, and getting out, saw her nakedness in the dressing mirror on the door. She ran her hand across her breast and wondered what Matt's touch would be like.

Someone coming upstairs startled her and she grabbed a

towel as Missy knocked on the door.

"Hey, Sis. What are you doin' tonight? Want to go out with me and Dave?"

Belle wrapped the towel around herself and opened the door to find Missy had gone into her room to change. She quickly got dressed in her new outfit and was dreamily pulling a brush through her hair when her sister walked in.

"Well, I'll be damned! Turn around, girl."

Belle slowly turned. "Waddaya think?"

"You look great!" Missy gave her a cagey look. "And who, may I ask, is the lucky guy?"

Belle responded with a coyly raised eyebrow.

"Matt?" asked Missy.

Belle gave her a smug smile.

"Oh, my God! Wait till Pap hears about this." She snapped her head around. "Where is he?"

"Out. He won't be back till late."

"When's Matt picking you up?"

"Eight."

Missy took the brush from her. "You haven't got much time. Let me do your hair." Missy started to brush and then stopped. "No. It looks beautiful just the way it is. Natural, like you."

A voice bellowed from downstairs. "Missy, hurry up. We're gonna be late!"

"I'm coming," yelled Missy. "Where are you two going?" she asked Belle.

"Where else? The Rusty Bucket."

"We're going to dinner with Dave's parents," Missy shouted over her shoulder as she skipped down the stairs, "but we'll meet you there later."

Belle had a good ten minutes before Matt would arrive, so she went through Missy's purses until she found a small leather shoulder bag that matched her boots. She went downstairs and decided to wait for him on the porch.

The thick layer of clouds hid the stars but held the earth's heat, making the night warm for that time of year. She pulled her phone out of the purse and checked the time. Matt was now twenty minutes overdue. Probably having a hard time leaving Danny at his parents' place. She went back in and dug out a treat for Mac, then mindlessly straightened the kitchen counters.

Another ten minutes and still no sign of Matt. The fear that he might have been in an accident wormed its way into her head as she phoned him. No answer. Maybe she should drive over to his trailer. No, then she'd miss him if he showed up. She decided to call Raphael at home.

Helen answered.

"Is Matt there?"

"No. He came for the boy and had dinner with us, but left about an hour ago. Is something wrong?"

"No." A pause. "Did he say anything about trouble at the farm?"

"Raphael is out in the garage but Carlos is here. He'll know."

She heard her call Carlos to the phone.

"Belle?"

"Carlos, did anything happen after I left this afternoon?"

"No. Matt showed up and gave everybody their checks. Wait a minute. He had my dad fire someone."

"Who?"

"That new guy who's been thinning the buds."

"Why?"

"Matt heard him say something about you he didn't like."

"What was it?"

"Come on. You know what some of these drifters are like."

"He's not exactly a drifter. He's from the valley. I went to school with his sister, who by the way, is the biggest gossip in town."

"What can I say? My dad let him go."

"Can you tell me what he said?"

"Nope."

"Did it have anything to do with the guy who bought Jake's place?"

"Maybe."

Belle said thanks and hung up. She felt the room slowly spin. Her cheeks burned. This couldn't be happening. *Dammit!* Matt's so straight-laced, all the gossip going around could drive him crazy. She grabbed her keys and ran out the door to her truck. She raced down the lane and spun out of the compound onto the main road. The Rome orchard came into sight with Matt's truck sitting in front of the dark trailer.

She parked and tried him on his phone again. She didn't get an answer, and the realization that he didn't want to talk to her made her swallow a scream. She steeled herself, slid out and ran up the steps. She listened for a moment, then gently tapped on the door. Danny had to be inside sleeping. She put her mouth to the crack. "Matt, please let me talk to you. You can't do this, Matt. Please, open up."

She raised her hand to knock again when the door swung open. He was standing back, and she barely made him out in the hazy light from the night sky.

"Matt, believe me, I never did anything with Ken."

"If you told me that yesterday, I might've believed you."

"Matt, don't let what that guy said bother you. None of this filthy gossip is true."

"Do you really think I give a damn what people say? What do you expect me to think when I saw you in that guy's arms this afternoon? You were drunk the first time. But you weren't drunk when you went back there today." He let out a bitter humph. "What did you want from him this time?"

"Matt, you're getting everything all wrong. I went over to ask for Jake's workbench."

He slowly shook his head. "You'd stop at nothing to get what you want." He paused for a moment. "We're finished, Belle. Leave."

Belle's face twisted in bewilderment. "Don't do this, Matt. I would never lie to you. I swear, I didn't do anything with him. Ever."

"Save it for some other sucker, Belle. I'm done with you and this place. I'll stick around until the harvest, and then I'm getting the hell out of here and starting a new life somewhere else."

"What are you talking about? That's crazy!"

"Carlos will stay. He knows the business as much as I do."

She struggled to hold back the tears streaming down her cheeks as his words sank in. She put her arms around him and tenderly pressed her head against his chest. "You can't go, Matt. I love you."

She felt him stiffen, and chills ran down her spine, making her hug him even tighter. He pulled her loose and shoved her against the railing.

"You've punished me enough. Now get outta here."

Belle froze in horror until she caught the sound of the door starting to close. What the cidery meant to Pap and Missy shot through her brain and she grabbed the door and stared at his hardened face.

"Matt, whatever you think of me, you can't walk away from the cidery. You'll never get a chance like this again." She grasped his arms and looked into his eyes. "It's your dream... and Dave's and Missy's. This is the first time she's shown any interest in the farm. You know how much that means to Pap."

He jerked his arms free.

Desperate, she grabbed hold of his shirt. "Stay, and I'll do whatever you want. You can run the whole show. I'll do the grafting and take care of the seedlings. Matt, you're the son Pap never had. It'll kill him if you leave."

All became quiet except for the chorus of peepers in the pond across the road. She studied his face, searching for the mask he'd always put on whenever his feelings were hurt, but all she saw was a crushing sadness and pooling eyes.

He looked away. "Please... go."

Belle, drained, trembled uncontrollably from the coolness of the air curling around the trailer. Yet, she stood unmoved, for she knew Matt's and her fate pivoted on this very moment. She slowly released her grip on his shirt, desperately searching for something to say that would change his mind.

"Matt, if you don't care about the McGradys, for God's sake, stay for Raphael and your mother. Think what a legacy the cidery will be for them... and for Danny."

A long silence left Belle breathless. She swayed, and for a moment feared she might faint.

At last he spoke, but in a voice so sad it broke her heart. "I'll stay till I get the cidery up and running. Then I'm gonna sell you my share and get the hell outta here."

The door closed, and her eyes remained riveted to it for a long moment, then she clutched the railing and blindly made her way down the steps. She drove home feeling numb all over. It was as if she were trapped in a bad dream. She dragged herself into the house and up to her bed where she rolled into a ball and sobbed uncontrollably. A paw kept running across her arm, and she looked up to see Mac's sad brown eyes and furrowed forehead. She buried her face in his fur and silently wept until she had no more tears.

The creak of her door woke her. The hallway light beamed across the bed, making her shield her eyes with her arm.

Missy rushed over and sat down beside her. Belle sat up, her puffy, streaked face clear in the light.

"Oh, my God! What happened?"

"He didn't come."

"Damn! I should've known something was wrong when you two didn't show up."

Belle gazed into space. "He doesn't trust me. He's never gonna get over that night at Ken's house. He wants to—I know he wants to—but he can't."

Missy rocked her in her arms as Belle quietly wept.

Belle suddenly pulled from Missy's arms and stiffened her back. She swiped the back of her hand under her nose and sniffled hard, as determination took over. She clutched Missy's arms and looked steadily into her eyes. "Nobody knows about tonight. Just the three of us. Promise me you won't tell Pap. This is important, Missy. All of our futures depend on it."

"What are you talking about?"

"Missy—this one time—you've absolutely got to do as I tell you. Promise me."

"I promise."

The room was quiet except for the sound of Missy getting undressed and slipping into the bed. She pressed up next to Belle and said, "Remember when we were kids, how you'd always let me sleep with you when I was unhappy? How you'd run your hand up and down my cheek till I fell asleep?"

"I remember."

As Missy's delicate hand gently stroked her face, Belle murmured, "I don't know how I'm gonna do it, Missy, but I'm gonna get him back."

CHAPTER TWENTY

R AIN PITTER-PATTERED on the tin roof like a dirge. Belle lay in bed for a while, hoping it would stop. She'd been able to hide from the world all week by thinning the buds in the spindle orchard overlooking the compound, but she could hardly do it in the rain.

Yesterday, she had stopped by the office, and when Pap told her Matt had closed on the fifty acres for the cidery that morning, she wanted to fall to her knees and thank God. And she sensed Pap felt just as relieved.

Matt wasn't around at the time, but when she noticed all the broken parts on his desk, she figured he had to be in the garage getting all their equipment ready for the season.

She rolled on her side in bed thinking that would occupy him for a couple weeks, then Missy would be getting married. Maybe after that, things would settle down to the way they were before Matt got his divorce—the best she could hope for right now.

She lay there wondering what she could do other than go to the office. She rose and thumbed through the Asheville phone book, found what she was looking for and called. It took forever, but someone finally answered.

"Carolina West."

"Hello. Do you have a patient by the name of Randy Gregg?"

"Just a minute. I've got to get my computer up."

Belle looked out the window while she waited. Matt's truck was parked next to the garage. He had to be in there working.

"Yes. Room 124."

"What are your visiting hours?"

"Nine a.m. to ten p.m."

She entered the address into her phone and got dressed, then tiptoed past Missy's closed door and went downstairs. Pap was already up and gone, his empty cup on the table. She went outside and found Mac waiting for her.

"You wanna go for a ride, boy?"

He ran to the truck wagging his tail.

Forty-five minutes later she pulled up to a cement block building. The way it was set back a couple feet from the sidewalk there was no allowance for landscaping. If it wasn't for the sign above the door, she wouldn't have known it was a nursing home. Inside, the reception room was already bleak with its drab barren walls, but when she spotted the dirty carpets, she wanted to turn around and go back out.

No one was at the desk, so she ventured down the hall on her own. An arrow with 100-130 on it pointed to a dimly lit hallway. Halfway down, a young woman in jeans and tee-shirt came from a room.

The woman looked at her and said, "Are you visiting someone?"

"Yes. Are you?"

The girl looked embarrassed. "I'm a CNA—a Certified Nursing Assistant. Please, don't say anything to anyone. I spent the night at my boyfriend's place and forgot to bring my uniform."

"My lips are sealed," Belle said. Then she thought for a moment. "Do you know the guy in 124?"

"There's two. A quadriplegic and an amputee."

"Randy, Randy Gregg."

"That's the quad. He's down the hall to the right." She started to go, then added, "He doesn't like anyone looking at him, so don't turn his chair around."

Belle continued down, and was just about to open the door

marked "124" when a woman in a uniform came out of the room across the hall.

"Who are you looking for?"

"Randy Gregg."

"You don't want to go in there right now. He's getting his bowels emptied."

"Oh." She paused for a moment. "How is he?"

"Who knows. He only talks to Connie."

"I mean his health."

"He's got a bed sore, but other than that, as good as he gets."

"Is Connie around?"

"She comes on at three." She made a slightly annoyed face and said, "I'd like to stand here and talk to you, darling, but I've got to get these meds delivered," then quickly disappeared into another room.

Belle leaned against the wall waiting for someone to come out of 124 when something crashed against the door. A young man emerged pushing a cart.

He gave her a quick look. "Mr. Adanti is in the dining room right now."

"I'm here to see Randy Gregg."

He seemed surprised.

"Is anything wrong?" she asked.

"No. It's just that... we thought he didn't have anyone."

"Actually, he doesn't know me. I'm a friend of his parents."

With the rough way he muscled the cart around, it was no wonder the hall walls were scraped.

"Can you come back in an hour? He's been sedated." He gave her a leery look. "Did they tell you he doesn't want anyone to look at his face?"

Belle was beginning to wonder if her coming was such a good idea. "Do you have Connie's phone number?"

He looked around. "I'm not supposed to give it out, but she cares about that poor guy." He kept a nervous eye on the hall. "I bet she'll want to talk to you."

"Damn," said Belle. "I don't have anything to write with."

He took a ballpoint from behind his ear and handed it to her.

"Hurry."

She quickly jotted the number on her arm and handed the pen back. Once back in the truck, she punched the number into her phone, and a sweet voice told her to leave a message.

It was eleven-thirty and still raining. She could pick up some lunch, trawl around an office supply store and make it back to the nursing home by three, unless she heard from Connie sooner.

She sat eating a hamburger in the front seat with Mac sitting at attention with his ears flopped forward in begging position. He had already wolfed his down, but she tore off a piece of hers and gave it to him.

The phone rang. Belle saw it was Connie.

"Thanks for getting back to me so fast."

"Your message said you're calling about Randy Gregg."

Belle picked up on a quiver in her voice, unlike the mellow tone on the recording. "Yes. I was a good friend of his parents and thought I'd check and make sure he's okay."

Connie's tone turned more furtive. "Can you meet me somewhere?"

A half-hour later, an old beat-up Ford Escort pulled into McDonald's and a chubby woman in her early twenties sat waiting until Belle came up to her door and slid in.

"Sorry for all the intrigue, but if I was caught talking to you, I could lose my job. We're supposed to refer everyone to management."

Belle had to admit to herself all the secrecy was starting to give her the creeps.

Connie turned off her windshield wipers and looked at Belle. "I'm glad he's got someone who cares for him. You're the first person who's showed up since he arrived."

"Hasn't his uncle visited?"

"No one has."

"Is he doing all right? One of the nurses told me he has a bed sore."

"That's the least of his worries. He needs to go back to the place he came from."

"I don't know if that's possible. It was pretty expensive."

"Well, if he stays in this place much longer, he's gonna die."

"What makes you say that? Aren't there regulations?"

"You don't understand. There just isn't enough resources for someone like him. He needs 'round the clock care. Everybody in that place is spread thin. They hire all us CNAs and medical technicians—sure we're certified—but does that mean all those kids'll show up after some all night rave? This is a tough job. A lot of them get sick of wiping people's asses and cleaning up their puke, and they just walk out."

She swiped away the condensation on her window and looked out searchingly. "They've got to have the minimum amount of people on duty at all times or they could lose their license, and when anyone doesn't show, somebody's got to pull a second shift. And, believe me, that somebody's already exhausted. What kind of care are they gonna be able to give? I worry most about the patients who need their pain meds."

The way Connie really cared about Randy and everyone else in the place made Belle feel guilty about not coming sooner.

"It's a no-win situation here. He needs to go back," said Connie.

"What's he like?"

"What do you think? Sad. This happened to him when he was twenty-two. Just think what it's got to be like, spending thirty years locked in a paralyzed body."

"Can he move anything?"

"His eyes. He can talk, but you have to be very patient. He can only talk when the ventilator is pushing air out, usually two or three words, and then he has to wait for it to recycle again."

Belle, feeling her throat tighten, wiped her window and gazed out while Connie continued.

"He told me his parents used to visit him every Wednesday. It's my day off, but I try to run in if I can. Even if it's only for a few minutes."

Belle thought about Ben and all the money in the trust fund, and she filled with disgust.

Connie continued, almost as if talking to herself. "I do my best for everybody in there, but there's only so much you can do.

I worry about Mr. Gregg. A lot can go wrong for him—and it can go wrong fast."

Belle gave her a quick glance. "Like what?"

"Look. He's only been here a few months, and he's already had two respiratory episodes. The last one I discovered when I came on duty. God only knows how long he'd been lying there, hoping someone would help him. Can you imagine what goes through someone's head when their oxygen runs out? We should have a compressor in there. That way he wouldn't have to depend on some med tech to change the tank."

Belle reluctantly asked her the question that had been on her mind ever since she ran into the first CNA. "Everyone keeps telling me he doesn't want anyone looking at him. Is it that bad?"

"I've seen worse. He's had all kinds of reconstructive surgery—eyelids, ears. But let's be honest, some people get a horrified expression on their face when they look at someone like him. Some even scream. It's devastating. There's a picture of him and his parents on his table. Evidently, he was very good looking. Some people have an image of themselves, and when something like this happens, more than anything, they're ashamed. They shouldn't be, but they are."

Connie craned her neck and looked into Belle's eyes. "Is there anything you can do for him? He's completely helpless. Even if you just come and visit. A lot of times I take my break in there and read to him. It's kind of heartbreaking the way he sits day after day with nothing to look forward to but me running in there and reading him a couple pages of a war story. He was in Nam. It's ironic, isn't it? He can't move a muscle and wants me to read him action novels."

Belle gave Connie her number and asked her to call if anything changed, then promised to do what she could. Right now, what she needed to do most was get Ben to put him back in the other nursing home.

Once on the road, she phoned Lucy. "What are the chances of you getting into that closet right quick?"

"I was gonna call you. He's in trial all week, and Ellie's going for a fitting tomorrow and wants me to sit at the desk. And if

I know her, she's gonna nit-pick that wedding dress to pieces."

"Lucy, I just finished checking out the nursing home that Ben sent Jake's son to. You need to get *everything* out of that box tomorrow."

"What if he looks in it?"

"He's not going to do that. That smug little bastard thinks he's getting away with it."

"I don't know, Belle. I'm getting nervous."

"Nervous? He's screwed everybody over. Your mother, the poor guy sitting in that shit-hole of a nursing home, me, you— *Goddammit! Everybody!"*

Belle took a deep breath and slowly blew it out. She had to calm down and be more convincing.

"Lucy, all your mother's got—all that guy who's been hooked up to a ventilator for thirty years has got—is you and me. And finding something in that damn box is our last chance to help them. I want you to get everything out of it tomorrow and stash it in your office. I'll meet you at midnight, and you can give it to me then."

They were quite for a moment until Belle asked, "Are you gonna do it?"

"Last week I took my mother's new prescription to the drug store..." Her voice cracked. "When they said it cost over two hundred dollars, I had to leave it. Yeah, I'm gonna do it."

The following night, Belle stood at her bedroom window in the dark and watched the lights go out in the garage. The door opened and Matt trudged in the moonlight to the three-quarter ton truck he used to haul equipment, and then took off. Good. Now she wouldn't have to worry about him following her. She slipped out of her room and crept down the dark hall to the stairs. She winced when the second step creaked. She stopped for a moment and listened. The only one awakened was Mac who stood panting at the bottom of the staircase.

She hurried down and into the kitchen. "Come on, boy," she said as the two scurried out of the house. She had parked far enough away so she wouldn't wake anyone when she started up, but she still took care not to slam her door shut.

Before long, she was cruising down Ridge Road like someone innocently coming back from a date, making her wonder how many others on the road that night were doing something they shouldn't. For the first time in her life she felt like she was a member of the criminal class. She pulled up in front of Ben's office building and was surprised to see Lucy jump out of her car hauling a big plastic bag. She ran to the passenger side of Belle's truck, opened the door and shoved it on the floor.

"That's everything," she said. She closed the door, jumped back in her car and pulled away.

Getting back in the house unnoticed was going to be a lot harder than getting out. She parked in the same spot, told Mac to be quiet and trudged with the bag. It was large but light. She tried to remember what Barbara and she had stuffed in the carton, but she'd been in such a daze at the time, it was a blur. Once in the house, she stowed the bag in a hall closet that no one ever opened and tiptoed up the stairs to her room.

She quickly undressed and got into bed, wishing she'd stopped in the kitchen for a shot of Pap's whiskey. She tossed in bed, trying to push the images and odors from the nursing home out of her head. She finally gave up and lay flat on her back staring out at the moon. She let all the memories that she had shoved aside all day ebb back to her. She watched Mary take a picture off her dresser like she always did and lovingly dust it off with her apron before showing it to her. "That's my boy," she said. "Isn't he beautiful."

All her troubles suddenly seemed miniscule, as she lay wondering if the man locked in his body in room 124 was awake in his bed, looking out at the same moon.

CHAPTER TWENTY-ONE

P AP WAS SITTING IN THE KITCHEN waiting for the coffee to brew when Belle walked in. "I'll make breakfast," she said, then put some bacon on to fry and scrambled enough eggs for Pap and Missy, who she'd heard earlier in the shower.

"I'll be working on the cidery orchard plans upstairs today," Belle mentioned as she put a heaping plate in front of Pap. She looked up to see Missy rush in and help herself at the stove.

Belle filled a thermos for Pap and handed it to him as he left with Missy, then she meandered to the window and watched Pap give her sister a rare hug—a sign he was happy about her upcoming wedding, and even happier about her newfound enthusiasm for the farm.

It had been painful to watch his disappointment grow over the years as Missy's interest drifted further and further from the orchards. It struck Belle as ironic that the answer to Pap's prayers lay within his sworn enemy's trove of antique apples. If she hadn't saved Jake's trees, it probably never would have happened. She closed her eyes and pictured Matt's cold, stony figure cloaked in the darkness of his trailer and felt a killing hurt for the price she paid to get them.

She cleared the table and let Mac out, anxious to retrieve the bag from the closet. She rushed up the stairs and cut the bag open, dumped everything on the bed and started sorting. First, she stacked all the hanging files that miraculously still held most of their contents. Next, she snapped up all the receipts. Mostly for office supplies and postage. She dug a box from her closet and started tossing in the photos, not allowing herself the pleasure of reliving a single happy moment.

The sheet she'd found in her desk was spread flat on the bed. This is what she had to look for. She shuffled through the clutter searching for pages torn from a steno pad, but found nothing.

Quickly, she thumbed through the hanging files—Electricity, Water, Taxes, Royalties, Speaking Engagements, Insurance— and stopped at a tab marked "Personal." She flipped it open. What appeared to be the sheets she was looking for stared her in the face. Numbered from one to seven, she was convinced that the one she found in the desk belonged with them.

She sank down on the bed and started to read the bulleted items headed with "Memo to Ben." She skimmed the items in disbelief—two bank accounts, Jake's life insurance policy, rights to his royalties. The item saying "Sell the house with two acres and give Belle the orchard and the rest of the land" brought tears to her eyes. She quickly got Lucy on the phone and arranged to meet her downtown at noon.

This time, Belle was the one waiting at a table.

"I already ordered for us," said Belle when Lucy sat down. She leaned toward Lucy and spoke just above a whisper. "I think we might have him. The rest of the sheets were in the bag. There's no signature, but there's enough incriminating items to scare the hell out of him." Belle had been toying with a way she could fake a signature, but decided not to share it with Lucy.

"I don't know, Belle. If you saw some of the thugs he deals with, you wouldn't think anything would frighten him."

"I haven't decided exactly what I'm gonna do yet," said Belle, "but right now I need to find out more about your mother's case."

"We relive it on a regular basis. Ask me anything."

"Okay. How much was he suing Nature's Seasons for?"

"Basically, it was a wrongful death suit, claiming that due to their malfeasance, my father was caused to die. The suit was asking for them to give my mother equal to what he would have earned if he were alive, up until his retirement. It also included health insurance for my mom for the duration of her life. This was pretty much standard in those days."

"Do you know what his retirement age would be?"

"At the time, mandatory was seventy."

"How old was he when he died?"

"Forty-two."

Belle made a quick calculation. "Damn. With interest, it could be as much as a million bucks."

Lucy's eyes pooled.

"Don't get your hopes up, Lucy. Like you said before, we don't have proof." Belle thought out loud. "But from what I gather, Ben and his wife aren't going to like bad gossip, and neither is Nature's Seasons—especially with all the bad press they're getting about stalling that baby food recall."

Their order arrived, and they both dug in.

"I've got to confront him," mused Belle.

"Not in the office. Ellie won't let you in. She's got a buzzer on her desk that locks his door. It's a necessity with the kind of clients he sometimes has. Especially irate husbands he just took to the cleaners."

"Do you know where he lives?"

"Uh-huh. Sometimes when he's in a long trial I have to take checks over to his house for him to sign."

After Lucy told Belle how to get to Ben's house, Belle asked her if she knew the name of the man he didn't call to the stand.

"Jack Hale."

"Do you know where he lives?"

"No. He left town right after he talked to my mother. I've looked for him for years, but no luck."

That's okay, Belle thought. Ben doesn't know that.

The unfairness gnawed at Belle as she walked to her truck. She got in, and instead of heading home, pulled onto the Spartanburg Highway and found the road Ben lived on just outside Flat Rock. Her truck slowly wound up the mountain past a string of high-dollar homes tucked in luxuriously landscaped settings.

The road made a sharp turn like Lucy said it would, and there to the right was Sunnyside Lane. She turned in and looked for the second driveway on the steep, twisty lane. The only thing to identify it was the number twelve on a tastefully decorated mailbox. The driveway disappeared behind a grove of trees, with part of a second story visible through the upper branches.

Ben wouldn't be there, but Barbara might. She drove past and turned around in a driveway up ahead. She decided to go see if Barbara was home and beg her to help Randy, when the pitiful scene of her pleading with Matt caved in on her. No. She was through begging.

She had to threaten him. He might not be afraid of the thugs he did business with, but she was sure he would think twice about disgracing Barbara and his two girls. That was the tack she had to take. Pap was famous among his poker buddies for being a consummate bluffer. Tonight, she had to see if it ran in the family.

For the rest of the afternoon, Belle found herself talking to Mary and Jake every spare moment, promising she'd take care of their boy. Things had to work out tonight. If they didn't, it would take years of litigation to get a dime out of Ben—that is, if Lucy could even find a lawyer to take her mother's case on a contingency basis, and she could get the D.A. to look into Randy's situation. After all, she had nothing but an unsigned rough draft of a memo. By then, Randy and Lucy's mom would probably be gone.

Belle didn't trust the printer in her bedroom. The last time she tried to copy something with it, her taxes got chewed up. She'd have to copy the eight sheets at the office; but first she had to find something.

She searched through the pile of papers on her bed, and not finding what she was looking for, she thumbed through the files in the folders, and then stopped. She went to the wastepaper basket and pulled out Jake's credit card receipts, recalling that some of them had his signature.

Finding it, she carefully cut it out and positioned it at the bottom of page eight. Damn! This wasn't going to work. It covered part of a line. She studied it. The lines were almost invisible. Maybe she could set their machine on "light" and get a copy without lines. She found another signature and stuffed everything in a file and left for the office.

There was a beat-up pickup parked outside the packing house with a couple farmhands leaning up against it. They had to be waiting for Pap or Matt. She gave them a friendly nod, then rushed up the steps to the office and hurriedly adjusted the level on the printer until the writing was legible and the lines were almost completely gone.

She heard a truck door slam shut, and then another. She rushed to the window and was relieved to see it was just the two who'd been waiting, taking off. She went back to the copier, and her hands shook as she started to paste Jake's signature on the bottom of page eight. She squeezed the little piece of paper too hard and it flipped into the air. She got on her hands and knees and tried to find it, but no luck. She quickly made another copy of his signature, carefully cut it out and stuck it on, then made the final copy. She was carefully collecting all the sheets when Connie from the nursing home called.

"Is anything wrong?" Belle asked, worried.

"No. That's why I'm calling. I told Randy about you and it made him cry."

"Maybe I shouldn't come."

"No! You have to come now! He told me he was crying because he wasn't forgotten. But he wanted me to call you and tell you not to look at him."

"I won't, but I think it's ridiculous."

"Can I tell him you'll be here on Wednesday?"

"Yes. It'll be late. After dinner."

That evening, Belle fixed Pap's favorite—chicken and biscuits—and wondered if it was intended to leave an enduring memory with him in case anything went wrong tonight when she was visiting Ben.

Belle found the pleasant conversation at the kitchen table that night an escape. Pap kept looking over at Belle with a twitch of a smile as Missy went on and on about her wedding plans.

Pam was helping with all the arrangements, even ordering the dresses for Belle and the other two bridesmaids. It all seemed so forthright and promising, not devious and scary like the scheme she was about to attempt.

But somehow, Belle felt no guilt. By a strange twist of fate, she had landed in a pivotal position where she was being called on to positively affect two people's lives. But this was Ben Gregg's game, and the only way she could possibly win at it was to play by his rules—no holds barred.

She studied Pap and wanted to grasp his gnarly, heavily veined hand and ask him to help, but she was too afraid he wouldn't be able to get past his hate for the man who was responsible for his little Mandy's death. A mindless kind of calm one feels when they accept the inevitable fell over her. If she won tonight, two people would be better off. If she lost, they would languish in the status quo. At any rate, she didn't see she had much of a choice. She was the next batter up.

"I'm going to visit Lucy Bishop for a couple of hours," Belle casually mentioned as she took her plate to the sink. She caught a look on Missy's face and quickly added, "I heard her mother's thinking of selling their old orchard behind the house. It's only a half acre, but she knows a lot about those trees. Lucy said some of them go back four generations."

On the drive to Ben's house, Belle asked herself how she got dragged into this quagmire. Fate was a big part of it. If that one single sheet hadn't slipped out and gotten stuck in the drawer when Jake stuffed it in the folder, she wouldn't be carrying the weight of Lucy's sick mom and Jake's son around with her, and most of all, she wouldn't be driving to that bastard's house right now.

From what Lucy had said about him, she understood why he would do what he did to her and even to Lucy's mom, but not to his own flesh and blood. Tonight she was playing in the evil kingdom's big leagues. She ran through her game plan once more and decided she had to get his attention the minute he opened the door.

She accepted the fact that once she mentioned Mrs. Bishop's

lawsuit, Lucy would no longer have a job. Lucy had to know that, too. Don't worry, Lucy, she told herself as she turned on her windshield wipers. I'll get Pap to find you something. Hopefully, better than what you have.

As Belle cruised through Flat Rock, Ben Gregg was pouring himself a stiff drink in his den. He settled down in his favorite leather chair as Barbara said goodbye to their daughter at the door. His girl had prattled on through dinner about their new pool and cabana, making him wonder if she had any idea of all the evil he had to rain down on people to give her the gift. She called out from the hall, "Love ya, Dad," and left.

Barbara was certainly aware of what it took to get them what they had in spite of all his gambling losses, but somewhere along their thirty-year journey, she had chosen to ignore the unsettling facts staring her in the face and look the other way.

Ben finished his drink and was about to pour himself another when the doorbell chimed.

"I'll get it," he shouted up the stairs as he went to open the door. At first, the beautiful girl standing on the stoop stunned him; but realizing it was Annabelle McKenzie, he got over it quickly enough and slammed the door shut. Only, she had put her foot in the way.

"I've been talking with Jack Hale about Mrs. Bishop's suit with Nature's Seasons, and he wants to know why you didn't call him to the stand," she blurted out.

He opened the door and studied her. There was something both appealing and off-putting about her audacity in coming to his home.

A voice from upstairs yelled, "Who is it, honey?"

He turned and shouted, "I'm taking care of it."

He looked back at Belle. "Come in."

She followed him into the den, and he waved her to a chair as he casually poured himself another whisky. "Do you want a drink?" he asked.

She told him no and desperately tried to remember the game plan that flew out of her head the minute he opened the door. She sat erect with her feet tucked under the chair trying to stay calm; however, her fingers kept twisting Mary's ring. Belle rarely wore it, but hoped it would bring Randy some luck tonight if his mother's ring were on her finger.

Ben sat down and eyed her, a drink in his hand. He didn't know what kind of a shakedown this was; but whatever it was, he had to nip it in the bud. The way she was fidgeting with her ring, it had to be a bluff. After all, it was at least ten years since Hale came barging into his office with questions about the Bishop trial. It had been easy enough to shut him up by getting Jim Stevens over at Nature's Seasons to give him a management job and transfer him to their Michigan plant.

"And just what does Mr. Hale have to say?"

"More than what you and Barbara want anyone to hear." Belle's voice cracked, and she tried to get her nerve back and stop shaking. Ben's icy stare didn't help. "You can read about it when the North Carolina State Bar sends you a copy of the grievance Mrs. Bishop intends to file." She clamped her jaw and gave him a steely stare back.

Ben read it as fear. He'd deposed hundreds of witnesses and knew fear when he saw it. He studied her every subtle body movement, a skill honed by observing hundreds of truthsayers and even more liars. Yet, he wasn't sure of this one.

One thing he was sure of, however, was she was in cahoots with that mealy-mouthed little accountant of his. He'd gone against every instinct in hiring her, but her mother had begged Barbara to get him to give Lucy a job. This night's encounter only reinforced his basic tenet for survival—never show pity.

"Dear, exactly what do you expect to gain from barging in here with these scurrilous accusations?"

Belle's instincts told her to put everything she had on the table. She pulled the sheets she had copied out of her pocket and tossed them over to him. "The same thing I'm going to gain by going to the district attorney with this—justice."

He casually picked it up and read. It was definitely Jake's handwriting and the items ran close to his letter, hitting all the issues involving money. He smiled inwardly when he studied the signature. It was either a forgery or a cut-and-paste job. No one would sign a jotted-down list.

He tossed it on the table, confident he was dealing with a rank amateur. But those were the most dangerous kind. She had no knowledge of, and therefore, no fear of the dangerous water she was treading in. One good thing, however; she obviously hadn't taken this to her grandfather, or he'd be the one sitting in front of him right now.

Belle surmised Ben was definitely worried, or he would have thrown her out by now, and it emboldened her. "As you certainly know, Mr. Gregg, they say every crime has a motive. I asked myself why would someone take his brother's helpless son out of the nursing home he was thriving in and stick him in some cut-rate dump where he was sure to die? Then I asked myself, after the poor devil died, what would happen to the big, fat trust fund that was put aside just so this wouldn't happen? And you know what? I bet it would probably be up to the executor of the estate to disburse it as he saw fit."

Ben wanted to slap her silly but thought better of it. His biggest worry was Mrs. Bishop's lawsuit he threw to get business from the canning company. There was a strong chance she was bluffing about Jack Hale. He studied her again. If she had the nerve to try to pass a forged signature, she wouldn't stop at a lie. He had to call Jim Stevens and confirm Hale's whereabouts, and that they had gotten him to sign the disclaimer he'd written up for him.

Belle was casually looking around the room trying to appear relaxed, but the constant tugging at her ring gave her away. Ben wondered if she'd crack if he stared at her for a while. He sat thinking about the $500,000 in Jake's trust fund. It would be a total waste to give it to a nursing home for someone who could do nothing but talk and move his chair around by triggering a mechanism with his mouth.

Government benefits had covered the place in Charlotte. One damn case of pneumonia and Mary had overreacted. He had advised Jake not to move him to Winston-Salem over Mary's insistence. But once she slipped into the advanced stages of Alzheimer's and Jake had the bout with heart failure, he stopped listening. Ben couldn't shake him of the fear that Randy wouldn't be taken care of in the Medicaid supported facility without their constant vigilance, and Jake agreed to the move, confident their two $500,000 life insurance policies and the sale of the house would carry their son through.

Belle listened to the ticking of the grandfather clock in the hall while counting her options. By all rights, he should have thrown her out by now. The fact that he hadn't, convinced her she had gotten under his skin. She grasped at the sudden looming possibility of at least getting Lucy's mom's medical bills paid, which she would consider a win. But, no matter what, she had to get Ben to authorize the trust fund to pay for a better place for Randy.

She leaned back in her chair to signal she was willing to sit there all night if she had to, when a smug little smile appeared on his face and made her snap, just like it was intended to.

She lunged forward.

"You want to know what my exact expectations are? Well, I'll tell you. First, I want you to get the same folks you were dealing with from Nature's Seasons to reconsider Mrs. Bishop's suit and pay her what she's got coming. And then, I want you to find a decent nursing home for your nephew here in Hendersonville so I can visit him."

She shook her head in disgust. "What I'd really like, is to see you go to jail. But there isn't enough time for those two to get the justice they deserve, now is there?" Her rage escalated along with her tone and she stood up. "With your connections, you may get away with these crimes, but I promise you, you're not going to come out of it clean. I'm going to see to it that the Bar hears about both of these dirty little deals, then I'm going to the D.A., to the papers, anywhere, everywhere. You may be able to walk away and not look back, but it's gonna cast an ugly little shadow over Barbara and your two daughters—rumors, whispers, innuendos—you know what I'm talking about."

A flustered Belle caught her breath and she tried to calm down.

He rose clearing his throat. "I'll get back to you in a couple of days. You keep your mouth shut and don't do anything rash... or you could get hurt."

Belle let out a bitter laugh. *"I could get hurt?* You have no idea how much you've already done to me. I've been hurt enough to last the rest of my life." She turned and left.

Ben rose and went to the window and watched her pull away. It was just past nine. He went down the hall to his office, looked up a number and phoned.

"Jim, I'm sorry to call this late, but something's come up."

"What?"

"Remember that Bishop suit?" Ben could tell he'd been drinking and offered more. "The one where we had to get rid of Jack Hale?"

"Yeah."

"Do you still have that signed disclaimer?"

"Of course. What's the problem?"

"Someone was just here telling me he's willing to make a statement countering it. I'm pretty sure they're bluffing, but you better track him down."

CHAPTER TWENTY-TWO

BELLE BACKED THE TRACTOR UP to the barn and skill-fully wrangled the trailer inside. She was going to move the grafted seedlings to a plot on the hill next to the compound's trestle orchard where they could be tied into the irrigation system. Pap had offered to send a couple hands to help her, but she didn't dare trust anyone but herself to touch the trees.

She found some music on the radio and started loading the trailer, wondering if the guy in Charlotte who threatened to kill himself ever got his wife back. The days spent grafting seemed like a lifetime ago. She didn't know it then, but looking back, she could see she had finally let go of the past and was allowing herself to fall deeply in love with Matt all over again. And that was where she now stood—and just like that guy in Charlotte, she wasn't going to give up on it.

The trees were nestled snugly against the trailer's sides and packed tight enough so they wouldn't tip over on the climb up the hill. Belle estimated it would take her six trips to get all three thousand moved. She took the hill nice and easy with Mac running on ahead, then stopped at the plot covered with a black tarp. A hose ran from a spigot for her to use until the crew finished running the irrigation lines, and once she had the trees unloaded, she gave them a gentle spray.

This was the highest point on the compound property and

would be the safest place for the trees to spend next winter. The view was glorious, with the valley spread out in front of her like a Gainsborough painting. The summer before she went to college, Pap had told her he was saving this plot to build a house for her and Matt. Her stomach churned. He was probably going to give it to Missy and Dave now.

Her phone rang and she could see it was Lucy.

"He fired me."

Belle had figured as much the night before. "I'm sorry. But don't worry, I'll help you find another job. A better one."

"I'm not worried, but maybe you should be."

"What do you mean?"

"I came in this morning and the key wouldn't open my door, so I went in and asked Ellie about it, and she sent me into Mr. Gregg's office. I knew I was going to be fired, so that was no surprise. But it was kinda weird the way he asked me for your phone number... and your address, too."

"What did you tell him?"

"I gave him your cell and told him you live with your grandfather."

Belle thought about that for a moment, then said, "I'm sorry about your job, Lucy."

"It's okay. I knew this was coming the minute you asked me where he lived. Belle, you did me a favor. I should've gotten out of there years ago. Now, I can at least draw unemployment till I find something else."

Belle couldn't get her mind off Lucy for the rest of the day, and had to keep fighting off a feeling of failure. Whatever possessed her to think she could bluff a wily lawyer like Ben with a "to do" list and a lie about someone who might not still exist? She didn't want to raise the issue with Lucy right away, but she had every intention of getting her mother to file a grievance. And she wasn't finished fighting for Randy, either.

She finished transporting the trees around five-thirty, switched the lights off in the barn and headed for home. Mac knew where they were going and ran to the house.

She was thinking about finding a book to take to the nursing home that night when she noticed Matt's truck was still outside the garage, and recalled him telling her to ask him if she ever needed help. Things were too dicey right now to talk to Pap about Lucy, but she knew Matt still hung around with friends he'd made when he studied accounting. Maybe one of them needed someone or knew about a job.

Matt's boots stuck out from under their three-quarter-ton truck as she entered. The door slammed shut behind her, and he rolled out, holding a wrench. He sat up and tossed the wrench in a tool box, his hands black with grease and his sweaty face smudged.

"What do you want?"

"You remember Lucy, don't you?"

He tossed his head and gave her one of his smart-alecky looks. "Oh, darlin', not only do *I* remember her, I'm sure Miguel is never gonna forget her." He pulled a rag from his pocket and wiped his hands.

Belle ignored the sarcasm.

"I know you're still mad at me, but—"

"Mad at you? That's the biggest understatement of the year."

"Don't be such a smartass. Lucy needs a job."

He looked up at her. "So you finally messed up her life, too?"

She turned to go. "That's okay. I'm sorry I bothered you."

"No! Don't go."

She turned and came near to him. Those were the same words she had uttered the night he didn't come to get her. She looked into the eyes she knew better than her own. The wrinkle lines at their corners said he couldn't let himself trust her, yet there was something in the way he said "Don't go" that signaled love.

He looked away as if he were reading her mind. "I erased her number from my phone. Put it in my notebook over there on the bench. I'll see what I can do."

Belle found his greasy notebook on the counter and started to write in it when she saw "Marsha—Friday lunch." Her head shot around to him, but he had already rolled back under the truck. She wrote down Lucy's information and started for the door.

"Now that you got her fired, I hope this is the end of it," Matt hollered out.

She opened the door and left without a word.

Minutes later, Belle walked into the house. An opened soup can and everything Pap would need to make a sandwich lay on the counter. She found him watching the news in the living room and eating off a tray.

"Honey, just grab a sandwich tonight, okay? Missy's eating with Dave."

She told him she would, then ran upstairs and took a quick shower before putting on a fresh outfit. Downstairs again, she looked through Pap's paperbacks and picked one up.

"How was this?" she said as she held it for him to see.

"Anything Clancy's written is good. But I don't know if you're gonna like it."

"It's for a friend, Pap." She hesitated for a moment. "Pap, has Matt ever mentioned a Marsha Johnson to you?"

"It's more like have I ever mentioned her to him. She's the granddaughter of one of my poker buddies. He asked me to let her talk to us about representing the cidery. She stopped by the office once when Matt was there, and I heard her out, but when she got into all that 'image' stuff I turned her over to Matt."

"Are they dating?"

"I hope not. She's engaged to Charlie Hasner's boy."

"Then why is he going to lunch with her, and why would he go to the Rusty Bucket with her on a Friday night?"

"Oh, heck. She's always asking me to lunch. That's the way those folks do business." Pap chuckled. "You want to know what I told her when she said she could give us an image?" He chuckled again. "Nah, you don't wanna know."

"Okay, Grandpa, you got me. What did you tell her?"

"That the way our Carolina Belle fought off a bulldozer, we already got an image."

"Thanks. Just how I want people to think of me."

He shrugged. "It got a laugh from Matt." Pap reached up with a devilish grin and squeezed her hand, "So you're still in the game, huh?"

"You bet I am, Grandpa. You're right, Matt's worth fighting for."

She grabbed the book, told him she'd be back around nine, and ran out.

IF THE NURSING HOME WAS DARK and gloomy in broad daylight, in the night it was downright scary. Again, the reception desk was deserted. The sound of talking and laughing came from what had to be a dining room down the main hall as Belle turned toward Randy's room. Part way down, a door was ajar, and what had to be a game show trailed out.

She reached 124 and turned off her cell, then took a deep breath and knocked. No answer. She opened the door a crack.

"It's Annabelle McKenzie," she said barely louder than a whisper.

An unmodulated voice answered, "Come in."

She slowly pushed the door open. The only light came from a small lamp over one bed. That and the whooshing beat of a ventilator gave the room an otherworldly feeling. A man sat in a heavily rigged wheelchair, his back to her. He wore a baseball cap and what appeared to be a jacket. She looked around. The other bed had been stripped. A tube ran down from the wheelchair to the ventilator that was hooked up to a tank. A lonely metal chair with a worn padded seat faced the man's bed.

"Sit down."

She didn't know how much Connie had told him about her, but as she got settled in the chair, she remembered her instructions to be patient and give him a chance to get his words out.

"I brought a book to read you. *Patriot Games.* They say it's good." She didn't dare tell him it was Pap's. Why dredge up sad memories; his situation was bad enough. She had to fight the urge to breathe in sync with the ventilator's cycle as she sat waiting for him to say something.

"Do you want me to read it?" she finally asked.

"No."

Belle bit her lip. They weren't getting off to a good start.

"I want..... you to..... close your..... eyes."

Belle tapped her fingers on the book and tried to relax. The gloomy place, the call from Lucy and the horrible moments in Ben's house came down on her, but she braced herself, took a deep breath and closed her eyes.

"Are they..... closed."

She swallowed hard. "Yes."

"Do not..... open..... them."

"I won't." There was a hint of nervousness in her voice.

The sound of the wheelchair turning around and the whooshing beat made her clench her teeth and grip the seat of her chair. She could feel him looking at her for what seemed like an eternity. A slight kick at the end of every whoosh sounded like a muffled drumbeat. Finally, she heard the chair rolling around again, and she released her grip.

"You can..... open them."

The door to the hall suddenly swung open and Connie rushed in. "Just wanted to check that everything was okay," she said in a forced cheery voice. She went over to Randy and craned her neck to look at him. "Is everything all right, Mr. Gregg?"

"Make her..... go."

Connie looked at Belle and shrugged, then followed her out to the hallway.

"What did you say to him?" asked Connie.

"Nothing. Why?"

"He was crying."

Puzzled, Belle left the nursing home with Connie promising to find out what upset him, and then to give her a call. She pulled onto the Interstate and headed for Hendersonville. Already shaken by the encounter with Randy and cloaked in the darkness of the night, she was reminded of Ben asking Lucy where she lived, then his warning for her not to do "anything rash." Her bluff the other night had gotten her nowhere but in the line of his fire. He'd evidently checked Jack Hale out and found he had died or disappeared, and had no immediate fear on that account. Lucy was right. He didn't scare easy.

The highway was practically deserted, just the usual string of tractor trailers moving America's goods. A car came up behind her and trailed a few lengths behind the whole way to Hendersonville. Curious to see if it would get off at her exit, she breathed a sigh of relief when it continued down the highway.

The next morning, as she collected her grafting supplies in the barn, Pap walked in and told her someone was coming to see him, then he handed her his truck keys, saying they'd gotten the wrong engine and for her to take it back and pick up a new one. He also wanted her to bring back some items from the tractor supply store—chores that would take all afternoon.

She drove down Ridge Road, and a car coming from the other direction slowed down as it passed. It was enough for her to get a good look at the driver, and for him to get a good look at her. Wearing a shirt and tie, she assumed he was a salesman.

The road straightened out beyond the curve. Something about the way the man had looked at her, made her glance in the rearview mirror, and it unnerved her when she saw his car come around the curve behind her. He must have turned around. An awful thought ran through her head. Whoever was following her could have been sent by Ben.

She hit the accelerator, and so did he. It was making her nervous until she remembered the car behind her the night before and felt a little silly. A thug would hardly be coming after her in a shirt and tie. But, it still pricked the back of her mind, and she made a turn on a rarely used road just to make sure.

The car turned with her. She slowed down, then sped up, each time with him sticking to her. She gunned the engine, then pulled aside and slammed on the brakes. It surprised her when he pulled up behind her and got out.

She felt under the seat for the wrench Pap always kept there.

He neared and flashed a badge identifying him as a detective from the Henderson County sheriff's department.

"Can I see your license?" he asked.

She retrieved it from her wallet and handed it to him, wishing her hand wasn't shaking so much.

He studied it, then looked up at her. "I ran the plate. It's registered to a Jeremiah McGrady. Ms. McKenzie, what are you doing with it?"

"He's my grandfather and I work for him. Now can you tell me what this is about?"

He started to walk to his car. "You wait right here while I make a call."

She watched him in her side-view mirror talk to someone on his phone. He came back and handed her the license.

"Sorry if I frightened you, but there's been a couple of equipment robberies on this road, and we've got an undercover operation underway." He gave her a wary look. "The way you were driving, I thought you were running from something."

She snapped the license from his fingers. "Really? What would I be running from?"

MISSY CAME OUT of the house toting a box of clothes. The wedding was coming up soon, and she and Dave would be living in his apartment until their trailer was set up. A car pulled in behind her, and Missy was amazed to see Mrs. Bishop in the front seat with Lucy. This was the first time she'd seen her out and about in years. Lucy had said she didn't even go grocery shopping anymore.

Lucy bounced out. "Hi, Missy. Is Belle around?"

"Not now."

"Please have her call me. It's important."

Missy's lips parted as she watched Lucy jump back in her car. She'd never seen her so animated. Her mother rolled down the window, and as they pulled away, gave her a big smile and blew her a kiss.

BEN GREGG WAS GETTING IMPATIENT with Jim Stevens as he drummed his fingers on the arm of his den chair, waiting for his secretary to get him on the phone. Ben had called him twice today from his office and left messages. But when he didn't return the calls, the strong possibility that he might be avoiding him gave him a headache, and he'd gone home early.

Jim finally came to the phone.

"Ben. Sorry I couldn't get back to you. You know how it is."

Ben didn't like the breezy way that sounded.

"Did you check on Jack Hale?"

"Oh, everything's fine with that. He's retired and living in Mexico, of all places."

"Just as I thought. It was a bluff. Did you find the disclaimer?"

"Of course, Ben. We never lose track of that kind of thing."

Jim cleared his throat. Another sound Ben didn't like.

"Ben, we settled with Mrs. Bishop this morning."

"Why in the hell did you do that?"

"You've got to understand, Ben, I'm number two right now, and the president's one board meeting away from retirement. The last thing I need is to have even a whisper of this case rear its ugly head. Believe me, our boys had her sign everything they could think of to release us from any past or future culpability. We're all in the clear... including you."

Ben was stunned and worried at the same time. Nature's Seasons would have had to hand her a bundle, and he couldn't see Mr. Number Two going for it if he had to take the hit.

"I'm sorry, pal," Jim said, "but I had to throw you under the bus. I told them you messed up on your offense, and new facts just came to light. Our legal department has their hands full right now on other problems—I'm sure you've heard about them—and it was decided to get this thing swept under the carpet as soon as possible. The dust is just starting to settle on that damn recall we were slow on ordering, and we can't afford any more bad press right now." He was quiet for a moment. "Needless to say, our treasurer is pissed off. If I were you, Ben, I wouldn't count on getting any more business from us. That shouldn't bother you, Ben. After all, you got a good ride off us from throwing Mrs. Bishop under the bus."

He hung up.

"Where's the damn ice?" hollered Ben as Barbara strolled in the den with the bucket.

He quickly dropped in a cube and poured himself a glass of whiskey.

"Aren't you going to pour one for me?" Barbara asked.

"Pour it yourself."

She smiled and made herself a drink as he sat down.

"So Nature's Seasons caved," she said as she went over and sat across from him.

He looked at her with an incredulous expression.

She picked some lint from the arm of the chair. "Oh, I heard it all, darling. In fact, I decided to check out that nursing home myself today. I had to call half the places in the phone book, but I finally found Randy. That was very enterprising of me, don't you think, darling?"

Ben didn't like where this conversation was heading.

She made a droll face. "I didn't have to go farther than the lobby, actually."

"What the hell are you trying to say?"

"Nothing. Just that now my girls won't have to worry about—how did Belle put it—rumors, gossip and innuendos."

"What have you done?"

"Nothing... just arranged for Randy to be relocated to Carolina Living tomorrow."

"And just who's going to pay for it?"

"You are, darling. I told them you'd be there in the morning to sign all the papers."

BELLE WAS FINALLY DONE with picking everything up in town and was on her way back to the compound when Missy called her and told her about Lucy's visit.

"Something's happened. She wants you to call as soon as you can."

"Thanks."

"Belle?"

"What?"

"Nobody's going to jail, are they?"

"Don't worry. Not before your wedding, anyway."

Belle was sorry she'd said that. It hadn't been a good idea to let Missy in on all that Lucy and she had been up to, and she had to spend five minutes calming her down.

After that, Belle thought it was best to drive over to Lucy's and handle whatever had come up in person. But first, she had to drop off the engine and parts to Matt.

She drove Pap's truck straight into the garage and jumped out. Matt was at his workbench.

"Here's the new engine and your parts. I left Pap's keys in the ignition." She headed toward the door. "Can you let him know it's here?"

"Wait." He held out a piece of paper.

She went over and took it and looked at him questioningly.

"Give it to Lucy. One of my buddies thinks he might be able to use her."

Belle looked in his eyes. In them, she saw there was something he wanted to say but couldn't. If it was regret that whatever there had been between them could no longer exist, she would refuse to listen. There was silence as she tried hard not to let her yearnings show in her eyes as she prayed that the thing he wanted to say was that he loved her.

"Thanks," she finally said, and then left.

Grateful for Matt's lead, she hurried to the house for her truck, and wondered how much of what was going on he knew about. If Missy had told Dave, he'd be sure to tell Matt.

Before long, she was at the Bishop place. It looked so much smaller than she remembered from the window of the school bus. It needed paint, and the way some of the shingles curled, she wouldn't be surprised if the roof leaked, too.

Belle went up to the door. It suddenly burst open, and squeals of joy jumped out at her. Lucy and her mother wrapped their arms around her. Over their shoulders she could see the kitchen counters stacked with bags full of groceries. An open bottle of wine and two glasses sat on the table.

"What's happened?"

Lucy ran to the cupboard and took out a glass.

"Not one word till I pour you a drink."

Her mother raised her glass to be refilled after Lucy handed Belle hers.

"Here's to winning our lawsuit!" Lucy toasted.

Belle needed the drink. It was hard to believe this was actually happening. She pulled out a chair and sank down. Lucy's mother sat down next to her and squeezed her hand.

Lucy beamed from ear to ear. "It all happened so fast. Late yesterday my mother got a call from Nature's Seasons. They wanted to come to the house to discuss the lawsuit. I couldn't get you on your cell, so I called your house and your grandfather said you wouldn't be home till late."

Lucy squealed and clasped her hands in ecstasy. "And just like they said, they showed up exactly at nine. They sat down at this very table and pulled out a stack of papers. They told us something had come to their attention about my father's accident, and they wanted to settle."

Lucy ran to her purse and whisked out a folded sheet of paper. She tossed it on the table in front of Belle. "We asked the man at the bank to make a copy of the check before we deposited it."

Belle studied it, struck with amazement. She looked at the two glowing women. "This is one heck of a lot of money. What are you going to do with it?"

Mrs. Bishop gave Lucy a hug. "My girl's goin' back to school like she's always wanted."

Belle drove back to the house, stunned. This outcome had to stem from her visit to Ben, but that kind of money wouldn't come from the goodness of anyone's heart. Possibly it had something to do with all the bad press about Nature Season's latest recall. Or was it just timing? She accepted that she'd probably never know, and lamented that there was nothing high-profile about Randy's situation.

She suddenly became aware of being at the house, yet didn't remember how she got there.

CHAPTER TWENTY-THREE

"**P**ap's not going to eat with us tonight," said Missy as Belle walked in after her visit with the Bishops. Missy put two pieces of chicken under the broiler. "Well, are you gonna tell me about Lucy and her mom or not?"

"All the Bishops' money troubles are behind them," she said with a nonchalance stemming from shock. "Nature's Seasons gave them what they had asked for."

"I don't believe it," said Missy. "All that cloak and dagger stuff actually paid off."

"I don't know how, but it did."

"What about Randy?"

"That didn't work out so well. I'm planning on visiting him on Wednesday nights. I owe that to Jake and Mary." She shrugged. "It's better than nothing. Connie says that by my showing up on a regular basis he won't be overlooked." Belle put some plates on the table. "I'm also thinking of hiring her to spend an hour reading to him once a week." Belle didn't want to tell Missy she planned on contacting the D.A.'s office and the North Carolina Bar about Randy at the end of the season when she'd have more time to deal with it.

Belle looked around. "Where's Mac?"

"He followed me when I went over to the garage to ask Matt if he could take a look at my car tomorrow."

Belle got out vegetables for a salad and dropped them on the counter, wondering if Matt was still giving Mac treats, when he barked at the door to be let in.

Finished eating, they went upstairs, Missy to do more packing, and Belle to work on her cidery plans. After a while, Missy came in and flopped down on Belle's bed.

"I can't pack another thing until I empty those suitcases at Dave's."

The mention of a suitcase reminded Belle of the one she'd stuffed under her bed. She swung around in her chair and eyed Missy. "You want to open Mom's?"

"Where is it?"

Belle jumped up, pulled it out from under the bed and slapped it on top. "There!"

Missy was now standing next to her. "I'm afraid to open it," she said.

"I know. It's kinda creepy."

"I wonder if it's locked," said Missy.

Belle tried the hasps. They were a little rusty, but sprung open after a little coaxing.

Missy lifted the lid. "Phew! Talk about musty."

Lying on top was a large color photo—the cheap kind that folks get from temporary photo studios in big chain stores. Missy was a toddler and Belle couldn't have been over five. Belle thought it odd that Pap didn't have one like it. She and Missy looked so different, Missy with doll-like blue eyes and blond curls, and her with dark hair and green eyes.

Missy ran a finger over their held hands. "We were tight even back then."

Belle nodded.

"Do you think she was ever gonna come back for us?"

"I guess we'll never know."

They finished laying the clothes around the room and tried to picture their mother wearing them.

"Are you ever going to tell Pap that Randy's still alive?"

"I don't know."

Belle pushed aside some shoes in the suitcase and saw a

small bundle of letters. She picked it up and showed Missy. "Should we read them?"

"Why not?"

Belle put the bundle down, untied a narrow pink ribbon holding them together and picked one up. "Look. It's got Aunt Pam's address on it." She smiled inwardly. Even her mother counted on Pam.

Missy picked up another envelope and studied it. "They're from Randy Gregg." She curled her legs underneath her and took out the letter. "Oh, boy. This is gonna be good."

"I feel funny about this," Belle said, apprehensively.

Missy let out a squeal. "Look, he calls her Baby Doll."

Belle couldn't bring herself to invade her mother's privacy. She studied the photo and tried to remember a mother, but drew a sickening blank.

"Give me another one of those letters," said Missy, reaching out to her. Belle picked one up and put it in her hand, noticing the glee had faded from her face.

"What is it?"

"Gimme a minute."

Belle sank on the bed and watched Missy read.

Missy looked up and eyed her keenly, her face pinched.

"I don't know how to tell you this, Belle, but it says here, Randy's your father."

Belle sat stunned.

"He keeps saying it over and over again. Look. Read it for yourself."

Belle took it and read: "I wish to God I had known you were pregnant before they shipped me out to Nam."

Missy had pulled out another letter. "Oh, look at this one. She must have written him that Pap forced her to marry my dad." She looked at Belle. "Geez, we're half sisters."

Belle rose and walked over to the window in a stupor. "That's why he wanted to look at me."

"Who?"

"Randy. When I was there the other night. Can you imagine, he hadn't seen me for all these years. No wonder he was crying."

Missy shook her head at the poignancy of her mother's plight. "Imagine being forced to marry someone you don't love." They were silent for a while. "If you think back, that must've been why Pap was always so careful about never confronting us. After what he did to our mother, he must have blamed himself for her running off with Randy and getting everybody killed."

Belle went over and sat down next to Missy. She put her arm around her and squeezed. "But she got you out of it. That had to make it worth it."

Belle sat holding Missy and staring out into the distance. "That's what Pap was talking about when he told me he would never make me marry anyone." She got up, went to her closet and took a sweater off a hook. "I gotta get outta here, Missy. You wanna come?"

"No. I'm gonna stay here and read."

"Put everything back when you're finished, and shove it under the bed."

"I hope you're not gonna go after Pap about this," said Missy, concerned. "The wedding's only a few days away."

"Don't worry. The last thing I want to do is jeopardize that wedding. It's the only normal, happy thing we got goin' for us right now." She stood at the door and looked back at Missy. "And, Sis, don't dwell on Mom having to marry your father. You're the best thing to come out of all this."

Belle pulled on the sweater and ran down the stairs. Mac pranced around, knowing by her stride they were going somewhere. The days had grown longer now and it was a beautiful evening. The last scent of apple blossoms had faded, their drying petals still lying on the ground. Slight whiffs of Carolina jasmine drifted in on a breeze from time to time as she climbed the hill to the new grafts.

The sun was giving its final salute to the valley and sinking behind this secluded chunk of the Southern Blue Ridge Mountains. Draped in vivid new leaves, the trees in the distance shone chartreuse against the blazing red sky.

From this vantage she could see most of the valley, and she wondered how many hidden tragedies and disquieting secrets were cradled in its womb. She thought of the first McGrady to land in this place and wondered how many lies had been told since that time, and how many secrets kept in order to wed the clan to these mountain slopes.

She wished she knew if Pap had been aware her father was still alive and kept it from her all these years. No matter what the answer, nothing would change the way she felt about him; but it would change the way she saw the world—a place where, out of revenge, a man could be left to languish alone and unloved. She looked across at the rolling rows of trees. The orchard's endless annual cycle was a metaphor for life—only, the misdeeds wrought on the orchard by nature were less capricious than the sins inflicted on humanity by fate.

Mac curled up at her feet, and she reached down and petted him as she thought about the pain fate had rained down on this one little family. She could still see Mary's eyes well up with tears when she asked her if she could call her Grandma. Why, God? Why couldn't I, just once, have called Jake Grandpa? Everything made sense—the truck, the rug, the orchard, the love. Why didn't I see it?

She thought about Pap. All these years, the guilt he was carrying had to weigh on his heart. And then she thought of herself and felt a sudden release. This was the way things went; she was just another bead in the McGrady necklace, taking things as they came.

It was now dark, and in the valley below, houses glowed from within like Chinese lanterns, making her wonder what kind of dramas were playing out within them. Little by little the lights were extinguished, and all the secrets locked away for the night.

She got up, brushed herself off and walked back to the house with Mac. A small lamp on the counter barely lit the kitchen. She switched it off, and the dancing shadows from the flames in the living room fireplace drew her there.

Pap was in his rocker. She approached it and lovingly placed her hands on his shoulders and gave his solid, thickset muscles a gentle massage, then she bent down and kissed his cheek. She tasted the salt of his now dried tears and knew Missy had told him about everything—her search for Mary, Lucy's mother, the encounter with Ben; but she knew that her discovery of who her father really was, touched him the most, for he was one of the major players in that tragedy.

She sat down on the worn oak arm of the chair, put her arm around his shoulder and stared at the dwindling fire until his low, raspy voice broke the silence.

"That's the way they did things in those days. Your daughter got in trouble and you either sent her out of town and gave the baby away, or you had a shotgun wedding." Except for the crackling of the fire, the room was silent for a long moment. "There was no way I was going to give a McGrady away. Jake's boy had been drafted and sent to Vietnam, so I got a farmhand we had just put on to go along with it instead. He wasn't much, but he was willing."

Belle felt a killing pang of gratitude and gave him a tender squeeze. If he had given her away, she never would have been of that place and of that clan, a prospect that seemed unthinkable, for that was her very essence. She lay her head on his shoulder and stared into the fire.

"I want you to know I had no idea that boy was still alive." He paused. "I wish you had let me help you with everything. Especially him."

"Would you've?"

"I'd of supposed that poor boy had suffered enough, and done what I could."

"Pap, we gotta help him."

"We will, honey. We will. There's plenty of ways to get that guy to release that money for your father. I'll talk to George."

Belle kissed his cheek. What he did to her mother and father was a heartbreak he'd have to bear, but he did what he thought he had to do to keep the baby that was his flesh and blood. She was overcome with love for this man who had taken care of her even before she was born, and she felt, more than ever before, she was a part of him. She hadn't done the same for her little seedling, and she had long accepted that it would always be her heartbreak to never know him.

"I love you, Pap."

"I love you too, sweetheart."

This was the first time she had heard Pap say he loved her, and she remembered all the years of yearning that he would. She smiled to herself. He had told her he loved her a million times in a million different ways.

IN SPITE OF BEING EMOTIONALLY DRAINED, the next day Belle made it into the office. That afternoon, she finished phoning in an order for some chemicals when her cell rang. It was Connie.

"Randy's not here!"

"What do you mean?"

"I just came in and they told me he was transferred this morning."

A fear that Ben had stashed her father somewhere she couldn't find struck her with terror. "Can you find out where?"

"Oh, I know where. Carolina Living. One of the nicest nursing homes in Western North Carolina! Right in Hendersonville."

Belle was speechless.

Connie rattled on. "His aunt was here yesterday and made all the arrangements."

Belle wondered why Barbara was doing this. Of course. She must have come downstairs and listened to the whole story. Then she again remembered what Barbara had told her after she had all Jake's cartons put in her truck—Jake said she had always been fair.

"I'm going to miss him," Connie said in a teary-eyed voice.

Belle sounded equally teary-eyed. "Last night I found out he's my father."

Connie was quiet and Belle suspected she was crying.

"I knew who you were the minute I listened to your message on my phone," said Connie, sniffling. "That's why I took the chance to meet with you."

"How could you know?"

"He'd told me he had a daughter named Annabelle who didn't know he existed."

"Why in God's name didn't you tell me?"

"I couldn't. I promised him I'd never tell anyone. I begged him to let me find you and tell you about him, but he wouldn't let me. He said it would just hurt you. Knowing you were out there somewhere, tore me apart. Your phone call was a godsend."

Struck by the simple loyalty this kindly person had shown her father, Belle was suddenly aware of and grateful for the legions of people who care for the forgotten.

"Thank you, Connie. I'll never forget you for all the kindness you showed my father." They didn't speak for a moment, then Belle said, "I'd like to hire you to visit him once a week and read to him for an hour. Can you do it?"

"I would like that."

Belle said goodbye and left for the nursing home. Earlier that day, Pap had gotten George on the phone, and she told him about the eight-page memo and the trust fund. He had said he would do the best he could, but felt the most they could hope for was to get Ben to put her in charge of the trust. The rest of the money, he felt, was gone and not worth a lengthy lawsuit they probably wouldn't win.

She pulled into the huge, nicely landscaped complex and went in the main entrance. Someone at the desk had her fill out a form and referred her to their continuous care unit.

A nurse greeted her with a smile as she entered the wing. "The main desk just phoned. I'll go ask Mr. Gregg if he wants to see you." She eyed Belle as if she wondered how much she knew about her patient. "We've got strict instructions... from him."

"Tell him it's his daughter, Belle. Also tell him I'm only coming in if he'll see me face to face."

The nurse gave her a sympathetic smile. "I wouldn't count on it, dear."

"That's okay; you tell him that just the same."

The nurse returned, trying to hide her concern. "Come with me." She stopped at a door and pushed it open a tad and stopped. "I'll be right out here in case you need me."

Belle nervously gripped the paperback book and walked in.

Her father sat staring blankly ahead. She went up to him, looked him in the eye and smiled. "Hello, Father," she said, then kissed him on the forehead. She pulled a chair near and sat down, then opened the book and began to read. *"Patriot Games* by Tom Clancy." Her voice cracked and she gulped hard, then continued reading. "A Sunny Day in Londontown. Ryan was nearly killed in half an hour..."

"YOU ARE A THING TO BEHOLD," said Pam as she studied Belle in her red bridesmaid dress.

Belle slipped on a pair of red high heels. "I hope I don't kill myself in these."

"Well, you've got four days to get used to them."

Hearing another car pull up, Belle pulled aside the ruffled chintz curtains in Pam's living room and looked out at the driveway. Missy's two best friends from the salon bubbled out. She looked over at Pam. "The girls are here."

"Okay. I'll take them upstairs. When the guys arrive, have them try everything on in the den."

Pam let the giggling girls in, and they ran up the stairs behind her, waving hello to Belle. Belle carefully took off her dress and hung it up. She heard someone pull in, and then someone else. She got a quick glimpse of Matt and Dave pouring out of their vehicles. Pap's truck came to a screeching halt right behind them. Quickly, she slipped into her jeans and top.

The three rushed in like they didn't have a minute to spare. Belle handed them their suits and sent Dave and Matt to the den before leading Pap to a small office next to the kitchen. She quickly hung the tux on a door and took the pants off the hanger. "Here, put these on," she ordered.

"Not with you standing there."

"Come on, Pap. I've seen you in your shorts a million times." She pulled a shirt from the package and shook it out.

Pap grudgingly took off his jeans and put on the pants. By the time he got to the shirt and jacket he had run out of patience.

"Can I go now?"

Belle said yes, helped him get everything off and went about putting it back on hangers. She came from the kitchen to see the two girls gleefully chasing each other to their car carrying their dresses and shoes and waving goodbye.

Pam looked contented. "Do you believe it? Everything fit." She looked around. "Where's Pap?"

"Gone."

Pam ran her hand affectionately down Belle's face. "You'll have him looking good on Saturday?"

Belle nodded. "You won't know it's him."

Matt and Dave came from the den dressed in their street clothes. Dave said hello to Pam and quickly announced he had to get back to work as he hurried out the door.

Matt called out, "You forgot your tux."

"Belle, can you give it to Missy tonight?" he hollered back. "I gotta get to work."

"He's a nervous wreck," said Matt.

"As his best man, you're gonna have to get him dressed and to the church on time," said Pam.

Just then, Pam's husband came into the kitchen from the back door. He went up to Belle and gave her a warm hug. "How's our big hero doing?"

Belle tried to hide her embarrassment.

He opened the fridge and pulled out a loaf of bread. "Don't look at me that way, sweetie. You should be proud. The Bishops are singing your praises all over the valley."

Pam got busy making her husband a sandwich while he answered his phone, and Belle and Matt drifted toward the door. Matt draped his tux over his arm and reached for the doorknob. He turned and gave Belle one of his chiding looks, and she prepared herself for an admonition from a man who spent eight years in a Catholic school.

"If they only knew how you two little vixens pulled that deal off." He looked up at the ceiling. "Let's see. There was breaking and entering... stealing a computer, oh yeah... let's not forget contributing to the delinquency of a minor."

Belle looked at him through squinted lids.

He threw his head back and let out a sarcastic laugh. "And

then there's my personal favorite—*forgery.*"

Belle's lips twisted.

"There I was, sitting at my desk, when I saw a little piece of paper on the blotter with Jake's signature carefully cut out." He looked at her. "Don't worry, honey, I chewed it up and swallowed it."

Belle smirked. "Not funny."

Matt was still clutching the doorknob. The wry look on his face dissolved. "Dave told me about your father. I'm glad you found him."

Belle's eyes swept from side to side.

"I would've helped you if you had let me." He opened the door and turned to leave, then stopped and looked back at her again. "You know what Pap said about everything?"

"I can imagine."

"She's my right arm," he said, "and she'll fight for me and this farm just as hard."

Belle put all the outfits in her truck, said goodbye to Pam and her husband and drove home replaying Matt's words. Was he sending her a message, that between the two of them, she was the chosen one. They'd never spoken of it; however, since they were kids they both knew that they were competing for her grandfather's approval.

It wasn't anything Pap had encouraged or even wanted; it was simply something the two of them couldn't restrain. Yet no matter how much Pap loved Matt, the birthright was hers, and Matt knew it ever since the day the hailstorm wiped out their Honeycrisps and Pap picked her over him to report on the damage.

But it was more than the sheer accident of birth, thought Belle. She'd somehow inherited the unique combination of genes that had made both her and her grandfather stubborn fighters and ceaseless risk takers, a fact that had been apparent to Pap since that day at the age of ten when she jumped on their new John Deere and drove it into the barn. More importantly, both Pap and she were keenly aware that these two characteristics were vital to the perpetuation of the McGrady legacy.

Then something else entered her mind. Could it be possible that Matt was sending her another message—was he asking her if she was willing to fight that hard to win and keep him?

CHAPTER TWENTY-FOUR

T HE McGRADY'S WEREN'T ONES to put on an ostentatious wedding. With all their land, trees and all else they had scraped together over the generations, they were worth millions, yet they were always careful to act in such a way that most folks would never even suspect it. But when it came to pictures that would be viewed by posterity, Missy didn't care what it cost and who knew about it, and she pulled out all the stops.

The wedding was held at the Methodist church Pap had sometimes taken the girls to, and the reception, on the lawn of Pam's country club.

Belle stood between Dave and another bridesmaid as the photographer got everyone into position. A cluster of guests milled around and watched the activity. A breeze kept billowing Missy's dress and the shot had to be taken a dozen times.

"Next, we need the Maid of Honor and the Best Man," announced the photographer.

Belle knew it was coming, but hadn't anticipated such a big audience. Matt, who was now standing next to her, didn't seem to know what to do with his hands until the photographer whispered for him to put an arm around her waist. Belle felt his hand on her—a touch she knew.

The photographer took a few steps back and said, "A little closer."

Matt pulled her close enough for her to breathe in his scent.

A broad grin appeared on the photographer's face. "Perfect."

Someone remarked, loud enough for her and Matt to hear, what a beautiful couple the two of them made, making Belle blush. She caught glimpses of Missy being congratulated by a series of guests, and when she turned and smiled at Belle, she knew her sister had engineered the pose. Several shots were taken, and Matt kept holding her until the photographer told him that was enough, and he self-consciously let her go.

Belle hung around and watched Pap and Missy get their picture taken, then Pap and Pam. Pap suddenly swept his sister up in his arms and she kicked her feet in the air, making everyone laugh. Belle had never seen him in such high spirits. The photographer announced that he was finished with the McGrady side of the family, and then started on Dave's.

Music from the D.J.'s booth played underneath the warm hum of conversations as Belle drifted over to the bar. She stood with a glass of wine, watching people stroll around or sit talking at one of the draped tables decorated with clusters of red roses. Helen and Raphael huddled with their brood and little Danny at the far end of the lawn. Belle wanted to go over and make them feel more at home, but not when Matt was with them, as he now was.

Everyone's attention seemed to be drawn to the dance floor.

"The bride and groom will now dance for their first time as husband and wife," a voice blared from the amp.

Missy took everyone's breath away as she walked onto the dance floor. Seeing that Pap was choking up, Belle made her way over to him and squeezed his hand. Knowing that he would soon have to dance with the bride, Belle whispered, "Are you gonna be okay?"

He took a kerchief from his pocket and wiped his eyes. "I guess I'll have to be."

Across the dance floor, she could see Matt leaving his parents' side. Her eyes kept straying from Missy and Dave as he wove through the crowd toward her and Pap. Now, with Missy's dance over, she couldn't take her eyes off him. He was no longer a shy, skinny kid trying to fit in. Never had he looked so stalwart and confident; never had she wanted him more. He reached them just as the D.J. made the announcement.

"Next, we have the bride's sister and Maid of Honor, Belle McKenzie, and the groom's Best Man, Matt Sanchez."

Belle was aware of his warm hand on the bare spot on her back as he led her to the dance floor. She turned to face him, then placed one hand on his shoulder. Somehow her other trembling hand found his as the music started. When Whitney Houston crooned, "I will always love you," Belle struggled to blink back tears. She gave Missy a quick glance and saw she had pressed her crossed fingers close to her heart. Belle's cheek accidently brushed against Matt's and she felt the heat, drawing her eyes to his for an instant before he looked away.

The dance finished, and they walked back to where Pap was standing with Pam who was kindly giving him support before his upcoming dance with Missy.

"Do you think Jeremiah's going to make it without breaking down?" Belle whispered to Pam as Pap left their side and took Missy's hand.

Her great aunt slipped one arm around Belle's waist and another around Matt's. "If he's made it through you two, he'll make it through anything."

Belle blanched. Only her great aunt would casually acknowledge what no one else would dream of mentioning.

Belle quickly changed the subject. "Pap sure looks proud of Missy."

Just then, George came up behind Belle. Tall and husky, he put an arm around her and gave her a peck on the cheek. "He's plenty proud of you, too." He noticed Matt, and they vigorously shook hands like old friends, not two people in a client/lawyer relationship. Something Belle took note of.

George gave Belle another squeeze and whispered in her ear, "Don't worry, honey, we'll get that trust away from that bastard."

The D.J. called for the rest of the wedding party to come onto the dance floor. Belle felt self-conscious, wondering if Matt was going to ask her to dance, when he put his arm around her waist and led her to the floor.

With the platform now crowded, there weren't as many eyes on Belle and Matt and they fell into conversation.

"How long have you known George?" Belle asked.

"They invite me sit in on their poker games when one of the guys can't make it."

"Well, well. You're certainly in high cotton these days."

He raised an eyebrow and gave her the smart-alecky look he always did when she hurt his feelings, and she was sorry she said it.

"Not bad for someone who wasn't born in it," he shot back.

She brushed something off his shoulder, making him scrunch up his neck and look. "What was that?"

"Just a chip."

He laughed. "I'll give you that one."

Someone bumped into her and she was thrown against Matt. The way his firm grip easily steadied her made her aware of the muscular strength he'd gained from the years of physical demands an orchard man has to face.

They accepted the teenager's apologies and continued dancing. Matt's grasp gradually loosened, but not to where it had been before the incident. She pressed her cheek against his, and the heat of him made her close her eyes and dig her fingers into his shoulder.

He stopped dancing and gently pulled her away from him. "I'm sorry. I can't do this." He led her off the floor and walked away.

She stood devastated, when two small arms suddenly came from behind and wrapped around her hips. She turned to see Danny grinning up at her. He was wearing long pants and a white shirt. She crouched down and clutched his shoulders. She smiled through tears as she studied him.

He tossed his head and made a little face. "You're doin' it again," he said.

She laughed and wiped her eyes with the back of her hand.

"It's because I'm so happy for my sister."

"You look pretty."

"And you look very nice," she said as she straightened his tie.

He stood erect and threw out his small chest. "Everything's brand new."

She laughed and hugged him, afraid she wouldn't be able to let go.

"Anyone wanting to join in the line dancing, come on up," spilled from the amp.

Belle jumped up and grabbed Danny's hand. "Come on, buddy. Let's have some fun."

Everyone was in high spirits and forgiving of Belle and Danny turning in the wrong direction and bumping into them. A deep row of onlookers encircled the dance line, and every once in a while Belle caught a glimpse of Matt in the background watching them. As for Pap and Matt's mother, they never took their eyes away.

The third line-dance ended, and Belle was walking hand in hand with Danny toward the Sanchez clan when Matt stepped in front of her. He took Danny's other hand and gently pulled him away.

"Come on, son. We gotta go."

By now, Missy and Dave had gone, and Pap and Dave's parents were saying their final goodbyes to the guests. Pam gave Belle a ride home, and she didn't hear from Pap again until he came in after she went to bed.

Belle made as much noise on Sunday as she could, not wanting Pap to feel the hollowness of the house with Missy gone, even though they had hardly laid eyes on her for the past month. Because Dave had already taken one week off and would have to use his only other vacation week to work at the roadstand in September, they were spending their honeymoon in town at his apartment.

By Monday, the farm was back in its usual routine with Pap on the phone talking to clients and Matt speaking in Spanish to pickers he was lining up for the season. Belle, sitting at her desk, scanned the list of items Pap had jotted down for her to order and was about to pick up the phone, when it rang.

"Hey, sweetheart. When are you gonna come pick up your stuff?"

Belle recognized Ken's voice. "We'll get it in the next couple days," she said and hung up without saying goodbye.

"What are we pickin' up?" asked Pap.

Belle made eye contact with him, then threw a glance over to Matt, hoping her grandfather would get the hint.

But he didn't and just stared at her. "Well?"

"They want me to get my workbench and shed out of Jake's place."

Pap's eyes quickly focused on Matt, who was bent over his desk, pretending he didn't know what was going on. Pap picked up his phone and got Carlos. "You still using the big flatbed?" He listened for a moment. "Good. Take it with a trailer over to the old Gregg place and pick up a workbench and shed." He looked over at Belle. "Where are they?"

Matt's chair rolled across the floor and slammed against the wall as he stood up. "I know where they are. Tell Carlos to load the forklift."

Matt went to the door and opened it. Looking blankly ahead into the stairwell, he asked, "Where do you want them?"

"In my orchard. Next to the water spigot," said Belle.

He left, and Belle bit her lip and turned to Pap.

He shook his head. "I hope he doesn't kill him."

MATT RAN DOWN THE STAIRS and drove over to the barn where Carlos was driving the forklift onto the trailer.

"I'll take it," Matt hollered as he got into the truck's cab. "Try and get a couple more guys and meet me over there," he shouted as he pulled away.

Other than the Volvo parked in the lot, there was no sign anyone was around when Matt pulled into Jake's place. A huge pitiful void lay where the orchard used to be. A lone dwarf apple tree sat in a newly planted perennial garden hugging the house.

Matt jumped from the cab and quickly unhitched the ramp at the rear of the trailer. He backed the forklift off, then went over and sized up the workbench. Seeing it had been built in two sections, he tried to figure out how they could be separated without damage. If they could get it into two pieces, it would fit on the truck's bed and leave room for the shed.

Carlos pulled in with only one of their farmhands, and he and Matt got busy on the bench with two pry bars. Once it was pulled apart, they hefted the shortest piece onto the truck bed. It was a struggle lifting the other section until Ken appeared, grabbed one corner and helped them heave it on.

Ken strolled over to Matt. "Ken Larsen," he said, offering a hand. "I figure you're Matt Sanchez."

Matt ignored him and told Carlos, "Let's get the shed next."

Carlos lined up the forklift and eased it under, but when he tried to raise it, it began to keel over.

"There's no floor and the forks couldn't reach the far wall to stabilize it. We're gonna have to go back to the farm and get some planks to shove under it," said Carlos.

Matt impatiently waved the comment aside. "Let's just pull up the trailer, tip the shed and drop it on. We can come back for the forklift later."

Matt made a sudden turn and bumped into Ken. They stood face to face, and for a moment, it looked like Matt was going to take a swing.

Ken, who was inches from Matt's face, said, "Okay. I get it. You can't stand me. Now, we can either bump chests and see who wins, or we can get this shed the hell out of here."

Someone called out Ken's name, and they all looked over towards the house. A beautiful girl in shorts and a tee-shirt that she more than did justice to, stood at the door.

"Are you coming, Kenny?" she sang out.

"I'll be right there."

Matt clenched his fists and clamped his jaw. "You bastard." He tossed his head toward the girl. "Is she next?"

Ken appeared bewildered. "What are you talking about?"

"What do you think?"

Ken gripped the back of his neck and spun halfway around. "I hope to hell you aren't giving that kid a hard time."

"Not as hard of a time as I bet you did."

Carlos stepped between them and put a hand on his brother's shoulder. "Come on, let's load the shed and get outta here."

"Oh, no, you don't," said Ken. "We're gonna get everything right out in the open, here and now." He glared at Matt. "What has she told you?"

"She didn't need to tell me anything."

"Listen, buddy. I never laid a hand on her." He looked away. "I admit... I got a good look..." His eyes shot back at Matt, "...but I never touched her. The only reason she spent the night, was because she was so shit-faced she passed out."

"And you took advantage of it."

"You know what stopped me? All she could mumble was, 'Matt, I love you.' That kind of thing really cools a guy off." He looked at Matt and shook his head. "In case you don't know it, buddy, that girl's really something. I don't know how she got so stuck on you."

For an instant, Matt was stunned, then the vision of them in each other's arms aroused his ire. "Is that why she kissed you here a couple weeks ago?"

"Sure. She kissed me. You want to know why?" He walked to the garden and pointed to the brass marker near the foot of the apple tree. "That little marker got to me, and I just couldn't push the damn thing over." He looked at Matt. "You want to know what it says? 'The Accordian. Annabelle McKenzie's First Graft at the Age of Twelve.'" Ken folded his arms and gazed at it for a moment, then looked around and saw Matt had gone.

He was talking to Carlos.

"Where are your keys?"

"In the ignition."

Matt raced to Carlos' truck, jumped in and took off.

PAP KNEW BELLE was doing her darndest to look busy. "Stay off your phone in case anyone needs to reach us," he said.

She stood up. "I think I better go over there."

"You sit right down. He's a grown man, and he's got to settle this himself."

Raphael walked in, looking concerned.

"Sit down," Pap told him. "They've got to work it out between them."

The sudden screeching of brakes made them all freeze, then the stomping of boots taking the stairs two at a time drew their eyes to the door. It flew open. Matt's face was flushed and his muscles taut. He gave Pap a fleeting look and then Raphael. He went to Belle's desk and stopped short. She looked up at him, frightened.

"Where's your wallet?"

She feebly pointed to the corner of her desk without taking her eyes from him. He reached for it and opened it to where all the cards were kept. He pulled out her license and looked at her.

"Where's your social security card?"

A bewildered Belle answered, "It's tucked underneath."

He pulled some items from a hidden pocket, took one, and stuffed everything else back in. He reached down and pulled her up. "Let's go."

"Where?"

"The county court house." The look between them lasted less than a minute, but in it was a yearning that could break a heart. "We're getting married."

He took her in his arms and gave her a kiss that made Pap turn away and Raphael make the sign of the cross. Matt finally released her and she fought to catch her breath.

He ran a knuckle down the contours of her face. "I was wrong, Belle. I was wrong about the spindles. I was wrong about the antique apples... and I was wrong about you. I love you, Belle, and I'm sorry... for everything."

He gently wiped the tears streaming down her face. "Can you still love me?"

She looked into his eyes. "I never stopped."

He gripped her arms and gently kissed her forehead and tenderly nuzzled her cheek. "Are you okay with getting married in the courthouse?"

She looked into his eyes. "I'd marry you anywhere."

A smile slowly crept across Matt's face as if he were coming to the realization that Belle was finally his. He suddenly let out a joyful yelp and swept her off her feet. "Then let's get it on! It's been one hell of a wait."

He swung around with her in his arms to face Pap and Raphael. "You two comin'?"

"Oh, yeah. We're comin'," said Pap.

As Matt started out the door with Belle in his arms, she frantically called out, "Pap, call Missy and Pam." Her cry for Raphael to get Helen and Danny faded as the door slowly closed behind them.

Pap went to the window and waited for the two to emerge from the building. He watched Matt let Belle slide to the ground and kiss her again. He watched Matt open his truck door, sweep her up again, and put her triumphantly on the front seat like she was the prize he'd always wanted. He saw Belle smile up at him, her face glistening with tears.

Raphael tapped him on the shoulder. "Jeremiah, we go now?"

Pap turned around, pulled out his kerchief and wiped his eyes. He smiled at Raphael. "Hell, yeah. I wouldn't miss this for the world."

EPILOG

Five years later

"HAND ME ANOTHER BAG, Danny." Belle reached over and took it from him. She carefully covered the pistil she had just crossed with pollen from one of Jake's antique apples. All four hundred of them had been planted in this, her new heritage orchard up on the compound's hill overlooking the valley. Danny had already torn off a piece of tape and was handing it to her. She took it and wrapped it tightly around the base of the bag.

"There. Nothing else is going to touch it now." She attached a tag. "That's my M-18, and I've crossed it with an apple called Arthur."

Danny smiled at her. "Mom, I love you and all your stories." He tossed his head. "Go on, tell it to me."

She winked at him. "It's named after a boy just about your age."

Belle gathered up some of her supplies. "He was a preacher's son who had snapped off a switch from a wild apple tree to use as a riding crop. At the end of the day, he stuck it into the ground and it rooted."

She put her arms around him and brushed back a shock of wavy blond hair from his forehead. "The tree turned out to have pretty decent apples and they called it the Arthur. There's sup-

279

posed to be a couple of them still growing in Ashe County."

She handed him an empty carton and he started collecting the rest of the supplies. Mac, who had been lying in the sun, saw it as a signal she was preparing to leave. He got up and took a couple stiff steps toward her.

She reached down and patted his head. "Your arthritis is bad today, huh, boy?" The dog's ears perked up and he turned his attention toward the top of the hill, making Belle and Danny look up. Matt was coming from their new house with their two little girls gleefully running out ahead of him. She watched him come toward her, and the years of yearning rolled over her like a tide. Never did he look so manly, and never did she want him more.

Matt strode over and gave her a peck on the cheek while the girls ran squealing into Danny's arms, knocking him over, laughing.

"How many did you get pollinated?" Matt asked.

"Twenty," she said as she walked over to Jake's old workbench and brushed it off with a whiskbroom. "What do you think of the floors?"

"They make the house, honey."

It was hard for her to believe that they were finally going to live on the very piece of land overlooking the valley that Pap had promised to give them all those years back. "When do you think we'll be able to move in?"

"They're gonna finish installing the kitchen next week, but now that the floors are down, we can start bringing things in whenever you're ready."

"Coming over here is gonna be tough on Pap," mused Belle. "He's been living in that house since his mother Myrtle gave his father the money to buy this place."

"Well, if he doesn't move out with us, he'll be waking up every morning in bed with Carlos and his family." He chuckled as he looked up at the new house. "He likes it. We took some of his stuff to his room yesterday, and he looked around and said, 'Not bad for someone who was born in a log cabin.'"

Matt checked his phone. "We've got to get going. Missy will

kill us if we're late for that big shindig of hers."

He called out. "Danny! Start back down to the house with the girls."

Belle folded Bubba's cover over and snapped it shut. "Can you believe it," she said, dreamily. "Our Missy putting McGrady's Cidery on the map. Who'da thought it?"

She put Bubba in the box of supplies and was about to start down with it when she noticed that Matt had wandered over to the first row of trees. He turned to her and they stood looking at each other. The trees behind him were in full bloom, and the sky above a heavenly blue.

The sun was warm on the blossoms, misting their scent into the air and drawing the bees. This annual rite of propagation stimulated Belle's awareness of the cycle of life all around her and she went to him. He understood and kissed her long and with promise.

Matt put an arm around her shoulder and they looked out at the heirloom orchard.

"I'm glad we planted Jake's trees here," said Matt. "Once we move in, every time you look out, you'll see 'em."

Belle gazed at the endless billows of white blossoms, but all she saw was Pap filling with pride as he watched tractorloads of apples rumble towards their cold storage building. She heard little Missy shrieking in joy as she chased her through the now-gone Rome orchard. And she saw Jake at his kitchen table showing her how to graft. The memories of what it had taken to save his trees and the thought of what McGrady's Cidery now meant to their little clan streamed through her head.

Little Elizabeth came running back to her father, and Matt picked her up. "Don't you want to walk home with Danny and your sister?"

"No. Danny's mean. He wouldn't let me pick the apple blossoms."

Matt laughed and patiently explained to her why she couldn't.

The sweet smell of the blossoms lingered in Belle's nostrils and she thought about Jake. She told him to tell Mary she was taking care of her boy and was now his guardian. She told him of the first time she visited Randy as his daughter, and then laughed to herself remembering how all the two of them could handle was her reading *Patriot Games.* The corners of her lips turned slightly upward and she told Jake about her two girls and Matt visiting his boy; and how, when Pap had gone to see him, she was sure that in his own way, her grandfather had told him how sorry he was that things had worked out the way they had.

Danny came running up to them. Breathless, he put a cluster of five petals in Elizabeth's hand. "Are you happy now? Let's go," he said as he lifted her from Matt's arms.

As Belle watched Danny take Elizabeth's hand and lead her down the lane, she told Jake she finally had her boy, for she had taken Danny as her own. Then she smiled again and told him all the empty places in her heart were now filled.

Matt put his arm around her waist and pulled her to him. "What are you thinking about, honey?"

"Nothing much."

A breeze ruffled a plastic bag on one of the trees.

"Honey, with these twenty, how many have you pollinated all together?"

"Hundreds. But it doesn't matter how many. I'm gonna live a long life, and somewhere out there—in that very orchard—is the Carolina Belle... and one of these days, I'm gonna find it."

ACKNOWLEDGEMENTS

Most of my research on the history of Southern apples was drawn from the book entitled *Old Southern Apples* by Creighton Lee Calhoun, Jr. In fact, the character of "Jake" is loosely based on "Lee" and his efforts to collect old Southern apple trees he'd found in farms and fields throughout the South and now grows in his orchard in Pittsboro, North Carolina. An agronomist, his book is a comprehensive study of Southern apples and a fascinating chronicle of their storied past. He has been a friend and mentor throughout the writing of CAROLINA BELLE, and I am greatly indebted to him. Another book that helped in my research is *The Botany of Desire—A Plants-Eye View of the World* by Michael Pollan.

The Apple Valley is an actual place on Route 64 in Henderson County, North Carolina, and many of the characters in this book have been inspired by the farmers whose families have been growing apples there for generations. Many of the charming and character-revealing stories related by "Pam" in the book are loosely based on Pat Freeman's memories of her mother Ida and her father Walter, and growing up in this apple community. The photo on the cover was taken from the Freeman Orchards on Route 64.

I greatly appreciate the hands-on knowledge of the industry imparted by Marvin Owings, Jr., County Extension Director, North Carolina Cooperative Extension Service-Henderson

County, during his weekly work projects in an orchard where he grows and tests experimental new apple varieties in conjunction with the Master Pomology course he teaches.

I want to thank Kenny Barnwell and Don Ward, whose reflections and knowledge of the industry contributed greatly to this portrait of this farming community. I am grateful to Sandra Coston, Tony Hill, Susie Justus Hill, Faye Dalton, Sonja Hollingsworth and Jean Marie Saltz, who were all kind enough to share their memories of growing up in Henderson County's Apple Valley.

I am especially grateful to my early readers who generously offered helpful suggestions and valuable criticism: Jackie Price, LuVerne Haydock, Annie Pott, Madelyn Owneby, Alice Garrard, Danny Holland, Pat Freeman, Ronnie Oechsner, Paris Capozziello and April S. Young, all of whom have gone on this journey with me and given me their support and considerable wisdom.

It's always a delight to visit book clubs and conduct discussion sessions on one of my novels that they are reading. At these gatherings, I have met scores of interesting and vivacious personalities. What a breath of fresh air and an honor it is for this writer to mingle amongst the very folks for whom I write. And when I do, I can't help bouncing off characters and plot twists from the book I am usually writing.

While writing *CAROLINA BELLE,* I mentioned to these book club members that I'd put the person who came up with the name of the apple my heroine was looking for in the book. I received dozens of excellent suggestion but chose the name put forth by Charlotte "Char" Wojcik, a member of a book club in the Carriage Park community of Hendersonville, North Carolina.

I am also honored and grateful to Emöke B'Rácz, the beloved poet and founder of Malaprop's Bookstore and Downtown Books and News in Asheville, for taking the time to read *CAROLINA BELLE* and for offering her kind endorsement on the back cover.

ABOUT THE AUTHOR

*C**arolina Belle* is Rose Senehi's eighth novel and the fifth "stand alone" book in her Blue Ridge Series.

"Chimney Rock has been my permanent residence for eight years, and I am more in love with these mountains and the people within them than ever before.

"How I happened to write about our apple farmers stemmed from curiosity. Coming from New York state, I enjoyed eating the Empire apple, but found they tasted differently here in the South. So, I went to one of the many apple stands on Route 64 in Hendersonville, NC, picked up an empty bag and went from bin to bin, selecting one apple from each and writing its name on the skin. After eating them all, I decided I liked the Winesap the best, but when I couldn't find them that winter in the grocery store, I looked them up on the internet and discovered they were an antique variety that the early Colonists grew.

"From there, my curiosity picked up speed, and I ended up spending almost two years researching the history of this prolific apple growing region and the apple in general. Along the way, I have met and learned to respect all the wonderful hard-working people who make up the apple growing community of Henderson County, NC.

"I'm hoping that once you read *Carolina Belle,* you'll never look at an apple the same way again... I know I won't!

"The five 'stand alone' novels in my Blue Ridge Series are part family saga, part mystery and part love story. Through them, I have strived to paint a portrait of the mountain culture I have fallen in love with, and portray historical events as accurately as possible. I do hope you enjoy them."

P.S. I especially enjoy leading discussion groups with book clubs.

BLUE RIDGE SERIES of Stand-Alone Books

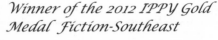

Render Unto the Valley. *Karen Godwell isn't as much ashamed of her mountain heritage as of what she once had to do to preserve it.* She reinvents herself at college and doesn't look back till her clan's historic farm is threatened. She returns only to come face to face with who she was and what she did. Cousin Bruce sees life through the family's colorful two-hundred-year past; Tom Gibbons, a local conservationist, keeps one eye on the mountains and the other on Karen. Her nine-year-old daughter is on the mission her dying father sent her on.

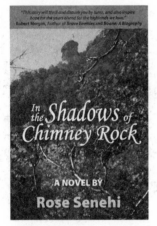

In the Shadows of Chimney Rock. *A touching tale of Family and Place.* A Southern heiress reaches out to her mountain roots for solace after suffering a life-shattering blow, only to be drawn into a fight to save the beauty of the mountain her father loved. Hayden Taylor starts to heal in the womb of the gorge as she struggles to redeem her father's legacy, never suspecting the man who killed him is stalking her.

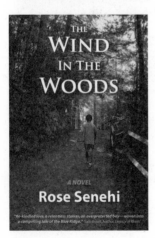

The Wind in the Woods. A romantic thriller that reveals a man's devotion to North Carolina's Green River Valley and the camp he built to share its wonders; his daughter's determination to hike the Blue Ridge—unaware that a serial killer is stalking her; and nine-year-old Alvin Magee's heart-warming discovery of freedom and responsibility in a place apart from his adult world.

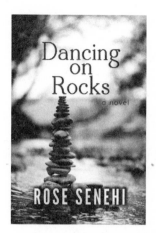

Winner of the 2014 Indie Reader Discovery Award

Dancing on Rocks. Nursing her mother back to health wasn't all that drew Georgie Haydock back to the little mountain tourist town. Hiding around every corner, are a family's painful memories of a child who disappeared in the middle of the night 25 years ago. The summer roils as her mother thrashes in her bed, insisting that the woman stalking her store downstairs is the missing sister. Meanwhile, Georgie aches to reunite with the hometown boy she never forgot.

ௐ

Other Novels by Rose Senehi

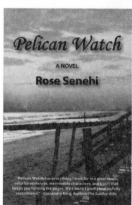

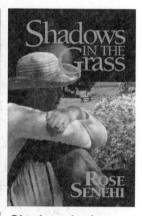

Pelican Watch. *Laced with the flavor of South Carolina's low country, this love story is told against a backdrop of murder and suspense.* Artist and animal lover, Nicky Sullivan arrives on a SC barrier island and discovers a kindred spirit in Mac Moultrie, a salty retired fisherman. From the moment she meets Trippett Alston, she's smitten, but the dark forces swirling around the island threaten to keep them apart.

Windfall. Meet Lisa Barron, a savvy marketing executive with a kid and a crazy career in the mall business. Everyone knows she's driven, but not the dark secret she's hiding. She's keeping one step ahead of the FBI and a gang of twisted peace activists who screwed up her life in the sixties, while trying not to fall in love with one of the driven men who make these massive projects rise from the ground.

Shadows in the Grass. Striving desperately to hold onto the farm for her son, a widow comes into conflict with the handsome composer who builds a mansion on the hill overlooking her nursery, never suspecting that the man who moved into the run-down farm behind her has anything to do with the missing children.

Visit Rose Senehi
www.rosesenehi.com
www.hickorynut-gorge.com
or email at:
rsenehi@earthlink.net